Also by SIMON RAVEN

Novels
The Feathers of Death
Brother Cain
Doctors Wear Scarlet
Close of Play
The Roses of Picardie
An Inch of Fortune

Alms for Oblivion sequence
Fielding Gray
Sound the Retreat
The Sabre Squadron
The Rich Pay Late
Friends in Low Places
The Judas Boy
Places Where They Sing
Come Like Shadows
Bring Forth the Body
The Survivors

Belle-Lettres
The English Gentleman
Boys Will Be Boys
The Fortunes of Fingel
Shadows on the Grass

Plays
Royal Foundation and other Plays

September Castle

A tale of love

Simon Raven

Blond & Briggs

First published in Great Britain in 1983
by Blond & Briggs Limited, Dataday House, Alexandra Road,
Wimbledon, London SW19 7JZ.

British Library Cataloguing in Publication Data

Raven, Simon
  September castle.
  I. Title
  823'.914[F]   PR6068.A9

  ISBN 0-85634-123-1

Photoset by Rowland Phototypesetting Limited
Bury St Edmunds, Suffolk
Printed in Great Britain by
Billing & Sons Limited, Worcester.

131748

N

Dieppe
Arques-la-Bataille
Rouen

Tours

Poitiers

Angouleme

Chlemoutsi
Albi

Saint-Gilles
Aigues Mortes
Saintes-Maries-de-la-Mer

M E D I T E R

"September Castle is fine and tall,
    And many a league is spread out for me;
But where is the fairest sight of all,
    O where is the never–resting sea?"

Henri Martel, Sire de Longueil,
The Ballad of the Lady Xanthippe

I

The Road From Ilyssos

ONCE UPON A TIME there was an English gentleman called Ivan Barraclough, who lived in a half-ruined tower house some two miles south of Vatheia in the Peninsula of the Mani. On a day in early autumn he received an unsigned telegram which he had long been expecting. It said: TIME TO GO.

Now, the Mani is the central prong of three which claw down from the base of the Peloponnese and into the Mediterranean Sea; and Vatheia is the last village which a man comes to in the Mani if he is travelling south by the main, the only, road. Althought Vatheia is quite a large village, you will never see anyone in it. This is because the houses go down into the earth further than they rise above it, and underneath the visible buildings is an extensive network of cellars in several layers, at which levels the villagers like to live, preferring the darkness of the earth to the light of the sky.

The main road south skirts Vatheia on the eastern side and then becomes a track; a track along which you can continue to drive a car for about two miles. When you have driven this distance, the track rounds a corner and runs into a little circus which provides ample space to turn round or to park. One or the other you must do, as thereafter the track becomes a mere footpath and in this form continues to the sea at the tip of the Peninsula, which is called Cape Taenaros and houses (so they say) one of the gates to the Kingdom of the Dead.

Drivers who reach the little circus would be well advised not to turn round immediately but to park their cars and admire the view to the south. Although they will not be able to see Cape Taenaros (let alone the gate to the Kingdom of the Dead), they will be able to follow the path, with their gaze, over hills and through valleys, up re-entrants, down spurs and along ridges, until it vanishes on the far side of a plateau on either side of which lies the never resting sea. To east and west

3

of the path the panorama is scattered with rough-hewn grey houses, each of which has a tower at one end, usually the end that overlooks the path. All the towers have had their tops lopped off, or to speak more technically, have been deprived of their platforms and battlements. This dismantlement was carried out on the command of King Otho of the Hellenes after an anti-monarchical rebellion by the Maniots, who were savagely suppressed by Spanish mercenary troops. By a curious irony the region is now celebrated for its loyalty to the deposed King Constantine, and almost every house between Vatheia and Cape Taenaros is decorated with a crude depiction of the Greek royal crown. One of the largest and most colourful of these crowns adorns the north wall of the house nearest the circus, a house about fifty yards down the footpath and twenty yards to the right of it, 'half-ruined' in the sense that, like all the others, its tower has been chopped, that same house in which, though it is empty now, Ivan Barraclough was living at the time my tale begins, having been happily engaged for something over two years in the study of the history, geography, demography, social custom, religious belief, sexual habit and superstitious practice of the southern Maniots, that is to say all such as dwelt below the town of Areopolis.

These were very few, and of them the Vatheians at least, as I have explained, apparently preferred to live underground; but Ivan enjoyed some acquaintance with them through the intermediacy of his body servant, or, more properly, his esquire, an eighteen-year-old Greek orphan called Nicos Pandouros, who came from Areopolis and did not share his master's bed. It was Nicos who had brought the telegram, for he knew, as Ivan did not, where to go in Vatheia in order to transact postal business, and had duly been there, this day early in September, on his weekly visit for the dispatch and collection of Ivan's mail. There were three letters of no interest or importance from learned but prosaic correspondents; and there was this telegram, unsigned, which Ivan had been expecting any time these six months and which said: TIME TO GO.

'That is final then. Can I not go with you?' Nicos said.

'No. I have always warned you that the message would

4

arrive and that I would have to leave you. But you shall have plenty of money until I return.'

'What should I do for it? I cannot take such money with honour.'

'Yes, you can. You will take it in return for your service. You will secure this house, you will maintain it, you will repair it, when necessary, all this against my return.'

'When will that be?'

'I cannot tell. I shall send you word. Meanwhile, although you may go often to Areopolis, or even to Kalamata if you wish, you will live in this house and keep it sweet and free from the damp and despair which come to houses where none lives. This will be your service for which I shall pay you.'

'It will be a lonely service.'

'And mine will be lonely business. But both are necessary. You may have a friend here, if you wish. Or a girl, if there be any hereabouts whose brother or father would not kill you.'

'I shall have my friend. From Limenaion. We can play tric-trac and make fantasies about young widows.'

'Good.' Ivan handed Nicos a thick pile of 1,000 Drachmae notes and instructed him that more would be telegraphed if he was not back within three months.

'What is this business, Kyrie, that takes you so long from this house?'

'I cannot tell you until it is done.'

'Why can you not take me with you?'

'Because one man travels swifter than two. And is more likely to return safely.'

'Why is this business "necessary"?'

'Because there is to be a rich reward which I shall need if I am to continue here making my studies. Such work feeds the mind but not the mouth.'

'Then go well, Kyrios Ivan.'

'Stay well, my Nicos.'

Nicos bent to kiss Ivan's hand. Ivan let him do this, then raised him, embraced him, and kissed his cheek. Then he walked alone (but watched all the time by Nicos) to the circus, climbed into his Land Rover and churned his way along the track towards Vatheia.

IVAN'S FIRST STOP was for luncheon at Gerolimen, some miles north of Vatheia. Had he been strictly practical, he would have had an early luncheon at home and thus avoided the need to stop. The reason why he had not done this was that he could not bear to remain a minute longer than necessary in the company of Nicos. The sullen and reproachful look in the boy's face, the accusations of treachery and desertion that emanated in waves from his moist and blinking eyes, saddened and irritated Ivan almost beyond endurance. He had warned Nicos, very clearly, on the very first day that he had brought him down from Areopolis to Vatheia, that the time would come, must come, when he (Ivan) would have to go away for a period of weeks, possibly months. He had repeated this warning at frequent intervals and had been given to believe that it had been well understood. And then, when at last the long-expected telegram arrived, what had happened? Nicos had gone into a black sulk, had behaved as if the possibility of Ivan's going away had never been mooted for a single instant at any time whatever, and had packed Ivan's kit so crossly and jerkily that he had broken the sole remaining bottle of Eau de Portugal.

True, Nicos had pulled himself together later on and their conversation just before parting had been more or less satisfactory. But even though the money paid and the conditions appointed had been liberal, indeed munificent, Nicos' face, his posture, his whole body had given off resentment and pique. The truth was, Ivan reflected, that the boy was being *left out* and knew it; something important was in train and there was no part in it for him and he was most bitterly hurt. Well, looked at like that his demeanour was up to a point excusable; and in any case, of course, he would soon get over it all. His friend from Limenaion would come to stay, they would talk of football and go on the bus to Kalamata or to Sparta, where

6

they would perhaps find a whore or, far better and more likely, a pair of juicy English girls 'on their way through'. All was really well in that quarter and would end well. For all of that, however, there could be no doubt but that Nicos' initial behaviour that morning had been tedious and upsetting and puerile to the point of making Ivan froth at the bowels – which only went to show that even if people listened to what they were told (rare enough) they never actually believed it if they didn't want to.

Further pabulum for disagreeable reflection was provided by the restaurant in which Ivan was eating, one of three on the quayside. A year ago none of them would have been there, and if any had the food would have been disgusting. But now, here they were, simple but clean, serving (at least the one which he had chosen) excellent prawns and skilfully dressed salad. This was bad, very bad: it meant that tourists and (far worse) foreign buyers of houses (Germans – ugh) had now penetrated south of Areopolis and down as far as Gerolimen, and would soon be knocking on the gate of Vatheia itself. It was of course quite possible that the inhabitants of Vatheia would be true to the custom of centuries, would stay in their deep dank warrens and ignore the knocking; but it was equally possible that the lure of hard currencies in lorryloads would tempt even the Vatheians from their lair. And if that happened, what followed? What followed was a tarmac road to the circus, which would be enlarged into a park for the coaches that would duly bring, from April to October, thousands of base mechanicals of detestable shapes and accents to gape at the view and snoop round his house and garden. In which case he would have to move on again. But where? One could not keep on running for ever.

Ah well: if he must think of troubles, better think of present ones. The trouble, here and now, was that although he was tolerably well off living the simple life that he did, the rate of inflation had already made it desirable and would soon make it obligatory that he should procure a sum of money of not less than six figures sterling (having a view to monetary hazards of the future) and that in order to get in sight of some such sum he had consented, some two years ago, to consider himself on call to assist in a project, preposterous but just feasible, thought out and got up by an old Cambridge chum of scholarly tastes comparable with his own and of wealth far exceeding. Since he had agreed to be on call he had been receiving a generous monthly retainer; he would now be paid a very substantial sum for his services even if the project flopped, through his own fault or another's; and should it succeed his prize could be princely. On the face of it, then, this morning's telegram had been not only an unrefusable summons but also exceedingly good news. There were, however, just two snags: firstly, the project was highly dangerous and not a little uncanny; and secondly, it necessitated his departure from a tranquil and decently ordered world into one of greed, stupidity and bustle.

Stiffen the sinews, summon up the blood. The sooner he took the plunge, the better. Pay the bill. Drive north to Areopolis and on to Ilyssos. Stop there to do what must be done. Then call on Paddy Leigh Fermor at Kardomele? No, better not. It would take him out of his way for one thing, and for another Paddy was the most hospitable man on earth, who would press him to spend a night, two nights, even more, whereas what Ivan had to do was to get on. From Ilyssos to Sparta and Mistra, from Mistra to Karyteina and Chlemoutsi, thence to Rhion and Naupactos, to Actium and Ioannina and many places more, until at last, knowing all he had to know and having heard all he had to hear, he would come, before the leaves were down, to September Castle.

THE ROAD ROLLED round and down from Areopolis to the little port of Limenaion and twisted up again into the hills. Then it forked: the left-hand prong would have taken Ivan and his Land Rover along the high coast road to Kardomele and thence to Kalamata; the right-hand prong, which he took now, led into the village of Ilyssos. An old Turkish fort crouched above the village. Old? Not by local standards. Ilyssos had been a flourishing city as early as the Middle Bronze Age, had sent ships and a fine regiment to sail with Agamemnon to Troy. Granted, that had been its high point of prosperity and fame; granted that it had been in decline ever since half the ships and three-quarters of the fine regiment had failed to return; granted that it was now the home, for the most part, of gibbering elders and peevish dogs: nevertheless it preserved a certain air of age-long grandeur, if only because of its site athwart the neck of an unplumbable ravine and the view which it offered of plunging rock and surging sea. Come to that, thought Ivan, it had retained, it had undeniably retained, considerable esteem on account of its privateering princes and admirals well into the thirteenth century and until the Franks left the Peloponnese . . . which was why, to speak in very broad terms, he had come here now.

He was here, more precisely, to remind himself of a monument. It was not a tomb, because the Lady whom it commemorated, though born and brought up in Ilyssos, had been buried far away in another country. It was just a plain slab of stone, a 'stele' as the Ancient Greeks would have called it, which recorded the name and rank of the Lady, the date, place and circumstances of her death, and the authority for this information. The stone was affixed to the south wall of a large and ugly church which, built at the expense of an Ilyssan who had struck gold in Australia in the mid eighteen hundreds, had replaced the tiny twelfth-century basilica where the Lady herself would have made her orisons. When the latter building had been criminally torn down to make place for its hideous successor, somebody or other had at least sensed that the tablet in its sanctuary was the record of a sad, a poetic and even an historic event, and this somebody or other had ensured the tablet's preservation by finding it the position which it now occupied in the new church.

Ivan tried the door of the church. Locked. But almost immediately a little old man came scuffling and muttering, the only person to be seen in the whole street, and unlocked the door with a crooked key which he took from under his armpit. Ivan entered. The old man trembled and babbled along behind

9

him, then made a low whine of protest when Ivan stopped by the slab on the south wall.

The characters were remarkably clear, if one considered that seven centuries had passed since they were inscribed; nor was the mediaeval Greek difficult to translate, so simple was its message:

ΑΓΓΕΛΟΣ ΕΚ ΦΡΑΓΓΙΑΣ ΗΛΘΕΝ

Ivan read:

A HERALD CAME FROM FRANCE
ON THE BIRTHDAY OF OUR LORD JESUS CHRIST
IN THE ELEVENTH YEAR OF THE REIGN
OF THE LORD [KYRIOS] PHAEDRON OF
ILYSSOS BY THE BLOOD OF GOD HE BROUGHT
WOEFUL TIDINGS EVEN THAT THE
PRINCESS [DESPOINA] XANTHIPPE
WAS TWO MONTHS DEAD THE ONLY
DAUGHTER OF OUR GOOD LORD PHAEDRON
WHO HAD GIVEN HER INTO THE KEEPING
OF THE FRANKS AS A PLEDGE OF HIS LOYALTY TO
VILLEHARDOUIN PRINCE OF ACHAEA
THE LADYS BODY
LIES IN THE FAR
CASTLE OF THE BOREAN
FRANKS WHERE SHE WAS
MEWED AND DIED
BUT PRAY FOR HER SOUL
THAT IT MAY RETURN IN
PEACE TO THIS HER OWN
LAND FOR DESIRE WHEREOF
SHE SICKENED IN HER
HEART AND PERISHED
BEING IN HER EIGHTEENTH YEAR

For some time Ivan had been aware that the old man's unease at his interest in the tablet had become active disapproval. A series of sharp tugs at his cuffs and his coat-tails indicated a strong wish to see him out and off. Well, he had seen what he had come to see, and there was no point in hanging around where he wasn't wanted.

Having given the scowling midget a coin of ten Drachmae, Ivan started the Land Rover and coasted down towards Limenaion, from which he would mount once more for Areopolis and thence take the road for Gytheion and Sparta, where he would seek lodging for the night. On his left the ravine opened like the Pit, while to his right, far below, the sea stirred and struck. Very odd, he thought: the correct Christian prayer should surely have been that the Lady's soul should dwell in the presence of her God, not that it should return to her home, to a place on earth. Only unhappy souls linger on earth, where they are not peaceful. Whose prayer was it then? No priest would have subscribed to such a wish. Was it the prayer of the Lord Phaedron, that of a lonely old man who loved his daughter and wished her to be with him, even if only as a shade, asking the impossible, that such a shade should 'return in peace'? Or had there been a lover? Or had one of her brothers, a younger brother, perhaps, whom she had bathed and petted, longed for her to come once more and fondle him in the night?

Answers to such questions would be interesting and useful. But of far more immediate import to himself and his endeavour was to confirm, as he now had, that the Despoina, Lady, or Princess had been definitely reported (1) as having died two months before the Greek Christmas in the eleventh year of her father Phaedron's Lordship (which could be computed from the reference books as 1255) and (2) as having died and been buried 'in the far castle of the Borean Franks where she was mewed'.

'But I wonder,' said Ivan aloud, as he drove past the tiny harbour of Limenaion and started to ascend the main street, 'I wonder who *did* compose that heterodox prayer for you, my Lady, and so wilfully and sinfully bade others to echo it?'

'HE'LL BE ON HIS WAY by now,' said Ptolemaeos Tunne to his niece, Jo-Jo Pelham. 'He'll be spending the night in Sparta and tomorrow morning at Mistra.'

'Is he coming here at all?' asked Jo-Jo.

'Only if things go wrong. If everything goes approximately to plan, we shan't see Ivan this side of the Channel till it's all over. Perhaps not even then.'

Ptolemaeos and his niece lived in the middle of the Fens east of Ely. Luckily Ptolemaeos had a very substantial private income, as the bills for the electricity and basic fuels needed to keep his large Queen Anne house warm and dry ran well into five figures annually. What made them even bigger than they might have been was the amount of cooking which had to go on. Ptolemaeos was a huge man and liked huge meals: at this very moment Jo-Jo and he were tucking into a dinner of seven courses.

'Pity,' said Jo-Jo. 'I'd like to meet him.'

'You will, poppet. Sooner or later. If he doesn't come to England, I'll take you to Greece to see him.'

'From what you say, Ptoly, his establishment in Greece isn't quite what you're used to.'

'He could meet us in Athens. Not that the food there is anything to bring on an erection.' Ptolemaeos considered the plate in front of him. 'I must say, darling,' he said, 'these frogs' legs are bloody marvellous. Crisp, as they should be, not sagging about in tomato pulp. Alpha plus – or at any rate pure Alpha.'

Jo-Jo did the cooking (her French nanny had taught her) because she loved cooking and loved to please Ptolemaeos. Some months since, when her mother and father died in a car smash with both her little brothers, she had come, as a matter of course, to live with Ptolemaeos, who was her mother's brother and the only relative she had left. After a few weeks a

Public Nose (female) came to the house and said that she must be placed in Public Care: she could not go on living with a bachelor uncle, said the Public Nose, revelling in the anguish which it hoped it was causing, because it wasn't for Her Own Good. What the Public Nose didn't realise, because it hadn't done its homework properly and took Jo-Jo, who was rather underdeveloped for her age, to be about thirteen, was that Jo-Jo was on the eve of her sixteenth birthday, after which she would be entitled to live anywhere she wanted, provided she had means for her support. Since she had inherited a cosy sum for her parents (not as cosy as what Ptolemaeos had in the bank but quite enough to be going on with) she certainly had that. When, therefore, the Public Nose had arrived a few days later with an ancillary Public Nose (also female) who was to escort Jo-Jo to a Special Place, she was able to put both of them roundly out of joint, metaphorically by producing her birth certificate, and then in physical fact for good measure, as she had two brisk little fists and two stout arms, undeveloped in some ways as she might be. A charge alleging assault, brought by the National Association of Public Noses, did not lie, as Jo-Jo was able to make out a plausible case that the Noses had been illegally abducting her against her will.

'*Entrecôte Marchand de Vin* next,' she now said as she removed the remains of the frogs' legs: 'I thought it would make a nice contrast.'

'Bless your little pussy,' said Ptolemaeos, and tickled it as she passed him.

I should now explain that, although Jo-Jo and Ptolemaeos lived on terms of total familiarity, both verbal and physical, although they had baths together and talked to each other while they were going to the loo, were for ever in and out of each other's bed and constantly practised the most intimate caresses – that nevertheless, despite all this, they were not and never had been lovers, in the sense that the world understands the term. They deliberately stopped short of 'the right true end of love': they didn't even come. This was the secret of their happiness; for as Ptolemaeos was fond of saying, '"The right true end of love" can indeed be the end of love. It needn't be, my love-bird, but often it is. It leads to satiation

13

and hence to indifference and hence, very often, to disgust.'

At the same time, Ptolemaeos was well aware that never to get one's nuts off was to invite a deleterious state of frustration. He took care of the matter by going, once a month, to a skilled masseuse in London. Although he was only thirty-five, he found that once a month was quite enough: as he remarked to Jo-Jo, 'After waiting a month a fellow goes off like a firework. It is one more instance of the rewards of self-restraint.'

The problem of providing such salutary combustion for Jo-Jo had also been solved in a different but equally satisfying manner, as will be demonstrated in due course.

'I thought we'd have watery nursery marrow with the *entrecôte*,' said Jo-Jo, coming back with two clean plates and beginning to serve.

'Clever girlie. One should always have one thing absolutely plain. Most people would have done the marrow in butter. Boiled in water is *right*.'

'You do know how to appreciate a girl,' said Jo-Jo. And then, when she had finished serving them both, 'I think my tits are coming on a bit. Shall you mind?'

'No. I adore them as they are, dear little chestnuts, but a gradual change will be very amusing.'

'What about the *other*?'

'Oh, I'm sure the *other* will feel the same. Which reminds me. We must have both the *others* to stay next week at the latest. As soon as possible really.'

'But that's a fortnight ahead of schedule.'

'I know, little honeypot, but you're only thinking of *that*. My point is that they will have to join Ivan Barraclough in ten days. Before then they must be briefed, and best briefed here. You do see?'

'Yes of course, Ptoly. I do see.'

'So you won't mind having *that* two weeks early for once? It may be your last chance for some time.'

'As for having *that* two weeks early, *mon vieux*, I'm entirely happy. But there are times, dear old beanie, they are just times when I could wish that the *others* weren't having any part in all this with Mr Barraclough.'

'It's Ivan who'll be running the risks. As the thing is presently planned, the *others* are responsible only for the admin.'

'Admin?'

'That's what Canteloupe calls it. (Have some of this La Tâche.) It's military lingo for administration. Canteloupe was a soldier, you know, about a century ago.'

'Well, if he's happy about it. . .'

'He longs for it. And you must see that he is so very suitable. I went over all the preliminaries with him in Pratt's the last time I went up for a rub-off. He understands the part perfectly and he fits it absolutely pat. His name, his air of distinction, that cool blasé, definitely *senior* presence . . . its beaut, darl', it's just beaut – as our Australian cousins say.'

'But is Baby Canteloupe just beaut? Well, beaut in one way she certainly is, *nom d' un nom*, but does she fit in . . . with this Barraclough affair . . . as smoothly as His Lordship? I mean, she does bounce a bit, Baby does. She might make a particularly noisy bounce at the wrong moment.'

'Good point. But there is . . . or there *may* be,' said Ptolemaeos gravely, 'one particular thing which only Baby can do. You could probably have done it too, only you're a little too inexperienced, I think, and you're not called the Marchioness Canteloupe.'

'Getting snobby, sweetheart?'

'No. It's just that Baby's job needs, or may need, a person with a heavy label as well as light hands. As for all that bouncing – well, Canteloupe will do his best to stop her being too effervescent. He said that for the duration of the project he was going to call her by her real name – Tullia, Tullia Llewyllyn she was christened – and that that might make her a bit less scaramouche.'

'Being called Tullia? I should think it would squash her flat. Poor Baby.'

'Not poor Baby. Rich, lucky little Baby, much loved and much loving. (Pass the La Tâche, my own bottykins.) Adorable, delectable baby, and clever with it. This *entrecôte* is point nought one per cent too well done, but the sauce is quite mythical.'

'Do you think Baby would like me to ask her Dad over from Cambridge for the night?'

'Old Tom? Ask him for luncheon, if you like, my darling, but not for the night. I've got a lot to go over with Canteloupe and Baby – I mean Tullia – and her old poppa might be in the way.'

'Right. I'll ring up and ask them for dinner and the night as soon as they care to make it. And I'll ask Tom to luncheon the following day, by which time, I suppose, you'll be through with the briefing?'

'By which time I should certainly be through with the briefing. Oh darling, a cheese *fondu*. I think I shall dip *you* in it and eat you.'

'Silly Ptoly. But look, if I spread some of it here . . . and under here . . . you could come and lick me clean, now couldn't you?'

PTOLEMAEOS AND JO-JO did not rise very early the next morning, unlike Ivan Barraclough, who, having dined rather more sparely than they in the Xenia at Sparta the previous evening and having none of their delicious dalliance to keep him from his rest, was up and abroad with the rosy-fingered dawn. For the site at Mistra would open at 7.30 in the morning; and Ivan, having far to go, was eager to be done with his business there and on his road.

It was in the Castro, the Castle at the top of the hill, that Ivan's business lay. This was not the Castle, September Castle, that was his goal, for that was still hundreds of leagues to the north; but there was something that the Castle of Mistra had in common with September Castle, something, indeed, that all the places which he would visit on his road had in common with it. What trace still remained of that something he must now determine – or rather, confirm, for he had several times visited Mistra on the same errand since he had been living in the Mani, and this visit was merely one of revision, part of a final check which he was making of all the links in the chain, so that he might be absolutely certain that it was sound and that he was not risking his life and honour to no purpose.

But although Ivan's business lay up in the citadel, Villehardouin's citadel, and although he had been determined to go straight up there, inspect what he had come to inspect and leave immediately, he loitered in the sweet autumn morning, he lingered on his way up the lovely hill: for Ivan regarded beauty and pleasure as the two elements without which life was unbearable, and he could never for long eschew either, no matter how exigent his affairs or immediate their burden. He dawdled in the quaint cathedral and tarried to listen to the fountain in the cloister; he brooded in the Courts of the Despots and all along the terrace of their palace; then he sat down and looked out over the valley below. A fine, rich valley for such a barren land. The Valley of Sparta, of Lacedaemon, of La Crémonie, as old Villehardouin and his Frankish knights had called it when they built the Castle over 700 years ago. Old Villehardouin, that was Prince William of Achaea, and of Lamorie, the Morea . . . what was it he had said at the time? 'Whoever holds Mistra holds La Crémonie.' Well, yes; yet Prince William had held neither very long. But while he had still held the Castle, a girl had come there on her way from Ilyssos to Glarentza and the coast, a girl with companions and baggage befitting her noble rank. She had stayed for seven nights, the Chronicle recorded, not because she needed so long a rest, but in order that Prince William might show honour to her and so to her father, for the code of chivalry required the generous entertainment of noble hostages. There was feasting, and there was a tournament on the terraced tilting yard; and each victorious knight dipped his lance in salute to the Despoina Xanthippe of Ilyssos, who was being taken far away from Ilyssos, from La Morie, from Greece itself, to be a surety for the peaceful behaviour of her father, the Maniot Lord Phaedron of Ilyssos, towards his Frankish overlord.

On the eighth day the little Princess and her companions and her baggage train were sent on their way, accompanied by a guard of knights which was commanded by the Banneret

17

Geoffery of Bruyère. Lord Geoffery and his mesne would escort her to his own Castle of Karyteina, then on to the port of Glarentza, where she would be put into the care of Messer Hubert of Avallon; for Messer Hubert had business in his fief at home, and had gladly consented to Prince William's request that he should have charge of the Despoina Xanthippe on her sea voyage from Glarentza to the north and then the west, and should later guide and guard her from her place of landing to the place where she must go.

All this was common knowledge (among such as cared for such knowledge) and beyond any possible dispute. What was not common knowledge, and would have caused considerable dispute if had been, was the existence, in a cell near the Castle chapel in Mistra, of an aumbry which had, in one side, a hinged stone that would turn at a touch to reveal an inscription on its rear. It was this inscription which Ivan Barraclough had come to examine, or rather to re-examine, in order to make quite sure that it said what he thought it said and that what it said was a sound link in the chain which he was checking.

And so now Ivan touched and turned the aumbry stone, and this is what he read:

Ego Theobaldus Episcopus Lacedaemoniae, Pontifex domicilis Principis Guilliami. . .
. . . I, Theobald, Bishop of Sparta and Chaplain in the Household of Prince William . . . *carnem laceravi et mentem pertundere fortissime sum conatus . . .* have rent my flesh and made most mighty effort to rack through my mind, to ensure that what I write is sooth and springeth not from trifling nor from false understanding and makes not affront to my God. For I write of this Mistress Xanthippe, and of what she brought with her hither and bears with her on her way hence. About her and it I have sensed that which must cause good Christom man to shrink as from the Fiend Himself; and I pray that God may deliver this amiable Lady, who in her soul is innocent, from the horror which voyages always with her and which (I fear me and despite this my prayer) *numquam a corpore ejus separari volebit . . .* will never willingly be parted from her flesh.

IT HAD TAKEN THE DESPOINA XANTHIPPE the better part of a week to proceed, under the Lord Geoffery's escort, from Mistra to Karyteina. Every night a camp was set up, in a forest in the hills or by a stream bed in a valley or near a crooked church; and on the sixth afternoon after they had left William's castle (as the Chronicle relates) she came ambling on her mare along the road from Megalopolis and into the Vale of Karyteina, riding side by side with Sir Geoffery at the head of his mesnie knights. The summer weather had been fine and the company (particularly Sir Geoffery's) had been fun, but she was not sorry (or so the Chronicle, the Chronicle of Avallon, affirms) to see Geoffery's substantial castle, which rose out of a rocky hill almost as though it had been part of it. She and her maidens were to spend three days there before again taking the road with Geoffery, this time for Chlemoutsi (Clermont) and Glarentza (Clarence).

It took Ivan Barraclough and his Land Rover about two hours to make the journey by much the same route, with one brief stop for a picnic by a small lake near which (had he known it) the Princess Xanthippe had spent her third night out from Mistra. He too climbed into the hills north of Sparta, then descended into the Plain of Megalopolis, then took the road north-west into the Vale of Karyteina, where a sharp hill rising from the floor of the valley still holds the castle up to Heaven. He too mounted by a winding rocky path through the village hovels to the castle gate, and he too made for the guest chamber (what was left of it), intending, however, to spend only three minutes where Xanthippe had passed three nights.

Adjoining the guest chamber was a little oratory and behind its altar was a crude reredos, carved in low relief out of the wall itself. Although time, damp, decay and dereliction had spoiled the work almost beyond interpretation, it was just possible to

19

make out a paunchy St George in the act of sticking a ratty dragon (always a popular theme in Greek churches) and a maiden on her knees who was presumably praying for deliverance. Greek capital letters scratched above her made Ξ Α Ν Θ, a plausible abbreviation of Xanthippe.

It was Ivan's belief (and also that of Ptolemaeos Tunne) that the Lord Geoffery, well known for his gallantries and sentimental turns of fancy, had chosen to romanticise his brief acquaintance with the Lady Xanthippe, to see himself, and later to have himself represented, not as her mere guide and guardian on the road, but as her Protector against Perils and Monsters, her True and Embattled Knight. When, therefore, he had delivered her to Hubert of Avallon at Glarentza and returned to Karyteina, he had ordered his mason (so Ptolemaeos and Ivan surmised) to carve the legend of St George above the altar in the oratory, and to portray him, Geoffery, as the Saint and Xanthippe (whose name was carved above her head to ram the point home) as the Lady in Distress. The mason, having a hankering for satire, gave philandering Geoffery a middle-aged spread and rendered the dragon a scabby saurian beneath contempt. He had also thought fit, inspired as he was by his native shrewdness and informed by close observation of his subject during her residence at Karyteina, to play the fool with Xanthippe herself: if one looked at the kneeling figure with attention, one could see, concealed in the folds of her robe, a tiny imp or demon, who was either snarling or grinning (decomposition had made it impossible to tell which) and was also probing with a spear the size of a bodkin in the region of the Lady's Mons Veneris. What the Lord Geoffery's reaction had been when these impertinences were unveiled for his inspection (as Ptolemaeos remarked to Ivan) must now remain forever obscure. But what was beyond any question (Ptolemaeos used to add) was that the mason, like the Prince William's Bishop-Chaplain, had received and had vividly recorded the impression that the Lady Xanthippe had one attendant too many. Unlike the Bishop of Sparta, the mason expressed no opinion as to her guilt or innocence: her carven face provided no clue, being totally vacant.

'THE GREAT POINT TO REMEMBER,' said Ptolemaeos Tunne, 'is that Ivan will follow Xanthippe's route exactly – provided that everything goes to plan. In every single place Ivan stops he will be able to confirm that an unbroken trail leads from Ilyssos to the end of his journey – to the castle then known as Arques, later, much later, as Arques-la-Bataille, on the Norman coast. September Castle, as the poet called it in his lay. This confirmation, this reminder of the firm and continuous thread that runs from place to place all the way from Ilyssos to Dieppe, will fill him with renewed confidence for the final task.'

Ptolemaeos was briefing the Marquess and Marchioness Canteloupe, with Jo-Jo in eager attendance. Earlier he had taken his guests to one side for some time and rather pointedly excluded Jo-Jo, who had wondered what he was up to; but then he had assured her that he had only been advising Canteloupe about the Stock Exchange, which would have bored her silly, and anyway here she was now right in on everything.

Lord Canteloupe, who had inherited his marquisate from a distant cousin and had previously been called Detterling, was a stringy and sardonic man of sixty-six. His Marchioness, like Jo-Jo, was sixteen, a lively little girl with esculent limbs, generally known as 'Baby' but henceforth, as Ptolemaeos had informed Jo-Jo at their conference a few nights before, to be called by her given name, 'Tullia', in order to render her less volatile and bring her into a suitable mood for the very serious work that would soon be at hand.

'Quite apart from that,' Ptolemaeos continued, 'he may discover something new, something that could assist him in assessing the . . . nature of the problem . . . and later in confronting whatever is to be confronted and removing whatever is to be removed.'

21

'And just what might that be, Ptoly darling?' asked Baby Canteloupe in a boisterous voice.

'More of that later,' said Ptolemaeos, rather evasively. 'Please, Tullia, do not interrupt.'

'Baby and me want to know now,' said Jo-Jo, standing up and prancing about.

'Sit down and shut up,' said Ptolemaeos, 'or you'll be turned out. Now then. Ivan will also be kept informed of any new knowledge that might come *our* way, of any new developments in our region. If necessary, agents will meet him to give him detailed accounts of what is toward.'

'At the risk of seeming dim-witted,' said Canteloupe, 'might one enquire why you set so much store on such a painstaking and pedantic re-examination of the Despoina's route? It is, after all, going to take up a lot of valuable time. And I can't believe that it is so essential to Barraclough's morale to confirm what he very well knows already.'

'As for time,' said Ptolemaeos, 'I have allowed ample margins . . . though there is one very mild cause for anxiety of which I shall apprise you all later.

'As for Ivan's morale, I agree that it is not essential that he should go over the entire course in detail, but I think it highly desirable. And there are considerations other than Ivan's morale. Whoever and whatever came with the Lady Xanthippe from Ilyssos to Arques obviously came by the same route as she did and halted at the same lodgings. Might not some part of them or their *esprit* have rubbed off (so to speak) on those locations? Or might not some wave or vibration have lingered on – some wave or vibration to which, with luck, Ivan might respond? We know that the Despoina, in her journey, made strong and peculiar impressions on her hosts and their servants, notably at Mistra and Rouen. Why should not similar impressions have been left on the places themselves, on their genius or their atmosphere?'

'Such impressions would be difficult to detect,' said Canteloupe, 'liable to mislead, and of no assistance as guides to practical action.'

'I disagree. Anyone can sense some impression from the

stones, for example, of Mycenae, nor is it in the least mis-
leading. Correctly and without equivocation it proclaims
murder and misery and lust.'

'Mycenae is an exception.'

'Nonsense. Delphi, the Colosseum, Ephesos, Nemi. . .
Not the same messages as those of Mycenae, I grant you, but
equally vivid.'

'All of them put out signals which could only confuse or
intimidate the visitor were any kind of action required of him –
as usually it is not. In Barraclough's case action *is* required; and
I suggest to you that if he should pick up the sort of . . .
residual oscillation . . . which you envisage, then it will at best
be disquieting and at worst quite paralysing.'

'Then we must agree to disagree. Ivan needs all the help he
can get in identifying the nature of the forces which he must
overcome and the prize to which he aspires . . . to which we all
aspire,' said Ptolemaeos with a sly pout. 'If this slow journey
north gives him any extra intuitions or inspirations, however
slight, then it will have been worth while.'

'Is he the intuitive sort?' asked glowing Tullia, while Jo-Jo
gazed on, her eyes enormous.

'When we were at Lancaster together he was a skilled
collator of apparently random and unconnected events. He
would say, "This, despite all appearance, has stemmed from
that, and the result will be the other." You'd be surprised how
often he was right.'

'That is not the same,' said Tullia, while Jo-Jo gazed her fill,
'as making accurate practical use of waves or vibrations from
the past. As Canteloupe says, however strong these may be in
particular places, they can only cause muddle – if not terror –
when precise interpretation is necessary or the need for action
is near.'

'Do not insist too much on accuracy or precision,' said
Ptolemaeos. 'Ivan may get what I believe is called "a gut
feeling".'

'And go berserk,' said Canteloupe, 'on the strength of it.'

'Anyway,' said Ptolemaeos, lifting his right hand and slowly opening the palm as if to emit or deflect a ray into Canteloupe's face, 'we are now committed there. Ivan is on his

journey. He has his instructions. He will make his visits. And that is all about that. Now let us discuss where you and Baby – where you and Tullia come in.'

Baby and Jo-Jo exchanged melodramatic looks and held hands on the sofa.

'The ship which carried the Despoina Xanthippe,' said Ptolemaeos, 'took a devious route from Glarentza to Corfu to Dubrovnik, where there was a change of plan, back to Corfu and thence to Bari; from Bari round the heel and toe of Italy to Scylla and Palermo; from Palermo straight across the Mediterranean to Saintes-Maries-de-la-Mer.'

'Why was there a change of plan at Dubrovnik?' asked Baby, and squeezed Jo-Jo's hand in her excitement.

'The plan had been to sail up to Venice,' said Ptolemaeos, 'and take Xanthippe the rest of the way by land. But the Chronicle of Avallon tells us –'

'Just how reliable is *that*?' Interrupted Canteloupe.

'It was dictated by Messer Hubert of Avallon, the knight who accompanied the Lady Xanthippe, to a monk of the Abbey of Vezelay. There is no reason why it should not be reliable, if we allow for occasional lapses of memory; and indeed we had better pray that it is, as our whole enterprise is based on the information which it and its sequel contains. So,' said Ptolemaeos patiently, 'we assume that Hubert is telling the truth when he says that in Dubrovnik they heard a rumour that there was plague in Venice, "wherefore they strait turned the prow back to Corfu, and thence made sail to Bari".'

'Why not direct from Dubrovnik to Bari?' said Baby, and again squeezed Jo-Jo's hand.

'Because the skipper was offered a fat payment to take a cargo of skins south to Corfu. There was, after all, no particular hurry. The speed of travel in those days was elephantine or at best equine, and a week or two more or less made no difference to anybody. So back to Corfu they went, thence to Bari, and thence, by the stages I have enumerated, to Saintes-Maries-de-la-Mer, a small port on the south coast of France, so called because the Virgin and the Magdalen once landed there having sailed from Joppa in a miraculous skiff made of rock.'

'South-east of Aigues Mortes,' said Jo-Jo knowingly.

'Yes: though at that time the ramparts were still a foot high. The town was building but didn't really exist.'

'Aigues Mortes means "Dead Waters",' said Baby; '*they* existed all right. Fever and cholera and God knows what.'

Ptolemaeos hesitated, then said, 'As you say, Tullia. "Dead Waters." Treacherous and remote marshes. And, what was more, Messer Hubert and the Princess and her companions had to ride straight through them. There is more than a hint in Hubert's Chronicle that they had some kind of unnamed and special protection, "Who ringed us round with his might", as Hubert puts it, "against drowning, flux or pest."'

'Ah,' said Canteloupe. 'Enter The Magician.'

'No. Not a magician. Hubert is very cagey about it all, but he makes it plain that in his view the Lady Xanthippe, whether or not she knew it, was attended by some kind of guardian spirit who smoothed the way for them.'

'Angel or Devil?' enquired Jo-Jo.

'He's too discreet to specify. Anyhow, they all arrived safe at the nearest town of substance, which was called Saint-Gilles. There they procured lodgings and rested for a week or so, to recover from their voyage.

'Now then. Villehardouin had long since sent word to his connections in Normandy that the Lady was on her way; and the Castellan of the Castle of Arques had been instructed to send an escort of knights to guard Messer Hubert and the valuable hostage in his care on the overland journey to Normandy, but the escort had, of course, gone to Venice in accordance with the original plan. This meant that for many weeks more Xanthippe would continue to be a wealthy young woman travelling with a friendly guardian rather than a captive Princess watched over by an official picquet. It might have been much better for her to have become earlier and therefore more gradually accustomed to the latter condition; for it is at least possible that much of the ill which befell her later was caused by the sudden and horrible shock of realising for the first time, as the gates of Arques closed behind her, that she was indeed a prisoner and not just a little lass on a jaunt with a jolly old uncle. However, that is mere speculation: the plain fact of the matter is that Hubert was still totally responsible for her safety and it was now up to him to find them a bodyguard; and he managed to engage a mercenary squad of serjeants-at-arms to accompany them as far as Rouen, after which the rest of the journey would be too short to present much problem.

'But what I particularly want you to remember, now, is this: that having landed at Saintes-Maries, and having crossed the sea-marshes round Aigues Mortes, Hubert and Xanthippe rested a while, and Hubert made important arrangements, at the town of Saint-Gilles, whither, in due course, will come Ivan Barraclough as he follows in their footsteps.'

'Is *he* going to land at Saintes-Maries off a miraculous rock?' said Jo-Jo.

'No,' said Ptolemaeos, po-faced. 'Ivan will travel the whole way overland, except for the unavoidable sea-crossings.'

'Then he won't be doing exactly the same as Xanthippe.'

'He will positively visit all the places and the ports through which she passed. From Bari he will drive to Palermo, taking the ferry from Scylla; from Palermo he will return to the mainland, taking the same ferry back, and he will then drive along the Italian and French coasts to Saintes-Maries. He will miss the experience of Xanthippe's sea-voyages, but these days it is impossible to take ship as she did.'

'Right you be, old bean,' said Canteloupe. 'One has the picture. But just where do Baby and I come into it?'

'You and Tullia come into it at Saint-Gilles, which is where you will meet Ivan. There is a modest but wholesome hostelry there, with one tower in the Guide Michelin –'

'Only one tower in the Michelin?' giggled Baby. 'Canteloupe will do his pieces. He's a four-tower minimum man.'

'A modest but wholesome and perfectly adequate hostelry,' insisted Ptolemaeos, 'where I myself have on occasion laid my head . . . and where *you* will meet Ivan Barraclough just seven days from now. You will remain with him, and he with you, over the rest of the Despoina's route through France, right up to Dieppe and the Castle at Arques.'

'September Castle,' said Baby, and squeezed Jo-Jo's hand once more.

'September Castle,' echoed Ptolemaeos grimly. 'You will

26

all three occupy rooms in the Hotel La Présidence in Dieppe. Three towers in Michelin.'

'Still one off par,' said Baby, 'but things are looking up.'

'Your primary function,' said Ptolemaeos, 'is to provide cover for Ivan. You are a rich and titled couple at the end of a long European tour. Ivan is your courier. He can have no safer explanation of himself; it will render him almost invisible.'

'Invisible?'

'From the moment you meet him at Saint-Gilles, he will be playing the role of Confidential Upper Servant to the Marquess and Marchioness Canteloupe; by the time you arrive in Dieppe Ivan will be so totally camouflaged that even the most suspicious observer will absolutely overlook him.'

'I suppose I'd better send my real man straight home alone from Saint-Gilles,' said Canteloupe. 'Perhaps he can give Barraclough a tip or two before he goes.'

For a moment Ptolemaeos was wrong-footed.

'What can you mean?' he said.

'What I say. I presume this Barraclough will be taking over as my valet along with all the rest of it. In which case I'd better send my own chappie straight home from Saint-Gilles. He might not like it very much, being replaced in the middle of a trip, but I dare say I can explain it all to him.'

'Why take him in the first place?'

'Must have someone to look after my gear on the way down, you know.'

Ptolemaeos opened and shut his mouth, like a fish.

'Now, now, Canteloupe,' said Baby, coming to the rescue, 'that's just silly. You know very well that poor old Corporal of yours would only be in the way, quite apart from the fact he's gone potty. An ex-soldier from Canty's old regiment,' she explained to Ptolemaeos and Jo-Jo, 'a terrific old darling and as loyal as the Flag itself, but he went funny a few years back, when Canty succeeded, and insisted on being called the Chamberlain of the Household. Not what we need on this sort of an outing.'

'Then who'll take care of my gear on the way down?' grumbled Canteloupe. 'And who'll explain it all to Barraclough?'

'I shall,' said Baby, patting his head very gently. 'I'll do Jeeves until Barraclough shows up. You know I'm jolly good at it, and it gives you a nice feeling to order me about. As if I was his study-fag at school,' she said aside to Jo-Jo, 'Gibbs Minimus. He once called me that by mistake.'

'How *sweet*.'

'So that's settled,' said Ptolemaeos, holding up a regal hand to quell the girls' chatter. 'You meet Ivan at Saint-Gilles, you travel north with him through France, you give him an absolute guarantee of respectability and *raison d'être* – and at Dieppe he busies himself unnoticed with . . . with what he must then do. Later, when he gives the word, you cross the water for home, possibly with Ivan, possibly without him but with . . . whatever he entrusts you withal.'

There was a long silence.

'You know,' said Canteloupe, 'you've been pretty clear about everything except the one thing a fellow wants to know. What, just what, might Barraclough be going to entrust to us . . . withal?'

Ptolemaeos' eyes dilated, then contracted and started to glint.

'First let me recap the history for you,' he said.

'You told us all that at the start.'

'It is important you should have it at your fingers' tips, down to the last detail I can dispense.'

'Very well,' said Canteloupe wearily. 'Re-run the history.'

'In the spring of the year 1255 an important Greek baron, Phaedron of Ilyssos, Lord Paramount of the Mani, agreed to give his daughter, the Despoina Xanthippe, into the keeping of the Villehardouin Prince, William of Achaea, as a surety for his good behaviour. Had Phaedron refused to do this, William intended to go down in the Mani and dispossess him. As William had a very powerful following and would almost certainly have succeeded, Phaedron toed the line and passed over Xanthippe. Prince William then despatched her to a Villehardouin Castle in Normandy, and notified Phaedron that it was at least possible that an advantageous match might be arranged for her. All right so far?'

'Yes,' said Canteloupe, 'except that I don't quite see why she had to be sent all the way to Normandy.'

'William was keen to marry her to a Norman vassal and cousin of his, called Henri Martel, Sire de Longueil, a small fief near the Castle of Arques – the very Castle in which he was going to park Xanthippe, so that she should be nice and handy for wooing and wedding. This Martel was a poor relation and a constant embarrassment, even at a distance, and William hoped to mend all that by handing him Xanthippe on a plate – and with her a fat dowry from her Daddy's treasure chamber, which was stuffed with the loot of generations of pirates.'

'And this was the "advantageous" match which William was holding out to Phaedron?'

'Yes. And advantageous it certainly was. This Henri Martel might be rather low on ready money, but he was a descendant of Charlemagne and had the noblest blood in Europe in his veins. Not at all a bad cop for a little Miss from the Mani.

'Now, all this we know from the Chronicle of Avallon, which was related to a monk at Vezelay by Hubert of Avallon, the chap who accompanied Xanthippe from Glarentza. According to Hubert, her father had sent her off in rare style. Six ladies-in-waiting, trunks full of expensive kit on a squadron of donkeys, and a bodyguard 200 strong to bring her up from Ilyssos to William's castle at Mistra, where she was officially handed over to William and then fêted for a whole week.

'From Mistra Lord Geoffery of Bruyère took her on to his castle at Karyteina, and thence to Glarentza, where Hubert of Avallon took her over, sailed with her by the devious route we have spoken of to Palermo and Saintes-Maries-de-la-Mer, and brought her over land, by way of Saint-Gilles, Albi, Angoulême, Poitiers, Tours and Rouen, to the Castle of Arques. There she arrived in mid-September of the same year, 1255, and was placed by Hubert in the care of the Castellan, a long service and good conduct hack on the Villehardouin pay roll.'

'And then, I suppose,' said Jo-Jo, 'round came grotty Henri de Longueil with his tongue hanging out.'

'He came to pay his respects . . . and barely had time to do so before she pined away and died. The news reached Phaedron in Ilyssos on Christmas Day, by which time she had been dead, according to the messenger, for something over two months. Someone composed an epitaph, in which he expressed the wish that the Lady's soul might return to her own country . . . "for desire whereof she sickened in her heart and perished" . . . and there is also a ballad on the subject written by – guess whom – none other than poor grotty Henri, who turns out to be a considerable minor poet, in his fashion. I've got a copy here,' he said, passing it to Jo-Jo. 'Rather your sort of a read.'

'None of which is making any clearer to me,' said Canteloupe, 'what Barraclough is looking for and what, in consequence, he may entrust us . . . withal.'

'I have told you that Xanthippe had six ladies-in-waiting and a mountain of gear. Somewhere in all that lot there was, or at least there subsequently appeared, a special item of which one special attendant had very special charge.'

'A special attendant?' said Jo-Jo, looking up from the ballad. 'You mean one of the six ladies?'

Ptolemaeos laughed rather awkwardly.

'There is some obscurity on that point,' he said. 'The matter has been, as they say, fudged.'

'How fudged?' said Baby.

'Well, the main text of the Chronicle ceases with the following passage.' Ptolemaeos opened a note book and read aloud to them: '"At the Lady's wish I lingered at the Castle of Arques, to be of what cheer I could to her, for we had had much adventure and merriment together on our journey. But now that this journey, with its perils and its wonders, was behind her and she was mewed in this said Castle of Arques, far from her father and her home of Ilyssos by the fair dancing waves of the sea, the poor Lady did sink with sadness. Messer Henri Martel did come to pay her court, but this gladdened her not – the greater pity, as he was a comely youth of good parts and quick understanding." Then he goes on to say that Henri, for his part, didn't care much for the Despoina, so that it was all no good anyway. But Henri hung about for a bit, trying to get something done for the poor girl – he was sorry for her, if nothing else – all to no purpose. "After the second time he came to her she would not receive him, nor could her maidens nor the Castellan nor I myself persuade her thereto. She neither ate nor drank nor took her pleasure in any wise; ever did she fade before our eyes, and was gone from us before the last leaves fell, as sweet a damsel as ever trod this earth, being scarce turned eighteen years.

'"Her body they buried near the chapel of the Castle. Her Treasure and its Guardian did stay with her. Her ladies the noble Henri Martel (who had made a ballade of her death) did escort back to Romanie, he being eager of adventure and strange lands, whereof he might devise new rhymes."

'You see,' said Ptolemaeos. '"Her Treasure and Its Guardian." "*Thesauros et Custos*" in the monk's Latin. God knows what they were called in Hubert's old French. Or perhaps he dictated in Latin, and the words were his. Anyway, "Her Treasure and Its Guardian" is the best that I can do. That is how the special item and its attendant are always described. Normally the phrase is easily construed as meaning one special item which one lady was detailed to take care of. But what can it mean *here*? "Her Treasure and Its Guardian did stay with her." As I say, the thing is fudged. Stay with her *where*? In the chapel? In a shrine near her tomb perhaps? The Guardian now taking on the job of a caretaker as well? One of the ladies, as normally? But they all went back to Romany with Henri Martel. Yet did they? Did they *all* go? Hubert just says "her ladies"; he does not say how many. Perhaps one or more stayed behind.'

'Or perhaps they didn't,' chuckled Baby, 'so then who or what *did*?'

'What you're saying,' said Canteloupe, 'is that something special came to Arques in little Xanthippe's luggage, something special with its own attendant or guardian, and that this is what Barraclough and you are after now?'

'Right. And *now* is the word. It's time to pick it up *now*, because now we know as much about it as we ever shall (though I still hope Ivan may come up with an extra tip or two on the strength of his journey) and it may not be there much longer.'

'But what makes you think,' said Jo-Jo, 'that it still is? Hundreds of people must have read that Chronicle. Are you going to tell me that this treasure – whatever it may be – has been left undisturbed all these centuries?'

'Yes.'

'How do you know?' rapped Baby.

'Special information. What you might call an Appendix to the Chronicle.'

'Let's have it.'

'No,' said Ptolemaeos, very sternly.

'Why not?'

'It might . . . trouble you. Just let's say that a special Appendix, to which I alone have access, puts me in possession of special clues and special knowledge.'

'I'm getting rather tired of that adjective,' said Baby. 'Everything in this affair seems to be "special", one way or the other. And you most of all.'

'Precisely so,' grinned Ptolemaeos. 'For unlike anyone else, except Ivan, I know *what* the Lady's treasure was. It wasn't just any little trinket, as you might assume from reading the Chronicle – something she made a silly, girly fuss about and insisted on appointing a joke Guardian for. The special Appendix, the special knowledge which neither I nor anyone else was ever supposed to come by, tells me what it was, what it is, and what it's worth. Believe me, it's worth having.'

'And the Guardian?'

'That's rather the problem,' Ptolemaeos said. 'It's also the reason why it's still there in the Castle. The Guardian has kept it safe. Most people assume that it, the Treasure, was some trivial but moderately valuable toy which has vanished with time and was probably pilfered. I know that it is still there, and I know why.'

'Because of this Guardian,' said Baby, like a good girl who repeats her lesson correctly but thinks it rather a silly one.

'Yes,' snapped Ptolemaeos.

'Then why,' said Canteloupe, 'if this Guardian is so effective, might it, the treasure, not be there for very much longer?'

'There is talk of restorations. That is the "mild cause for anxiety" to which I referred earlier. In the event of restorations, even the Guardian might not be able to prevent its being found – by the wrong persons.'

'They don't know there's still anything there to look for. Only we know that.'

'They may find it nevertheless. By accident. Or they may destroy it without knowing. The Guardian could not prevent that either.'

'What chance of these restorations?' asked Canteloupe.

'Restorations are the idea of the French authorities at Eu. The Department of Monuments and Antiquities, equivalent to our Ministry of Works. As it stands, the Castle is extremely dangerous. There are whacking great blocks of donjon just waiting to drop on a fellow's nut and crush him flat as a flounder; there are hidden pits to fall into, enticing staircases which shoot you over sudden precipices or lead into Minoan labyrinths.

'A few months ago Master Théophile Didier, aged twelve, threw his baby brother down an open well in the keep. That does it, said the authorities: we'll close the place down; and slam went the portcullis. Oh no you don't, said all the urchins, picknickers, antiquarians and country copulatives who enjoyed the place; and they got a battering ram and opened it up. All right, said the authorities: carry on going there, but for Christ's sake be careful, and one of these days we'll get round to tidying it up and making it safer: restorations.'

'One of these days?' said Canteloupe.

'Yes. When I first heard what was proposed, I was worried. Restorations were the last thing to suit my programme. But I have an ally who lives there – you'll probably meet him when you go to Dieppe – called the Marquis des Veules-les-Roses.'

'Pretty name,' said Baby, and tickled Jo-Jo's palm with her forefinger.

'He sits on some local committee to do with preservation and so on, and as soon as he heard what the authorities were thinking of doing with Arques, he persuaded them (a) that the

33

money needed would be better used to shore up the church at Varengeville, and (b) that Arques was past being restored anyway.'

'So that's all right.'

'For the time being, I think. But sooner or later they'll have to make some token gesture to make Arques less perilous (remember Master Didier's baby brother) and even a token gesture could wreck our enterprise. So we act now.'

'And our big worry,' said Canteloupe, 'is the Guardian. How is it that this Guardian makes such problems for us, and has protected the treasure against predators down the centuries, and yet will be incapable of fending off these restorers, if they ever come?'

'The Guardian,' said Ptolemaeos, 'is alerted by the *intention of the seeker*. The intent to find the treasure puts out psychic waves which send the Guardian into action. The restorers do not know of the treasure –'

'Why not? Haven't *they* read the Chronicle?'

'Not necessarily. Do civil servants, even French civil servants, bother to read such things? And even if they have, they assume, like everyone else who has read it, that the treasure was some piece of frippery which has long since vanished. A lost vanity. So they have no *intention* of seeking it: no waves emanate from them, the Guardian sleeps on. And then perhaps the restorers accidentally find it and smash it with one of their bulldozers – and it is too late.'

'But in our case,' said Baby, 'we're going to be anticipated. Our knowledge, our deliberate purpose, put out vibes and get this Guardian jumping about. How *near* do we have to be before the Guardian wakes?'

'Good question, Tullia. I wish I knew the answer.'

'And what in any case,' said Baby, 'can the Guardian actually do?'

'Another good question. There are hints . . . in this Appendix I have spoken of. They imply that it can be very disagreeable.'

'In what way?'

Ptolemaeos hesitated.

'It is not specific.'

Jo-Jo eyed Ptolemaeos, whom she suspected of evasion, but decided to let it pass for the time being.

'And another question,' said Baby, who enjoyed going into things: 'is this Guardian the same one that protected Xanthippe's party when they were crossing the sea-marshes to reach Saint-Gilles? I believe you quoted the Chronicle to that effect?'

'I did. Yes, Tullia. I would imagine it was the same protector.'

'One of the ladies-in-waiting was a white witch perhaps? And commanded her familiar to protect them all . . . and later to become Guardian of the treasure?'

'The Appendix does not deny such a conception. Nor does it remotely encourage it.'

'Look,' said Baby, 'if Canty and I are going to help out in all this, can't we just read the jolly old Appendix, find out exactly where we stand, and take it from there?'

'No,' said Ptolemaeos, 'no, no, no, no: no.'

'I think you're mean.'

'It's for your own good. You'll probably find it all out in time, and very sorry you'll be that you have. You may very well have to be told at some stage, particularly if things go wrong. But not yet. Not yet.'

Baby pouted. Jo-Jo stuck out her tongue at Ptolemaeos. Canteloupe crossly examined a recently scuffed patch on his left toe-cap.

'So that's all for now,' Ptolemaeos said. 'All you have to remember just now, Canteloupe, is that you and Tullia must be dining in the Hotel Cours in Saint-Gilles not later than eight p.m. this day week. Reservations have already been made for you. Just drive yourselves down there, clock into the place on the right day – late afternoon, I suggest – and wait for Ivan to introduce himself.'

35

'ISN'T ALL THIS EXCITING?' said Baby to Jo-Jo.

'Oh, *yes*. That poor little Xanthippe, and the treasure and the Guardian and the Castle –'

'No, no, you fool,' said Baby; 'I meant *this*.'

And she planted a huge wet kiss between Jo-Jo's tiny breasts.

'Oh, darling,' Jo-Jo said, 'I wish mine were like yours.'

She cupped one of Baby's in her palm.

'You're lovely,' said Baby: 'just like a fine strong boy with a cunt.'

'Would you sooner it was a cock?'

'I like everything,' said Baby with zest, 'that's good in its own kind. Your cunt,' she said after affectionate investigation, 'is really super.'

'I am glad you still like it. I thought perhaps that since we're doing it two weeks ahead of schedule you might not be so keen.'

'Keen,' said Baby, wriggling her finger in Jo-Jo's fundament, 'is not the word. I'm ravenous. And so must you be. That's if Ptoly and you still have the same old thing about not coming with each other.'

'We still have it,' said Jo-Jo. She passed her forefinger down Baby's spine. 'There for you too?'

'Um,' Baby said.

'Oh, yes. We still have it. No one goes over the top in this house – unless you're here. Ptoly still goes to his massage parlour once a month, though he says the expense is now wicked, and I just wait for you.'

'No wanking?'

'No wanking – except a little pretending, to amuse Ptoly. He's really quite right. If you don't come you don't get tired of each other, and if you're living in the same house it's very important you shouldn't. What about you and Canty?'

36

'Canty's taught me to toss him off the way his study-fag did. Making a mess, he calls it. "Canty wants to make a mess on Baby's tum-tum," he says – but only about once in six months, so I don't think he'll get tired of *that* in a hurry.'

'What's in it for you?'

'He's very grateful and very loving . . . but he won't actually do anything to me, except undress me and kiss me goodnight. *That's* it, sweetheart. Not too hard. Just waggle.'

'You can put yours in further if you like. Ooooh. Do you think Canty and Ptoly are really happy about us. I mean . . . about *this*.'

'Of course they are,' Baby said. 'They both love us very much and they both want us to enjoy ourselves. For reasons of their own they limit what they do with us, but of course they understand that a girl needs a real throberama from time to time.'

'Suppose a girl wanted a real throberama with other *men*?'

'*That* might be a little difficult. Myself, I think we're very lucky as we are. Imagine the ghastliness of having a lover – some boring and conceited stockbroker with smelly feet.'

'One might do better than that,' Jo-Jo said.

'And one might do even worse. One might get carried away and start carrying on with a jockey or a bruiser or a journalist or something foul like that.'

'One could always get rid of him.'

'Not so easy sometimes, cherry pie. People will *cling*. Promise you'll never cling. And I'll promise you,' said Baby.

'I'll never cling, darling. Would you like me to show you something really special?'

'Yes.'

'It's a new trick of Ptoly's. We'll have to take our fingers out, so that I can get off the bed and find the kit.'

'What kit?'

'The bicycle pump,' Jo-Jo said. 'Ah . . . Now, what I do is, I screw on the flex, like this, and then I pop the other end of the flex into your thing –'

'Which thing?'

'Front thing this time, darling. Just feed it in . . . that's right . . . and now I start pumping.'

'Zow-*eeee*,' said Baby after the first few strokes. 'What happens when Ptoly does this to you? How come you don't come?'

'Ptoly's very clever at knowing when it's near. So he stops. Do you want me to stop?'

'Yes,' said Baby, 'because I want you to get on the bed again . . . so that we can both be very close . . . darling Jo-Jo. . .'

'Darling Baby. . .'

'Very, very close . . . and stroke each other, very, very gently, making it last . . . and then be together at the end, which men call the little death.'

THE NEXT DAY Tom Llewyllyn, Baby's father and a Fellow of Lancaster College, came over from Cambridge for Luncheon.

'How is the old place?' asked Ptolemaeos.

'Even worse than when you were there.'

Ptolemaeos had been there in the early sixties.

'Galloping Socialism?'

'Terminal,' said Tom, with a look of genial displeasure.

'But I thought,' said Ptolemaeos, 'that you were a Socialist yourself.'

'Poppa was a member of the Labour Party,' said Baby, fondling her father's wavy head of hair. 'He was a great admirer of Major the Earl Attlee . . . if you take my meaning.'

'And,' said Tom, 'of Provost the Lord Constable. Our Provost at this moment. An old Labour man with no nonsense about him, who's just managed to hold the College together – till now. But now . . . he's sixty-five and his time's up. Lord Constable must pack his traps and leave his lodging. God knows what sort of monster will be put there in his stead.'

'Luncheon is ready,' said Jo-Jo, who had just come in looking rather sweaty. 'We must eat it at once or it will spoil.' She smiled at Baby. 'Your favourite,' she said, 'quenelles of pike with lobster sauce.'

'Darling,' said Baby. 'Where on earth did you find the pike?'

'I caught one when I knew you were coming. There's still a lot of them in these Fen rivers round here.'

'I call that rather grand of you,' said Canteloupe. 'Live bait or a spinner?'

'Spinner. It gives you exercise, spinning. I get restless, just sitting there watching a float.'

'It's a great moment when the float dips,' said Canteloupe.

'That's true,' conceded Jo-Jo: 'rather like starting to come.'

'What an extraordinary comparison,' said Canteloupe.

'Not at all. Just think of that . . . certain moment . . . when something quivers inside you – like the float in the water – and you feel it's on its way.'

'Ingenious, I admit. Poetic too. Whatever made you think of it?'

'Love,' said Baby, 'that's what made her think of it. Love, sweet love. God, I could *rape* those quenelles.'

'But surely,' Ptolemaeos was saying to Tom Llewyllyn as they sat down, 'the Statutes of the College provide for Constable's retirement to be deferred by the Council for a term of up to five years after his sixty-fifth birthday.'

'No one wants to defer it,' said Tom, 'except for a few old hands like me. The junior Fellows are red in tooth and claw: the social scientists are on the march in jeans and gym-shoes, and Provost Constable, with his hand-made brogues and his tweeds, must cry goodnight "and leave the world for them to bustle in".'

'How depressing you are,' said Baby. 'It's too bad of you, Poppa, when Jo-Jo's made this delicious lunch,' of which she shovelled a huge forkful into her wide, pretty mouth. 'Now tell me a thing,' she said, hoovering down her food with a great suck at the same time; 'Ptoly's friend Ivan Barraclough – what's he like?'

'Ask Ptoly.'

'Oh, I have. Ptoly says he's tough but sensitive, and supplements considerable powers of intuition with immaculate use of reason.'

'There you are then,' said Tom.

'*But*,' said Baby, 'if this Barraclough was at Lancaster with Ptoly, you must have known him too. I'd like a second opinion.'

'Why?'

'Canty and I are going to meet him very soon.'

'Why?'

'For purposes of research,' Ptolemaeos put in smoothly. 'Ivan and I have an antiquarian project, in which Tullia and Canteloupe are also interested. I too,' he added, 'would be glad to know your view of Ivan.'

'I was a married man when the two of you were up,' said Tom with a discernible note of bitterness. 'I wasn't in College very much.'

'But you knew them both,' said Jo-Jo, 'because you taught them. Ptoly said so. Tell us what *both* of them were like.'

'Ptolemaeos was much as he is now: ample in girth and mean in spirit, affable but not amiable, lavish but not generous, furnished with considerable abilities which he exercised in a condescending and dandified but (I am bound to admit) highly effective fashion. In a word, he was, as he doubtless is, a liege man of Belial.'

Ptolemaeos chuckled. Jo-Jo reddened.

'But he's lovely,' she cried. 'He's so good at understanding a person.'

'Understanding in order to exploit. This antiquarian project: I'll wager my weight in gold that he's using Ivan Barraclough to do all the hard work and using Baby and Canteloupe –'

'Tullia and Canteloupe,' emended Ptolemaeos mildly.

'– Using Madam and Canteloupe to keep an eye on Ivan in case he tries to claim the loot or the credit, as the case may be.'

'So Barraclough's that sort of man, is he?' Baby said. 'Grabby?'

'Not grabby. He knows his worth and insists on his deserts,' said Tom. 'If he thinks Ptolemaeos has not contributed a fair share of effort, he will deny him any share of the prize.'

'A just man?' said Baby.

'To the point of obsession.'

'A fanatic?'

'No. There is no emotion here. Justice, with Ivan, is not a matter of passion but of analysis. He himself will do what is right, just as he would avoid errors of logic or syntax – because he feels intellectually obliged. He will work out the factors and the denominators and will proceed as they instruct. And if they instruct him that no share is due to Ptolemaeos, then Ptolemaeos will have a share only over Ivan's dead body.'

'Fortunately,' said Ptolemaeos, 'he is well aware of my very substantial contribution, in time, research and, *évidemment*, finance. It was my network, originally established for purposes of scholarship and enquiry, which traced the course of Xanthippe's journey from the Mani to Dieppe, and also did most of the groundwork for Ivan's more particular investigations later on. He will be the first to acknowledge his huge debt to my agents . . . one of whom unless I am much mistaken, is approaching Ivan at this very moment.'

IVAN BARRACLOUGH sat in a tavern on the island in the Lake of Ioannina and ate lake trout, which tasted like cotton waste arranged on a frame-work of barbed wire.

He had caught the boat from the jetty under the walls of the castle which had been Ali Pasha's Headquarters and he was now sitting on or near the spot where Ali Pasha once loved to come and dally with his women and his boys. But Ivan's thoughts were not of Ali Pasha, or not for long: he did indeed reflect on the assassination of that interesting adventurer, which had occurred in the midst of his dainty pleasure and in the precinct of a monastery not a stone's throw from where Ivan now sat; but having briefly mused on the moral of the incident (that a stiff penis is a wand that waves the Gods themselves into infatuate negligence of their proper business and security), Ivan turned his thoughts to the task which had brought him to the island.

The Princess Xanthippe, he first reminded himself, had of

course never visited Ioannina. She had taken ship, with Hubert of Avallon, a long way south, at Glarentza. Ivan had in fact just come from Glarentza, now called Killini, though there could be no clues there for him as the place had been twice destroyed, by Constantine Palaeologue in the fifteenth century and by the Germans in the twentieth. Even so, however, he had decided that a courtesy visit to the little harbour town could do no harm, and he had taken the opportunity to walk in the handsome nearby Castle of Chlemoutsi (or Clermont) which is sometimes confused with Glarentza (or Clarence) and at which, he supposed, Xanthippe just might have been lodged for a night or two while waiting to take ship. But he caught no whiff of her ghost there, nor had he seriously expected to; and he now decided that he must finally accept, as the most he could ever know about this stage in her journey, the bald statement of Hubert – that the Despoina had been duly delivered to him by Lord Geoffery de Bruyère at the port of Glarentza and that 'with present exigence' he had taken her on board and bade the master set sail for Corfu.

So Xanthippe had sailed away to Corfu, and Ivan for his part now motored to Ioannina, which lay on the way to Igoumenitza and the Corfu ferry. But he had business in Ioannina beyond mere transit. For although Xanthippe herself had never been there, she had received a gift which came thence – a gift from this very island.

Ioannina, during the Frankish rule of Romany, had remained in Greek hands and had been a popular place of refuge or passage for Greeks from Constantinople or the Morea. To Ioannina from Byzantium in 1255 came the Thessalian-born Necromancer Aristarchos of Veroia, on his way to investigate the ancient oracle of the dead at Ephyra, where Cocytos merges with Acheron. Aristarchos had heard from a colleague, who had for a time been a refugee in Ioannina, that there was to be found on the island in the lake there a rare herb of which the fragrance had strong appeal for spirits such as he, Aristarchos, might encounter at Ephyra; and he therefore broke his journey at Ioannina to gather some of this little known and valuable flora.

Aristarchos, being sage and scientist as well as magician,

suspected, from the description which he had been given of it, that the herb was a Convolvulus variant listed by Leon of Argos in his "Αυθη Ελληνικα (Flowers of Greece) Chamaetisos Hyptios. Since this was not known to possess anything much by way of fragrance (of appeal whether to dead or to quick) Aristarchos inferred that if his informant had been speaking the truth the herb to be found on the island must be a special sub-variant of the variant; and this indeed he discovered to be the case. Chamaetisos Hyptios Spanopouloēdes (his extended version of the name) had a narrower and more sharply pointed leaf than plain Chamaetisos Hyptios, and a pinker flower. It also had a pronounced fragrance, displeasing to his own nostrils but, for all he knew, delectable to ghosts; while the leaves, as he elicited by ingenious experiment, contained a zestful sap which had various and powerful effects on physiological and cerebral function, the variations depending on the manner in which the leaf or its sap were administered, i.e. by whom and to whom. When the leaf dried, it retained its flavour if chewed, and it could be preserved, if carefully put up, for months and even for years. What was more, the effects on the human body, mind and (as Aristarchos believed) soul or spirit, were just as powerful when the leaf was taken or administered in its dried and preserved form as when it was applied fresh. Although the actual chemistry remained obscure to Aristarchos, of the herb's therapeutic (and other) potential there could be no question: Chamaetisos Hyptios Spanopouloēdes had certainly merited the detour.

The authority for all this, Ivan knew, was what Ptolemaeos and he used to call 'The Special Appendix' of Hubert's Chronicle. According to this, Aristarchos went on his way from Ioannina to Ephyra, conducted his investigation there (with what degree of satisfaction or success was not related), then took ship from nearby Previsa to Corfu, where he wished to inform himself about a particularly ferocious cult of Artemis-Hecate which had flourished in a temple near the Capital during the sixth century B.C.

In Corfu, by sheer chance, Aristarchos had encountered Xanthippe and Hubert, who were staying there while Hubert pondered an alternative route to bypass plague-ridden Venice.

As soon as Aristarchos had clapped eye on Xanthippe he had obviously received the kind of impression that certain others had already received in the course of her journey. But his reactions were those of a man well versed and trained in these matters: as far as Aristarchos was concerned there was neither moral scruple nor religious aversion, there was merely professional interest. 'He was long closeted with my Lady,' stated Hubert in the Special Appendix, 'who was attended by two of her hand-maidens to ensure that all intercourse might be virtuous.' It later appeared that Aristarchos had done a deal with Xanthippe: in return for a full account of 'her condition, vision and possession' Aristarchos had given her a quantity of the herb from Ioannina, with the remark that 'being situate as she was, the Lady might well find use for it ere long'. A few days later Hubert and Xanthippe had sailed from Corfu for Bari; neither of them ever saw Aristarchos again.

There had been some problem, Ivan remembered now, about how to preserve the herb in good condition. Aristarchos himself kept the dried flowers in an airtight phylactery. Xanthippe owned nothing similar, but decided that a small onyx box in which she used to carry sweetmeats –

'Good afternoon, Kyrie Barraclough,' said an obese Greek in a slick blue suit and winkle-picking shoes. '"The Iniquity of Oblivion blindly scattered her poppy."'

'"Man is a noble animal,"' rejoindered Ivan, completing the agreed code, '"splendid in ashes, and pompous in the grave." Please to sit down, Kyrie. Some refreshment?'

'Café Grecos, if I may. Sweet.' And after Ivan had ordered this, 'You found our trout to your liking?'

'Lacking in savour.'

'Ah. You should have tried the *écrevisses*. They abound in this lake.'

'I find the shells too annoying.'

The Greek inclined his head in polite acceptance of this sentiment and fondled the coffee cup which had just been set before him.

'I have two messages for you,' he said, 'from the Fat Pharaoh of the Fens.'

Not for the first time, Ivan wondered why Ptolemaeos

insisted on these infantile rigmaroles. Perhaps it was to reassure the Greeks, who liked devious methods and suspected simplicity. But then not only the Greeks but all other of Ptolemaeos' agents had to use these absurd and arcane formulae. Perhaps, thought Ivan, he makes us do it because the continued use of an imbecile nursery idiom is, after all, an anodyne, and serves to ease one's spirit and soothe one's nerves in face of the really rather hideous concepts which underlie this whole affair.

'How says His Divinity?' he said now, observing the prescribed form.

'The news from France is good,' said the Messenger, on whom, once the introductory code had been got through, precision was strictly enjoined. 'The Marquis des Veules-les-Roses is convinced that no attempt will be made, for many weeks at least, to interfere with the Castle. You are therefore to proceed absolutely as planned, and to be at the inn in Saint-Gilles six days from now. Which brings me to my second item: the other Marquis, the English one, will be meeting you there with his wife as previously arranged.'

'I see,' said Ivan.

But in truth he did not see. Ptoly's rule was that established arrangements and conditions should not be repeated, confirmed or even referred to: only if they had to be changed should they be the subject of messages or discussion. Now here was this Greek, who had sought him out with expense and difficulty, merely telling him what he very well knew already, i.e. that restorations to the Castle of Arques-la-Bataille had been indefinitely postponed and that he was to meet Lord and Lady Canteloupe at Saint-Gilles according to schedule. The repetition was quite pointless: Ptoly must have had some other reason for ordering the man to come to him.

'I see,' he said again. 'And does the Divinity vouchsafe no other message?'

The Messenger frowned. He looked puzzled, dissatisfied, uneasy.

'Yes,' he said at length. 'I was to say to you, "Now gather round me, you, my Myrmidons, Here at the setting of the sun." From your poet Shakespeare, I think.'

'From *Troilus and Cressida*. A lesser known but very intriguing piece.'

'You understand what the words are intended to convey?'

'Oh, yes.'

They were the words which Achilles had used when instructing his warriors to kill Hector; what they conveyed was that Ptoly wanted this fat Greek dead before sunset.

AFTER ALL THEIR GUESTS had gone, Ptolemaeos walked with Jo-Jo in the garden, in the evening of the day.

'How was it with Baby, sweetheart?'

'Prima,' sighed Jo-Jo, 'oh, prima.'

'Good. It is always a great comfort to have pleasant memories of someone.'

'What do you mean . . . "comfort" . . . "memories"?'

'I mean . . . that it's a long time, according to the schedule, before you're due to meet Tullia again. But meanwhile you do have the comfort of these memories.'

'Is that all you meant? Play square, Ptoly.'

'There could be . . . complications. Someone has been sticking his nose in where it isn't wanted. Ivan Barraclough has instructions to lop it off.'

'Just his nose, Ptoly?'

'Ivan will know what to do, pratty-pie. It should be dead easy, the way I've set it up for him. But if things *did* go a bit wrong, and if some nasty officious friend of the nose's *did* perhaps follow Ivan to Saint-Gilles, then I suppose that Tullia and Canteloupe might find themselves in the line of fire.'

'You haven't warned them?'

'No. In my view, it would only cause deleterious worry when the odds are there will be absolutely nothing to worry about. But because you love Baby Canteloupe – and don't think I can't see the galaxies in your eyes when we discuss her – because you really love Tullia, my darling, and do not merely

46

hanker after her luscious bold limbs, I will warn them if you ask me to.'

'Oh, I love Tullia. But I believe, I absolutely believe, lovely Ptoly, in you. If you say it's better not to warn them, then that's all right by me.'

'Good girl. Give us a kiss. Give us a hot deep kiss, "just like what you gave your Baby last night".'

'IF YOU CARE TO COME WITH ME,' said Ivan to the Greek Messenger, 'I will show you what the Fat Pharaoh meant by his quotation from Shakespeare.'

The Greek nodded. Ivan held up his hand for the bill. Messenger, he thought: in Greek, αγγελος, angelos, angel: some angel: I think I know why Ptoly told him to meet me here: here, rather than anywhere else: yes: it must be that.

When Ivan had paid the bill, they walked down a narrow street and out of the little village.

'There are several monasteries on this island,' Ivan explained to the Greek, who nodded in courteous admiration, as if amazed that Ivan should know. 'There is the Monastery of Pantaleimon, where they killed Ali Pasha, which is near the water of the lake.' The Greek nodded again. 'But just beyond it,' Ivan continued, 'even nearer the waters, is the Monastery of the Prodromos, of the Man Who Went Before.'

Ivan now went before the Greek: into a wooden kiosk, at the entrance of which he bought tickets for them both, down steps and into a tunnel, up steps again and out on to rock. The cliff which now faced them was plumed by huge plane trees and pierced by a wide cave. In front of the cave, trying to nestle into it, was a chapel.

'Agios Ioannis Prodromos,' said Ivan. 'Come.'

He led the way towards the chapel, into the nave and up to the screen.

'Thirteenth century, this part of it,' Ivan explained. The Greek nodded gravely. '1232, or thereabouts. And almost at once they found that a kind of plant had started growing in the earth which gathered between the stones, a plant which put out a pinkish-grey flower, a pungent fragrance of tar, and a pretty leaf in shape rather like a spearhead. So they called the leaves "Myrmidons" after the Spearmen of Achilles. The Fat Pharaoh wants me to gather some, as they are of great botanical interest.'

Ivan started to pick the leaves off the creeper which trailed round the lower part of the wall. It was not of course true that they were called 'Myrmidons': he had said so only to explain the appearance of the word in Ptolemaeos' message. But everything else he had said about them was true as far as he knew: the plant and the leaves had started to grow (according to the Special Appendix of the Chronicle of Hubert of Avallon) shortly after the building of the chapel. And again, the leaves were indeed of great botanical interest. They were also, as he would not be telling the Messenger, of other interest, so much so that many men had come gather them, among these men Aristarchos of Veroia, in 1255.

'They are famous, among other things, for a pungent yet delectable flavour,' said Ivan. 'Try chewing one.' Unseen, he tore a leaf very slightly to release the sap; then offered it to the Messenger.

The Messenger looked as if he would have preferred to refuse the offer; but such a refusal would have been against Greek laws of courtesy, the more so as Ivan had now put a leaf in his own mouth.

After Ivan had pretended to chew (leaving the flesh of his leaf uncut by his teeth) for three or four minutes, and after the Greek had pretended to chew but had nevertheless absorbed the sap of his torn leaf for a like period, Ivan said:

'Why does the Fat Pharaoh of the Fens wish you to be killed?'

'Because I found out what you were seeking,' the Messenger said bleakly.

'How did you find out?'

'I went to the Pharaoh's great house in England to receive

instruction. I found the Chronicle – and the special part of it. A safe had been left unlocked.'

'You understand what I must do to you?'

The man nodded dully.

'Or rather, what you must do to yourself.'

For one minute Ivan told the Messenger exactly how, when and where to commit suicide. There was no question, he told himself as he left the chapel, but that he would be obeyed. The effect of the leaf, both fresh and later when dried, had been tested, time and time again, though with less deadly intent, by Ptolemaeos and himself. What remained to be seen, thought Ivan, as he walked under the murmuring plane trees towards the village and the quay, was whether the *other* effect of the leaf had been correctly reported in the Appendix of the Chronicle: whether the Mage Aristarchos had been right in the special directions he had given the Despoina Xanthippe for its use in the extremes of her affliction.

MAURICE BERTRAND MARTEL, Marquis des Veules-les-Roses, Comte d'Offranville et de Cany-Barville, Vicomte de Barville, hereditary Capitaine de Fécamp et d'Etretat, and Sire de Longueil, walked down the drive of his huge and handsome house (early eighteenth-century; twelve bays) near Cany-Barville, in the company of his elder sister (late nineteenth-century; two bays, amazingly prominent) and even elder dog. Which is to say that the Marquis was eighty, his sister (Magdalene Françoise, Princesse d'Héricourt-en-Caux) was eighty-five, and the dog, a golden labrador, was seven times eighteen equals one hundred and twenty-six. Yet the trio was spruce, and kept up a brisk pace *en route* for the nearby chapel of Barville, where they were to inspect some damage done to the wood carvings, allegedly by some German hitch-hikers.

'Male and female,' said Madame la Princesse. 'Young and

filthy. Claudine watched them go in, she told me on the telephone, from the door of her cottage.'

'If she had the wit to observe that they were young and filthy, she should have had the wit to go in after them. Anyway, how did she know they were German?'

'They conversed in grunts.'

'So does every nation north of France. None of this explains why she did not follow them.'

'Oh, she did. But when she reached the porch she heard the girl wailing like a banshee, and the man bellowing like a hippopotamus, and she felt that it would be indecorous to witness what was clearly going on inside.'

'But if they were so agreeably occupied, why, and when, did they damage the carvings?'

'The bellowing ceased almost at once, whereupon the wailing turned into a grizzle of disappointment which was succeeded by shrill insults – there was no mistaking the tone, Claudine said – in the Nordic tongue aforesaid. Clearly the damage was done as the result of deprivation in the female or failure in the male, or both. I diagnose premature ejaculation followed by discontent on the one part and humiliation on the other.'

They turned off the drive and walked across a meadow to a stream that was lined by weeping willows. The chapel was about a hundred yards up-stream, partly visible from the point they had reached, partly masked by rhododendra.

'If this sort of thing is to continue, Magdalene, we may have to keep the place locked.'

'Or have the carvings removed, Bertrand. They are the only things of value inside.'

'How badly are they damaged?'

'That is what we have come to ascertain. Good-day, Claudine.'

A woman of about sixty, so ill-favoured and malformed that she could only (one might hazard) have been spawned on a witch by the Devil, bobbed a courtesy to the Princess and her brother.

'Madame la Princesse. M'sieur le Marquis. I shall show you.'

With long, hobbling strides Claudine led the way into the

porch and thence into the chapel. She passed up the nave and into the chancel, where she made a sudden dart to the right, pounced on the southern choir stall, and lifted one of the seats to reveal the carven misericord beneath it. The labrador, who had followed hard on Claudine's clogs, began to tense its left rear leg against the woodwork, then remembered where it was, snuffled, and withdrew.

'*Quelle cochonnerie* did you intend!' the Princess admonished the animal. 'Not but what your instinct in the matter was apt.'

The carving represented a rather bedraggled lady who was peering through a gap in the parapet of a rampart. Closer inspection revealed that she had hoisted the hem of her robe over the crook of her left arm, the hand at the end of which she was unmistakably applying to her pudenda. The damage, now indicated by Claudine, consisted in the removal of a very small piece of the lady's hair, which had left a minute area of splintered wood.'

'Accidental, not malicious,' said the Marquis to his sister. 'Let me suggest an alternative scenario. The young people came to admire the misericords, which are mentioned in the guide book. Excited by the subject of this one, the male fingers it, does so clumsily, unintentionally removes a small piece of rotting wood. After which, his excitement being unabated, he proceeds to rut with the female, who is wailing, not in pleasure, but in distress at such blasphemous conduct in a holy place. But very soon it is finished for him, whereupon the wail of distress subsides and becomes, first a whimper of reproach, then, as she sees the confusion which he had made about her person, a sharp rebuke that he had taken no precautions. On the available evidence this interpretation is in every way as rational, *chère Magdalene*, as yours.'

'How did they look,' the Princess asked Claudine, 'as they left?'

'Tired and cross, Madame la Princesse.'

'That would fit either rendering,' said des Veules-les-Roses.

'The trouble with yours,' his sister rejoindered, 'is that these days the young take no precautions, *comme d'habitude*, and she would never have rebuked him on that count. All this however, is but idle conjecture. The immediate lesson to be learned from this sorry affair is that the carvings need treatment for rot. I believe we can have them injected or anointed.'

'I shall telephone the office at Eu and find out?'

'Which office?'

'Our own people. The Norman Committee of Historic Preservation.'

'*Cher Bertrand*. That committee is well enough for deciding what should or should not be done, but it knows nothing about how to do it. For that we must go to the Office in Eu of the Department of Monuments and Antiquities.'

'*Chère Magdalene*. If I go to that Department, they will send somebody, almost certainly that nosy young man Jean-Marie Guiscard, to examine the damage. He will come, he will be reminded, quite properly, of the legend of the Despoina Xanthippe at the Castle of Arques-la-Bataille.'

'Why should he be reminded?'

'Most of these misericords, as you well know, have defied interpretation. But *this one*, it is understood, represents the Despoina Xanthippe while she was imprisoned in the Castle of Arques.'

'It represents a young woman standing on a wall and pleasuring herself. It has never been established that the sculptor had in mind the Despoina Xanthippe.'

'Nevertheless, it will remind Jean-Marie Guiscard of the story, and the story will remind him of the Castle, and he will start thinking, once again, of how restorations are needed there, and by association of thought he will equate the immediate necessity of *les reparations* here with the immediate necessity of *les reparations* there, and before we can turn round he will have his men and his machines in the Castle – just when M'sieur Ptolemaeos Tunne and I least want them there.'

'But you have persuaded M'sieur Guiscard and the Department to leave the Castle alone for the time being.'

'With great difficulty, yes, I have persuaded them. I particularly do not wish their interest in the Castle to be re-aroused. So I must send for this affair' – he gestured at the delinquent lady on the rampart – 'to the Norman Committee.'

'Who can and will do nothing for us. *Viens, Coco*,' the

Princess called to the dog. 'Your master would leave the family treasures to rot to pieces, and all because of some fantastical scheme he has with a fat, mad English to possess themselves of what is not there and would do them no good if it were. *Bon jour*, Claudine. Be diligent, *mon enfant*, and pray to God to forgive your parents their sin.'

'*Bon jour*, Madame la Princesse. We shall lock the chapel from now on? It will save me from having to watch all day.'

'That,' said the Marquis, 'is what you are employed to do. To unlock the chapel at dawn and to watch who goes in and ensure that they come out. You will continue.'

'*Comme tu dis*, *papa*,' said Claudine spitefully. '*Au revoir, Maman. Au revoir, Coco.*'

IN THE END, the Princess won her way, by the simple expedient of telephoning the Department of Monuments and Antiquities at Eu without any further reference to her brother and requesting that an expert on woodwork be sent to Cany-Barville. The expert who came was indeed 'that nosy young man' Jean-Marie Guiscard, and he was indeed reminded by the misericord, as the Marquis had predicted he would be, of the Despoina Xanthippe and the sad state of the Castle of Arques-la-Bataille. But to be fair to the Princess, none of this made any difference to the course of events that followed; what happened would have happened in any case, whether she had summoned Guiscard or no: for at much the same time as Coco was tensing his leg against the Despoina Xanthippe's image in the choir stalls at Cany-Barville, and several days before Jean-Marie actually came to the chapel to make his inspection, the following conversation was beginning in the Office of the Department of Monuments and Antiquities in the Rue de Tréport in Eu.

'ARQUES-LA-BATAILLE,' said Jean-Marie Guiscard to the Director of that Branch of the Department, Monsieur Socrates Besançon.

'What about Arques-la-Bataille?' said M. Socrates warily. 'We have just agreed with the recommendation of the Norman Committee of Historic Preservation that the case of Arques is hopeless and that the money at present available will be better applied to the church at Varengeville. That is *all*, dear Jean-Marie, about Arques.'

'We must reverse the decision. The Norman Committee has no authority. It is just a self-elected gang of rich busybodies. *We* have the power to decide, *cher Directeur*, and we must decide to do something for Arques while there is still . . . just . . . time.'

'But why this obsession about Arques, Jean-Marie?' M. Socrates wiped his bald head with a mauve silk handkerchief. 'Many would say that it is better as is – a picturesque and crumbling ruin.'

'A very dangerous ruin . . . that may crumble away altogether.'

'If people will go there, they must risk the danger. They have been comprehensively warned of it.'

'But if it rots away to nothing?'

'That donjon will last for ever.'

'But the barbican? The arch? The guard room? The observation towers?'

'Agreeable but unimportant. *Écoute*, Jean-Marie: we have neither the duty nor the resources to preserve every pile of ancient rubble in Normandy.'

'Arques is special. Because of what happened there. It is . . . a place of poetry. In the name of poetry it must be preserved.'

'Convince me, dear boy. You have ten minutes to convince me.'

So Jean-Marie rose from his chair and propelled his gawky frame round and round the Director at his desk, gesturing and declaiming and pleading, telling the story of the Despoina Xanthippe of Ilyssos and how she came to the Castle of Arques. With some of this story you are now familiar, but parts of Jean-Marie's narrative may open up new angles of vision, may suggest new attitudes to be adopted.

'This same vexatious Marquis des Veules-les-Roses,' said Jean-Marie, 'the one who so constantly pesters us with his inane suggestions and opinions, had a thirteenth-century ancestor called Henri Martel, who, like his insufferable descendant, was Sire of Longueil, at that time a small barony not twenty miles from Arques which Henri ruled over justly and liberally – so liberally that he never had a silver piece to call his own. The other important thing about him was that he wrote poetry, and was a source of high embarrassment to his many royal and noble connections both at home and abroad, who relished the poet as little as they did the pauper.'

'How so?' said M. Socrates. 'Surely the Art of the Troubadour was much prized at that time. A singer was held in honour; the composition of songs was considered an accomplishment very desirable in Princes.'

'Cousin Henri's songs were unacceptable – at any rate the early ones. They were radical. Under the guise of telling tales or celebrating *amours* he was quite clearly deprecating feudal conditions and proposing extensive reforms. He was a traitor, as his relations saw the matter, to his and their whole class. They considered dispensing of him in summary fashion, but they were a good-natured lot and in the end decided that what Cousin Henri needed was simply to make a suitable marriage and settle down – too many romps in the hay with pretty peasants, that was one source of his silly egalitarian notions. So in 1255 he was notified that his Villehardouin kinsman, William, Prince of Achaea, had decided to do something for him. The Prince had a Greek hostage or surety, the Lady Xanthippe of Ilyssos, whom he was sending for safe keeping to the Castle of Arques, which was at that time a Villehardouin stronghold administered and commanded by a one-time Serjeant in the family service, who had by now risen to be a kind of commissioned quartermaster and enjoyed the title and privileges of Castellan. All Cousin Henri had to do was to hack over to Arques, where the Castellan would make him very comfortable, and pay court to the Lady Xanthippe, whose father, Lord Phaedron of Ilyssos, was only too happy with the idea of a well connected French son-in-law and was prepared to find a very handsome dowry from his own and his forefathers' piratical profits.

'For Ilyssos, as *M'sieur le Directeur* knows well for himself, overlooks the Ionian Sea and is situated just above a very handy little harbour called Limenaion in a very comfortable little bay, all of which had much facilitated the Lords of Ilyssos in their nautical adventures over many generations. So the Lady Xanthippe had centuries of seafaring ancestry and had, as a matter of course and case, been born and bred by the sea . . . a fact of which no one took much account when making the arrangements for her future. A lamentable oversight.

'Anyhow, in due time the Lady was brought to Arques, and Henri Martel de Longueil rode over to welcome and perhaps to woo her – for although he did not approve of mercenary marriages he felt that he could not altogether ignore his powerful cousin's well-intentioned offer. Besides, he was curious to see this Princess from far Romany. So to Arques one golden September afternoon, trolling his ditties and jingling his spurs –'

'Careful, *cher* Jean-Marie,' the Director warned. 'One must not allow oneself to be carried away.'

' – So to Arques he came and asked permission to wait on the Lady. He found her in grave distress. She missed the sea. As Henri was to write when telling the story later:

> She was a Lady from Grecian land,
>   And her delight in her own countrie
> Was e'er on her father's tower to stand,
>   And gaze on the never-resting sea.

'But now, in Arques, she could not see it, although – and this made it much worse – she knew it was not at all far away. Cousin Henri was touched by her predicament. For some reason which the Chronicle does not make very clear he did not like the Lady –'

'The Chronicle?'

'The Chronicle of Avallon. Transcribed by a monk from the spoken narrative of Hubert of Avallon, who escorted the Lady from Greece to Normandy. Generally clear enough but occasionally evasive, and certainly so in this area . . . "Albeit the Sire of Longueil found her person to be fair and tender, yet did he not relish her company, vowing that another watched him from behind her eyes."'

'Rather striking.'

'But not easy to interpret. Anyway, though he didn't care for her he did pity her, and he thought it was a shameful cruelty that she should not be allowed to look at the sea. He tells us in his poem about her – a very odd combination, by the way, of the ballad and the ballade – how she had arrived in the early autumn and called the Castle "September Castle" from the month of her coming. The name suggests a liking for the place, and at first, it seems, she enjoyed herself there . . .

> . . . And walked all day upon the wall,
> And laughed with her Maidens merrily;
> But soon her joy began to pall,
> And she spake her heart to her company;
> 'September Castle is fine and tall
> And many a league is spread out for me;
> But where is the fairest sight of all?
> O where is the never-resting sea?

'It was about this time, the time when she first began to complain, that Henri had first come to see her. As I say, he didn't like her, but he was sorry for her and felt she was being badly treated. He advised her to go to the Castellan and ask to be taken on a visit to the nearby cliffs at Dieppe. Although she in her turn did not much like him – once again, the Chronicle is obscure about the reasons for this – she felt his advice was well meant and sensible, and she took it:

> She told her woe to the Castellain:
> Lord of this Castle as ye be,

57

Can ye not bring me once again
To gaze on the never-resting sea?

'But of course Lord of the Castle was exactly what the Castellan was not. He was simply an old and reliable ranker who had been put in charge of the place because his masters knew he would obey his orders to the letter. As he now did. His orders said nothing about trips to Dieppe or anywhere else: they said the Lady must be kept close in the Castle, allowed and encouraged to entertain Henri Martel but none other, and that there she should stay until her espousal to Henri – and probably till the day of their marriage, suitable arrangements for which would later be promulgated from above. So although Henri too tried to persuade him, the Castellan was firm: "Sorry, my lord, but it's more than my job is worth", the traditional whine of the underdog all down the millennia.

'Still, the Castellan liked Xanthippe's pretty face, and he hadn't noticed anything untoward behind her eyes (unlike Henri the poet, very few people did) and he wished to spare her pain and give her hope: so he told the Lady that the Channel was indeed very close and that soon she would be able to see it from the ramparts. When the leaves fell from the Great Oak that stood on the slope North by West of the Castle, the sea would become visible on a clear day. Sheer humbug, of course, lying treacherous humbug, kindly intended but solving nothing, merely delaying disaster and meanwhile feeding it more full of cruelty. The typical stratagem of an ignorant, insensitive, sentimental, sycophantic Jack Martinet.'

'What did Henri Martel make of it?'

'Henri is not much mentioned in the Chronicle at this stage. The Lady had made it clear she didn't fancy his company and he knew well enough that he didn't fancy hers; so what with one thing and another, and what with the sickly smell of impending calamity, which Henri's sharp nostrils would surely have picked up by now, I imagine he made himself pretty scarce. Nothing he could do – except exercise a poet's appreciation of the scene and prepare to make a ballad of the whole affair later. With this in view he kept in discreet touch, through servants and so on, with events inside the Castle, one of the more melancholy of which must have been the Lady's display of grief when she finally realised that she had been tricked by the Castellan:

> Then spake the Lady to all her train:
>   The leaves have fallen from off the Tree,
> Yet still I look from these walls in vain –
>   O Christ for the never-resting sea.

'After which she pined away and died?' said the Director, consulting his watch.

'After which she pined away and died. No one could help her and she would not, in any case, be helped:

> Prince, who walkest those walls to-day,
>   Gazing over fair Normandie,
> Pray for the soul of the Kyria
>   Who yearned for the never-resting sea.

'I see. The traditional *envoi* appropriate to a ballade. A ballad with a ballade's refrain and conclusion. And it is for the sake of this poem that you wish to save Arques?'

'For the sake of the poem. And the poet. And for the sake of the Lady . . . who is buried in the Castle.'

'Where?'

Jean-Marie shrugged sadly.

'There was a chapel near the donjon. We know the rough location, though nothing is left of it. The Chronicle implies that there was . . . some kind of shrine to her.'

'Now utterly vanished?'

'Yes. The shrine and everything in it. Except the Lady. *She* is still there.'

'Dust and ashes.'

'The tower she stood on, when she realised that although the leaves had fallen she would never see the sea – that is still there too.'

'Is it indeed? You know,' said the Director carefully, 'there is one aspect of all this which really intrigues me. It is hinted at in that passage of the Chronicle which explains, or fails to explain, why Henri disliked Xanthippe . . . because, he vowed, "another watched him from behind her eyes". There is something, something *pas honnête*, about this lady. Something "fishy", as the English would say, the uncovering of which, if only it turns out to be as truly disgusting as I hope it will, would make my reputation – and, just possibly, yours.'

AND SO WHEN Jean-Marie Guiscard came to Cany-Barville three days later to examine the damaged misericord he was able to cause the Marquis great annoyance by announcing that it had been decided, after all, to commence operations at Arques-la-Bataille in '*quinze jours*' to the day.

IVAN BARRACLOUGH descended some steep and narrow stone steps and stood in the darkness on a little quayside underneath the ramparts of Dubrovnik. *Twelfth Night*, he thought: 'This is Illyria, Lady.' 'And what shall I do in Illyria?' What indeed . . . if once I am found out?

Nothing can be proved, thought Ivan, as an operatic moon sailed out from behind a turret above him. That fat Greek with the winkle-picking shoes cut his own throat in his own house a whole day after I parted from him, twenty-four hours, at least, after I left Ioannina in the Land Rover. But . . . his friends will know that he met me. He is . . . he was . . . the head of Ptolemaeos' wide and intricate Greek network, and he will have maintained, to judge from his air of self-importance, many men at his HQ. These, his staff officers, his sycophants, his bodyguard, he would certainly have informed of the exact circumstances of our rendez-vous. 'I have received instructions from the Fat Pharaoh,' he would have told them: 'I am to look for the Kyrios Barraclough in the restaurant on the island, and give him a message. I do not trust this message. Some of it is too simple to need saying. Some of it is obscure. Watch closely for my return from the island . . . which should be by the boat after the boat that brings the Kyrios, as he will expect us to separate for the sake of discretion. I shall humour him in this. But if I am not on the boat after his boat, act at once.'

And the friends, watching from the Old Fort, watching the landing stage for the boats from the Island, would have seen himself, Ivan, disembark from one such boat late in the afternoon, climb into his Land Rover which was parked under the walls of the Fort, and drive away on the road to the west. So then: 'He will come by the next boat,' the friends would have said; 'and if he does not, we must act.' But sure enough, there he would have been to reassure them, the Fat Angelos with the pointed shoes, disembarking from the next boat half an hour later.

'How was it?' the friends would have asked. 'How was it, Stratis/Theodore/Andrea?' – Whatever the fellow's name was, for Ivan had not enquired.

And Stratis/Theodoros/Andreas would have shaken his head dully and started for home.

'What is the matter, Stratis/Theodore/Andrea? Why are you silent? Has the Fat Pharaoh discovered that we know his secret, that we too are on the search?'

And now the Messenger (Stratis, Theodoros or Andreas) would have answered. 'There is nothing of substance to report,' he would have said, for so Ivan had instructed him. Then he would have gone home, gone in, and shut his friends out; and some twenty-four hours later his wife/daughter/son/catamite/concubine/cook/maidservant, seeking him out for whatever purpose, would have found him with his throat cut.

And then the friends would have said: 'It is something to do with the meeting he had on the island. Now we must act. We must find this Barraclough and question him. We have friends in the Army and the Police. Let them see to it that he cross no border.'

61

Anticipating some such danger, Ivan had abandoned the route which he had originally planned (and which would have taken him west to Igoumenitza and then by the ferry to Corfu) and soon after leaving Ioannina had branched off the road for Igoumenitza and set course north by east for the town of Niki. There he had crossed the border into Yugoslavia many hours before the Messenger would have killed himself, many hours before the Messenger's friends would have sought aid from official confederates or started in pursuit. His intention was to drive north-west through Yugoslavia, to cross the top of Italy from east to west, and to proceed along the south coast of France to Saintes-Maries, where he would wait for Lord and Lady Canteloupe to arrive. Ideally he would have driven straight up the centre of Yugoslavia by Belgrade and Zagreb; but the one place on his original list which he *must* visit, among the many which he could afford, albeit reluctantly, to miss, was Dubrovnik. Surely there could be no risk in taking the longer road west to Dubrovnik and then north up the coast? And surely he could linger a few hours in Dubrovnik without danger? The Messenger's friends, even when alerted by the Messenger's death, could not conceivably trace him now.

So he had thought . . . until, leaving his favourite fish restaurant in the middle of Dubrovnik, he had known that he was being followed by a youngish man who wore a sea captain's hat, a dark blue roller-necked sweater, gum boots and black jeans. Ivan, who knew Dubrovnik well, had dodged into a complex of alleyways and had now come to the tiny quay (barely larger than the Eton Fives' Court which it somewhat resembled) under the ramparts. Either he had lost the follower, in which case he could attend to his business in Dubrovnik and leave that very night; or the man in the captain's hat would be upon him at any minute. Would he be peaceful or violent? Inquisitive or threatening? Conciliatory, reproachful or vindictive? 'This is Illyria, Lady,' Shakespeare's land of idyll and fantasy . . . until a man is found out. *Then*: What shall he do in Illyria?

PTOLEMAEOS came into the kitchen where Jo-Jo was cooking the dinner.

'Out of bounds,' said Jo-Jo. 'You don't come in here without invitation – any more than I come to your study without your say so first.'

'Come to the study.'

'The food will spoil. We're going to have a *Gratin des Queues des Écrevisses*. I caught them in Quy Fen.'

'Put them by. We can have something cold later. Come to the study.'

And when Jo-Jo came five minutes later, after she had sadly 'put by' her *Queues des Écrevisses*.

'Telephone call from des Veules-les-Roses,' Ptolemaeos said. 'The French authorities are, after all, going to excavate and restore September Castle.'

'How soon?'

'"*Quinze jours*." A fortnight.'

'So you'll have to speed the whole thing up?'

'I can't speed up Ivan. We've lost him. He should be in Corfu, at the Corfu Palace Hotel. I telexed just now. They telexed back. He didn't arrive to take up the booking.'

'What's happened?'

'I think I know – roughly. I asked him to do something rather tricky for me as he came through Ioannina, something which may have got him into trouble. If so, he'll have changed his route. God willing, he'll get to Saint-Gilles to meet Tullia and Canteloupe on the day arranged, but until then, prettikins, he may be anywhere. So speeding him up is impossible.'

'Then they'll just have to move faster than they would otherwise have done after they all meet at Saint-Gilles.'

'Easier said than done. Come and sit on Uncle's lap and let him explain.'

Jo-Jo pulled off her slacks and went to sit on Uncle's lap.

'From Saint-Gilles up to Dieppe,' said Ptolemaeos, tickling Jo-Jo's thighs round the hem of her knickers, 'they can indeed move faster. They can be there in a day. But even so by this time "fifteen days" will have been reduced to nine; and the whole trouble is that what has to be done in Dieppe and the Castle itself *cannot* be speeded up, will if anything slow itself down, and at the most optimistic estimate conceivable requires eight days. So the margin, you see, is very narrow.'

'I do see,' said Jo-Jo, gently scratching the inside of Ptolemaeos' right calf. 'Now tell me *exactly* what it is that has to be done.'

Ptolemaeos drew breath.

'We were going to leave that until later,' he said.

'So we were. But then we had plenty of time, or so we thought. Now we know the heat's on, and you're going to need all the help, every little bit, that you can get. So start by telling a girl what's cooking. Come on, Ptoly: what's on the menu?'

'*Écrevisses* for one thing.'

'Don't be so silly. Those are – were – for our dinner.'

'I'm not being silly. Be patient, and sooner or later we shall come to the *Écrevisses* in all this.'

'So you're going to tell?'

'Yes. I would have done anyway, fairly soon. Why not now? I need to relieve my tensions,' said Ptolemaeos, plucking a tiny hair from her flesh.

'Yow. Shall you also tell Baby and Canty?'

'As to that, we'll see. I may have to now it's crisis time. You can judge whether I should.'

'I'd tell Baby everything. She's that cute up top and as tough as a jack-boot.'

'You haven't heard what there is to tell yet.'

'Fire away then.'

'You load my cannon.'

'Okay,' said Jo-Jo, nimbly manipulating its breech.

'Clever little gunner. Yes . . . just . . . like . . . that. And stop at once when Uncle tells you, or it might go off by mistake. So where were we?'

'At the beginning.'

64

'Ah yes. Well, little powder-monkey, one autumn long ago Uncle went with his old college chum, Ivan Barraclough, to the Abbey at Vezelay to look at the pretty (if much restored) Romanesque carvings, and thence to a museum nearby; and in the museum, on display, was a beautifully bound and illuminated manuscript volume of the Chronicle of Avallon, being the story, as told to a learned monk by Hubert of Avallon, of how the said Messer Hubert brought the Despoina Xanthippe of Ilyssos from Glarentza, or Clarence, in the Principality of Achaea in the land of Romany to the Castle of Arques in Normandy, wherein this Lady pined and died – all of which you know well enough already, and most of which was well enough known to Uncle and Ivan at that time. But what they didn't know, and were never meant to know, was that there existed a supplementary or appendicial volume of the Chronicle. This fact emerged only by accident and through the light-headedness of the Curator, whom Uncle and Ivan invited to dinner at the excellent local inn as a means of thanking him for allowing them to look right through the manuscript of the Chronicle, which was normally confined to its glass case. This Curator, rendered irresponsible by many glasses of heavy Burgundy, which he would never have drunk had he not been flattered by the hospitable and deferential attentions of the two *milors Anglais* –'

'He can't have thought you were lords. Anyhow, the French hate them.'

'He loved us well enough after the second bottle. And after the fourth, which was ordered up out of sheer self-indulgence and with no intent to uncover a secret which neither Ivan nor I knew was there to be uncovered – after the fourth bottle, I say, this Curator opened his mouth, dribbled a little, and said: "Come with me now, and I will show you something which only I can show yet have shown to nobody during the thirty years of my Curatorship, nor any of my predecessors since 1817, when the Maison was founded, nor any of the monks before the Revolution, being held to secrecy by Love of God and Fear of the Devil. Come," said he – and we went.'

THE MAN in the sea captain's rig walked jauntily down the steps and on to the moon-lit quayside. Ivan cringed into the shadows.

'"A long time ago the world began,"' said the man, in a light voice and with creditable accent.

'"The rain it raineth every day,"' said Ivan, responding to the Yugoslavian code. He came out of the shadows and shook hands. The Sea Captain's hand was moist and very soft.

'Why did you run away?'

'I've had a nasty shock,' Ivan said.

'Oh?'

'I've been given reason to suppose that some of the Pharaoh's men in Greece have turned against him . . . and may have followed me here. Unlikely, highly unlikely, but I suppose just possible. So when I spotted you shadowing me, I at once assumed that you were one of them.'

'And what now makes you think that I am not?'

'You have given the Yugoslavian code. You are clearly one of the Pharaoh's Yugoslav agents, having nothing to do with the Greeks.'

'And why should not the Greeks have been in touch with us long since? Why should they not have persuaded us to be their allies against the Fat Pharaoh? Why should we not have exchanged knowledge of each other's code words? And why, come to that, should I not be a Greek masquerading as a Yugoslav?'

'Why not indeed? After all, you should not have been looking for me. According to my schedule, as laid down by the Pharaoh and made known to all his agents, I am not due here in Dubrovnik for two days yet.'

'I know. I was *not* looking for you. But I recognised you from the photograph which I was given, and I said to myself, "He should not be here yet, something has gone wrong, I must find out if he needs help."'

'Perhaps I do. But you have just given me a number of reasons why I should not trust you.'

'Then let me now give you some,' lilted the Sea Captain, 'why you should.' He brought his fresh but rather jowly face closer to Ivan's. His breath smelt agreeably citrous. 'We in Yugoslavia,' he pursued, 'have been told by the Fat Pharaoh about the dissidence in Greece. We have also been told of the Pharaoh's plan to kill the Greek leader – by instructing you to do so through that leader's own mouth. We have been warned that you might be compelled to break your schedule in consequence, and we have been instructed to keep an eye open for you before – and after – your proper time. So although, as I said just now, I was not looking for you in the sense of deliberately seeking for you, I *was* looking *out* for you just in case. Does all this make sense?'

'Admirable sense. What more can you tell me of the Greek dissidence?'

'It is dead with its leader. He alone has the necessary knowledge to compete with the Pharaoh in the search. As you may know, he has a large staff of assistants quite apart from his forces in the field (for the Pharaoh has been generous with funds), and many are expert in the history and lore which are required to further this enterprise. But he, the dead leader, was the only one who knew enough about the enterprise itself to set himself up in opposition to the Pharaoh, for he had once visited the Pharaoh in England and by luck or by treachery had acquired special knowledge there. This knowledge he refused to pass on even to the closest of his colleagues (in case anyone should be tempted to dispose of him and take his place) and now the Greeks are powerless through sheer ignorance.'

'Might they not still pursue me, if they could? For revenge . . . or in the hope that they might extract their dead leader's secrets from me?'

'Yes. They might try to follow you. But you have a good start and you have friends in Yugoslavia to assist you. I do not think that you can be in much danger now.'

And yet, thought Ivan, there is something wrong with all this. This man is not my friend. Why do I know this? Instinct? Vibrations in the aether? That soft, moist handshake? The

Skipper's outfit, worn to win the confidence of the gullible? No. None of these things, Ivan thought: something he has said and which I hardly noticed at the time has set off a belated alarum bell in my brain. What was it. . . ? YES. 'We have been told of his plan to kill the leader – by instructing you to do so through that leader's own mouth.' Now, thought Ivan, Ptolemaeos might well inform loyal Yugoslav agents that the Greeks had turned treacherous and that he had decided to eliminate their leader: but he would never take them into his confidence to the extent of explaining, even in part, the methods he proposed to use. Ptolemaeos was very close, he was as tight as a cockle, when it came to what he called 'Trade Secrets'. 'Tell them what, where, why and when if you absolutely must,' Ptolemaeos used to say, 'but never how.' Never how. This Sea Captain claimed that he and his friends had been told how. By Ptolemaeos, by the Pharaoh. This could not be. Yet the man knew how. Apart from Ptolemaeos, only the Greeks could know more or less how the thing had happened; *ergo* this Yugoslav must have been told by the Greeks, with whom he was in complicity, by whom he had clearly been entrusted with the task of pumping Ivan for the information that was lost with their leader, a task for which he was now carefully making the initial preparations, by soothing and finessing his victim. Later, when he had Ivan well and truly under his control, would come the time (if all else failed) for threat and torture; then, when Ivan, induced by whatever means, had told all he could, the time for Ivan's swift disposal, probably in a weighted sack some miles out to sea from this beguiling maritime city. 'This is Illyria, Lady.' 'And what shall I do in Illyria?'

'HANDS OFF,' said Ptolemaeos Tunne, taking Jo-Jo's into his own, 'or there might be a nasty accident.'

'Sometimes I wish there would be. With me too.'

'No. We agreed. Neither of us would come with the other. The orgasm is the enemy of happy cohabitation. The orgasm, even when closely disciplined and severely rationed, leads to weariness, waste of spirit and loss of love.'

'All right. But you needn't stop playing with me. I'm a long way off. . . Yes; like that. Oh *Ptoly*, you are clever. What fun it is, being with you. Now go on about this Curator. You got him pissed and he offered to show you something which no one had ever been shown before. Oh *Ptoly*, I think you'd better stop after all. I'm beginning to drip.'

'Right you be, let's give it a rest, girlie. Now, this Curator. He took us up the hill past the Basilica, and on to his museum, and down into a vault. And there, on a shelf, locked into an airtight metal box, was the Appendix to the Chronicle of Avallon. As soon as Ivan and I had taken a peep we knew it was dynamite, but already the Curator was regretting what he had done and was trying to get us out. What to do? It wasn't the kind of stuff you get the measure of in five minutes flat: it needed close study, days and weeks of concentration. Clearly we couldn't steal it, or the Frog police would be on to us the next day, as soon as the Curator was strong enough to dial their number. We couldn't photograph it – no equipment. We couldn't copy it – no time. Could we borrow it? Not on your nelly, the Curator said. So then I got firm. I needed a transcript, I told him, for *bona fide* research. Did such a thing exist? No. Then he must allow me to make one during the next few days. *Jamais*; it would be violation of his most sacred trust, etc, etc, and anyway he was forbidden to admit anyone into the vault *or* to take the Appendix out of it.

'So firmness having failed, I became brutal. I began to bash him about –'

'Oh Ptoly –'

'– Whereupon little softikins, he threw off his trousers and begged me for more and more of it – which I then promptly refused except on the strict understanding that he would admit us to the vault secretly every night until we had had time to take a competent copy of the Appendix. Yes, yes, *milor*, if only I would continue doing that thing to him, that wonderful, wonderful thing. . .'

'What wonderful thing? Punching him on the jaw?'

'I'm sorry to say it had all become more . . . sophisticated than that. It turned out that our Curator was a pioneer of a beastly and scarcely credible American practice of which you may or may not have heard rumours.'

'Oh no,' cried Jo-Jo, 'not that fist business?'

'The very same. So every night we went to the vault, and while Ivan copied out the Appendix the Curator and I . . . busied ourselves with the fist business, my fist and his fundament. Do you know, little soppy, it gets quite fascinating. The fact that it should even be possible. . . After a time I became quite fond of the little man, and really very anxious that he should have the most marvellous time I could give him, if that was the way he wanted it: so that when Ivan had finished copying and we had no more need of the Curator's services, I nevertheless went down there with him for one final work-out – a huge success, I'm happy to report. The next morning, when we all said goodbye, he was absolutely streaming with tears. And do you know, little sweetheart, I shed a few myself.'

'God be praised,' said Jo-Jo, 'for giving such diversity of love. Now then, Ptoly-Woly. Tell your little niece exactly what was in that Appendix. . .'

'THE BEST THING,' said the man in the skipper's outfit to Ivan, 'will be that you should put yourself in our hands just in case the Greeks should pick up your trail.' The young face was unctuous and earnest under the moon, like that of a priest who woos a possible convert. 'We can conceal you for as long as is necessary to make the arrangements. We can take you off by sea –'

I bet you can, thought Ivan.

'– And put you down on the Italian coast, anywhere between Bari and Venice, beyond the reach of any possible pursuit.'

Yes indeed: dead. Ivan looked up at the moon.

'Thou that makest day of night,' he thought: 'Goddess, excellently bright.

But not what he wanted at the moment. He looked into the corners of the little court. He looked at the quayside against which the little waves washed and lapped. No way out: except by the steps down which he had come.

'You could leave your hotel,' the Sea Captain was saying. 'and come to my home for the night. I shall invite some of our friends there who would like to meet you. And then, in the morning, we can begin to arrange for your discreet departure.'

In a sack.

'You are very kind,' said Ivan, 'and very prudent. But before I come with you to your home, I have one duty to discharge. I must visit a shrine which is some miles up the coast.'

'You wish to pray?' said the Captain, puzzled.

'Perhaps to pray. In any case at all to confirm my previous impression of the place.'

'Why should this be necessary?'

'In the shrine is a tomb and on the tomb is an effigy. The Lady Xanthippe visited shrine, tomb and effigy when she passed this way in 1255. Her behaviour there is relevant to our quest. The effigy is indicative of her behaviour.'

'What is this shrine? It will be closed at this hour.'

'No. It is a ruin. A ruined Chapel of Our Lady of the Sea-Marsh, formerly a pagan temple dedicated to Diana in her role of Hecate.'

'I do not know this place.'

'Very few people do. I will take you there with me, if you wish.'

The man hesitated. He shook his head in perplexity and annoyance.

'It is better you should come straight to my home,' he said.

'On the contrary,' answered Ivan, affably but ungainsayably, 'it is essential that I should visit the chapel.'

'At night?'

'That is when it is seen to its best advantage. Besides, I do not wish to be observed approaching it. There could be

71

interference . . . by the idle or the inquisitive.'

'It is getting late. Your hotel will be closed when we return from this shrine. It is important that you should get your luggage tonight, to be in readiness to leave at any time.'

'A very sound point. We shall go now to my hotel,' said Ivan, 'where I shall collect my luggage and pay my bill. Then we shall pay our respects to Our Lady of the Sea-Marsh, before we seek your home and your amiable acquaintance.'

'IF YOU ARE TO GATHER the full meaning of the Appendix,' said Ptolemaeos, quietly goosing Jo-Jo on the nape of her neck, 'you will first have to be introduced to one or two rather difficult conceptions.'

'Try me.'

'Well now: Socrates used to say that we all have our personal daemons – spirits which guide our thoughts and influence, even dictate, our actions.'

'No difficulty there. Daemon equals moral character.'

'But what happens when you postulate a daemon that is totally exterior and independent, one that is indeed allotted to an individual man or woman but, instead of abiding permanently with him or with her, comes and goes on the orders of its master . . . who may be a god or a devil.'

'Like the dreams which the gods send in Homer?'

'Very like. Or like certain recurrent illnesses – epilepsy, for example. One could easily conceive of epilepsy as a daemon or spirit allotted to a certain person and under orders to visit him at certain intervals.'

'One could. Where is all this getting us?'

'The Lady Xanthippe was intermittently attended by a daemon – or so that Appendix insists – of a distinctly unusual kind.'

'What kind?'

'Before I answer that, I have another conception to bring to your notice. Have you ever dreamed that you had had some piece of good or ill fortune, and dreamed it so convincingly that you actually believed it, for a few seconds only but nevertheless believed it, after you awoke?'

'Yes. I once dreamt I'd married Prince Charles. For a split second, until I was properly awake, I really believed I was holding his –'

' – The point is well taken. Now, it is normally held for granted these days that our dreams emanate from ourselves in some way; leave aside the details and the perversities of the mechanism, we assume that our dreams are set off by our own fears or problems, our own deprivations or desires. So when I dream that I have been created a peer of the realm, the peerage starts in my own vainglorious soul and ends with the dream – except for a few seconds before I am truly awake, during which time I can still, as it were, clasp my coronet.'

'Scratch my scalp.'

'Tickle my buttocks . . . with the points of your fingernails. Have you understood so far?'

'Yes, lovely Ptoly.'

'But more ancient theories of dreams held that some at least were sent by the gods – as indeed you mentioned just now, with reference to dreams in Homer. Their purpose was for the most part mantic – to promise, to apprise or to warn – though sometimes, as with the dream sent to Nausicaa, the purpose was disciplinary, to forbid or to command. In either case – and here we come to the nub of the thing – the dream sometimes left behind *some concrete proof* of its divine source and its good faith. Thus, if Apollo wanted to direct my attention to a horde of gold coins, he would send a dream to show me where they were and the dream would leave behind it a few *actual coins* in my hand or my bed, as a sign that it wasn't generated by my own cupidity or wishful thinking but was an accurate piece of information sent by a truthful and beneficent deity.'

'What has all this to do with *Écrevisses*?'

'*Écrevisses*?'

'You did say we'd be getting on to them sooner or later.'

'Very much later, my mouseykin. Now then. Suppose one

had a daemon that visited one at irregular intervals, the god –
or the Devil – who controlled it might well decide to send a
dream along with it, as well as whatever concrete proof of its
truth was thought appropriate. Suppose it was a bad dream
and presented one with some token or talisman of evil. When
one awoke, one might, for a few moments, actually believe in
the dream and the evil talisman which was its gift; but very
soon one would say, "But it was only a dream, thank God, and
dreams, good or bad, leave nothing behind them in the real
world." Something like that one might say . . . and one would
therefore be very disagreeably surprised when one found that
the evil talisman thrust upon one in the dream was in very
truth *still there in one's sweaty hand*. One would, you will allow,
have to think twice about a dream which left a visiting card of
that nature.'

'Is this what happened to Xanthippe?'

'Something of the kind. Apparently she was visited by a
daemon who acted, quite indifferently, as a messenger both
from God and from Satan, and both God and Satan sent her
dreams, along with concrete proofs of the dreams' veracity, in
their competition for her soul.'

'She was simply imagining it. Or making it all up.'

'But was she? According to Hubert of Avallon's Appendix
the objects which come with her dreams were very solid.'

'I'm too hungry to listen to any more until I've had a snack.
There's some caviar in the fridge. Okay?'

'Okay.'

'How can you be sure,' said Jo-Jo, going, 'that Xanthippe
wasn't somehow faking these . . . these talismen that her
dreams brought? How can you be sure she wasn't planting
them herself?'

'Of course I can't be *sure*, my dear, but if I believe this
Appendix – and why shouldn't I after all the trouble we went
to in order to get a copy? – if I believe this Appendix, I have to
conclude that one such talisman, the most solid and sensational
of all, was responsible for her death. There was no faking or
fiddling about that.'

'But Hubert's Chronicle says she simply *pined* to death, out
of yearning for her home and the sea.'

'That's the official version. The Appendix states, unequivocally, that she was killed, actually and physically killed, by an extraordinary object which was found near her bed one morning when the ladies-in-waiting came to wake her.'

'You mean . . . she was dead when they found her?'

'No. Death came quite a long time later.'

'But Ptoly, this extraordinary object. What was it and how did it kill her? And why, for Christ's sake *why*, are we to believe that it came to her or was given to her in a dream?'

'I am *very* excited, little plum pie, by the prospect of that caviar. It is bad for men of my age and temperament to be kept waiting.'

ABOUT TEN MILES NORTH of Dubrovnik, Ivan put the Land Rover into a left turn along a narrow isthmus. A Venetian Campanile loomed ahead; the isthmus turned suddenly into a circular Campo; two churches, one Palladian and one early Gothic confronted each across it, while in the dead centre and plumb in line between the churches a marble column stood pedestal to the Lion of Saint Mark.

'Why do you bring me here? This is a bad place. Everyone is gone from here except the old – and the young children of unspeakable marriages.'

Ivan drove on. As soon as they left the Campo they were driving through a heath of pine and shrub. To their left were occasional glimpses of the sea under the moon; to the right the ground mounted to a ridge. As they drove on it became flat. No more pine; just reeds. They were driving along a raised track through mud and salt-marsh, of which there was about half a mile, on either side, between the track and the sea. After driving for another few minutes, during which the width of the salt-marsh diminished slightly, Ivan stopped the Land Rover and dismounted. He signed to the young man in the Sea Captain's rig, who stepped sullenly down from his seat and took a few dainty steps to join Ivan on the left-hand side of the track.

'Follow me,' Ivan said. 'Don't loiter, or you'll lose the path.'

He led the way down the embankment. At the bottom a single plank was laid across the marsh. Ivan walked along this, then turned sharply left where it ended and proceeded down an invisible path which lay under the brackish water. His companion followed, muttering. In a few minutes a small island, little more than a tussock in the marsh, appeared, as if from nowhere, ahead of them. On it was a wall pierced by a single arch, above which a small recess housed a bell. Ivan led the way through the arch.

A box tomb, sunk so far into the damp earth that only six inches still protruded above ground level, was surmounted by the marble effigy of a man dressed in a curious garb of breeches and jerkin, the head and throat being protected by a skull-cap-cum-collar.

'A sailor,' said Ivan, 'a real one. A pirate. One of Xanthippe's ancestors. He was the most bold of all his adventurous race. Too bold. He made the mistake of leaving his own waters and poaching up and down the Dalmatian coast. When they caught him at last, the Byzantine despot had him put to death by force-feeding him with live crawfish.'

'What is this to me?'

'However, some years later the man's son, Xanthippe's great-great-grandfather, obtained permission, in exchange for a large bribe, to build this shrine and bury him here. He's in the box, under his own effigy. So of course when Xanthippe broke her journey in Dubrovnik she persuaded her guardian to bring her out here, to see the tomb and pray for her ancestor's soul.'

'Do what you have to do, and then let us be gone.'

'According to the Guardian – Hubert of Avallon – something very curious occurred. Mind you, he says nothing about it in his published Chronicle, but he describes it vividly in a suppressed Appendix. According to this, the moment the Lady appeared the effigy began to show signs of violent displeasure. There was a terrible rumbling sound . . . "and the statue did shake and shudder; the face whereof, when the

76

disturbance ceased, was found to bear an aspect of loathing and disgust, in place of the tranquil sweetness which had hitherto informed the visage."''

'An earthquake. It would have caused the rumbling and altered the relation of the features.'

'Of features carved in marble? Let's have a look.'

Ivan bent over the effigy and turned a pocket torch on to it. Two stone eyes glared up in hatred and the mouth writhed in repudiation.

'No question about it,' said Ivan. 'If the face really was "tranquil" before the Lady's arrival – the normal monumental convention, so why should we doubt it? – then her appearance certainly started something. What did she do? one asks oneself. Or was it just . . . something about her . . . that got her ancestor so worked up?'

'What difference can it make now? What do you want here, Mr Barraclough?'

'I want to try to get some sense, from looking at the face of this effigy, of the kind of thing which might have caused it to take such a ferocious form.'

'Time and damp. The salt air. Damage by some thief or hooligan.'

'No. It is all of a piece. No hooligan damaged it. As for time and erosion, they would have softened the expression if anything. But see how strong it still is. Not just disgust; real horror. As if it feared lest the Lady Xanthippe might have some power over its soul . . . or the body that lay beneath it.'

'This is mere fancy. Let us go. Our friends will be waiting.'

'I think I have it now. Loathing; offended family pride, that a female of the family should do or be what the Despoina had done or been; terror, suppressed and controlled by that same pride.' Ivan straightened himself up and backed away from the tomb. 'I do not care to meet your friends,' he said, 'and I am rather at a loss what to do with you. Although I have already, on the Pharaoh's instructions, superintended the death of one member of your conspiracy, I cannot go through Europe leaving a trail of corpses, for I find the notion offensive. On the other hand, I cannot endure this continued pursuit and persecution. So I have decided on the following course. First, you will swear on your oath, on this tomb, not to pursue me further. Second, you will swear another oath, to inform these "friends" we were to meet that I gave you the slip and that although you found me again, it was just too late to stop me boarding the ferry to Bari –'

'Why are you saying all this? You are mad. I tell you, we wish only to help you.'

'I know different. And third, I shall leave you behind when I go. Since you do not know the path through the marsh, you will be well advised not to attempt to escape until the morning. Even then you will find it difficult. By the time you are able to break your oath, if you dare, and inform your friends what has happened, I shall be well on my way – and I promise you I shan't give you a second chance to find me.'

'You can do none of this.'

A slender hand came out of the belt of the jeans and pointed a pistol at Ivan.

'Now you will come away from here,' said the lilting voice. 'I have borne with you so long and so far in case information of interest should come of it; yet there has been nothing but superstitious nonsense. Now you will come to my friends and give proper information about your task. We may even let you continue in it – provided it is clear that you are working for us and not that fat degenerate in England.'

Good, thought Ivan; he is showing his hand too soon.

'Come,' said the man. 'Let us go back to your vehicle.'

Ivan looked at his watch.

'In thirty minutes,' he said, 'when the tide has started to ebb.'

'There is no tide in the Mediterranean.'

'There is a *small* tide in the Mediterranean. Our path was only just passable when we came by it. Since then the tide has flooded it completely. We cannot leave for at least half an hour.'

Ivan went back to studying the stone face of the marble pirate, while the seaman minced uneasily up and down the wall on which the moon threw his shadow, slim and jerky like that of a puppet on a screen.

'NOW LOOK, Ptolykins,' said Jo-Jo as she spooned the last three luscious eggs of Beluga into her mouth, 'this whole thing is the most infernal muddle. On the one hand is the official Chronicle of Hubert of Avallon and that poem, that ballad, written by this Sire de Longueil, in both of which Xanthippe is presented in much the same way – as the tender and innocent hostage, the poor little damsel who died of homesickness and/or because she missed the sight and sound of the sea. So far, so good. But on the other hand, Ptoly-pie, there is all this stuff in the Appendix of the Chronicle, to say nothing of those clues which Ivan Barraclough is checking on his way home, the burden of which turns her into some kind of monster – or at least into somebody who is being haunted by some kind of monster. Dream-treasures which are still there when she wakes up and later cause her death; inscriptions hinting at some horrible curse or taint which she carries everywhere with her – God knows what all.

'And on top of all this,' Jo-Jo continued, vigorously scratching the crack in her rump, 'you tell me that Mr Barraclough is having "complications" on his journey and is having to cut off protruding noses – by which I've little doubt you mean heads. So for Christ's sake, Ptoly darling: what *is* going on? And what exactly *was* going on with that poor little Greek Princess seven centuries ago?'

'As you must already have gathered,' said Ptolemaeos, 'these are not easy questions to answer. The best way is for me to deal with the second question first. So stop scratching your arsehole, little pusskin, and go and get your Uncle Ptoly some more vodka – the cayenne vodka – and then he will resume his efforts to guide you through the labyrinth to its centre, where lies the enchanted garden.'

'With poor Xanthippe underneath it, I suppose, pushing up the flora.'

WITH SOME DIFFICULTY, Ivan Barraclough turned the Land Rover round and drove back along the embankment across the salt-marshes, making for the Venetian Campo and the main road up the coast.

Poor little brute, he thought.

The moon was almost down now but he refrained from turning on his headlights; for although he had done nothing culpable (if one considered his situation) there were nevertheless questions which he could reasonably be required to answer, and he had no wish to attract the attention of potential inquisitors. If he could slip unnoticed through the Campo (surely deserted at this hour) and make a hundred miles up the coast road to the north before dawn, then he had every chance of escaping from Yugoslavia without further trouble. He could find a boat from one or another port for Bari or Venice and embark on it, with or without the Land Rover, before the wretched Sea Captain's colleagues had any idea of what had happened to their friend or any cogent motive for Ivan's pursuit.

He glanced to either side. He was now passing through an area of shrub and pine, which meant that he must be nearing the Campo. There was a low ridge to his left, behind which the moon now modestly retired. He slowed down, decided he must use the fog light, switched it on, and picked his way among the pot-holes.

Poor little brute, he thought again. Deceived by Ivan's plausible lie about the tide, he had fidgeted restlessly round the remains of the chapel, constantly asking how soon they could leave. Then Ivan had the piece of luck for which he had hoped. An earth tremor; common at this latitude and at this season of the year. An earth tremor, accompanied by a low rumbling and by a sudden and absolute eclipse of the moon by a thick stray cloud. In the pitch dark Ivan delivered a ferocious jab at where he calculated the capering Captain's solar plexus would now be, felt his fist sink into a surprisingly soft stomach, heard the Captain gag horribly as if about to vomit, and then followed up with a back-hander which was intended for the jaw but in fact struck the temple . . . and was none the less effective for that. As the moon emerged from behind the cloud, the Captain slumped at Ivan's feet. Ivan disarmed him, then took a leaf of the herb from the island at Ioannina, tore it slightly, and thrust it between the man's lips. 'Sleep till noon,' he told the unconscious figure, 'then tell your friends, when you meet them, that I am at sea and beyond their reach.'

He had no confidence, however, in the herb's efficacy to enforce obedience to instructions which were given to an unconscious person. Before the herb could act, he told himself, the brain must presumably register. The brain of a sleeping man could in some cases register; but could the brain of a man rendered unconscious by violence? Not knowing the answer, and concerned to prevent any possibility of early pursuit, Ivan stripped the Captain stark naked and gathered up his clothes, which he dumped in a pool of sludge half way back to the Land Rover.

'So that's you out of the way,' he said to himself: 'you poor little brute, you.'

And now, some ten minutes later, he was driving into the Campo (deserted as he had hoped, or so it would seem), past the central column half way between the Palladian and Gothic churches, out the other end and on to the isthmus which would take him to the main road. Yes, he should be half way across the Adriatic before any pursuit could start.

But would that be the end of it? They would know, these people, which way he was heading; they would know his goal. Very possibly they had allies in Italy and France. Perhaps *all* of Ptolemaeos's agents were now in conspiracy against him; or perhaps the rot was confined to Yugoslavia and Greece. Who could tell? But even in the latter case there was nothing to prevent his continued harassment. Yugoslavs, it was true, might have certain difficulties in leaving their country, but there were ways and means, particularly for those who lived on the coast, particularly for men who would stop at nothing (and most of them, it could be reckoned, would be of sterner stuff than the Sea Captain), particularly for people who had a prize in view such as they had.

Ivan turned left off the isthmus and drove, very carefully but at the top speed the Land Rover could manage, towards the north.

'AT FIRST SIGHT,' said Ptolemaeos Tunne, as the cayenne vodka lapped into his glass, 'the contradictions in the various accounts of the Despoina Xanthippe are not difficult to explain. We know that certain Greeks wished to discredit Phaedron of Ilyssos for doing a deal with the Franks. We can easily suppose that the method they adopted was to vilify his daughter, and that they tricked, bribed or blackmailed many Franks into helping them. Thus Prince William's Bishop-Chaplain went on record as hinting that she had some sinister or supernatural accomplice – though he, at least, was decent enough to express a belief in her personal innocence. Or again, a sculptor who did a carving in the chapel in the castle of Geoffery de Bruyère at Karyteina shows her in the process of being pricked by a kind of sexual imp. Or yet again, there is an interesting and very rude carving in the family chapel of my friend des Veules-les-Roses at Barville, a piece of work done long after the Despoina died but inspired by the local legends about her, which clearly included substantial elements of bawdry.'

'And such obscenities,' said Jo-Jo,' would have been invented by Greeks and crooked Franks far away in Romany . . . but would still have been powerful enough, you think, to spread as far as Normandy?'

'Oh yes. Some of the knights or mercenaries who accompanied her could have been paid or suborned to tell the stories on the march. So the rumours would have travelled with her . . . false rumours that she was a woman abandoned to lewd practice (the carving at Barville shows her masturbating on a castle wall), that she was attended by a daemon or familiar who egged her on, and that she was, therefore, almost certainly a witch.

'But the trouble is,' pursued Ptolemaeos, 'that this explanation just don't fit. If people were out to vilify Xanthippe, they could have recorded anything they cared to imagine. Harlotries, orgies, adulteries. But we have nothing of the kind. All we have are rumours of masturbation, artefacts showing her at it, and, in inscriptions and so forth, the implication that she was accompanied by some supernatural *doppelgänger*. Pretty tame stuff for those days.'

'Perhaps,' said Jo-Jo, 'Phaedron's enemies thought that a relatively quiet and consistent series of charges would be more convincing than sexual spectaculars.'

'Possibly. But in the end the theory that the accusations against Xanthippe were merely anti-Phaedron propaganda fabricated by his political enemies founders utterly on the rock of Hubert's Appendix. You see, Hubert was as absolutely on her side as a man could be. He adored her. Granted, his official Chronicle does contain a few hints that people sometimes found something sinister about her, as when he quotes the Sire de Longueil's remark that "Another watched him from behind her eyes"; but this is presented as *someone else*'s view, not as Hubert's. As far as the author of the official Chronicle of Avallon was concerned, the sun shone out of her navel. And yet in the end Hubert was too honest and clear-sighted to give her a clean bill. He knew there was something wrong all right – and hence his dictation of the secret Appendix. He had to tell the truth under God even if he tried to conceal most of it from man.'

'But couldn't the Appendix have been a forgery by the propagandists? Or couldn't they just possibly have managed to bribe Hubert to make it all up?'

'No, no, sweetheart. If either of these things had happened, the Appendix, like the Chronicle itself, would have been much copied and had wide publicity. The propagandists would have seen to that. But the great point about the Appendix is that it has been kept almost entirely secret right down the centuries. While the Chronicle was much read by the literate, and while rumours and tales in bawdy supplement were bandied about by the general public, the actual Appendix was all the time mewed up in its box in Vezelay, and never saw the light, save when it was inspected by its guardians, until the drunk Curator got it out for Ivan and your uncle.'

Ptolemaeos took a bumper of cayenne vodka.

'Besides,' he went on, 'Hubert comes out as a straight man who was devoted to Xanthippe both in love and in duty. Strictly *not* a venal number who would have crabbed her for cash. As for any suggestion of forgery, all the internal evidence – style and manner, methods of narration and so forth – indicates that the man who dictated the Chronicle also dictated the Appendix, and, to judge from the orthography, dictated it to the same monk. And so, heart of my heart: if there is one thing in which I trust as surely as I trust in red gold, it is Hubert of Avallon's Appendix, a clear and honest account, I will stake my cod on it, of all that he saw happen . . . much of which was not pretty, my own one, my *liebling*, not pretty at all.'

'Then *why*, Ptoly, did so many other people – Lord Geoffery de Bruyère for example – find her wholly entrancing? I mean, if she had all these things wrong, how could they?'

'Oh yes they could. The point is that she *was* entrancing, much and even most of the time. So the answer to your question is that Lord Geoffery saw nothing sinister about her, because there was nothing sinister to see, during the brief period he was with her.'

'That sculptor in his castle saw something pretty peculiar. The one who carved the imp.'

'Perhaps he caught her at a bad moment, when Geoffery wasn't present. Perhaps his sense of such things was sharper than Geoffery's. Or perhaps they both had the same vision, but Geoffery took a more lenient view of it. You must remember that even some of her accusers – like that Bishop-Chaplain of the Villehardouins – believed that she herself was innocent even at the bad times, even when the daemon was with her. And you must remember, too, that the daemon, according to Hubert, sometimes brought her good dreams, good messages, good impulses: the daemon came from the Throne as often as it came from Gehenna.'

'Yes. . . Intermittent visits, you said earlier. Some from Heaven, some from Hell. So that most of the time there was either no daemon or the daemon was being a good influence. A man could consort with her for days or weeks before the daemon turned up with something nasty.'

'And even when it did, she might be in her private quarters, and no one else know of it except her ladies-in-waiting, who were all old friends of her family.'

'Certainly Lord Geoffery never seems to have known . . . or not enough to have minded. . . Are you sure it was the same daemon, Ptoly, for good and bad? Couldn't there have been two?'

'No. The daemon always announced itself by the same name.'

'A trick?'

'No. Daemons set great store by their names, which bestow certain powers upon them. So they have to take nomenclature seriously.'

'I see. And Hubert found all this out. How?'

'He was with Xanthippe for a long time. For the whole journey from Glarentza to Arques. And then at Arques until she died. Sooner or later he had to be present when the daemon appeared. And one day, later rather than sooner, he was.'

'What happened, Ptoly?'

'Wait. I'll get the Appendix from the safe.'

While Ptolemaeos was gone, Jo-Jo collected the caviar plates. That safe, she thought: how could I have left it open that time . . . that time when the Greek was in the house? I'd simply gone to it for some of Ptoly's special pills, something I do almost every day, nothing to be excited or nervous about – and yet somehow I was in such a flurry I forgot to lock it. I found it open the next morning, just ajar. Thank God Ptoly never noticed. But that Greek agent did. Or so it seems. He must have got at the Appendix and found things out, much more than he was ever meant to know; and then started scheming when he got back to Greece; and Ptoly must have learned about this and sent Ivan instructions to . . . cut his nose off; and Ivan has done what he was told and now he's in trouble. All my fault. Shall I own up? No good now. Christ, I hope no one ever knows. But if anything happens to Ivan, the blame, the guilt, will all be on my head. *Mea culpa, mea maxima culpa.* God, please let me off this hook. I couldn't bear anything to happen to Ptoly's friend because of me, and what I really couldn't bear is for Ptoly to be angry with me, send me away perhaps, oh Christ I do love him so much. Jesus, how could I have been such a careless little fool? HOW COULD I? Stop, girl, stop, or you'll drive yourself mad.

'Massage my shoulders,' said Ptolemaeos, 'while I read you a bed-time story.' He opened a ragged exercise book. '"And on a fair day early in September,"' he read out, '"we came to the city of Rouen and there found lodging prepared for us, on the order of Guy de Villehardouin Captain of Les Andelys, near the Western gate. And on the evening after we arrived, I waited on my Lady Xanthippe in her apartments, where she had dined with her women." – Just a little harder and higher, darling. "And at first she was full of courtesie and merriement, recalling a party of players we had met by the way, who had enacted for us the Tale of Ulysses of Ithaca, how he escaped from the Giant who would devour him by clinging 'neath the belly of a ram. But by and by my Lady quietened and seemed about to sink into a sleep. A glaze came upon her eyes and her face fell empty. Her women signed to me directly that it was time to depart and let their Lady rest, and indeed I had all but risen to take leave when a most curious thing occurred. And that I tell truth I vow by Mary, sweet Mother of Christ. I swear in that holy name that the Lady Xanthippe did draw up her robe above her knee and then still higher to the fork, and began to fondle and probe her secret parts, as though none else were present.

'"And I was uncertain, whether to remonstrate with her for unseemliness, or to welcome this as a sign of lust, that she would have me do the like; for I was both saddened in my heart by this lewdness and yet much fired in my loins by the fresh silken cuisses which she revealed. But before I could move or speak, the tallest of her maidens rose and signed to me to be silent, shaking her head as one who, being well acquaint with such 'haviour, would fain warn that great danger might lie in any disturbance of the Lady. And this same maiden went to a chest and returned with a device of horn fashioned like a rampant cod and furnished with a fine ruby at the tip, which she did offer to the Lady. The Lady, not seeing it (for her eyes were now closed) yet did take it in her hands and, with a low growling of her breath, did ease it full into her *cunnis* and then thrust it against it most mightily, two, three or four times, until she gave a gasp, and then a groan and then a howl, as of an animal in hunger, and did tremble all over, then jerk and shudder and shake as one who is stricken with the falling sickness, save that she fell not. Again she howled like a beast, then opened her eyes, and there was another there behind them.

'"I am Masullaoh,"' she spake in a deep, melodious voice, such as would have befitted a Chancellor or mighty Judge: 'this time of my coming hither I bring messages neither of good nor ill. Yet I must be refreshed for my next venture."'

'"Whereupon the tall maiden nodded to two others, who went forth and returned with a sheep; and the Lady Xanthippe rose from her chair – by God's Mother I speak only the truth – the Lady Xanthippe rose from her chair, and seized and rent the sheep, and devoured it while it yet lived in great gobbets of raw flesh and streaming blood, bowells and bladder and entrails, cramming the meat down her throat as though she were an ogre that had been starved for a twelve month" – okay, poppet, now up to the neck and head,' said Ptolemaeos, and closed the exercise book.

'Oh Ptoly, go on. If you don't, *I'll* stop.'

'It now becomes a bit dull by comparison and is better abbreviated,' Ptolemaeos said. 'After gorging herself on the sheep, Xanthippe falls into a heavy slumber, and the senior maiden – the tall one – takes the opportunity of repossessing herself of the horn and ruby dildoe (which was still where Xanthippe had put it) and placing it back in his chest. She then decides that Messer Hubert had better be treated to a word or two of explanation.

'It seems that according to this handmaiden, who, by the way, was called Hero, Xanthippe had been visited by the daemon Masullaoh ever since she was thirteen years old. The visits always took a similar form. First of all Xanthippe would

87

grow quiet and dozy, then she would just lift her clothes and start wanking, regardless of where she was or with whom; then she would have an enormous orgasm, and there would be Masullaoh inside her, looking out through her eyes.

'He always introduced himself formally, "I am Masullaoh", and often went on to announce some message, usually theological in type, that had emanated from God or the Devil. These messages conveyed something of the relation between the two, and also of the state of the struggle between them; for according to Masullaoh Satan was definitely not a mere demiurge acting under God and with God's indulgence, he was self-created, co-eternal and equally powerful. In the beginning he could, if he had wished, just have lived at peace with God, each in their separate ethereal domain, but he had chosen instead to create the physical universe and challenge God to try to rescue the damned and doomed souls of the people whom he placed in it. Masullaoh, who was apparently morally neutral, had access to both camps, and hence his excellent intelligence as to the state of the contest.

'After he had delivered these bulletins, Masullaoh would require "refreshment", which was invariably consumed through the body of Xanthippe and in the bestial fashion which Hubert had just witnessed. After this Xanthippe would go into a deep sleep, in the course of which, as she herself avowed, she was treated to more curious instruction about Satan's Universe and God's efforts to save its inhabitants. Towards the end of her dreams she would often be presented with a gift of some kind, either Divine or Satanic, which she usually found in her hand or in her bed on her awakening. The phallus of horn had been one such gift – the first – and she had been very exigently instructed to teach Hero to present it to her for insertion at the first indication that her orgasm was coming, as it facilitated Masullaoh's passage into her.

'After the long sleep Masullaoh's custom varied slightly. Sometimes he would be gone when the sleep was over. Sometimes he would still be there, looking out through her eyes, and would linger for hours or even days, but at this stage he seemed to allow Xanthippe to reassume autonomy. She could think and act for herself, while Masullaoh remained passive and uncommunicative inside her – though when he was finally ready to leave he always spoke a message of farewell.'

'Like telling them when he was coming next?'

'Not exactly. What he would tell them was the sort of "refreshment" – generally a sheep, sometimes a lamb, on one occasion a hare and on another a whole ox – which they should have ready against his next visitation, and by what date, at the latest, they should procure it. He was very reasonable about recognising when things would be difficult – at sea, for example – and ordered his menus with great consideration for Hero, who was responsible for the Commissariat, and expressed much gratitude to her. The thing was, you see, that he depended on these meals of flesh, for somehow or other they were transmuted into the spiritual energy which he had used up in his latest venture or would need for the next.'

'Had he other sources? Or was Xanthippe his only supply-station?'

'No one liked to ask. But since the amounts of flesh he ordered varied, it was thought that sometimes he must have made visits and meals elsewhere in the intervals between coming to Xanthippe.'

'So when he left the message was, "Please expect me again some time after the first of next month, and have the following goodies available"?'

'Right.'

'And where was all this getting Xanthippe?'

'It was getting her very knowledgeable about the Powers which were disputing over the fate of the Universe – or at least that of its inhabitants.'

'I meant, Ptoly, where was all this getting Xanthippe *in regard to our present purpose?*'

'You'll see. But first a few snippets of occultist theory. There was an ancient Greek belief, prominent for a time in the early sixth century B.C. and summarised by the pundits as ςωμα – ςημα, or "flesh the tomb". According to this, the body, or *sōma*, is the tomb (*sēma*) of the ψυχη, the psyche or soul.'

'Nothing very original in that.'

'Wait for it, sweetheart. The body is the tomb of the soul, *which lies dead within it*, and will be released and given life only when the body dies. The soul was alive in a previous state, before it was mewed up in the body, and it will be alive again when it is set free, but while it is actually in the body, it is *dead*.'

'What a very disagreeable notion,' said Jo-Jo, toying cleverly with the lobe of Ptolemaeos's left ear.

'Isn't it just? But let us, for a moment, assume that it is true. How would the dead soul, lying in the tomb of Xanthippe's body, react to the comings and goings of a live daemon, who inspired Xanthippe to acts of colossal indecency and had caused her to devour, in the most bestial fashion, several entire raw sheep and on one occasion an ox?'

'If Xanthippe's soul were dead,' said Jo-Jo, 'it would not react at all. Far more to the point to enquire how it would react if it were alive – which is far more likely.'

'So you might think. But the point is that in the part of the Mani where Xanthippe was born, the belief in the flesh as tomb of a dead soul had endured from the sixth century B.C. right on into the Christian era. Several times it had nearly perished, but it had always been revived and re-inculcated by various sages, notably Semandios of Mistra and Dionysios of Kythera, just in the nick of time. It was particularly strong from about 50 B.C., when its exponent, Apollodoros of Paros, came to live in Ilyssos, so strong that it had to be accepted and accommodated by the Orthodox Church, after the establishment of Christianity, in the whole area from Gythaion south to Taenaros. This, then, would have been the belief of Xanthippe herself, and of her attendant damsels, and, of course, of her father.'

'Ah. Daddy. Did *he* know about the daemon?'

'Yes. And very much hoped she would be safely married off before she made a public exhibition of herself. Hero had strict instructions to guard against that, and had pretty well succeeded (though the odd nose here and there had been set twitching a bit) until her mistress broke out in front of Hubert . . . which wasn't as bad as it might have been, as Hubert, by then, was almost part of the family. But back to Xanthippe and the daemon, and her dead soul, as she believed it to be.

How, one asks oneself, would she have viewed the situation in her saner moments?'

'First tell me what was supposed to be keeping her going at all . . . when the daemon wasn't there . . . if her soul was dead.'

'The θυμος, the *thymos* or living personality, a sort of superficial soul, which, they thought, initiated and controlled all mental and physical activity in a person – until that person died. The theory was that the *thymos* died with the flesh which it transformed, giving place to the newly resurrected and now independent psyche or soul.'

'But Ptoly, darling delectable, desirable Ptoly, all this is NONSENSE ON STILTS. Please can we be rational for two seconds at a time. Plainly, what we have here is a disordered girl, given to fits of masturbation (not uncommon), which were followed by an insane craving for raw meat. A deplorable phenomenon, most embarrassing for friends and relations, but nevertheless explicable in medical terms (if allowance is made for obvious exaggeration) and requiring no bizarre apparatus of daemons, dualisms and dead souls.'

'What about the presents which she received in her dreams – and found in her hand when she awoke?'

'Some hanky-panky of that dismal bitch, Hero.'

'What have you got against Hero?'

'Bossing everybody about. She probably wanted to gain some ascendancy over the Princess; so she encouraged her naughty habits and put valuable presents in her bed while she was asleep – and then persuaded her, when she woke up, that she had dreamed about receiving them.'

'There is a great deal, as it happens, in what you say. Hero was certainly up to something, though you will be rather surprised when you know exactly what. But in any case, poppety-poo, you must *accept* the terms in which I am talking as the terms in which Xanthippe would have been thinking. As far as she was concerned, with one catastrophic exception, she was a perfectly ordinary girl who had inside her a dead soul, which could be released and revived only by her own death, and a living *thymos* which, for all present and practical purposes, fulfilled the functions of soul, mind and spirit

91

altogether. It ran the show for the time being, though it was mortal as the flesh was mortal and would eventually die with the flesh. So far, so good; all this was perfectly correct form according to the beliefs in which she had been brought up. But then we come to the exception, the anomaly: this visiting daemon – *not* a thing a normal girl should have.

'And clearly the *thymos* was no match for it. The daemon took over as and when he wanted, and either allowed the *thymos* to function or prevented it just as he pleased. He made her do hideous things, used her as a fuelling station, so to speak, by converting the animal matter which she consumed into some kind of ethereal energy, he looked out at people through her eyes and ordered everyone about as if he owned her. Which indeed it seemed likely he did. Certainly her poor futile *thymos*, her own living personality, could do nothing about it.

'And then, one day, something must have occurred to her. What about her *soul*? Even if the *thymos* was powerless, surely the eternal, the God-given soul would have something to say about this . . . *when*, that is, it came alive again. It would certainly be angry with the daemon for telling theological lies, for suggesting that God was no more than the equal of Satan; it would want to punish the daemon and drive him away, to free her of him, to destroy him – only the trouble was that by then she would be dead, because she could not bring her soul into action (so she believed) except by dying. And this brings me back to my original question: how would the dead soul have reacted to the demon?'

'It also brings us back to my original answer: if the soul was dead it could not react. Which must have been what Xanthippe believed too.'

'Yes. Until one day she thought she felt it stir in protest. And then she remembered a certain herb, which a magician called Aristarchos had given her on Corfu. It's all in the Appendix. He had spotted her out as an odd one and persuaded her to make a full confession of her condition, in return for which he had given her some leaves of this herb, which she put away in a little onyx box. "Use this," Aristarchos had said, "to command yourself. To command your true self, your true soul. If you give it to another, you may command his whole being. If you give it to yourself you may command *your* whole being, you may (which is given to few men or women) command your soul.'''

'Where did this Aristarchos stand in the matter of the soul's being dead?'

'Nowhere. It would never have even occurred to him. As far as he was concerned that concept (if ever he knew of it) had died seventeen centuries before. But of course our little Princess from the Mani took a different view; and when Aristarchos gave her the herb, Xanthippe, while too polite to mention it, knew that it would be useless. She could not command a soul that was dead, so she put the leaves of the herb in an onyx box and forgot them. Until, that is, many days later, long after she left Corfu, long after she arrived in France, long after she left Rouen and came to Arques, a remarkable, an impossible thing occurred: she felt her soul stir in protest. If it could stir in its death, perhaps it could live. Perhaps Aristarchos' herb, forgotten till now, could help it to live. It was, at any rate, worth a try. She would take the herb as instructed by Aristarchos, she would command her soul to come to life, and if it did she would then request it to cast out the daemon on his next appearance.'

'For goodness' sake, Ptoly. You are talking the most utter ballocks. When do we get to the treasure?'

'Patience, darling. Unlike those Greeks, you must be patient. They were in too much of a hurry, and so they got things wrong and came unstuck. Calm, calm, calm.'

At the mention of the Greeks, Jo-Jo turned her eyes guiltily to the floor. But Ptolemaeos, it appeared, had no idea that someone might have seen the Appendix in his own home, through the carelessness of his own niece. He explained to her that the leader of the Greek faction, having some notion of the wealth to be won, had decided that there might be more to be learnt from the museum Curator at Vezelay, who, after all, had the MS of the Chronicle in his keeping and could reasonably be supposed to be expert in this area. So the Greek had applied to him, had insisted that there must be more material than merely the official Chronicle, had bullied and pleaded, had rattled his sabre and clinked his gold. That makes sense, Jo-Jo thought: clearly that Greek who came here only got a very quick and nervous look at Ptoly's copy of the Appendix; so he went to Vezelay, hoping for a long and leisurely read. Which, as Ptoly now told her, the Curator, part in duty and part in loyalty to his English chums, had persisted in denying him. In the end he had had to have him turned off by the police, after which he had written to Ptolemaeos to warn him of the man's violent and excessive curiosity.

'Too fierce, too unsubtle, too greedy,' said Ptolemaeos now. 'He gave his game away, and I've had Ivan deal with him – with the one that matters, the leader. He was the one who came here,' he said to Jo-Jo. (As if, she thought, I didn't know.) 'I expect our manner of living gave him ideas above his station. But never mind him. Where was I?'

Jo-Jo gave a sigh of relief at the safe passing of the topic, converted it quickly into an erotic mew, and said: 'Xanthippe was going to use the herb to wake her soul from death. Or that's how she saw it.'

'And we must try to see it the same way if we are ever to understand.' Ptolemaeos flexed his shoulders and signed to Jo-Jo to continue the massage. 'However,' he said, 'before she tasted the herb she told two people of her intention: Hero, her old friend and senior maid-in-waiting, and also the avuncular Hubert. Hubert seemed uncertain about the idea. Hero didn't like it at all.'

'Ah-ha. I knew that Hero was up to no good.'

'Her motives for opposing Xanthippe appeared to be strictly honourable. She told her mistress that it was a dangerous, even a blasphemous thing to do – to try to arouse a soul which, as they both knew, was intended to lie dead inside her until she herself should die.'

'What did Xanthippe say to that?'

'She fell silent and started fretting. The daemon was on his way. They had been expecting him about now and a lamb which he had ordered was ready for him. So Hero went and fetched the dildoe from the chest, and told one of the girls to bring the lamb. Xanthippe went through her bit with the dildoe – even more violently and noisily than before, Hubert

94

tells us, and then started talking in the voice of Masullaoh.'

'And what had he got to say for himself?'

'That he had a particularly exacting task ahead of him and required nutriment of a particularly delicate yet sustaining kind: he didn't want the lamb after all; he wanted Hero.'

SOME TIME after the dawn broke, Ivan realised that he was being followed. A powerful Lancia was pacing the Land Rover at a distance of about a furlong. He knew that the driver of the Lancia was deliberately tracking him, as opposed to dawdling fortuitously along the same route, because twice he made detours from the main road into villages on the shore, and twice the Lancia turned off after him, drew a little closer, then attended him through the village and back on to the road north. From repeated scrutinies of his mirror in the rapidly improving light Ivan eventually ascertained that the Lancia contained four men as well as the driver.

All of which, Ivan now told himself, suggested two questions. First, how had these people come to be on his trail so soon? The Sea Captain, even if he had early recovered from his swoon, and had been rendered immune by it from the power of the herb, simply could not have escaped from the chapel, through the deadly patch of salt-marsh, and so back to the Campo (stark naked at that) quickly enough to raise an alarm that would have brought this Lancia – a maroon Lancia, the morning now revealed – on to his heels so soon. Again, he was certain that no one had followed him and the Sea Captain out to the chapel. He must conclude, then, that a general watch was being kept for him and his Land Rover up and down the coast (and probably up and down the inland road north through Belgrade and Zagreb) as a result of an alert broadcast by the friends of the dead Greek, and that almost certainly these men in the Lancia knew nothing yet about the excursion to the chapel and the unedifying fate of the sea dog. They were looking for him quite regardless of all that: they were looking for him, and had been for some time, because they needed him to tell them what the dead Greek could no longer tell them about the nature and whereabouts of the treasure which he had promised them. Which being the case, he came to the second question: how would they proceed?

They wanted him alive, to start with at any rate; they wanted him to talk. So the thing was very simple: they would loiter along behind him until he ran out of petrol or stopped to buy some more; and then, surrounding and outnumbering him, they would quickly and quietly escort him to the maroon Lancia and convey him to a place where they could put the question at their leisure.

'BUT WHY HERO?' said Jo-Jo. 'Hero was on Masullaoh's side. Or at least she helped him to come to Xanthippe, *and* she was opposed to Xanthippe's trying to rouse her soul, with that herb, into making resistance. So why should Massulaoh wish to destroy his ally – in that particularly revolting way? Hero had deserved much better than that.'

'Massulaoh wanted Hero dead,' said Ptolemaeos, 'because he had a special task for her soul – and she was the only person around of the calibre to do it.'

Ptolemaeos swept back the curtains. Dawn struggled with a yellow fen-mist at the bottom of the garden.

'Still, she must have felt a bit hard done by when he announced that she was the next item on his menu?'

'No. He reassured her, through the mouth of Xanthippe, that he would be in touch with her to comfort and command her on another plane. Then he bade Xanthippe fall to. And a very messy business it was. Apparently Xanthippe started on Hero's jugular, and "the blood issued like a great fountain gushing crimson".'

'Hubert was watching, of course?'

96

'Hubert was watching. He'd been there when her fit started, while they were discussing her intention of taking Aristarchos's herb. So of course he stayed on for the rest of the show – absolutely powerless, he assures us, to stop it.'

'But by this time they were all at Arques. You did say that?'

'Yes. They had been at Arques some weeks.'

'Then where was the Castellan while all this was going on?'

'Minding his own biz-whacks. His job was to keep Xanthippe in the Castle and admit Henri de Longueil into her presence. He'd done exactly that. He had nothing with which to reproach himself. He couldn't be held responsible for characters like Masullaoh, who were in any case unstoppable. So the Castellan just didn't want to know. Hubert, he thought, would see him in the clear with the Villehardouins, and that was all he cared about. Obviously the wretched girl was possessed, and if anything nasty happened to her then as far as he was concerned it would only be good riddance.'

'What about Henri de Longueil then? Was he taking any interest?'

'Henri was sorry for the girl, but you remember that he didn't much like her and had been dismissed by her. He too was minding his own biz-whacks – in Longueil, most probably. As I told you, he'd been keeping in touch with the situation, but only from a distance, and he didn't turn up at the Castle again until he had news that she was dead and buried. He was told a relatively anodyne and quite plausible version of the whole thing, which he turned into a ballad.'

'He forgot that "another had looked at him from behind her eyes".'

'Perhaps he didn't choose to remember. It probably suited him to believe what he was told. At any rate, he just wrote his pretty poem, and later on he took Xanthippe's ladies-in-waiting back to Greece . . . the five that were left of them. But I'm jumping too far ahead. Back to the death of Hero.

'By the time Xanthippe had finished there was nothing left of Hero except a pile of bones, which Masullaoh, still speaking through Xanthippe's mouth of course, ordered the girls to hide, for the time being, in one of Xanthippe's trunks. Xanthippe then went off into a deep sleep.

'When she came to, she told everyone, speaking in her own voice, that she had dreamed of a lake in her own country, a lake far from Ilyssos but nevertheless in Greece. While she was swimming in that lake, she said, a great hand had drawn her down and a voice had told her not to be afraid, as she was about to receive a highly privileged revelation. She was going to be introduced to Satan in person, and he was going to make her a gift which would prove, to herself and to all men, that Satan was not a fallen Angel originally created by God, but another and equal God in his own right, like God self-created, as powerful as God if not more so, and thus representing principles which had as good a title to paramountcy as the so-called Christian virtues. Well, Xanthippe was fairly used, by now, to hearing such pronouncements from Masullaoh and others, but she had never yet been offered an introduction to Satan in person and was expecting rather a lot of him. She was rather disappointed, therefore, when she was taken into an underwater grotto and shown a small black stone, ovoid in shape.

'Now we know, of course, that this was probably the Primal Atom which exploded to produce the Physical Universe – Satan's creation, you recall. And not merely his creation: there was a sense in which the physical Universe *was* Satan, was of his substance; so that at least part of himself must have gone to make up the Primal Atom before it exploded. Now this, of course, had happened aeons before, but it is reasonable to assume that Satan was still capable of taking the same form, in retrospect so to speak, and chose it now as being more convenient than most for presenting himself to Xanthippe. After all, if he had appeared as his real self he might have dazzled her to death, as Jove did Semele. Anyhow, there was this black ovoid, the egg of Satan's Universe and in effect Satan himself; but of course poor Xanthippe's physics weren't up to understanding any of this, and she was horribly disappointed – as indeed she was at first with her present. For she was given, by a hooded attendant, a basket which contained what she thought was an enormous lobster but which she soon recognised as an *Écrevisse* or fresh-water *langouste*. Since the only remarkable thing about it was its colossal size – far more freakish in an *Écrevisse* than in a lobster – she could not imagine, for the life of her, how this creature was going to prove the Independence of Satan and his parity with God.'

'I'm glad about that *Écrevisse*,'' said Jo-Jo; 'I was impatient for its promised appearance.'

'There you are then. When Xanthippe woke up and started telling the story, she kept looking around as if she expected to see the *Écrevisse* somewhere about the place, being accustomed to find that her dream-gifts had assumed material shape. And sure enough, in the ewer of water which stood near her bed, was a gigantic crustacean – not a real one but one made, according to Hubert's Appendix, "of gold and enamel and all manner of rare jewels and precious metals, being two cubits in length by nine inches in width and six in height, most deliberately wrought and dightly carven, and of most curious mechanism: for when a small key or lever in the tail was turned thrice this wondrous toy would crawl slowly along the ground while from within an instrument of tiny chimes would play an elegy or dirge – I know not what – that did entice the soul at once to delicious melancholy and to wanton fancy; the former soothing the soul and acquainting it that all the world is transience and there can therefore be no need of earnest striving or weary prohibition; the latter inviting the flesh to delights unspeakable, to all that is forbidden to us on pain of hell fire everlasting, as to lie in lewd sport with our mothers or newly bosomed daughters or tender sons, all of us together, pleasing each other about and about without cess or shame, laughing and throbbing in quenchless joy, for that Satan has ordained that lust as soon as satisfied shall straight return."'

'A very enviable state of affairs,' said Jo-Jo.

'Quite so. But Xanthippe would have none of it. Masullaoh had gone – but not before he had made her devour her childhood friend and had presented her with this insidious oracle of Satan's indulgence. Though it might well prove the existence of Satan, she now affirmed, it did not prove his parity with God. She must and would hold by God, the supreme King. In any case whatever, Masullaoh was a torment and temptation of which she would have no more. She would wake her dead soul to fight for her: where was the onyx box containing the herbs which Aristarchos had given her, the herbs that enabled a man to command his own true soul and which, she hoped, would now empower her to revive and activate hers?

'Gone. Nowhere to be found. Briefly Masullaoh returns to explain, through Xanthippe's mouth, that just as he can conjure dream-objects into the material world, so he can take real objects, like herbs and onyx boxes, back with him into his own etherial one. Let Xanthippe cease to resist; only let her do his will without further fight, and all will be well.'

'Ptoly . . . O Ptolemaeos, Angel of Evil, is the Treasure which you seek this monstrous toy crustacean?'

'Yes. Yes . . . BUT. We have to find it, to make sure of finding it, in certain prescribed circumstances or conditions. If the circumstances or the conditions are wrong, then the *Écrevisse* will be useless and worthless. It will have no meaning.'

'You can hardly hope it still plays a tune.'

'That is exactly what I hope, if only metaphorically. And all depends on the conditions and circumstances of which I speak. Listen and learn.'

Ptolemaeos beckoned her to come and stand with him in the window. Together they looked down the lawn to the ochre mist which oozed from the fen beyond it.

'And now back,' said Ptolemaeos, 'to our little Princess. She mistrusted the gift, she feared its message. She wanted to fight Masullaoh; but the special herb which might have helped her to rouse her soul to combat had been stolen. Day after day she walked on the walls of the Castle and found no comfort anywhere. Not even a sight of her beloved sea. And then she succumbed.'

'Succumbed? To death?'

'Not just yet. First she succumbed to temptation. Satan's gift had been well chosen. To start with it was of extreme beauty and immense value –'

'How can you be sure of that? You've only Hubert's word for it.'

'Patience, girl. All will be made plain in due time. As I was saying, not only was Satan's gift a most beautiful and glittering toy, it was also the image of a creature which dwelt in water, not indeed a creature of the sea, but of lakes and rivers, the next best. After a time Xanthippe sent for the *Écrevisse*, looked long at it, and was delighted by it. She listened again to the tune it played and was intrigued by its message. Soon she was inseparable from it. I must have something to please me in my misery, she kept saying, someting dainty and beguiling to look at, something sweet and tuneful to listen to. And who is to say this image is evil? Perhaps the voice in my dream spoke truth: perhaps Satan is indeed the Peer of God; and then who is to say what is sin and what is virtue? Or who is to say that the tune of enticement from the little bells within the *Écrevisse* is not the voice of true wisdom which announces the true happiness?

'One stormy day in October Xanthippe went to bed at sundown, complaining of a slight headache. The senior maiden attended her. This was now a girl called Lalage, a plump, merry hoyden, very different from the statuesque and tactiturn Hero. As was now the custom, Lalage placed the golden *Écrevisse* on a table near her mistress's bed, leaving a lighted candle nearby which made of the bright gems and enamels a fantasy of colour amid the surrounding darkness. Lalage kissed the Princess goodnight and left her just as the sun dipped beneath the western rampart. Some hours later, while Lalage and the other four girls were preparing for bed in their dormitory, there was a hideous scream from Xanthippe's chamber. Lalage, who, as Hubert tells us, "had left her companions for a while and been at stool in the Tower jakes", came rushing down into the dorter, grabbed a candle and called to the others to follow her. She led them down a stone corridor which ran inside the western rampart for some ten or fifteen yards and then into Xanthippe's bedroom. Xanthippe was lying quietly on her back, holding the giant *Écrevisse* in her left hand. As they approached, they saw by the quivering light of the candle that her hand had been ripped, as by sharp metal, and that her throat had been most horribly clawed. The poor little Despoina was dead. There seemed to them to be no possible explanation other than that the *Écrevisse* had somehow come to life and attacked her, had opened her throat with its scales or its tail, and had also savaged the hand with which she had tried to prise it off.'

'Leave aside that that explanation begs about a million questions,' Jo-Jo said, 'why should the *Écrevisse*, or those that had sent it, wish to kill poor Xanthippe?'

'One answer, which is suggested by the events which now followed, is that Masullaoh, the daemon, wished to put on a particularly powerful and diabolic exhibition . . . which began when Lalage summoned Hubert to Xanthippe's chamber later the following night. Xanthippe's body had by now been lying in state for well over twenty-four hours and something, it appeared, was very badly wrong.

'You see, according to the belief of Greek Orthodox Christians the soul of a dead person lingers near the body for quite a long time, being afraid to leave it. It is very important that during this period friends of the deceased should be in the same room as the body, to encourage the soul by their prayers and to protect both it and the body against the undesirable attentions of evil spirits who may happen to be passing. Later on the soul is endowed by the prayers said on its behalf with the courage to set out on its journey, which will be over Wilderness and through peril to the Throne of God – but with that we are not just now concerned. What does concern us is to understand that when the soul is about to set out on this journey it makes some sign to those gathered round the body, so that they may know it is now departing and is finally leaving its body to their ministrations.'

'But as we know,' said Jo-Jo carefully, 'some Greek Christians from the Mani have an additional belief. They believe that the living body is the tomb of the dead soul – which is only released and brought to life by the death of the body. This surely makes a difference?'

'It does indeed. Whereas the normal Orthodox belief is that the soul, regarding the body as its old friend and home, lingers near it anything up to three days, the belief of the Maniots (or at least of the Ilyssans) is that the soul, hating the body as its tomb and its prison, hangs about only for long enough to get its bearings, after which it takes off to visit the places frequented, as it instinctively knows, by the body during its lifetime, in order to see what it itself has been missing.'

'What about the Wilderness and the Throne?'

'Ah. The soul is, of course, free to make straight for these and quite often it does so. Usually, on the other hand, it leaves the journey to the Throne until after its round of earthly visits; and sometimes it never attempts it at all. But we are not concerned with such details now. Our present business is to realise that according to the Ilyssan belief the soul stays by its body for twelve hours at the most. However, though its attitudes and destinations may be different from those posited by standard Orthodoxy, in one way it behaves precisely the same as any Orthodox soul: when it is about to depart it makes some sign to the friends who are praying by the cadaver and must now prepare to dispose of it.'

'What kind of sign?'

'A noise as of wings. A violent disturbance, without the extinction, of the flames of the candles which surround it. A sudden and marked drop in the temperature. When the soul goes, Orthodox or Ilyssan, everyone present knows all about it.'

'And I suppose,' speculated Jo-Jo, 'the trouble with Xanthippe was . . . that her soul had not gone as it should have done.'

'Correct. After over twice the period allotted for an Ilyssan soul to take its departure *en règle*, there had still been no sign, not the very slightest. From which Lalage and her chums concluded that Xanthippe's soul was still hanging about in the death chamber.'

'Which would have been perfectly all right on the Orthodox belief but was very much not all right in the Maniot or Ilyssan version?'

'Correct again. So there was Lalage, summoning Hubert to explain all this, and there was Hubert, saying how sorry he was but really there was nothing that *he* could do about it.

'Ah, but there was, she told him. In crises like this one there was prescribed a formula of incantation, in which the soul was courteously but very firmly exhorted to be on its way before it became an embarrassment. The trouble was, a priest was needed to lead the incantation – not a Roman priest (who would refuse to conduct an Orthodox rite) but an Orthodox one, which in their case they had not got, as priests were thin on the ground in Ilyssos and there had been none to spare for Xanthippe when she left home. Which things being so, they would have to make the best of Hubert, who, though a Roman, was not in Orders and could have no conscientious objection. But was he worthy to stand for a priest, enquired Hubert. Well, they all knew him for a just, kind and righteous man, much loved by their late mistress, and they could only hope that he would be acceptable to God as a minister for this present purpose.

'As it happened, Hubert had a goodish bit of Greek from his time in the Morea and was pretty well able to get up the refrains and recitative required of him. So off they went. First of all, they addressed Xanthippe's soul with polite wishes for its welfare, then expressed a fear that all was not quite *thik hai* with it – for why had it not gone about its business as it long since should have done? Was there, in short, anything which Xanthippe's friends could do to help?'

Ptolemaeos paused and shuddered. He led Jo-Jo away from the window.

'Come to bed, sweetheart,' he said.

'Not till you've finished about Xanthippe.'

'I'll finish there.'

As they climbed the stairs, Jo-Jo said: 'But what did they think they could possibly do to help?'

'Nothing. It was just a rhetorical question put out for the sake of good manners, and like all rhetorical questions it neither required nor expected an answer. The nub of the incantation was still to come – and for that good manners would be shelved and Xanthippe would be told in pretty brisk terms to take herself off as she ought to.'

Again Ptolemaeos fell silent. They undressed hurriedly, crawled into Ptolemaeos' enormous bed, and discreetly cuddled each other.

'The trouble was,' said Ptolemaeos, drawing his right forefinger slowly down Jo-Jo's spine, 'that just for once the rhetorical question got a most unwelcome answer. Xanthippe talked back.'

IVAN BARRACLOUGH was beginning to feel hungry. He had had nothing to eat since his dinner the previous night, and the morning was now far spent.

So was his petrol. By his reckoning he had perhaps an eighth of a tank left; enough for another sixty miles, which would take about an hour and a quarter at the speed he was now averaging.

Still the maroon Lancia loitered patiently along behind him. An hour and a quarter, Ivan thought. Well, as long as he had petrol he could at any rate choose where he would stop. For at least another hour he could choose the place of confrontation. Surely he could devise something, surely he could come up with some ruse or another (with the help of a suitable location) in that period. Eyes front looking, then: watch for the right spot.

> 'And no discouragement,' he sang,
> 'Shall make him once relent
> His first avowed intent
> To be a pilgrim.'

Feeling much better, he launched into the second verse. He was just rendering his favourite line about 'hobgoblins and foul fiends' when there was a discreet thud from his rear offside. The discreet thud of an undramatic puncture. He looked left: salt-marsh and the distant sea. He looked right: pine forest gently rising among sand-dunes. Well at least, he thought, as he coaxed the wounded Land Rover on to the verge, they may fix me up with some breakfast.

'OH PTOLY, for the Lord's sake,' said Jo-Jo for the twentieth time.

'*For the Lord's sake*,' repeated Ptolemaeos for the twenty-first time, 'XANTHIPPE TALKED BACK.'

The mist swirled against the bedroom window, mist shot with sunbeams; for now it was day and had been for some time. I must sleep, thought Jo-Jo. No, not yet: I must hear this out.

'All right,' she said: 'I'm sorry for interrupting. Please go on.'

'According to Hubert, Xanthippe lay on the bed, dead and motionless . . . motionless except for her lips, which said something so appalling that at first they could none of them take it in.'

Jo-Jo slowly withdrew her arms from Ptolemaeos' neck and chest and felt for his hand.

'Yes?' she said in a small voice.

'She told them what had gone wrong. When her body died, her *thymos*, i.e. her whole system of physical and mental and nervous responses, had of course died with it, while her soul, her psyche, had duly come to life.'

'Which was just as it should be.'

'Yes. The bother was, though, that her soul could not leave her body. It wasn't hovering around the room, as they had supposed, and getting ready to go: it was still in her body and could not escape.'

'Could not escape?'

'It was prevented. Prevented by the soul of Hero, who had been sent to watch her. You see, since Xanthippe had devoured Hero, Hero, with some assistance from Masullaoh, had become intimate with Xanthippe's being and was able to exercise certain powers over it. And one of these was to ensure that Xanthippe's soul, though now awake and fully alive, remained a prisoner in her body.'

106

'How? Had Hero entered Xanthippe's body to constrain her?'

'I think . . . that Hero somehow enveloped her. Hubert is not precise about their relationship. But three things he does make clear. First, Xanthippe's living soul is confined within her dead body. Secondly, since the soul cannot take over the vital function of the now dead *thymos*, which was to inform and quicken the limbs and senses, her body will soon begin to decay in the usual manner –'

'– And her aware of it, for Christ's sake, Ptoly, aware of what's happening? As if I suddenly started to rot while lying here with you?'

'Pretty much the same as that. You see, in these circumstances, with the *thymos* dead but the psyche or soul now living and trapped in the body, the soul begins to assume certain *mechanical* functions of the *thymos*. This is the third point on which Hubert of Avallon is very clear. Although Xanthippe's soul could not co-ordinate mind and nerves and sinews as her *thymos* had done, and although it could not keep the flesh and blood healthy and in proper operation as the *thymos* had done, it *could* achieve a certain physical control of the cadaver. It could learn to activate it. Xanthippe had already started to talk: soon, she said, very soon, she would be able to use her dead limbs and sense organs.'

'Like a zombie or a vampire?'

'No, sweetheart. Zombies and vampires have ways of keeping their bodies in good condition. Although they are dead, they have some special physical dispensation. The hideous peculiarity of Xanthippe's condition was that she had no such dispensation: that although her soul was in control all right, what it controlled was not her body but her *corpse*, something which would decompose until it became a skeleton of bones which would finally fall apart.'

'And would her soul *still* be imprisoned?'

'Yes. It was doomed to stay linked with the body as long as Hero watched over it . . . i.e. as long as Masullaoh willed it.'

'But why was Masullaoh doing this to her?'

'Because she had rebelled, she said. Because she had planned to become captain of her own soul and her own fate through the use of the herb which Aristarchos had given her. She was being made an example. She wanted everyone to know and be warned. She also hoped that if she acknowledged Masullaoh's powers in this way, he would eventually relent and release her.'

'But Ptoly, how were Hubert and the hand-maidens behaving during all this?'

'It seems that thirteenth-century Greeks had a strong stomach for this kind of affair. The girls, after the initial shock, stood their ground and listened, while Hubert, being the man of the party, was in honour bound to conduct himself as steadily as his inferiors.'

'But what in God's name did she propose that they should do with her?' Jo-Jo let go of Ptolemaeos' hand and joined her own two in supplication over his breast. 'I mean . . . they couldn't bury her alive, so to speak. And they couldn't have her walking around dead – or not for very much longer.'

'She proposed that they should make a shrine with a crypt and a little cloister for her. If they would do this, and if they would let her have the beautiful *Écrevisse* to help her pass the years, perhaps the centuries, of the suffering which was in store for her, she would promise to confine herself to this precinct and never to issue out and show herself in the increasingly repellent form she would assume. She was not yet sure whether she would need nutriment: if so, the creatures of the crypt and the cloister would probably provide it. Masullaoh was perfectly content, she said, that this accommodation should be come to: for even if she did not exhibit herself in her full horror, the shrine, crypt and cloister would give rise to a legend quite powerful enough for his purposes. One final condition: let no one ever try to take her beloved water-creature from her. It was her murderer, by the will of Masullaoh, but it was also her joy, her solace, her treasure, from which she could never be parted.

'And she then, according to Hubert, gave point to her address by slowly pivoting her trunk to a vertical position, then horizontally pivoting her nether limbs, and finally rising from the bed and stalking away to the ramparts, in a series of ungainly and jerky movements like those of an arthritic. This, she promised, would be her last walk at large in the Castle, provided only they did what she had asked in all matters.'

'And so they did?'

'And so they did. In those days labourers and craftsmen were cheap when not gratuitous (if firmly approached) and swift in operation. For a week the Despoina Xanthippe lay in her bed-chamber, attended by Lalage and the other girls, surrounded by autumn flowers and smoking censers, making occasional rather heavy conversation about her condition and gazing always on her beloved *Écrevisse*. At the end of the week the shrine, the crypt and the cloister were ready. The Princess immediately took possession of the crypt, which was crudely furnished with couch, chair and table, and from which she had easy access to the shrine and thence to the cloister: but the only exit to, or entrance from, the outer world was a door at the west end of the shrine, which looked on to a jousting yard north of the donjon; and this door, with Xanthippe's full knowledge and consent, was to be sealed. "And so," says Hubert, "her maidens and I attended her to the tomb in which she must live and left her there with her beloved water-creature (which was scaled in such richness as would purchase a fair dukedom). There were many tears at parting, and her maidens were eager to give and receive the final kisses; but 'No,' quoth she, 'this may not be, for already my lips harbour the poison of decay, and I would not sully your fair flesh. Go your ways, and pray for my soul that is mewed in so foul a coffin; and may God give you goodly husbands.'"

'Do we know any details?' asked Jo-Jo. 'Could she sleep, for example? Did she in the end require food?'

'Hubert thinks not. Sleep and nourishment are requirements of a living organism: Xanthippe was just a cadaver which was propelled by the power of her pent up soul.'

'This sounds absurd . . . but was she given books?'

'There would not have been many of those at that time in a place like the Castle of Arques. She had much food for thought, and she had her *Écrevisse* which a daemon had brought her from the Court of Satan. Let us hope these kept her occupied.'

'And you are still expecting me to believe all this?'

'It is a matter of interpretation. I'll come to that in a moment. Meanwhile, you should know that Henri de Longueil turned up, the day after Xanthippe was immured, and started asking a lot of awkward questions. After all, there had been talk of marriage and settlements and so on, and now he was absolutely left flat.'

'So what? He never liked her.'

'He was sorry for her – and he might have liked her dowry, for all his protests against arranged marriages. Anyway, he was inquisitive about what had gone on. So Hubert told him the tactful story that subsequently inspired his ballad, and suggested that he might like to escort Xanthippe's young ladies back to Ilyssos, where he could have a word with Xanthippe's father, Phaedron, and then present himself to his Villehardouin connections. Either Lord Phaedron or Prince William might well prove glad of his services, and besides, Hubert pointed out, travel would be of inestimable value to Henri *qua* poet. Henri, having nothing much else to do, pronounced this a topping idea, and they engaged to travel together as far as Avallon, where Hubert must give his belated attention to the affairs which had originally called him home.

'So they set about the final arrangements that had to be made before their departure. It was decided to send an express messenger on ahead to the Lord Phaedron of Ilyssos, to tell him that Xanthippe had died of homesickness, and that her former suitor was coming to pay his respects and deposit the hand-maidens in due course. Henri busied himself with his ballad (which he intended to present to Phaedron) while Hubert took the Castellan on one side and adjured him, on pain of horror worse than death, to keep clear of Xanthippe's shrine. This was popularly supposed, by inmates of the Castle, to be a conventional mausoleum of a conventionally deceased Princess who had been interned there with some of her valuables, in those days a standard incitement to all and sundry to come looting. Hubert tried to make the Castellan understand that anyone who broke the seal on the door of the shrine would find, too late, that he was playing in far too tough a league; and the Castellan in turn undertook to spread the word down the line. At first to no avail. A gang of imbeciles tried to break into the shrine the very night before Hubert, Henri and the girls were due to leave – and the whole bloody shower was found the next morning, outside the door, which they had torn open, with their throats ripped out.'

'The Lady's work – or that of her pet?'

'Either way, *that* put a stop to further incursions. The Castellan and Hubert sealed the shrine again, and as far as we know no illicit attempts have ever been made since.'

'Though one is intended now?'

'If we can find the shrine.'

'By the jousting yard, you said. North of the donjon.'

'There have been many things added and many taken away in seven hundred years.'

'No one would have dared disturb the shrine.'

'Shrines subside. Cloisters crumble and crypts gape. But of this more later. Meanwhile, picture to yourself the re-sealing of the shrine by Hubert and the Castellan (the incident was tactfully concealed from Henri); then a ceremony of farewell in one of the outer courts; and then the procession moving under the raised portcullis and winding down the hill to take the road east for Paris and then south for Avallon: Hubert and Henri leading, the ladies on palfreys behind them, then a troop of local knights, vassals of Villehardouin led by the Constable of Eu, and finally a squad of mounted serjeants in the rear. Picture this, oh heart of my heart; assume (since it was still October) that the party had untroubled passage to Paris and on to the south; imagine Hubert taking farewell of Henri and the girls at Avallon; wave the gallant Sire de Longueil and the ladies on their way, for now we must part from them for this time; and then, then, my poppety-poo, think of Hubert, his journey over and his duty done, home at last in his manor on the western slope of the valley that lies between fair Avallon and towered Vezelay. Think of him, as he walks in his orchard or sits in his hall, while the autumn creeps damper and colder along his valley. He has finished, by now, the business that brought him home; he has already tired of the dumpy wife who has waited so long to welcome him; and there is nothing to keep him from setting out on his journey back to the Morea, to reclaim the fief which he has left in the charge of his steward.

'But he does not go. He has no heart for voyaging. He loiters in his bare orchard and drinks in his draughty hall until it is too late to leave, even if he wished to. He must wait until the springtime now. He has three long dark months to ponder what he has seen and heard since he left Glarentza with Xanthippe and her maidens many months before. He has a burden on his soul; he must discharge himself of this before he sets out again for Romany; that it is why he has lingered – anxious to discharge himself but uncertain how best this may be done.

'But at length he thinks he knows. One morning in December, just before the Birthday of Christ, he comes to shrive himself in the Église Saint-Lazare in Avallon. "O Ghostly Father, I me confess. . ." He has a tale to tell, he says, a tale that should be preserved. But the priest at Avallon is busy with preparations for the Festival of the Birth of God, and is in any case no great hand with a pen. He directs Hubert to seek out a certain learned monk in the cloister of the Basilica Sainte-Madeleine in Vezelay, and dictate his history to him. So Hubert comes to Vezelay –'

'–And tells two stories to the same man. He tells him a nursery version, which pretty well accords with Henri's ballad but has a few faint hints that all is not quite so straight forward as it seems: the Chronicle of Hubert of Avallon. He also dictates an Appendix, full of wonderments and horrors and daemons, daemons who frequent the Courts both of God and of Satan, and bring jewelled gifts from realms beyond the Universe. Was he romancing, Ptoly? Had he flipped? What did he think he was up to?'

'Luckily we have a point from which we may begin to conjecture. We know that the jewelled *Écrevisse*, two cubits long by nine inches high by six inches wide, actually existed. It is recorded in a Byzantine catalogue of the eighth century as having been fashioned for a certain Sebastocrator Demosthenes Commenos from jewels and metals which he looted while suppressing a rebellion at Trebizond. Its value was computed at the rough equivalent of six million sterling of today's money.'

'Did it play tunes which encouraged incestuous orgies? Like Xanthippe's?'

'We know from the catalogue that it could move with the aid of a clockwork mechanism, and that while it moved little bells inside it played music – the nature whereof is not specified. We also know, from the same source, that the Sebastocrator and all his treasure were seized by pirates while he was later voyaging from Constantinople to Smyrna. The pirate chief is named as Crito of Ilyssos. We infer that the *Écrevisse* passed to Phaedron of Ilyssos as an heirloom fire centuries later –'

'And that he put it in the Lady Xanthippe's luggage to make part of her dowry. He wanted to marry her off quick because of her peculiar habits. So he said to Hero, the senior hand-maiden, "Keep her out of trouble, for Christ's sake, and take this golden *Écrevisse*, and this jewelled horn" – the one she used to do it, Ptoly – "and this that and the other, and use these things, if you have to, as an impressive and ready dowry, cash on the table, so to speak, to get her married off to this Henri de Longueil or any other fucker that may fancy her, because, sweet Hero," he would have said, "I love her very dearly, but boy, oh boy, oh boy, is *she* an embarrassment." Right, Ptoly?'

'Roughly, I think.'

'But then her illness, her madness, got worse and worse. She frotted herself in public, and devoured raw meat in a frenzy, and made up more and more appalling commands from Masullaoh. So Hero, to humour and soothe her, brought out the objects from the chest. She encouraged her to dream of such things, and then pretended they had come from her daemon and his world beyond time and space. Like a mother quietens a child with toys which she says have come from Father Christmas, to give them a sort of faerie glamour. For a time this worked, if rather uneasily. Finally, though, Xanth-ippe turned on Hero and rended her . . . at which stage Lalage, the second-in-command, decided it had to stop. For good and all. So one night she said she was going to the loo, killed Xanthippe with the sharp edges and claws of the scaly *Écre-visse*, and herself raised the alarm. She hoped that everyone would connive and more or less believe in a tale whereby the magic shellfish would seem to have destroyed Xanthippe; and she wanted both it and her buried good and deep and there and then, and so an end of it.'

'Whooaah there, sweetheart. Stop to consider a simple question. Did *Hubert* know any of this? And if so, why does he mention it neither in his official Chronicle nor in his Appendix?'

'Hubert loved her. So at first he gave a simple and harmless version of her death – but realised that it might not be believed. There are always odd people, loitering servants and so on, who see or hear more than they should, and Xanthippe's behaviour might well have given rise to rumours. So in case this had happened, in case some of her enormities came to be known about, he devized a version which explained them in a mysterious and grandiose manner. As I see Hubert, as I *feel* him, Ptoly, he was not going to have his Xanthippe written off as a mere common madwoman, as a Bedlam drab subject to vulgar seizures, he was going to present her as something splendid, diabolical but splendid, as a medium of mighty spirits which moved between God and Satan. So he perjured himself to the monk who took his dictation. He said to this monk, "Look, here is one story, the story that the Princess died of yearning for her home and her sea. It will be better for her memory if this is believed. It is not true, that I know, but as men of charity you and I would wish that some such history of her, if any, should survive. However," he would have gone on, "there was that in her life which may cause great scandal if ever it be known . . . and known it well may be. So having wished all this upon you, I must in fairness tell you the entire truth, and you must record it. If you record only what I have so far told you, you may hereafter be taken for a booby or a crook. Hear, therefore, the full sum of all."

'But then, Ptoly, Hubert proceeded to tell the monk a great pack of fibs. And his aim was this: if ever the preferred tale, the tale told by the Chronicle and the Ballad, should be discredited –'

'And there was plenty of evidence, of the kind Ivan is reviewing on his way home, to discredit it –'

' – Then the monk could release Hubert's second version,

114

the Appendix, which was a huge fabrication explaining the poor girl's miserable affliction in such a fashion as to make her a mighty figure of myth. *Not* just a squalid little epileptic who showed off her honey pot and had bestial cravings, but the chosen companion of Archangels of Good and Evil, of the Messengers of God and Lucifer.'

'Ingenious, pretty Jo-Jo. But why should Hubert have found it necessary to make up this horrible story of her survival after death? By all means let us agree that Hubert wished to present her as a kind of superior Sybil to save her from being thought a mere lunatic: but why on earth should he make up this revolting tale that her soul was imprisoned in her decaying corpse? What good could that do her memory?'

'You have a point,' Jo-Jo said.

'What we have to consider is the possibility that Hubert's Appendix is, in some senses, a true version of what happened – that although he knew all about Hero and the trunkful of dowry and Phaedron's instructions to marry her off good and fast, he nevertheless saw the thing on a higher, on a mystical or celestial plane, so that out of poor Xanthippe's lunacy he created a kind of cosmic allegory.'

'Which still does not explain,' said Jo-Jo, 'why he presented her death and immurement in such a sickening way. Don't tell me *that*'s an allegory.'

'It could be an allegory of a great many things.'

'All of them quite disgusting. It could not possibly help to enhance her memory.'

'There remains the possibility,' said Ptolemaeos, 'that Hubert was quite simply telling the truth about Xanthippe's death – or at least what he believed the truth to be. Perhaps his conscience caught him. Having deceived the monk with all the earlier stuff – the spirits of the vasty deep and so on – he decided that in the matter of her death and her survival of it he must tell the truth, if only to warn the world what lay in the Castle of Arques.'

'But if we are right, if Xanthippe was just a madwoman (the simplest and most likely explanation of her behaviour), *then why should she have survived in this ghastly way*? Why should her soul have been trapped in her rotting flesh . . . and be able to announce the fact through lips that were already putrefying? There is no reason, no sense, no purpose in any of it.' Jo-Jo paused and grasped at the empty air as if for an explanation. 'Perhaps she was alive, really alive, all the time. Perhaps she just put on an act in order to get them to shut her away, so that she could at least die alone and in peace, and shed her torment and misery?'

'If she'd wanted to make away with herself, there were simpler ways than that.'

'Are you saying, Ptoly . . . that you think . . . that whatever else he made up . . . Hubert is telling the truth about the way she ended – as a walking and talking corpse?'

'I'm saying, Jo-Jo . . . that I think . . . that one would be prudent . . . to concede the possibility – and to make preparations accordingly.' Ptolemaeos rubbed the palm of his hand gently over both her nipples. 'For whatever the terms in which Hubert is talking,' he continued carefully, 'whether literal or figurative or allegorical, the inference is that what happened was so distasteful that one must be very wary indeed when going (as Ivan is going) to encounter the aftermath, wherever it is, buried in September Castle.'

'So what precautions is he taking?'

'He will carry some of the herb from Ioannina, the same as that with which Aristarchos presented Xanthippe on Corfu. That part of Hubert's story turns out to be true – or at least the herb grows where he says it does. We have identified it, basically, as a member of the Convolvulus family – Chamaetisos Hyptios – but in a slightly different form, with a powerful smell and special pharmaceutical properties that possibly derive from the peculiar silt of the lake, which penetrated the Chapel of Saint John the Baptist, where the herb is found. These special qualities are marked by the addition to the name of the epithet "Spanopouloēdes", a word meaning from the dwelling place of the Anticipator (φθανων), a suitable description of the precinct. As you remember, Xanthippe was at one stage about to use this herb to awaken her soul to fight the daemon. But before she could do this, it disappeared . . . stolen, we are told, by Masullaoh.'

'Hero's work, you think? Or Lalage's perhaps?'

'I don't know that it matters. The point on which to concentrate is this: according to Aristarchos, that herb could enable one absolutely to command either one's own soul or that of another. There must, of course, be some doubt about all that, but experiments which we have conducted prove this much at least, that the herb, if orally administered, can be very effective as an aid in persuading people to do the most improbable and bizarre things, even when these are totally against their own interest. It is therefore permissible to hope that it may have the absolute power over the human soul which Aristarchos claims for it.

'And so,' said Ptolemaeos in a patient and everyday sort of voice, 'if Ivan should be confronted with what is left of Xanthippe, and if he should be informed by her that her soul is still imprisoned there, he will administer the herb to her, and command her to command her soul to free itself.'

'This will not please Hero and Masullaoh – if they are still around.'

'We do not need them to explain what happened to Xanthippe. As we agreed, when rationalizing the earlier part of Hubert's Appendix, there is no Masullaoh, only a girl having fits, just as there were no supernatural gifts from beyond space and time, but simply a series of valuable objects brought out of the trunk in which they had been transported from Ilyssos. As for Hero, who got the objects out of the trunk, she was merely Xanthippe's nurse, who perished at the hand of her patient. Quite a common thing to occur.'

'And yet, Ptoly, you seem to think that the *last* bit Hubert dictated, the bit about the trapped soul, could be true. How could it, unless all that it says about Hero and Masullaoh is also true?'

'There could be other explanations of Xanthippe's condition after her death . . . or her apparent death.'

'Like what?'

'That herb. The last we heard about it is that it had disappeared, spirited away by Masullaoh. But as you plausibly suggest, it had probably been hidden by Hero or Lalage; and even in the former case it is likely enough that Lalage knew where. Now then. Suppose that Lalage, as we think possible, had decided that Xanthippe must be got rid of, being by now really too much of a bad thing. Suppose that she went to Xanthippe's chamber, picked up the *Écrevisse* and wounded the sleeping Princess with it, wounded her quite seriously and very messily, but not fatally; suppose that when her mistress awoke as a result of the attack she administered the herb to her, in a glass of water perhaps, and then instructed her that she was now dead.'

'Xanthippe would have replied that she was very much alive, thank you, and enjoying her glass of water, but what was all this blood?'

'Then the boot goes in. For the herb takes charge and makes Xanthippe believe whatever Lalage says. And Lalage says that she, the Despoina, is indeed dead, dead of the wounds from which the blood has issued; and that the reason Xanthippe thinks she is still alive is because her soul, though awakened by death, has been imprisoned, by special command, in her deceased body.'

'Why should Lalage do this?'

'Jealousy. Jealousy of the noble and quasi-royal House of Ilyssos. Boredom. Resentment and fury at being the servant of a lunatic, at being made to fetch and carry for a so-called Princess who often conducted herself like a common whore. Revenge. Do you see? Lalage, with the help of the herb, was going to persuade poor Xanthippe, to convince her, that she was a living soul shut up in a decaying carcase. She was going to submit Xanthippe to the most hideous punishment to avenge her own fancied wrongs: she was going to confine her, while yet she lived, to what was to all intents a tomb, and leave her to die by slow degrees there, during which time she would have the agony of thinking that her entombment would last for ever and would also endure terrible throes and pains (from her untreated wounds and creeping debility) which she would attribute to the fancied decomposition of her flesh. Can you imagine a more horrible way to die? Thinking, up to the very last, that her torment would persist for ever and that the obscenity of her bodily state would daily spread until she could see her own bones through the worm-eaten flesh. That was what Lalage condemned Xanthippe to.'

'*Might* have condemned her to. Why, if all this was Lalage's work, did the Despoina babble on about Hero and Masullaoh? We'd thrown them out, remember?'

'Hubert would have described her as talking like that in order to give continuity to the whole scenario – in order to bridge the gap between his earlier fictions about Xanthippe's daemon and his later and true account (true from where he stood) of her fate after death.'

'So,' said Jo-Jo thoughtfully, drumming the fingers of her left hand on Ptoly's fair-haired chest, 'we have two superlatively beastly possibilities. Either Xanthippe's soul has been living for the last seven centuries chained to her own rotting corpse; or else she died in agony, already more or less entombed, *believing* that she must for ever dwell amid the garbage of her person. If the former, Ivan can expect an uncivil reception. If the latter – well, if there *are* ghosts, this is surely the sort of situation that creates them, and he might find something even nastier.'

'I rather agree,' said Ptolemaeos. 'I can only assure you that he is being well paid and will be given a fair share in the prize, if any.'

'If any? I thought you said that *Écrevisse* was definitely the real McCoy. Assembled by Byzantine jewellers for this Sebastocrator, worth six million sterling, pinched by the Ilyssan lot, *et cetera, et cetera.*'

'I also told you, earlier tonight, that its value depended on the conditions of its discovery. Quite simply, darling, if there are lots of nosy Frogs quacking about the place, as it now seems there may be, we haven't much chance. They don't know about the *Écrevisse* because they haven't read the Appendix; but try smuggling two cubits by nine inches by six – well over 1,500 cubic inches – of gold and jewels and enamel over the drawbridge under your shirt – with vanloads of Frog officials looking on. They'll be on to you like flies on to shit, and they won't believe it's baby's new rattle.'

'What with the quick and the dead,' said Jo-Jo, 'Ivan has much to contend with. What about my darling Baby Canteloupe? I don't want her frightened by anything horrid.'

'Baby don't frighten easy.'

'Well, I think I'll tell her what's going on and leave it to her. That all right?'

'I said I'd leave that decision to you. You tell her whatever you think best. As you know, Ivan has his role, and Baby and Canteloupe have theirs.'

'Yes . . . as cover for Ivan.'

'Baby might well have something nearer the front line.'

'Jesus, Ptoly,' said Jo-Jo, digging her nails into his chest, 'if anything happens to Baby I'll fucking well kill you. I think I shall warn her to clear off before it's too late.'

'It is too late, angel-pie. Baby is *committed*. Tell her what you like, she can't get out of it now.'

'Get out of what?'

'Baby has promised me . . . that if I tie up some little money worry of Canteloupe's –'

'I thought Canteloupe was rolling.'

'He has made one or two mistakes – errors of omission – in the last two or three years. We were talking about it when he first got here the other day. And since then –'

'Since then you've grabbed him by the balls. So Baby's promised you – what?'

'That she'll go in there with Ivan, if he needs her, and . . . well . . . soothe any nasty female tantrums.'

'Ptoly, *what can you mean*?'

'Whatever version of Xanthippe's death and its aftermath is the true one, there could be affronted female feelings to be dealt with. Hero or Xanthippe, either of them, for one reason or another, might make herself very unpleasant. Now, my little love, you of all people know how clever Baby can be at . . . reassuring fellow females.'

'Dead fellow females?'

'Oh yes. *Mutatis mutandis* the problems are presumably analogous.'

II

Hallowed Ground

WHILE JO-JO AND PTOLEMAEOS slept in the fenlands, Jean-Marie Guiscard had greater joy of the bright morning, as he walked on the ramparts of the Castle of Arques.

September Castle in September, he thought: the season in which the Lady Xanthippe arrived here, seven hundred and twenty-five years ago, almost to the day. O the red sun rising and the white pockets of mist, loitering among the turning trees over the moat. No wonder she found it beautiful, no wonder she was pleased with it when she first came. Yet soon she wearied of it. Why? Unappeased longing for the sea . . . could that truly have been the cause of her death? Well, true or not, it made a sad, pretty tale. . . A *pretty* tale? 'There is an aspect of all this,' M. le Directeur had said in Eu, 'which really intrigues me.' It was that Henri Martel had disliked Xanthippe because 'another watched him from behind her eyes'. 'There is something, something *pas honnête* about this lady,' the Director had said. That was why he, the Director, had given instruction for the restorations to be begun after all. Restoration would mean excavation, and excavation might turn up something peculiar to do with Xanthippe, something – what were the Director's exact words? – 'something "fishy", as the English would say . . . the uncovering of which, if only it turns out to be as truly disgusting as I hope it will, would make my reputation – and, just possibly, yours.'

And so orders had been drawn to commence work on the Castle in just two weeks' time ('*quinze jours*') and now, with thirteen of those days still to go, Jean-Marie Guiscard was pacing the walls (while the woodland mist melted into the red and gold of the morning) and devising programmes and priorities for the forthcoming course of repairs.

As far as that went, Jean-Marie was very happy: he wished to make the Castle a safe and comely place in which the people could walk in peace, having tender memories (those few that

123

knew of her) of the Despoina Xanthippe of Ilyssos. What did not make him very happy was the attitude of the Director, that learned antiquary M. Socrates Besançon: true, had it not been for that attitude there would be no restoration in prospect; but it was nevertheless deeply distasteful to Jean-Marie to think that anyone was eager to dig up matter injurious to his beloved Princess . . . which was most certainly ('something "fishy", as the English would say') what the Director had in mind.

Nevertheless, thought Jean-Marie, who was a man of truth as well as chivalry, if there is something 'fishy' to be found then it should be found, for one should not give one's affection, whether to the quick or the dead, on the strength of false premise. Therefore let us combine sound work for security and amenity with a thorough search for any trace which may be left of the Lady's tomb – or the Lady.

Very well then: to these ends he must now consider the structure of the Castle throughout, beginning with the western gate, proceeding gradually east, and ending with the eastern donjon. Such a scheme, he thought, is topographically convenient and also happens to present the features of the Castle in ascending order of importance from the point of view of those who are responsible for this operation. So. The fourteenth-century barbican or gate house at the west point of the Castle offers no problems, provided we fence off the crumbling stairway down to the adjacent dungeons, in which children (or lovers) might well be injured or trapped. Similarly, as we march along the path to the east, we must block access down to the cells, chambers, serjeants' and footmens' quarters (*et cetera*) which are contained in the low body of the walls to north and south. We should also clear much of the brush, which has an agreeably forlorn air about it but conceals perilous pits and shafts.

Alors. Let us take the central archway which leads into the Court of Honour: the vaulting is sound; and all we need do is scour up the lettering on the Chevalier's tablet on the north wall within, and restore the monument to the Battle of Arques over the eastern arch without. As for the area between the archway and the tilting yard, once again a clearance of brush, and the prevention of access to chambers or corridors within the ramparts, will suffice.

It is when we begin to cross the tilting yard (or meadow), with the twelfth-century turret of the watch over the Lesser Forest straight ahead of us, and the eleventh-century donjon or keep ahead and to the right of us – it is then that the great problems, whether of security or search, beset us. For the turret of the watch over the Lesser Forest (the Forest of Envermeu to the south-east) is a round and gay little tower which we enter through an enticing Romanesque door at its north-west – only to find ourselves within a few feet of an ugly breach (formerly a window) from roof to floor of the south-east section, a breach through which any child who had entered too eagerly might take off on a precipitate flight over the ramparts to eternity at the bottom of the empty moat, some hundred yards below. The simple answer is, of course, to brick the breach up to the level of (say) a six-year-old child's chin; yet quite apart from the difficulties of matching the stone and finding a craftsman with the style and delicacy needed for the task, one has to reckon that the windowledge of the new barrier would make an irresistible temptation to all older children of proper spirit to ride hobby horse over the void, bringing inevitable fatalities which would be blamed on the Department.

Here, reflected Jean-Marie, is all the trouble. As long as the Department does nothing about Arques apart from warning people that it is dangerous, no guilt or discredit can attach to it in case of calamity; but from the moment the Department takes the place under its official wing, anything that goes wrong will be rubbed with sanctimonious relish right up our nostrils. And so one concludes that in order to prevent children diving into the moat (and but one such incident will be blown up into a Massacre of the Innocents) one must either forbid the tower altogether (a thousand pities), or put bars into the window (thus damaging the fabric of the roof), or just possibly (thought Jean-Marie with uncharacteristic malice) make the sill taper to a knife-edge ridge which will cut into those dear little *culs* and *cons* so sharply that none, once the word gets round, will attempt to bestride it. As to all that, the decision must rest, in the end, with M. Socrates Besançon, who was most welcome to it.

The next problem which Jean-Marie had to consider was whether to rebuild the turret's long vanished sibling, the turret of the watch over the Great Forest (the Forest of Arques to the north), which had once stood on the northern battlements and commanded a fine view over the valley and on to the ridge which 'the Great Forest' still covered. The decision here was easy and could be taken at once: since the valley had been choked by projects of labour and the breeding boxes of the labourers, the view was ruined and there was therefore no point in erecting a new tower (leave aside the expense) from which to view it.

And now, thought Jean-Marie, now for the real menace, the donjon or keep. This was a huge hollow cube of jagged flint, perhaps fifty yards square by fifty yards high, which stood in the south-east corner of the perimeter. Its south wall descended flush with the southern rampart; its east wall was rooted some twenty yards only from the eastern rampart; its west wall looked across scrub and debris towards the central archway; and its north wall lowered over the yard or meadow that had once accommodated tournaments and jousts.

If the exterior was merely brutish, the interior of the shell was treacherous and vicious. There were mouldering staircases which mounted to tilting platforms flimsily attached to oblique walls. There were high and mighty projections of stone which trembled at the bare sound of the human voice and threatened to fall from the sky like the bolts of Jove to crush the prying wretches beneath. There were steep ridges of grass and earth, treacherously muddy even in the driest weather, from top to bottom of which the unwary might slide as down a chute and over a ski-jump, to fall ten feet on to stalagmitic formations of rock, rusty iron and broken glass. Worst of all, perhaps, there was the well: an open well of ample circumference, approached by an insidious path through a tiny meadow in an inner recess of the keep, inefficiently guarded by a low parapet over which an infant might crawl with ease, variously reckoned to drop for between forty yards and seventy to a puddle of slime and shingle suppurating in a concave rock.

Well, there was only one answer to the donjon: a heavily roped or railed walk along its four inner sides, YOU COME IN HERE AND YOU GO OUT THERE – BY ORDER, and an ex-*sous officier* or traffic policeman to make sure no one tried to take a diversion. This in turn raised the whole question of how many such officials would have to be employed, their scales of pay, their hours of work and the hours and days of the restored Castle's opening and closing – but these were problems for his superiors, *et Jean-Marie, il s'en foudra*.

Having thus settled security's hash, Jean-Marie started to consider the more entertaining topic of excavation and search. What, he asked himself, were they searching for? They were searching, in the main, for the burial place or tomb of the Despoina Xanthippe of Ilyssos. He, Jean-Marie Guiscard, wished to find it out in order that it might be rescued, re-appointed and distinguished as the resting place of an heroine of French poesy. The learned M. Socrates Besançon wished to find it in order that he might deduce scandal from it, in order that he might dig up something ('fishy' or 'truly disgusting') which would make for the posthumous disgrace of the Despoina and for the fame, as Scholar and Archaeologist, of M. Socrates. As to that, thought Jean-Marie for the second time that morning, so be it: he must simply abide the event. If they should discover (as surely they would not) any evidence of wantonness or evil doing, well, as he had already told himself, the truth must be served and preserved, a law both moral and academic from which even forlorn and exquisite Princesses were not exempt. In any event, it would be time to taste *that* particular mess of potage when and if it was ever cooked; meanwhile, let him gratify himself, and oblige the superior on whose good will and offices the whole exercise depended, by intelligent prosecution of the search.

So. All the Chronicle said about Xanthippe's grave was that it had been 'near the Chapel of the Castle', and that 'Her Treasure and Its Guardian did stay with her'. As for the first, the topological item, it was clearly indicated by vestigial foundations that the Chapel had stood on the flat summit of a low and circular mound which lay between the turret of the watch over the Lesser Forest and the north-east corner of the donjon. It was built on an exact east-west axis, and the east wall had been only a few yards from the eastern rampart, which rose out of the eastern slope of the circular mound and would have towered right up above the Chapel. To the south of the Chapel and the east of the donjon (between it and the rampart) had been and still in part was an elevated and fortified platform for the deployment of engines of the defence such as catapults, giant arbalests and devices for squirting boiling oil (etc.) on to the intrusive; while from the northern and western walls of the Chapel the mound sloped gently away into the tilting yard or meadow.

A grave or tomb 'near the Chapel', Jean-Marie told himself, must have been either (1) between the north wall of the Chapel and the turret, or (2) between the east end of the Chapel and the rampart, or (3) between the south wall of the Chapel and the raised platform, or (4) west of the Chapel and north of the donjon. In cases (2) and (3) the situations were (a) unsuitable, for one did not erect tombs where the fray would be hottest and the missiles thickest, and (b) too exiguous (a tomb or grave between the east of the Chapel and the battlements, for example, would effectively block all martial passage there). Of the remaining possibilities, situation (1) was commodious but must be disqualified for the same reason as (2) and (3) – it was too exposed to the hazards of battle. This left only situation (4), the area west of the Chapel and north of the donjon; presumably, then, the grave must have been either on the western slope of the mound or at its foot, just on the edge of the tilting meadow. One could reasonably assume that there would have been no objection to siting a tomb near a place of *simulated* combat when the only alternatives were clearly going to be slap in the middle of the real thing. It would, of course, have been very easy to bury the Despoina anywhere in the whole Castle and so somewhere far more peaceful than the edge of the jousting lists: but obviously they needed hallowed ground for the purpose, and this enjoined proximity to the Chapel.

Enfin, thought Jean-Marie, the thing is very plain: unless the remains of the Despoina have been disturbed or removed, they are somewhere in the earth just to the north of the eastern section of the northern wall of that donjon.

Thus it will be observed that Jean-Marie Guiscard, who had not the benefit of the Appendix to the Chronicle (of the very existence of which he was ignorant), had nevertheless been able correctly to deduce, from the official version of the Chronicle, the approximate whereabouts of the Lady Xanthippe's resting place. What he could not know, of course, was that this had not been a mere hole in the ground or a mere box above it, but a shrine complete with crypt and cloister. Another thing he could not know was the condition of the Lady, as alleged by the Appendix, when she was consigned. Nor could he know very much about 'Her Treasure and Its Guardian', a phrase which had puzzled him from time to time and the precise significance of which he now began to ponder.

According to the Chronicle of Hubert of Avallon, the Lady Xanthippe had brought from Ilyssos a sumptuous dowry for bestowal on Henri Martel. It further appeared from the Chronicle that one particular item, or perhaps set of items, was distinguished from the rest as the Despoina's special Treasure ('*Thesaurus*' in the Latin of the transcribing monk of Vezelay), and that she had appointed someone, presumably one of her girls, as its special 'Guardian', '*Custos*' in the Latin. But the immediate difficulty then arose that the Chronicle stated absolutely flat that 'The Treasure and Its Guardian did stay with her' after her burial; and surely it was unthinkable (it had to be unthinkable) that one of the hand-maidens had been buried alive with her mistress.

So *what* stayed with her? Come, come; common sense. Consider what it was *practicable* to bury with her in a grave, a tomb or possibly a small mausoleum. Obviously the 'Treasure' was some favourite jewel or precious object, or a set of such; an eikon or series of eikons, perhaps: and obviously the 'Guardian' would have been something of outstanding holiness, a crucifix or a relic or perhaps the paramount eikon of the collection, which radiated a divine and protective influence over the entire bag of tricks. What fault could be found with that explanation? No need to suppose the interment of living hand-maids or the unhealthy presence of ambiguous spirits: all that had happened was that two or more of Xanthippe's most treasured possessions, one of which had a sanctity that protected the rest, had been placed in her coffin or in some part of her tomb. *Pari passu*, let it be added, this interpretation of the phrase worked equally well throughout the entire Chronicle.

And just what difference, if any, did this make to the forthcoming search? If the objects were of interest or of value (quite possible), was it his duty to see that they stayed where they were, to prevent their being rifled from the Lady's tomb on the pretext of research or in the cause of gain? Or was it permissible, after all this time, to remove them from the Lady, who had had long centuries in which to enjoy them, and exhibit them for the public pleasure?

Such problems he could mull over as the days went on: meanwhile, there was one wholly practical decision which must be made here and now. These various and sometimes complex tasks of restoring and making safe, of excavation, sifting and search – in what order should they be performed? He was charged to draw up a memorandum for M. Socrates about this and to present it immediately. The form which the memorandum should take was quite clear, reflected Jean-Marie as he paced slowly across the tilting meadow and the Court of Honour, then under the central archway: the obvious and sensible thing to do was to start with the simple tidying up operations at the west end of the Castle and work eastwards, through restorations of increasing difficulty, until finally they could take on the challenge of the labyrinthine and murderous donjon. This done, they could begin the trickiest tasks of all – a dig beneath the ruins of the chapel (there might be a crypt of some note) and the probing for, and then (God willing) the excavation of, the Despoina Xanthippe's place of burial north of the donjon (as he had deduced that it must be), on the edge of the jousting yard and near the bottom of the western slope of the Chapel mound. This scheme (thought Jean-Marie as he peered into the dungeon nearest the barbican) had the triple advantage of simplicity, continuity, and ascending interest and importance: the most demanding jobs would wait until the workers were thoroughly practised, and the fascination of the final probe would compensate for the accumulated tedium of repetitious labour.

Full of self-satisfaction at the way in which he had passed his morning and at the conclusions to which he had come, Jean-Marie passed under the suspended portcullis and along the causeway across the empty moat. A few months now, he thought as he turned for a farewell look at the gatehouse, and the ticket machines will be whirring and the postcards selling, the walls and the walks will be safe and spruce, eager queues will be filing round the refurbished donjon, and there will be a worthy memorial for all to gaze on of the little Princess from Romany, who journeyed so bravely to this Castle of the north, then pined and died for the never-resting sea.

But as he walked towards his car, which was parked in a meadow beneath the Castle wall, a small voice spoke in his heart and said:

There needs no stone, Jean-Marie, for all to gaze on. I like this pretty wilderness, and so do the lovers and the loiterers. I like this grim old donjon, and so do the high-voiced children, who are far happier with its quirks and snares than they will be with your primly fenced galleries. If you really love this place, Jean-Marie, as I know you think you do, go away and leave it, leave it and us, alone.

'AND SO,' said Jean-Marie Guiscard to M. Socrates Besançon over his well earned luncheon, 'as a result of my reconnaissance this morning I recommend that we start with the gatehouse or barbican, near which there are some dangerously exposed dungeons, and then work by degrees towards the keep, leaving the excavations which interest us both so much until the very end.'

'Thus giving us plenty of time to investigate the nature and lie of the ground before we actually begin to dig.'

'Indeed, M. le Directeur.'

'So. Given that work is to commence in thirteen days' time, how soon shall we be finished with reconstructing the interior of the donjon and ready to excavate the Chapel and the Lady's tomb?'

'In three months' time, if all goes well.'

'In December. Not a propitious season.'

'A discreet season. There will be no watchers.'

'There will be no watchers in any case, esteemed Jean-Marie. We shall close the Castle gates – shall we not? – as soon as we commence work . . . or indeed well before.'

Jean-Marie licked his lips.

'With respect. The closing of gates, M. le Directeur, has never yet deterred serious snoopers. Besides,' he said very carefully, 'I do not think, after my . . . experiences . . . this morning, that the Castle – or shall we say the Genius of the Castle? – will look favourably on such a proceeding. Could we not leave as much as possible of it open, even while we work?'

M. Socrates examined Jean-Marie and sucked at his teeth. After a long pause, 'You may well be right,' said M. Socrates, who had not arrived where he was in the Department for nothing; 'one should always be mindful of the Genius. I remember a time when we tried to close the bridge between Beaucaire and Tarascon – but never mind that now. Now we are concerned with Arques, and with Arques in mind I will give the question thought. For the time being we shall leave the Castle open, but we shall issue very strict and precise warnings against each and all of its dangers. You will see to that?'

'Happily, M. le Directeur.'

'As for the operations, whether we leave the Castle open or partly open, or close it altogether, we shall, I now think, observe the schedule which you propose. December is, as you remark, a discreet month, probably a more effective inhibitor of snoopers than any number of bolted gates.'

'AND SO,' said the Marquis des Veules–les–Roses to his sister at tea time that same day, 'my spies tell me that the castle may well remain open during the operations of the Department; also that there will be relatively little attention paid to the eastern end – *our* end – until much later in the winter.'

'Who are these spies?'

'One spy, to be precise. A female typist of quite astounding seniority.'

'Reliable?'

'So I care to think.'

'What do you pay?'

'I do not pay. I was once briefly *et il y a mille ans* her lover. In memory of which time I provide her, every Christmas, with a rare and expensive brand of rumbustious and ejaculatory vibrator. She seems appropriately grateful, and her information has always been broadly sound. So I have little doubt that matters *in re* the Castle of Arques are much as she has just reported . . . which will, by and large, please the gross Ptolemaeos.'

'AND SO,' said the gross Ptolemaeos to his niece Jo-Jo, having received a telephone call from M. des Veules–les–Roses shortly after tea (anchovy muffins), 'they are leaving our bit of the Castle until the last.'

'Good?' she enquired.

'Only on the face of it. They are bound to start making surveys and preparations from quite early on, so that they will be buzzing round the area all day. That will make Ivan's work impossible.'

'Could he not work at night?'

'He could – if unimpeded. But once the works begin, the Department will maintain a night watchman to protect its equipment and deter *visiteurs du soir*. So the thing is quite clear: Ivan must be finished before the Director and his gang begin. He will need eight days. On his present schedule he will have exactly that – *if* he can still get to Saintes-Maries-de-la-Mer and on to Dieppe at the times planned. If only I knew where to find him, I might have got him there sooner. But as it is . . . let the thing run as previously reckoned, if only it will, and Ivan and the Canteloupes will have the bare eight days.'

'LEN HAS A PROBLEM,' said Ivor Winstanley to Tom Llewyllyn in Tom's rooms in Lancaster College.

Tom surveyed his two guests equably and passed the port to Ivor, who filled and passed it to Len, who filled and passed it back to Tom. Ivor was a Latin don in an advanced state of fruitiness: Len, his protegé, was a stringy man of just under thirty, who was dressed in stylish bad taste and had a face of sly intellectual distinction.

'Like the pitch is this, man,' said Len to Tom in an immaculate Cambridge accent. 'I've stowed enough bread in the bank to feed me high off the hog for a lifetime, with a lot more besides. So what's to do with me and it? Any ideas?'

'Surely,' said Tom, 'when you first . . . first became affluent . . . you intended to travel and live the good life. Art, music, literature, wordly pleasures of every kind – you had them all before you, and Ivor as an expert guide and tutor.'

'That was the notion. But how it all turned out was different. In the beginning, before I made it, old Ive, like you say, was my guide and tutor. Dear old Ive, he taught me everything. What to eat and drink and read, and how to finish up a letter to a Royal Princess that's married a Baronet. And pretty soon he raised me up from being a shitty-arse cunt-hungry bum, spewing cant and envy all over the place and crawling with left-wing bugaboos, drooling my life away as a so called graduate student researching into social garbage and squeezing out a few more scabby pennies by looking after the College Manuscripts in some smelly hole in the heap – he raised me out of all this into being my own man who knows what was what and where to get it. And then he put me – and him – in the way of a big pile of loot. After which we had a lot of fun for a while, up and down Europe, expensive and memorable fun, and not for the world would I have missed it.

'But by now old Ive had long since ceased to be my guide and tutor, Tom. By now I knew it all myself – and was in a fair way to getting sick of it. The trouble with the good life is that once you've had it for a few minutes you don't want it, or not all that much, and only at intervals; a man must have some occupation other than feeding his mind and his face. The good life is no fun, Tom, unless you've got something else as well to keep your wits sharp and your sword bright. So what am I to do, Tom, in the intervals of the good life? Don't tell me to make money, because I've got all I need.'

'Do you wish,' said Tom, '"to reign in Hell" or to "serve in Heaven"?'

Ivor Winstanley giggled.

Len looked blank for a moment. Then, 'You mean . . . do I want flashy work or solid work?' he said. 'Do I want excitement or duty?'

'Very roughly, yes.'

'A bit of both. I'd hoped I might find them back here in the College.'

'You want to come back to Lancaster?' said Tom. And to Ivor, 'Has Len mentioned this to you?'

'Yes,' said Ivor. 'He thinks – and I think – that he could handle the young quite well in his own way.'

'Helping them. That would be duty all right,' said Len.

'And where is the excitement?' enquired Tom. 'You did say you hoped for both?'

'Like Ive says, I can handle the young,' said Len shamelessly. 'He was speaking metaphorically: I'm talking straight.'

'So,' said Tom, 'you envisage some post in this College, presumably of an administrative rather than strictly academic nature, which would enable you to act as arbiter and mentor among the young, and also as their sexual impressario?'

'Not for all of them,' said Len complacently: 'mostly the girls. Since they've managed to nag their way into the place, they may as well be put to some use. I see myself as a kind of house-father. Just as an unmarried master at a public school employs someone called a house-mother, so I'll be employed here as house-father. Drying the tears and changing the knickers. But we'd better give me a more classy name: say, "Counsellor".'

'And who,' said Tom, 'is going to persuade the College Council to ratify this interesting appointment?'

'Provost Constable still owes me and Ive from the old days,' said Len. 'We had him by the crinklies and we let him down light.'

'That may well be,' said Tom. 'It may also very well be that Lord Constable, who finds your brand of rascality rather engaging, would agree the debt and engineer the appointment: after all you could certainly teach the undergraduates of either gender much that they should know about the world; and since their sexual activities are these days so comprehensive in any case, they might just as well, and possibly with advantage, comprehend you.'

'I'm glad you see it my way,' said Len.

'But there is, my dear Len, a worm in this nice, rosy apple, a worm of which Ivor, with his kindly and tactful character, has apparently forborne to warn you.'

'I fear so,' said Ivor, in a tone so mildly self-deprecatory as to be virtually self-gratulatory, and reached by stealthy degrees for the port.

'Well then,' said Tom, putting the decanter firmly into Ivor's hovering hand, 'it falls to me, as his host and advisor of the evening, to explain to Len why his elegant little scheme is just so much piss up the wind. Lord Constable can in no way assist you, Len, whether he owes you or whether he don't, because he is on the way out.'

'Not until the end of the academic year,' said Len, 'next June.'

'Founder's Day,' said Tom, 'December the Sixth, as you doubtless recall. Little more than two months from now. That is what the Statutes rule in his case, if strictly interpreted. Normally these would be waived and he would be allowed, indeed pressed, by the Council, in its courtesy, to remain until June or even later. But as it is, since Provost Constable, although a Socialist, is also a Scholar, a Peer of the Realm, an ex-officer of gallantry and distinction, and a man, *man*, Len, of discipline and mettle, the present rabble of philistines and levellers want him out of the way at the first possible moment, so that they can start their dismal antics unimpeded and with the minimum of delay. A new Provost will therefore be elected in a very few weeks' time: from the first moment the election is called, the Provost *in situ*, though still technically reigning until December the sixth, is forbidden by Statute from proposing or promoting any new measures or appointments, even if the Council be willing to underwrite them.'

'Right you be,' said Len. 'That still leaves *some* time before the election is called.'

'You forget. Full Term begins on October the twelfth. Nothing can be done for you until that date falls. *As* that date falls, the election will be called . . . and thereafter nothing can be done for you. The thing is quite clear, Len: your horse does not even get into the starting box.'

'Nor even into the race card by the sound of it,' mused Len. 'What hope with the next regime?'

'Nil. Zero. *Niente*. As far as the young set are concerned you are not only a reactionary but also a class traitor. As far as the older men see, you're a jumped up nothing –'

'Thank you very much, Ethel –'

'Who's made some shady money. Without Constable, Lenny mine, you're absolutely without hope.'

'So that's flat,' said Len without rancour. 'You just sling your hook, Len Cunt, you fascist parvenu oik, you, and don't slam the door as you go out.'

'You're much better out,' said Ivor, 'than in. It's going to be horrible here. Nothing but brutes canvassing other brutes to elect the most brutish brute of them all. And the standards pretty high these days, I can tell you.'

'Or,' said Tom, 'the brutes will carefully arrange to elect some dripping wet slob, so that they can run the whole place over his head. Either way the College is going to be ridden with tertiary Socialism within six months.'

'They'll forbid the May Ball,' moaned Ivor; 'they'll cancel all the Feasts and sell the College Cellar.'

'They'd sell the College Chapel if they could find a buyer. They'll certainly sell the Rubens and the glass out of the windows . . . and give the money to Oxfam.'

'To terrorists, my dear, I shouldn't wonder.'

'I think that's rather overdoing it, Ivor. They may be perfect sods, but they're not assassins. Not yet, anyway. But Ivor's quite right, Lenny,' said Tom, retrieving the port from Ivor and pouring Len a liberal back-hander. 'They'll be nothing here worth hanging about for, not with Constable gone.'

'Point taken,' said Len, 'and thank you for the tip. I think I shall go somewhere east of Suez and turn native. Fuck myself to death, like Gauguin.'

'Very boring. If you really want excitement,' said Tom, suddenly remembering something, 'I might be able to fix you up. My daughter and her husband have a friend, an old Lancastrian, called Ptolemaeos Tunne. Rather before your time but very much to your present taste. He'd like you too, I think.'

'So what's with this Tunne?' drawled Len.

'I'm not quite sure. But from the little I overheard while lunching there the other day, there's something bubbling that's right up your own stinking alley. It's indecent, insanitary, illicit if not criminal, and much beset about with ghoulish apparatus. Just your cuppa, me ole Len.'

'You think they could fit me in?' said Len.

'With the greatest of pleasure, I should imagine, if once you acquaint them with your range of hideous talents. Why not apply to Ptolemaeos? Just forty minutes' drive from here; I'll give you his number and address, and you can say I sent you. He's got a nice little bit of hot twat living with him,' said Tom, momentarily reverting, in Len's honour, to the tone and taste of his own youth, 'who may well fancy a sharp fellow like you.'

'What would this Ptolemaeos say?'

'He's not the jealous type. He'd probably come along and watch. But just one word of warning, Lenny doll,' said Tom in a voice of marble. 'My daughter Tullia's going to be in on all this somewhere, and if you put your greasy prick anywhere near her, I'll slice the fucking thing off.'

AT ABOUT THE SAME TIME as Tom Llewyllyn and his guests finished dinner, Ptolemaeos and Jo-Jo started theirs.

'I've been thinking,' said Jo-Jo. 'All this chat about what Ivan Barraclough may or may not be going to find in that Castle is great stuff for an autumn evening, but isn't it time we asked ourselves exactly how and where he's going to find it?'

'We know where the shrine was built. Though the official Chronicle is vague, the Appendix makes it absolutely clear that the shrine and cloister were set up north of the donjon and on the edge of the tilting ground, which lay towards the eastern end of the Castle. It is also clear that the shrine lay at the bottom of the western slope, or perhaps a little way up the slope, of a mound on which stood a chapel. The inference is that the shrine was placed there so that it should be on Holy Ground.'

'Then it would have been a little way up the slope,' said Jo-Jo. 'If a chapel stands on a mound, then you can say that the mound is holy or sacred, but somewhere there must come an end of the holiness – obviously at the bottom. So they would have put her at least a little way up the slope. Right?'

'I dare say so, and I know Ivan agrees with you. So what with that and all the other co-ordinates, we can say that we have the shrine more or less pin-pointed.'

'So then we ask ourselves, how was the thing designed. We know that the only entrance to it was a door looking on to or over the tilting yard. What else do we know?

'We are given no precise measurements but we do have some notion of spatial relations. The shrine was built on an east-west axis. In the middle of its south wall there was a door leading into a cloister, which must have been built at least partly into the hillside.'

'To be of any use at all, that cloister must be at least five yards square,' said Jo-Jo. 'Did it have proper galleries?'

'Neither the time nor the space available would have sufficed for the construction of these. It can't have been much more than a walled yard, half roofed over, perhaps, to give the Despoina shelter when she walked there.'

'Did she need shelter? I mean, to what extent could she feel damp or cold or heat? Obviously these . . . affected her corporal condition . . . but could she *feel* discomfort?'

'A nice question. If, as we think possible, she was really alive when first confined, then plainly she could. *But the assumption on which the place was built for her* was that she was dead (though still mobile). In which case, does one assume that her nerves no longer operated? Probably not. And yet her senses would seem to have worked: in some fashion she saw and heard. But either way, sweetheart, I don't think much attention would have been paid to her comfort. She was an embarrassment, not least to herself, whom all concerned, including herself, wanted safely out of the way as soon as possible. So up went the shrine, up went a crudely walled cloister adjacent – with the minimum thought of amenity.'

'And up – or rather down – went a crypt,' said Jo-Jo. 'Where was this in relation to the rest?'

'Underneath the cloister, apparently. But to get to it you had to go back from the cloister into the shrine, in which there were some steps that led down under the altar at the east end and into a little passage, along which you – or rather she – turned right and walked south to the crypt. This was entered at its east end, where there was another altar, and formed a rectangle longer than the cloister east-west but not so broad north-south. Apart from the altar the only other things in the crypt were a couch, a table and a chair for Xanthippe's . . . domestic occasions.'

'How was it lit?'

'She was given a supply of candles. Apparently she liked to look at her *Écrevisse* candle-lit in the crypt far more than in the daylight of the shrine, which itself was lit by a circular east window over the altar, or *al fresco* in the cloister. However, as Hubert points out in the Appendix, the supply of candles would have run out after a time – and by then everyone who knew and cared about her predicament was on the road south.'

'What about the Castellan? Couldn't he have been asked to deliver a supply?'

'The Castellan was a simple soldier, whom no one wished to burden with sophisticated problems. All he had been told, both before and after the one attempt to rifle the shrine, was that there was something abominable about it and that nobody must tamper with it. The place had now been resealed, so let it stay that way. If parcels of chandlery could get in, God knew what might not get out – despite Xanthippe's promise to keep herself to herself, which she might find irksome as the years went on. Sooner or later she would have to accustom herself to doing without candles, however prettily they played on her shimmering and many-hued *Écrevisse*, and that must simply be that.'

'Anyway, Ptoly, for how long, one now wonders, would she actually have been able to *see* the *Écrevisse*? I mean, if she really was a corpse, albeit with a soul attached. . .'

'That whole area is very dubious. All we can say is that at the time she was consigned to her quarters – seven days after her supposed death – she was still seeing, hearing and talking with pretty fair efficiency . . . according to Hubert. And since then, of course, nobody at all has seen her.'

'Ah,' said Jo-Jo: 'this brings us to the *echte* practical question: what happened to the shrine, and to Xanthippe (in *whatever* state she might have been) inside it? One would expect there to be ruins or traces. But from what I gather, there is now neither sight nor sign of anything.'

'A very good point, my dear.'

Ptolemaeos helped himself to a pile of *praires farcies* and poured his niece and himself tall glasses of Montrachet.

'The frustrating thing,' he continued, 'is that there are no accurate records or explanations. There may have been once, but the library in which they would have been housed, in the premises of the Department of Monuments and Antiquities in Eu, was destroyed during the Invasion of Normandy. After the war the loss of the records was simply shrugged off (*enfin, qu' est-ce qu' on peut faire?*) and no one in the Department took much interest in the Castle of Arques for many years. Indeed, no one would be taking much interest now, or so my friend des Veules-les-Roses tells me, were it not for a romantic attachment which a young official called Jean-Marie Guiscard has conceived for the place. His imagination was fired by Henri Martel de Longueil's ballad and by the Chronicle of Hubert of Avallon, both works of fairly wide circulation in scholarly circles. Of the Appendix, of course, he knows nothing, and his recent and exhaustive search of the archives at Eu only confirmed what was already well known, that all specialised records of Arques, its construction, its alteration, its military and architectural development, were blown to atoms by a two-inch mortar bomb during street fighting in the city in the autumn of 1944. So, the fate of the shrine, and of its occupant, would be completely unknown to us, were it not for one rather remarkable circumstance . . . or chain of circumstances.

'For the first link we have to go right back to the Mani, to Ilyssos. In a church in Ilyssos there is an inscription, probably composed or commanded by Xanthippe's father, the Kyrios Phaedron. Ivan has read and checked it quite often. Carved on a plain tablet of marble, it begins with a lamentation for the death of the Despoina Xanthippe and continues with a prayer – a very odd prayer – for her soul: PRAY FOR HER SOUL THAT IT MAY RETURN IN PEACE TO THIS HER OWN LAND. . .'

'What's so odd about that?' said Jo-Jo. 'You yourself told me that the Ilyssans believe that the soul, being at last brought to life by the death of the body, often tours the places where the body has spent its life "to see what it has been missing". It knows instinctively where the body has been, you said, and goes off on a check-up round.'

'But the belief also holds, my darling, that the soul needn't do this . . . that it does not always do it, and it certainly needn't, and that the important thing is, from the point of view of itself and its well wishers, that as soon as possible after leaving the scene of demise it should brave the Wilderness and commence its journey to the Throne. Pottering about the former haunts of its now defunct body is quite irrelevant. Whoever composed that prayer, which was Phaedron almost for certain, should have wished Xanthippe's soul all speed into the presence of its Maker, not expressed a hope that it should come to Ilyssos. As it is, what the prayer asks is that the soul of Xanthippe should "return in peace" to Ilyssos, thus implying *not* just a casual visit, which might not matter much, but a definite and even prolonged sojourn. We conclude that Phaedron desiderated an event that he should have deprecated. Why?'

'He may have loved her very much . . . and perhaps he hoped to make some kind of contact, which would have been more likely if she hung around for some time, nice and calmly, than if she flitted straight off on the long trek to Heaven.'

'Right. He hoped to make contact. Perhaps he loved her, as you say; and perhaps he also wanted something from her. Information: just what did you do with that very beautiful and valuable *Écrevisse* which went with you to Normandy?'

'Ptoly . . . how too squalid.'

'Of me – or Phaedron?'

'Both of you.'

'Nothing squalid about a brilliant work of art worth six million quid. And to Phaedron the disappearance of that *Écrevisse* would surely have been a misery and a mystery. All the other items of Xanthippe's dowry (all those of any importance) had come back to Ilyssos with Henri and the girls. But no sign of the *Écrevisse* – not a single jewel off its back. Where on earth was the fucking thing? Now, neither Lalage nor any of the other girls was going to tell him, because they knew how important it was to Xanthippe that the creature should stay where it was, undisturbed. So they didn't want Phaedron to get it back, and they may well have been scared about what might happen to him if he tried. Anyone who knew anything about that shrine also knew that it was not to be interfered

143

with; and mum was the word about any aspect of that affair, for everyone's sake, including the Lord Phaedron's.'

'Could Henri have told him anything?'

'No. As you remember, Henri withdrew from Arques before the fun and games began, and returned only after Xanthippe . . . had been disposed of.

'*Dunque*. No one tells Phaedron where the *Écrevisse* has gone to. They simply do not know, the girls tell him. Oh yes, they all knew it was there in the chest as part of the dowry when they set out from Ilyssos with their mistress; and oh yes, they all saw it from time to time on the journey or at Arques: but no, they have no idea what became of it. Pressed to state a definite time after which they saw it no more, they improvise: it disappeared, they depose, round about the time that Hero died.

'Aha, thinks Phaedron, perhaps there is some connection or explanation there. What happened to Hero? he enquires. She . . . had a nasty accident (the usual formula, at that period, for accounting for anything awkward) . . . and her remains were not recoverable. (In fact the bare bones of Hero, all that Xanthippe had left of her, had been put in a weighted sack and thrown by the girls into the moat.) Could the *Écrevisse* be with these remains, asks Phaedron, desperate for a lead, wherever they might be? But the girls just shrug and pout and shake their heads and mutter and titter and give nothing. Phaedron starts to fume with impatience. For some time he has hoped (and prayed) that the soul of Xanthippe might come along and give him a clue, but it hasn't and he now reckons (quite rightly) that it won't, and he makes a snap decision. He will go to Arques and look for himself. Whatever has happened to the *Écrevisse*, it can't have gone far without *somebody*'s having noticed it, even if he can't get anything out of these dumb (or dishonest) hand-maidens. So he will go to Arques, on the respectable pretext of making a pilgrimage to his daughter's tomb, and investigate the matter in person.

'He further decides that Henri, who has found no gainful occupation in the Peloponnese, can accompany him as guide and courier. Henri's social standing in Normandy will be a useful asset. As it happens, Henri has now married Lalage (a cross-bow wedding, if you take me) and there must be some question of whether or not she should come too. But to everyone's relief she pleads her advancing pregnancy as an excuse for staying behind. In fact she is as strong as a horse and quite fit to travel, in a litter at least, but she is not going to get mixed up in the kind of *grand guignol* with knobs on which she reckons may be in store for anyone who goes into that shrine by the tilt yard. Henri, who is only too happy to off-load her and be free for fumbles and tumbles on the trip north, accepts her plea and leaves her with her parents in Ilyssos. Either he will return when Phaedron does or he will send for her after the child has been born. So here are loving kisses, one, two and three, and off prances Henri with Phaedron and a train of young Maniot knights and nobles, some time around Michaelmas of 1256.'

'How on earth do you know all this, Ptoly?'

'As it happens, I am just about to tell you. The story, as you will see, provides its own authentification.'

'All right. But tell me first: does Lalage give Henri any hint, before he goes, of what he may be getting into?'

'No. She leaves him to find out for himself. She wants Henri to go, and she don't propose to put him off by telling him scary stories.'

'Why does she want him to go?'

'Because Phaedron will pay good money, because she thinks Henri should check up on his (their) estates in Normandy, and because she has some zestful entertainments planned for the time of his absence.'

'While she's pregant?'

'The best time, provided no one gets faddy. There can never be, you see, any tangible evidence of misdemeanour.'

'Surely, in those days Henri would have left her padlocked?'

'Padlocking a Greek is like putting a paperweight on a shadow. Anyway, her parents would have objected (family honour), and don't forget that Henri was a liberal progressive.'

'So. Hey boys for Normandy. What happened next?'

'One of the things that happened was that Henri started writing a kind of diary in verse of the events of the journey.

Not a day-to-day record, but a series of poems, of varying lengths, which described and celebrated the salient occurrences. For centuries after Henri's death these poems were lost. But as my friend, the Marquis des Veules-les-Roses, also Sire de Longueil and Henri's descendant, was well aware, there had always been a legend in the family that there was, somewhere, a lost collection of manuscript poems by Henri Martel which had to do with his later adventures, after escorting the hand-maidens back to the Mani; and indeed they were eventually discovered, along with a copy of the 'Ballad of the Lady Xanthippe', in the library of a monastery near Areopolis. Ivan Barraclough found them while engaged on his historical research in the region.

'There was also an Epistle, written or dictated by Phaedron's son and heir, the Lord Meno, which explained what had happened. Henri's poems contained a great many blunt remarks about Phaedron's motives and conduct, and a pretty comprehensive exposé of the eccentricities which went on after they had all arrived at Arques. For although Henri had been allowed to set off north in total ignorance of what might be cooking for him, he began to wise up as time went on (since Phaedron's conversation was not always very discreet), and when they finally got to Arques he saw – well, what he saw – and set it down in his verse. According to the Kyrios Meno, his father discovered what Henri was up to and realised that the manuscripts of those poems were dynamite. But since there was as yet only one copy of them, preventive measures were clear and easy. Phaedron seized the poems, had his attendants murder Henri, in case he should re-write the poems or otherwise broadcast their substance, and then, his business in Arques being concluded, rode back to the Mani. Once there, he locked away Henri's injurious verses, along with his presentation copy of the Ballad of Xanthippe, which Henri had given him when he first turned up at Ilyssos. This latter item was quite harmless in itself, and in any case other copies of it had already been widely distributed; but I suppose Phaedron felt that all souvenirs of Henri might as well be kept together in one place . . . where they were duly secreted and in due course forgotten.

'Meanwhile, Henri's wife, Lalage had dropped a fine bold baby son, and the Villehardouin Prince of the Morea (or Lamorie) had claimed the pair of them as kin. After a time a male guardian or warden was appointed for the child, who, with his mother, was sent back to Henri's Manor in Normandy and continued, when grown, to propagate the line of the Martels, Sires of Longueil, later Viscounts of Barville and Counts of Offranville and Cany-Barville, finally Marquises des Veules-les-Roses – a line of which my friend at Barville is, I think, the last. However, before Lalage and the boy were moved on to France, Lal had of course enquired pretty fiercely of Phaedron what had become of Henri in the course of their expedition. She was told, inevitably, that Henri had "had a nasty accident" and with that she had to be content – probably didn't care all *that* much so long as her position and her son's were properly recognised. But one lead she did get: a strong hint from a handsome friend in Phaedron's guard that things hadn't been quite as simple as she'd been told and that if ever she could get hold of Henri's poems these would a tale unfold. . . No doubt she was curious, but then she and the boy were sent for by the Prince, there was a new world now for her to bustle in, and off she went without ever seeing her husband's *oeuvre* –'

'But she did know of the poems, and very roughly what they were about, so the rumour that they existed was started by her and passed down in the family for centuries?'

'Right. And then canny old Ivan happened on them about eighteen months back, when he was looking for something quite else, a manuscript history of some convent in Gythaion where the nuns had practised white magic. That manuscript he did not find, but Henri's poems he came across one April morning, written in Henri's own bold hand and old French, stacked in an unlocked casket which was sitting on a shelf in the linen cupboard of a tiny monastery on a cliff over the sea just south of Areopolis. There they were, fortunately in an excellent state of preservation, and with them was Meno's Epistle of provenance and explanation. He had come on the poems after his father's death, had enquired and discovered (from a surviving member of the expedition to Arques) how and why they had come to be where they were, had thought of destroying them, had enjoyed them far too much to do so, and had finally given them into the discreet care of the learned monks of the little monastery on the cliff. Learned they might have been in the Kyrios Meno's day, but seven centuries later, when Ivan made his find, they were illiterate and drunken boobies, who neither knew nor cared what the manuscript was, whence it came or whither it went – which was by the hand of a trusted guest of Ivan to the place in which it properly belonged, des Veules-les-Roses' Château at Cany.'

'And of course the poems narrated all that you've just been telling me –'

' – Narrated or suggested all that I've just been telling you –'

' – About why and how Phaedron set off for Arques, and all the rest of it . . . which Henri had gradually come to learn, and to record in his verses, as the journey went on.'

'Right. Now, when Ivan discovered the MS, the Arques project had been long decided upon and was already far advanced. But as you may imagine, those poems were a real bonus. They told us what happened when Phaedron arrived at September Castle and asked to be taken to his daughter's tomb . . . and what happened when he was.'

'Well, what did happen?'

'The narrative value of the poems is variable, as Henri is vague in places, and often prefers the poetic image to the concrete fact –'

'For Christ's sake, Ptoly. What happened when they got to that Castle?'

' – And of course,' said Ptolemaeos, serving himself to tench pie, 'Henri the poet was not much exercised about architectural structure and detail. Nevertheless, it is easily possible to infer from his poetry an explanation of why the shrine has now completely vanished.'

'Ptoly. If you don't tell me what happened, I'll never play with your balls again.'

'All right, heart of my heart of my heart. I shall now tell you.'

There was a knock on the door and Len came in.

'Sorry, folks,' said Len, 'but the front door was open, and Tom Llewyllyn said you were late night people. So I hoped you wouldn't mind if I popped in. Now, I don't know quite what you're up to, but I do know, if I can believe Tom, that it's in an area where I could be very helpful.'

'The devil you could,' said Ptolemaeos. 'You're a friend of Tom, you say?'

Len introduced himself. 'A friend of Tom,' he said, 'and of a lot of them at Lancaster. Balb Blakeney and Ive Winstanley and Jake Helmut.'

Jo-Jo goggled at Len. The witty bad taste of his apparel, his crooked intelligent features, the combination of ardour and treachery in his eyes, struck her pretty nigh catatonic.

'Ah,' said Ptolemaeos, 'I remember. *You* were in with Helmut in that matter of the rubies – the Roses of Picardie★.'

'And all the rest of it.'

'Tell me the details,' said Ptolemaeos. 'Tell me chapter and verse, and then I'll consider in what way, if any, you might be able to help us. My affair is very different from that of the Roses, you see, at least in terms of broad exploration. But it is possible that both quests require similar talents of intellectual sleight-of-hand. So convince me, my dear Len, pray convince me that you are qualified to assist us.'

'Oh yes,' sighed Jo-Jo, 'pray convince him.'

Then Len began.

JEAN-MARIE GUISCARD paced the ground north of the keep and considered the plan which he carried. Of all the documents which related to the history and architecture of the Castle at Arques, this was the only one still in the possession of the Department, the only one to be turned up by Jean-Marie's recent check-up of the archives. Everything else had gone up in smoke in 1944. And really, thought Jean-Marie, it might

★*The Roses of Picardie*, by Simon Raven. (Blond & Briggs, 1980) *Vide passim.*

have been as well if this had gone up too. 'This' was a map of the Castle and its immediate *environs*, drawn by a Royal Surveyor in 1773, on a scale of 1 to 1,000, too large to carry with convenience, too small to convey any but the general information which two eyes and a little common sense could gather unaided: for any fool knew that *that* must be the gate house or barbican, that *this* must be the keep, that the Romanesque ruins with an eastern altar, situated on top of the mound, were the remains of a Chapel, and that the flat rectangular area between his present line of march and the northern rampart would have been designated for the joust.

Why then had he brought the map with him this morning? He now had only twelve days to prepare for the forthcoming restorations and excavations, and here he was, having frittered away almost the entire afternoon with a commonplace eighteenth-century plan, drafted by a surveyor who had, by the look of it, only the barest modicum of the talent, taste and technique required by the exercise.

Well, he repeated to himself for the twentieth time, I brought it with me in the hope that it would tell me something about the Lady Xanthippe's shrine. As I well know, there is not the slightest sign of this anywhere on the ground, but I did work out yesterday approximately where it might have been: to the north of the keep or donjon, near the bottom of the western slope of the Chapel mound, overlooking the jousting meadow or tilting yard. Now, it so happens that this map, drawn just over 200 years ago, has the symbol △ marked in crimson on that very area, and that in the margin, against a second and precisely similar crimson △, are the following words:

> *Così l'aer vicin quivi se mette*
> *in quella forma che in lui suggella*
> *virtualmente l'alma che ristette. . .*

Dante, as M. le Directeur had informed him; somewhere in the *Purgatorio* (the Director thought) and meaning:

> So the air nearby puts itself
> into that form which the soul,

> that is there fixed, impresses
> upon it by its virtue. . .

After a painful search through the *Purgatorio* in his lodgings
the previous evening, Jean-Marie had found that the passage
was lines 94 to 96 of Canto XXV, and came in the middle of a
tedious discourse, by the soul of the Roman poet, Statius, on
the Aristotelian doctrine of generation and embryology, sup-
plemented by an exposition of the Christian notion that Soul is
breathed into the animal form by God. Since none of this
seemed to have even the most tenuous connection with or
application to the story of the Despoina Xanthippe (or any
other aspect of the Castle), Jean-Marie had concluded that the
lines must be taken clean out of Dante's context and considered solely for what they stated in and by themselves, which
was that 'the air in the neighbourhood takes a shape impressed
on it by virtue of the soul . . . *che ristette* . . . which is confined
there'. So: apply this statement to the map, or rather to the area
of it marked by the crimson △, and one deduced that there was
some kind of soul fixed, confined or imprisoned in that spot,
and that this soul had somehow shaped, formed or affected the
air or atmosphere of the neighbourhood.

If, as Jean-Marie had calculated, the area was that in which
the Despoina's shrine had once stood, it was tempting to
suppose that the statement referred to the soul of Xanthippe.
Tempting but appalling. Why and how, thought Jean-Marie,
should her soul be confined there? What did she feel about its
detention? And what effect did it have on the air about it?
Visible, audible or sniffable? Agreeable or disagreeable? Since
the effect was apparently produced 'by *virtue*' of the soul, one
assumed the former. Yet one never knew: 'by virtue of' was an
ambiguous phrase, and virtue itself could take the most
hideous shapes, e.g. the Furies.

But however all that might be, as far as he could make out
after a whole morning of promenade there was no effect
whatever. Perhaps it only manifested itself at night or at
certain seasons? Well, one thing was certain: he hadn't the time
to hang about until it did. In any case, on what authority was
the cartographer making the statement? Local knowledge (or

superstition), or his own experience? And was he talking about the soul of Xanthippe (knowing, from calculations similar to those of Jean-Marie himself, perhaps, that her tomb could have been in that area), or was he talking about a soul, any soul, the effect of which upon 'the neighbouring air' had been reported to him or observed by him?

The answers to some of these questions might have been available if only anything had been known of the cartographer himself, who he was or whence. But the map was unsigned. It was the work, so one learned from a brief note at the bottom, of a

SURVEYOR APPOINTED
to this task by
THE CAPTAIN SUPERINTENDENT
of His Most Catholic Majesty's
COMPANY OF GEOGRAPHERS.

Four copies had been made, the note said: one for the military archives in Paris; one for those of HMCM's Company of Geographers; one for the Mayor or Chief Burgher of the Township of Arques-la-Bataille; and one for the (largely titular) Constable of the Castle, which by that time was already superannuated but could conceivably be restored and reanimated as a strategical reality in certain most remote and improbable circumstances.

And that, thought Jean-Marie, is that. I have spent a whole morning in the expectation of some phenomenon or vision or apparition which might guide or help me in the search for the Despoina's grave; and nothing has been vouchsafed to me. And yet . . . and yet only yesterday, as I have left the Castle walls, a voice seemed to speak to my heart. It asked me to go away and leave the place in peace. The voice of my conscience? Or of my love? Or that of this soul 'which shapes the air'? But then this soul is confined (according to the map) to the area by the mound and the donjon, whereas I was a good 300 metres off. But then again, perhaps it can throw its voice, so to speak, at least for a short way. Well, I cannot go away and leave you in peace, whoever you are, because my Department is now committed. However, I have, or so I think, persuaded my Director that the Castle shall not be closed to those that love it while the work proceeds; and I have obtained his agreement to a schedule under which whatever lurks in the area marked by the crimson △ will not be seriously intruded upon for many weeks, and will therefore have plenty of leisure in which to decide whether to assist us in our operations or to protest against them – even if it has not thought fit to show itself or its airy shape this morning.

AFTER LUNCHEON (taglierini with white truffles, broiled sturgeon and assorted savoury soufflés) Ptolemaeos, Jo-Jo and Len went for a walk over the fens. Len had stayed the night, which, by the time he had convinced Ptolemaeos that he was indeed qualified to assist him, had been very far spent. They had all risen late, and then Ptolemaeos had used what was left of the morning to start filling Len in with everything he needed to know of the legendary, historical and archaeological antecedents of the search that was shortly to conclude within the Castle of Arques-la-Bataille. By the beginning of luncheon, to which Jo-Jo called them at Ptolemaeos' usual hour of two-thirty, Len had mastered the necessary corpus of knowledge up to and inclusive of the death of the Despoina; by the end of luncheon (a quarter to five) Ptolemaeos, with occasional assistance from Jo-Jo, had brought him to Henri Martel's marriage to Lalage in Ilyssos; and now, as the three of them walked along a dyke, having a slow grey canal below them on one side and greasy flat fields on the other, they had come in their minds to the point at which Len had interrupted Ptolemaeos and Jo-Jo the previous evening: they were poised, with Henri and Lord Phaedron, to wind their horns under the ramparts of September Castle, to request entry of the Castellan, and to complete their pilgrimage at the shrine of the Lady Xanthippe.

'Henri, by this time, was disturbed and suspicious,' Ptolemaeos was telling them; 'more than suspicious – he was angrily apprehensive, as he now knew exactly what Phaedron wanted and pretty well how he proposed to get it. If we follow the sequence of Henri's songs on the road from the Mani, we find a gradual but definite downward curve in his moods and in his affection for Phaedron. He started by being happy and carefree:

> As I ride out in the autumn morn
> I greet the winding road with glee;
> For we now depart from this land forlorn
> (Where the Portal of Hell gapes over the sea)★
> Heading north for the ranges of Lamorie. . .

'And at Corfu he is still lyrical, telling us of

> . . . the pomegranates of Kerkyrā,★★
> Which the West Wind quickens to rich and ripe,
> While under the branches the maidens play
> And foot to the tune of Silenus his pipe
> The dance of the Princess Nausikā.

'Oooh,' said Jo-Jo, and shivered slightly.
'Cold, baby?' said Len, giving her a quick sideways hug.
'Warm, much too warm,' said Jo-Jo, and looked anxiously at Ptolemaeos. But Ptolemaeos smiled like a serenely bloated seraph and went on with what he was saying.
'By the time they had reached Avignon, however, Henri was beginning to get the message about their mission. In

---

★This line could refer either to the ravine near Ilyssos, or to the fabled entrance to Hades at Cape Taenaros, not far to the south of Ilyssos.
This note is reprinted by courtesy of P. Tunne from *The Ballads and Ballades of Henri Martel de Longueil*, edited by P. Tunne and published by the Fitzwilliam Press, Cambridge, in 1979.

★★It is a convention of translating poems from late Latin, Provençal, or, as in this case, early French, that a final long 'ā' may be pronounced to rhyme with 'ray' instead of with 'car'.
Note reprinted by courtesy of P. Tunne from his edition of Henri Martel's poems.

general terms at least he realised that Phaedron was up to no good at all. In a poem called "The Ballade of October" he laments the waning year and compares it with waning love, still beautiful at times, but melancholy, and shortly to turn chill and treacherous. Such, he says, is the state of his own friendship with the Kyrios Phaedron. He had come to love the old Ruffian in Ilyssos and had hoped for magic things from their journey together; but now something grey and steely has entered Phaedron's heart, something which has all but placed him beyond the reach of Henri . . . who no longer wishes, no longer dares to show Phaedron the poems he is writing, even though most of these are still nominally addressed to him as the poet's benefactor and patron. . .

> Prince, to whom I have pledged my truth
> To bring thee safe to my own fair land,
> I pray thee, come in love and truth,
> Ne with eyes that pierce ne with raking hand.

'That was the kind of thing which Henri was writing in Avignon. He was still not entirely without hope, you see, though already too fearful to show his envois and his prayers to his "Prince". By the time they had struck west for Chartres and Rouen, Henri has become totally disillusioned. In a passage of rare precision he explains what Phaedron is after – a gigantic and magnificently wrought metal *Écrevisse*. This he knows because Phaedron, drunk, has told him about it and described it. Here is Phaedron talking:

> A creature fashioned of silver and gold,
> Of ruby and emerald and deep sapphire,
> Carnelian, diamond, enamels bold
> With crimson and purple, forged in a fire
> That had scorched off the very Devil's cock
> And made Troytown's blaze a laughing stock.

'Racy chat,' said Len.
'Yes. It is most touching,' said Ptolemaeos, 'to reflect how Henri shows a kind of vestigial love and appreciation of

Phaedron by giving him colourful and challenging and au-
daciously phrased speeches. But the burden of the poem is not
at all in Ptolemaeos' favour. Phaedron, Henri says, means to
have that *Écrevisse*, wherever it may be. He will be very
grateful for any help Henri may give him, and will richly
reward it. On the other hand, let Henri impede him, for
whatever reason, or betray his purpose to any that might
disapprove of it – well, says Phaedron,

> Ye see my knights riding two by two,
> Thirty lusty paladins –
> Who will cut out the heart and tripes of you.

'Ugly chat,' said Len.

The low fields receded into a gathering mist, a 'mauve-
frosty Bank' thought Jo-Jo, no, no, what *is* that phrase from
Tennyson, 'a purple-frosty bank', that's it, 'of Vapour,
leaving night forlorn'; but that was on Hallam's birthday, in
the middle of the winter, and now it's only September. But
then it is so cold on these gloomy old fens, I wish Ptoly would
live somewhere else, abroad perhaps, fair Verona or sandy
Pylos or sweet Argos or even windy Troy. No, no, I must
think no thoughts disloyal to Ptoly, I must be like Tennyson to
Hallam, I must *not* go all wet just there every time this Len so
much as looks at me, because what would Ptoly feel, what
would Baby feel, if I let them down?

Perhaps they wouldn't mind, thought Jo-Jo: they love me,
they want me to be happy, they wouldn't want to spoil my
fun, and they know I'd share with them if they asked me.

No. I must at least try, at least for a time, to go on loving
Ptoly and Baby and no one else. I must not behave like this
Kyrios Phaedron behaved, getting greedy and eager for other
things and forfeiting the friendship of dear sweet Henri Martel.

'So that was how things stood,' she said aloud, 'when they
came to Arques? Phaedron had spoiled everything, but Henri
was still there for very fear of being served with a premature
quietus? In a state of deep depression?'

'Yes. That's more or less it,' said Ptolemaeos. 'When they

reached the borders of Normandy, near L'Aigle, Henri did manage a brief bout of euphoria because he was home again, but it lasted only long enough to produce one quirky little song about "country matters":

> I took my Heloise
> Beneath the cider trees
> And gave her a good bang
> While the nightingale sang;
>
> It sang a dismal song
> Of what might go wrong:
> It did not sing for me –
> Dieu merci.

'After which his misery and forboding returned and deepened as they covered the leagues to Arques:

> And so we came to the Barbican
> On a bitter night of wind and rain;
> And the Kyrios called to the Castellan
> That we came as friends to his terrain.

'Unlucky in their weather,' said Len. He dabbed his right forefinger at the nape of Jo-Jo's neck and gently tweaked her between the tendons, inviting her assent in more ways than one.

'No,' said Jo-Jo, willing herself to contradict: 'if they left the Peloponnese at Michaelmas, of course they should have expected rough weather by the time they reached Arques. They were lucky not to have snow. I must say, the whole thing seems to have been very badly planned.'

'Remember that Phaedron had become very impatient,' said Ptolemaeos. 'Once he'd decided to go, he wasn't going to hang about till next spring. Corsairs are not easily deterred by weather forecasts.'

'Anyway, there they all were, turning up on a dark, wet, windy night, and a villainous crew they must have looked. Thirty-two mouths to feed,' said Jo-Jo, 'to say nothing of esquires and pages. If I'd been that Castellan, I'd have slammed down the portcullis.'

'They'd probably sent word on ahead to warn him. "The Kyrios called to the Castellan" is just poetic licence,' said Ptolemaeos. 'Anyhow, the Castellan knew Henri well enough.'

'Surely, this was Henri's big chance. He should somehow have got a message to the Castellan – "This lot's up to no good. Don't let 'em in. Love from Henri."'

'What?' said Len. 'With thirty lances and the old man's cutlass ready to dig his guts out if he put a toe wrong? Strictly a time for a man to zip his lip, girlie, and keep pen well away from paper.'

Jo-Jo cringed with pleasure at the note of reproof in Len's tone. They crossed the canal by a wooden bridge and turned for home along a footpath which led past high reeds on one side and a long black pond on the other.

'And now for the *scènes à faire*,' Jo-Jo said. 'What happened, Ptoly, whatever happened, O sweetest of Ptolies, when Phaedron and his thirty butchers got into the Castle?'

'The morning after they arrived,' said Ptolemaeos, 'Phaedron waited on the Castellan, presented his best compliments to him as representative of the Villehardouin Lord of the Castle, and intimated, very politely, that he would like to be admitted to the shrine and tomb of his daughter, the Lady Xanthippe of Ilyssos. Now as far as that went, it was a perfectly reasonable request, not to be faulted even by Henri – who, let us remember, did *not* know of the weird circumstances in which the shrine, according to Hubert, had been built and occupied, since all of that had deliberately been kept from him. As Henri saw the matter, Phaedron was entitled and indeed obliged to visit Xanthippe's shrine – provided he didn't start pulling the thing apart in his search for the *Écrevisse*. But obviously, Henri would have thought – did indeed think, according to his own verses – obviously it's early days for *that* kind of carry-on, and to judge from Phaedron's present behaviour he means to play it all calm and gentle, just like the book of manners says – at least for as long as he can. He will visit the shrine to make himself look thoroughly respectable in person and in purpose, spend several hours praying there, and then, the next day or the day after, he will start diffidently enquiring whether anyone has seen a spare gold *Écrevisse* lying about. Only if he doesn't find it will he turn nasty and tear the place to pieces.

'So perhaps things aren't too bad after all, Henri thought: it is *his Écrevisse*, when all is said, and if only it can be found and handed over without fuss, then he'll go away happy, and I shall be given my rake-off, and no one will be any the worse for it. In which case, should he send for Lalage or return to Ilyssos with Phaedron? Well, there was no need to worry about *that* just yet.

'So Henri now has a different perspective on the matter and is far happier than he has been for many a day. The Castellan, on the other hand, is in it up to the eyeballs. He does not know what is in the shrine; but he does know that he has been warned, on pain of death and worse, to keep absolutely out of it; and he also knows that a gang which tried to break into it some fifteen months ago came to a very sanguinary end – each and every one of them. On the other hand, *this* is not a drunken foot-soldier after loot, it is the Lord Phaedron of Ilyssos, ally of the Villehardouin Lords of Achaea, accompanied and vouched for by Henri, Sire de Longeuil, requesting to visit what purports to be his dead daughter's shrine, where he will kneel and pray for her soul.

'So if you were that unlucky Castellan, what would you do, chums?'

'Send to Hubert at Avallon?' suggested Jo-Jo. 'It was Hubert who put the embargo on the shrine. Let him come and do the explaining.'

'But, nittikins, it would take weeks to send to Avallon – and for anything they know Hubert has long since returned to Romany, thankfully leaving his stumpy, boring, patient dame behind him.'

'I think,' said Len, 'that I'd have given this Kyrios number the key, then told him it was shopping day and vanished into Dieppe.'

'There wasn't a key. The shrine had been sealed and then re-sealed, remember. There was indeed a west door that faced the tilting meadow, but it was now secured by three colossal bolts on the outside, all of which had been welded into place by a master ironsmith – something else which the Castellan was going to have to explain, without, poor sod, having any idea of the reason, beyond Hubert's exhortation to stay out at any price.'

'Yes,' conceded Len, 'that Castellan was certainly on a crappy wicket.'

'Right. And not the type to jump down it and hit the ball on the volley, which would have given him much the best chance. Look, he could have said, I'm afraid there is something wrong with that shrine, I saw what happened to the last lot that tried to get in, and I don't want God knows what let loose in my nice Castle now; so if you'll take my respectful advice, my Lord Phaedron, daughter or no daughter, you'll go sensibly back home. And by the way, if you don't like that advice, I've got a garrison here of twenty knights and forty mounted serjeants, and I can raise help from a score of castles within a dozen miles. That's what he could and should have said, knowing what he did; but no. He was the ex-ranker, naturally deferential to the likes of the Lord of Ilyssos and the Sire of Longueil, he was the man "who knew his place and had his job to do", who got his orders and obeyed them to the letter. When the orders were contradictory or inconsistent, he obeyed the set given by the higher-ranking superior. Messer Hubert of Avallon had said one thing, but now here was a noble relative of the Villehardouins and a Sovereign Greek Baron saying another – and having come a very long way to say it.

'So. He puts on his hat and he leads Henri and Phaedron to the tilting yard, where he halts some ten yards from the shrine and then points to it – with that shifty, self-satisfied, spiteful mien that subordinates assume when they're doing something on your orders and your responsibility but which they know to be against your interest. "There's your rotten old shrine," the Castellan's sullen face seemed to say: "and now just what are you going to do with it?"

'Henri and Phaedron, seeing the massive holts and not knowing when and why they had been fitted, both came to the same conclusion – that inside the shrine there was not only a tomb and a body but something which somebody wanted to keep safe. Who? And what? Obvious answer to first question: the Castellan, either on his own behalf, or on that of his masters, the Villehardouins, or in conspiracy with Hubert. Obvious answer to second question: something very valuable, quite possibly the *Écrevisse*. Third question – now put to the Castellan for the form of the thing: why? why has my daughter's shrine been sealed up in this monstrous fashion? The Castellan shrugs: he doesn't know and he doesn't want to know. Very well: send for the master ironsmith to open it up. But at this stage Henri sees something in the Castellan's face which Phaedron, heavily engaged in ordering people about, does not see: fear. And he remembers something; he remembers one of the reasons why he did not care much for Xanthippe: "another was watching me from behind her eyes." So could there be . . . something not quite *comme il faut* . . . about her tomb? Best to be on the safe side: should we not, he says to Phaedron, send for a priest as well as the master ironsmith? Phaedron pauses for a moment, and then, since this is obvious good sense when one is tampering, however licitly, with the fittings of a sacred edifice, nods in agreement.

> Let him bring the blessèd Cross this day
> And sweet incense and Holy Book,
> And let him chant a prayerful lay
> To her that lies here so long forsook.

'Phaedron speaking, or Henri?' Jo-Jo asked.

'Henri's poem, Phaedron's lines. In any case, a very proper sentiment. For it was evident from the state of the bolts that no one had entered the shrine since a long while. The incumbent had indeed been forsaken. For whithersoever the soul may depart, both in Henri's view and in Phaedron's you paid respects to a dead person at his or her shrine or tomb. This had not been done here, by anyone at all, for a disgracefully long time. . . So fetch the Castle priest, now that we *are* here, and make it all look as pukka as possible.

'And now, a Joker in the pack. As you may remember,

Xanthippe had had no priest of her own in attendance, for no Orthodox priest had been available to accompany her from the Mani. Neither Xanthippe nor her girls seemed to miss such a ministrant very much, but they were in any case adamant that in no circumstance would they sit under the prayers, preachments or personal admonitions of a priest of the Church of Rome. When a real crisis arose, after the apparent death of Xanthippe, Hubert, as an honourable lay man, had been called in to assist, rather than the Catholic priest of the Castle chapel, who had been roundly warned from the start to hold himself utterly apart from the Greek girls, their quarters, their everyday affairs and their religious practices. This the priest, a drunkard and an idler and a toyer with kitchen wenches, had been only too glad to do, rather than have a lot of extra work with people who didn't even speak his lingo; and so he knew nothing at all of Xanthippe's interment, except for the bare fact that she was reported to have been buried in the shrine near the foot of the mound. As to the shrine itself, it was Greek Orthodox territory, as far as he was concerned; he had had nothing to do with its conception, erection or inauguration; it was part of a scene from which he, as a priest of Rome, had been specifically excluded.'

'And so he refused to come?'

'On the contrary. Bad priest though he might be, normally unconcerned with his office, he did resent the intrusion of a rival ecclesiastical edifice slap in his own domain and hardly a stone's throw from his own chapel. The feeling was personal (a matter of face) rather than religious, but it was none the less fierce for that, and he was determined to take his chance now that he had got it. Certainly he would bring the blessèd Cross and sweet incense – he would also bring Bell, Book, Water and Candle, and thoroughly exorcise the place of whatever foul foreign profanities were lurking in it. Since he was not sober when summoned (if not yet drunk), any theological qualms were easily set aside, leaving him full of zeal, hate and bombast.

'And so the scene is set. Phaedron and his knights gathered outside the shrine; Henri looking on, perplexed and curious, hoping for the best; the half tipsy priest gabbling preliminary incantations; the Castellan fidgeting about at a very safe distance; and the master ironsmith going to work on the bolts.'

'Now just hang on a tick,' said Jo-Jo. 'You told me that after that first attempt was made on the shrine none had ever been made since. Ours would be the second, you said. But here you are now, describing another one in full swing.'

'I think I said – I certainly meant – that no *illicit* attempt had been made since. The original gang who unsealed the shrine were common thieves. So shall we be. But on the occasion of which I am telling you now, a father was opening up his daughter's shrine to pray, as he thought, at her tomb, and to recover, as he hoped, a piece of his own property.'

'Try telling that to the Guardian. You did say that any conscious effort to find the treasure, the *Écrevisse*, would set up vibrations which roused him?'

'So Hubert believed, apparently.'

'Well, what was the Guardian doing while all these people were monkeying about outside?'

'I simply don't know, sweetheart. I am not sure whether the *Écrevisse* constituted its own Guardian, being animated, perhaps, by Masullaoh or some other spirit, or whether the Guardian was entirely separate. Do please remember, we agreed that all that apparatus of spirits and so forth, though to be regarded with tactful wariness, could probably be discarded. But in any case, I do not know what the Guardian, if any, was up to at this stage, because Henri, who knew nothing of him, does not tell us, and to judge from his narrative there was no visible or audible manifestation from the shrine.

> The 'Smith he toiled at the massy bars
> And my lord, he watched with eager e'en,
> And the Priest, he called on the Thrones and Powers;
> And else was aught neither heard nor seen.

'If that priest knew his job,' said Len, 'no evil spirit would have been able to act anyhow.'

'Ah. Remember that Masullaoh and his attendant spirits, if they existed, were neutral, not diabolic.'

'Sure, Ptoly man: but a neutral spirit, who enjoyed right of access both to God and Satan, would presumably think it proper to behave himself nicely if so requested by the agent of *either* party.'

'Good point, good point. Anyway, nothing whatever happened until the last of the three bolts had been loosed. Then Phaedron, as was his right, strode to the door and opened it.'

Ptolemaeos ceased talking while he negotiated an awkward stile. The black pool was gone now and in its place was a wilderness of huge weeds, angrily thrusting and clutching, slily exuding a low grey mist.

'Within a second of opening it,' said Ptolemaeos, after Len and Jo-Jo had lowered him to the ground, 'he let out a long, deep grunt.'

'Like he was cross,' said Len, 'or like he was just going to come?'

> As if from his belly a rumble arose,
> Making his girth to ripple and quake,
> And then from his throat and ears and nose
> A doughty hog's bladder of wind did break.

'So at all events it was clear that he had seen or felt something worthy of remark, and since he had evidently sustained no damage, Henri was bold enough to come up behind him and peer round him. And then Henri saw it too: a giant, jewelled *Écrevisse*,

> Its limbs enamelled in crimson hose,
> Its head encrusted with carbuncles
> Of purple and saffron and cerule and rose,

all the monstrous two cubits by nine inches by six inches of it, crouched under the altar at the top of the steps that led down to the passage and the crypt.'

'Crouched?' said Jo-Jo.

'Well, sitting. Or whatever *Écrevisses* do when they're on dry land. So Henri looked at Phaedron and Phaedron looked at Henri, but before either could do anything more the boozy priest, frantic to get on with his exorcism of Orthodox harlotries or whichwhat, came busting through and issued a tremendous anathema:

In the Name of the Father, the Ghost and the Son;
By the Essence of Three and the Essence of One;
By the Blood of the Christ and the Tears of His Mother;
By the raw Wounds of God and the Ark of Jehovah;
By the Flesh and the Bones and the Bowells of Our Saviour:
By the Book and the Bread and the Wine and the Bell –
Nunc Retro Satanas: BEGONE BACK TO HELL.

'Well now,' said Jo-Jo: 'if it was Masullaoh or one of his subordinate spirits acting as Guardian in there, either animating the creature or hovering around it, he would have been pretty offended by this. It would have been one thing for the priest to request his good behaviour, as Lovely Len puts it: a neutral spirit would obviously accept that, from God's agent or the Devil's. But to be seen off, to be absolutely ordered back to hell as if he were some squalid number like Belial or Beelzebub who had no business anywhere else – *that* would have got right up his nose.'

'Nevertheless,' said Len, 'he might have been bound to obey the formula (which, incidentally, would have been a great deal more precise and technical than Henri's flamboyant rendering). The Rules might well have required any spirit who was not positively pro-God and anti-Satan to take itself off when accurately addressed in the proper style for dismissing devils.'

'Let me remind you both,' said Ptolemaeos, 'that we think we have explained away all that sort of paraphernalia . . . though of course we shall continue to insure against the *possibility* that it exists and operates. Either way, what we *know* is that the *Écrevisse*, whether having spirit or no spirit within or around it, whether offended or warned off or whatever, now vanished. Or rather, it moved off down the steps that led beneath the altar to the passage, pursued by the Priest, Phaedron and Henri, in that order. But before they'd any of them essayed the steps, which were in pitch darkness, Phaedron had whistled up a couple of his boys and had the turbulent cleric removed. He then went down two or three steps, came back, ordered a lantern, and drummed his heels until somebody arrived with one. Having told off Henri to hold the thing and light the way, Phaedron proceeded down the steps, turned right – the only way he could turn – along the little passage, and so came to the crypt. Nothing in the passage; nothing, except for the couch, the table and the chair, in the crypt.'

'And a second altar, you said?'

'And a second altar. But no *Écrevisse*. And, now Phaedron came to think of it, no Xanthippe – unless she was entombed in one of the altars. But there was no inscription or any other indication that this was the case. Perhaps she was under the floor of the shrine? Or the floor of the crypt – which, by the way, was just earth? But again, there was no indication of any kind. And of course, nobody could tell him anything. Neither the Castellan nor Henri had ever been inside the place before or knew anything about the arrangements for the Lady Xanthippe's burial. Clearly, a thorough search would have to be made – and could quite properly be made, with no raised eyebrows, on the ground that Phaedron was looking for his daughter's body, even if in truth he was more interested in the *Écrevisse*.'

'And so,' said Jo-Jo, 'he started pulling things apart?'

'But both reverence for his daughter's remains and care for the *Écrevisse* (for damage was desirable to neither) necessitated a very slow and painstaking process. There was none of the smashing and ripping which Henri had been dreading. Phaedron, though a quick-tempered man, was much too canny for that. First the cloister, then the shrine, then the passage, then the crypt were totally dismantled, stone by stone, piece by piece. But there was no Xanthippe and no *Écrevisse*: neither inside the altars, nor under the floors, nor concealed in the walls. Nothing . . . except towards the end of the search, one possible lead. A piece of loose stone, under the couch in the crypt, was shifted, and underneath it was what looked like a rabbit's burrow.

'For eight days the workmen, closely supervised by Phaedron, dug into the ground beneath the crypt, following the direction of the burrow. As before, they had to work with

great thoroughness and caution, leaving not a pebble un-
turned, scraping their way inch by inch, constantly mindful
that a careless blow with a pick or a shovel might violate the
poor body which they sought.'

'*Or* the rich *Écrevisse* which they sought.'

'Only Phaedron and Henri knew about the *Écrevisse*, for
only they had seen it.'

'What about that priest?' said Len.

'The priest, who became and remained even drunker than
usual for several days, reported that he had seen the head of a
dragon or of a snake, in either case that of the Great Beast of the
Greek Communion, at the foot of the altar. Since people were
used to his drunken hyperboles, they discounted this vision
accordingly.'

'Phaedron's lads who whisked the priest away,' said Jo-Jo;
'had they seen nothing?'

'No. The *Écrevisse* had vanished down the steps before they
were even summoned. In effect, then, only Henri and Phaedron knew that this was a treasure-hunt. Everyone else thought
that the search was for the vanished corpse of Xanthippe. The
theory was, in so far as there was one, that some animal had
dismembered it and dragged it piece-meal down the burrow
and into its lair.'

'What about the coffin? We know there wasn't one; they
didn't.'

'The body *could* have been merely draped, as far as they were
concerned, and left in the crypt – on the couch.'

'Like Juliet in the family tomb?'

'Precisely. Something like that they must have assumed,
and if the theory of the animal were true they had a good
chance of recovering Xanthippe's bones, which could then be
honourably reburied. So down they went, inch by inch, clod
by clod, following the burrow. The motive was respectable
and Phaedron enjoyed the sympathy of all and especially that
of the sycophantic Castellan . . . who, however, on the
evening of the eighth day, told Phaedron that now there must
be an end of it; the dig must be called off forthwith.

'At first Phaedron looked cold and dangerous and simply
asked in one word, "why?" Because, said the Castellan, the

167

direction of the burrow and therefore that of the dig was no longer vertically downward but for some days now had been slanting further and further towards the south, i.e. under the foundations of the donjon and towards the shaft of the well that watered it. Now, anxious as the Castellan was to oblige his lordship, he could not endanger, or even run the slightest risk of endangering, the water supply of the Castle.

'There were, observed Phaedron, other wells in the Castle. Indeed, my lord, and so there were, but this was the only one in the keep, and the whole point about a keep, as a warrior of his lordship's experience and sagacity would certainly know, was that it was a last resort and must therefore be absolutely self-sufficient. The Castellan was sorry to disoblige, but his standing orders were clear beyond any possible qualification, *nothing* must ever be allowed to derange the water supply in the donjon for two seconds together, it was more than his job was worth. And so, with the utmost respect for his lordship and the deepest sympathy for his lordship's cruel bereavement, the Castellan proposed to withdraw, as from dusk of that day, the sappers and labourers whom he had so far placed at Phaedron's disposal.

'Oh, did he? Then Phaedron would be compelled to report this exhibition of insolence to the Castellan's master, the true Lord of the Castle – and meanwhile to continue digging with members of his own retinue, his own knights if need be. It was, Phaedron insisted, his sacred duty to his daughter. If the Castellan would only understand that and renew his cooperation, then Phaedron would happily forget their little disagreement and indeed give the Castellan very liberal proofs of his gratitude.'

The mist rose from the marsh below. It was almost dark now, but they were only half a mile, thought Jo-Jo, from home. She must cook a really special dinner for beautiful Len, who had expressed generous and knowledgeable appreciation of the lunch. They walked over a ditch on a bridge of two planks. Jo-Jo looked down and saw a glutinous yellow scum. God, these fens, she thought: I must get Ptoly and myself out of them. Yet Ptoly seemed to thrive on the Fenland air, and she herself had yet to take harm from it. So much the more reason for leaving, she thought: let her depart while youth was still on her side, let her go while the going was good. But Ptoly must come too. She would not leave without her Uncle Ptoly.

'"Sacred duty to his daughter,"' she now said aloud. '"Liberal proofs of his gratitude." That Phaedron had a strong hand.'

'He did. But the toady had turned. The Castellan was an old soldier and had not reached his present rank and post for nothing. If Phaedron had a duty to his daughter, the Castellan had a prior duty to the Villehardouins and their Castle: he must obey one of the fundamental laws of soldiering, the one which states that until the Last Trump sounds you guard your water with your life. And that's what he now told Phaedron . . . who lost his patience and flew into a ghastly tantrum.

> If a Giant had spawned a brawnsome brat
> And his mother's bubs refused him suck,
> And the booby frotted and squealed and spat
> And squirmed and wailed and drooled his zluck –

for that was what Phaedron put Henri in mind of, wrote Henri later that evening. The Castellan, by contrast, had kept his cool and his dignity, and had quitted Phaedron's presence with veiled intimation of his intent:

> Let the Gryffon lordynge tell 'aye' or 'nay',
> The morrow would be another day.

'And on the morrow, when Phaedron and his squad came to the site of the shrine, they found it surrounded by the Castellan's mesnie knights and two hundred men at arms from Arques itself and friendly neighbouring castles. The Castellan was polite and regretful but very, very firm. The excavation had got to stop, he said; and though he would gladly entertain Phaedron and his knights (as his master would doubtless wish) for as long as they desired to linger in this agreeable countryside, he could not but think that Phaedron would by now be having business at home.

'That was what Phaedron thought too. He was playing a

losing game: he had better cut his losses, however bitter (one jewelled *Écrevisse* and one dearly beloved daughter) and push off back to Ilyssos before anyone down *there* started getting big ideas. He would leave, he said, the next morning. For some reason, wrote Henri that afternoon, he seemed quite hurtfully indifferent to Henri's plans or wishes. Henri himself is uncertain what to do:

> Shall I remain in my ain countrie,
> Where the maidens' fesses are wet and warm?
> Or shall I ride South to Romanie,
> Where the wife of my bossom is seven months gone?

'Phaedron, Henri tells us, had made it clear that he neither knew nor cared:

> 'Tis one to me whatever ye wist:
> Tarry or sally, ye'll ne'er be missed.

And of course we know why. These were the last lines that Henri would ever write. As Meno's Epistle makes clear, his father, who had probably bribed Henri's servant or one of his "wet and warm" wenches to keep an eye open, had now been informed of Henri's mocking and injurious verses. Anyway, Henri knew altogether too much and was a loose sort of fellow who might tell it abroad. So, "Come, gather round me, you, my Myrmidons, /E'en at the setting of the sun", and see to it that a suitable "nasty accident" is arranged for Henri Martel, Sire de Longueil, instanter. Then secure *all* his beastly verses, and make sure they are put right and tight in my luggage – which must be good and ready and packed for the off tomorrow at half past eight.'

The lights of Ptolemaeos' house were in sight. They went through a postern in his wall and started up a lawn. Red caviar first, thought Jo-Jo: then Prawns Provençal (the frozen ones will do quite well for that), *Zuppa Pavese*, those early partridges (they're *just* well enough hung), scotch woodcock and *Tarte aux Pommes*. Aloud she said:

'A pity about poor old Hen. I was getting very fond of him.'

'*Requiescat*,' said Ptolemaeos; 'but from the way he went on he was rather asking for something of the sort to happen. Anyway, Phaedron and his knights departed, leaving Henri and the Castellan behind; and the Castellan rolled his old soldier's eye over the mess and started to clear it up. First of all he cleared up "poor old Hen" after his nasty accident, and sent round to Hen's local friends and relations to certify that this had apparently been random and was in any case final. Then he turned to the stuff round the site of the shrine. Clearly, all of his horses and all of his men could never put *this* together again, and in any event, what was the point? The body had vanished; all the people who cared for Xanthippe were, in one way or another, gone; and there was a better use for valuable building materials. So bit by bit, as one may fairly conjecture, the whole of Xanthippe's shrine, her cloister and her crypt would have been parcelled off to repair the battlements, the watch towers and the barbican; while the burrow which the sappers had been following would have been stopped up at the point they had reached (for after all, whatever *might* have gone down through it *might* just come up through it), and the tunnel which they had dug would have been carefully filled in and the earth tightly packed, under the old soldier's knowing eye, to prevent future subsidence.

'And then? And then the months passed and the grass grew and very soon there was no trace of the shrine whatever. As for the *Écrevisse* which had disappeared in it, the only living people who knew of its existence were Phaedron, who had abandoned it; Lalage, who later came to live at Longueil with her son and Henri's but steered clear of Arques, for her memories of it were not agreeable; the four other surviving hand-maidens, all of whom were far away in the Mani, growing prematurely old and crooked with repeated childbirth; the drunk priest, who thought it was some kind of devil which he had exorcised; and Messer Hubert of Avallon, who, having dictated the two versions of his Chronicle and caused the first to be copied and distributed, thereafter held his peace.'

'And so,' said Len, 'if we believe Henri and do not accept supernatural accretion, we tell ourselves, as Phaedron must have done, that some kind of animal, who lived deep in the earth, made a burrow which came up in Xanthippe's crypt; that it ate what was left of her body; that it separated the bones and dragged them down the burrow to its lair, where it proposed to gnaw them during the weeks to come; and that it also took a fancy to the *Écrevisse*, and was in the act of carting that off as well when surprised by Phaedron, Henri and the priest . . . all of whom spotted the *Écrevisse* but not the creature which was busy bagging it.'

'Not too difficult to explain,' said Jo-Jo, as they turned for a last look down the lawn towards the slowly coiling vapours at the end of it. 'It could have been lurking down the steps which led to the passage. A quick flick of its paw from underneath could have dislodged the *Écrevisse*, which it could then have dragged off to the mouth of the burrow. It was given quite a long time, you see, while they found that lantern.'

'Granted. But on Henri's showing it was almost unbelievably nippy getting off the mark in the first place. During a couple of seconds at most, while the invaders ran to the head of the steps, our nimble beastie shifted itself and that great load of loot into the dark and out of sight. Now you see it – all two cubits by nine inches by six – and now you don't. Good going, girlie; far too good from where I sit. Nevertheless,' said Len, 'we might, for the sake of a working hypothesis, accept your theory as far as it goes. Which is not far enough to solve the following conundrum: what kind of creature lives deep in the ground, eats dead human beings, and also has a taste for artefacts?'

'Rats?' suggested Jo-Jo. 'They're said to be intelligent . . . to like looking at pretty things.'

'No,' snarled Len angrily, 'not rats. Not here.'

'No need to bite my head off.'

'Sorry, girl. It's just that I'm rather touchy about rats. As I told you both last night, I once had something very unpleasant* to do with them . . . so unpleasant that I don't want any kind of repetition.'

'Forgive me,' said Ptolemaeos; 'the mere fact of your not

*The Roses of Picardie, by Simon Raven (Blond and Briggs) *Vide passim*.

wanting anything more to do with rats does not disqualify them from being the agents here, but might disqualify you from continuing to assist us, if rats it really were.'

'Agreed,' said Len. 'But it's not rats. During that other business I learnt a lot about the kinds of rats that like the flesh and bones of dead humans. They wouldn't have been hanging about Xanthippe's shrine, they'd have been down at the local churchyard or in the Castle burial ground. Where was *that*, by the way?'

'Outside the wall, about a quarter of a mile to the north-east. The prevailing wind was westerly, you see, so that the Castle was well up wind of the dead – an arrangement they very sensibly preferred whenever it was feasible.'

'Well, that's where your intelligent rats would have been. Xanthippe's shrine was strictly a one-off number – not worth the trip.'

'But what was done,' said Jo-Jo, 'about burying people during a siege?'

'I honestly don't know,' said Ptolemaeos. 'I imagine they made temporary arrangements.'

'In which case,' persisted Jo-Jo, 'flesh-eating rats might have found their way into the Castle during some siege, then perhaps liked the place and hung about afterwards – and would have been very glad of Xanthippe.'

'Look, Miss Jo-Jo,' said Len. 'If you and I are going to get on as well as I hope we're going to get on, you must drop this natter about rats. Just accept that I have a special understanding of them – though I very much wish that I hadn't – and that I should *know* if rats had been mixed up in any of this.'

'Right,' said Jo-Jo, flushing with pleasure at this admonitory address, 'no rats. Then what?'

'It will be,' remarked Len, 'amusing to find out. Meanwhile,' he said, turning to Ptolemaeos, 'what's with this "eight days" bit? You have insisted that this Ivan Barraclough must be in Dieppe with eight days to spare before the Froggies show up to do their restoration. Why eight days?'

'Call it a hunch,' said Ptolemaeos. 'I like seeing patterns in things. It took the Castellan's sappers and serfs eight days to dig from the mouth of the burrow to the point, dangerously near the shaft of the well, where the Castellan called a halt. And here's another hunch. If the sappers were nearing the well, they were probably nearing their goal, as it is unlikely that this was on the other side of the well. So there it is: eight days I reckon as par for the dig. Call it, if you like, a matter of tradition.'

'But this is crazy, Ptoly man. If it took a crowd of sappers and the rest eight days, it will take Ivan about eighty.'

'No. The sappers had to proceed inch by laborious inch, testing everything for fear of doing damage, Ivan need have no such inhibition. Until he gets pretty near the place where the treasure now must be, he can go as fast as he likes.'

'But how is he going to find the right direction? That tunnel from the crypt was filled in.'

'He won't be starting from the crypt. He won't be following the old tunnel or the burrow. He knows that that tunnel led from Xanthippe's crypt (the location of which we have pretty well), under the foundations of the donjon, and on towards the shaft of the well – the head of which is still plain to see. So he will start to dig inside the donjon, fairly near the wellhead, and at a point immediately above the line which the tunnel must have followed as it approached the well's shaft. He will therefore hit this line at some point near where the Castellan stopped the last dig, which was probably, as I said just now, very near the actual goal.'

Ptolemaeos opened the back door and they all marched into the kitchen.

'Hit or miss,' said Len.

'There is an element of that – inevitably.'

'And what sort of cunt is this Barraclough going to look, digging away like a ghoul in the donjon? He'll be *noticed*, man; word will go round there's a freak in the Castle, and they'll probably send a man to carry him off to the bin.'

'One: he will be working at night – and there will be no night watchman to hinder him until the French have brought in their equipment, which, des Veules-les-Roses tells me, will not be until the first day of their schedule.

'Two: the donjon is not visited by many people, as it is awkward of access. It is rather a favourite with adventurous

174

children, but these will not be up there at night – nor indeed will anyone else.

'Three: even if someone does visit the donjon while Ivan is working there, he probably won't see Ivan . . . whose starting point is in a little hollow near the wall, a hollow largely concealed by a gorse bush.

'Four: even if a visitor does see Ivan, or hears him at work in his hole, he won't take it in, because Baby Canteloupe will be there to make imploring eyes at him – to imply that she and Ivan have come up there for a tumble and would the kind stranger please leave them to it.'

'He'd probably hang around in the hope of watching.'

'As you say. In which case something must be improvised. Baby is good at improvisation. And now,' said Ptolemaeos crossing the kitchen, 'as Jo-Jo will tell you, this kitchen is not my domain. I have some letters to write in my study.'

'Tell me first,' called Len, 'who is this Baby Canteloupe? I mean, I know she's Tom's daughter, but what else about her?'

'Hang around while I get going on the dinner,' said Jo-Jo, 'and I'll tell you what else about her. That's all right,' said Jo-Jo, looking forlornly at Ptolemaeos, 'isn't it, Ptoly? Len staying here with me? Perhaps he can do little things to help, and sometimes, you know, a girl gets lonely cooking, however much she –'

'Soul of my soul,' said Ptolemaeos, holding up his left palm to cut her short, 'I am neither a possessive nor a jealous man, and those that are I despise, from the bottom of my corrupt old heart. But please remember my old warning. Please remember, in this case as in all others, that to reach what they call the right true end of love is often, indeed, to reach the end of love. Or to approach it. Or at least to begin to approach it. So beware of orgasm . . . of orgasm, that is the drain of pleasure in the short term, and, in the long term, the death of love.'

175

SO THIS IS IT, thought Ivan Barraclough: I can't complain; I've not had at all a bad innings as the game goes. Still, it would have been pleasant to have had just a little longer; I had plenty of interesting questions still to ask, about the history, morals and religion of the Maniots, notably about pagan survivals, whether superstitious or philosophic, in the liturgy and rituals of the local Orthodox church. I'd already unearthed some very curious beliefs about the soul – comparable with, though often in contrast to, that weird notion entertained by the Ilyssans and others that the soul was a dead thing entombed in the body until the body's death resurrected and released it. This and other matters would have absorbed my attention for many happy years, provided we'd found Ptolemaeos's treasure and I'd had my share to live off.

But now this treasure hunt of Ptoly's has been my undoing, Ivan Barraclough thought. These people, these agents of Ptoly's in Greece and Yugoslavia, have somehow discovered the magnitude of the prize and think that they can win it for themselves if they only have enough information. They think I can provide that information. They require certainty: they do not understand that this whole enterprise has been built of speculation, of the tentative interpretation of dubious texts (Hubert's Chronicle and its Appendix) the original motive behind which is as highly conjectural as is the method of narration; for how far the latter is literal truth (or at any rate supposed to be) and how far it is purposeful metaphor (but to what purpose?), it is now impossible to discriminate. Yet where doubt is of the essence, these men want certainty. I have told them that they cannot have it; they do not believe me. They wish me to say, 'Dig *there*, and at *this* level you will find *that*.' They have convinced themselves that the matter is that simple; they will not be dissuaded; and now, since I refuse to tell them, cannot tell them, anything precise, they are going to torture me in order to extract precision. What they do not know is that I have a dicky heart and a low pain threshold (as Mr Bone the dentist used to say), and that even quite elementary experiments in this kind will probably kill me instanter.

Why am I so resigned? Because having taken a large dose of Aristarchos's herb (when I heard that tyre go off and realised that capture was inevitable) I am still in absolute control of my own soul: I tell it to be at peace, and it is so. But how much longer will the dose last? It might be advisable to renew it before they start their work; but the herb is in a phylactery on a chain round my neck, and my hands are bound behind my back. And yet . . . if somehow I could come at the herb in the phylactery, I should have the means – why did I not think of this before? – of controlling not only my own soul but also theirs. If somehow I could persuade them to chew a flake of the leaf, I could command them utterly.

The eldest of Ivan's four guardians, a frizzy-haired man with an '*Homme qui rit*' moustache, crossed the room from the fireplace and waved a pair of red-hot tongs under Ivan's nostrils.

'This is an end of patience,' he said. 'Tell us exactly where and how and what we may discover.'

'I have told you,' said Ivan, 'that it is not possible to be exact. But in so far as advice may be given, it is to be obtained from a small metal cylinder which you will find, if you open my shirt, on a chain round my neck.'

The frizzy-haired man unbuttoned Ivan's shirt, then summoned another from the group by the fire, one with a wide mouth and protruding underlip, beneath which the chin was dotted with ripe blackheads. Together the two men looked at Ivan's phylactery. Then the second man put out a furry paw with stubby fingers and long filthy nails and tentatively began to fondle the metal object, breathing heavily the while.

'BYE-BYE, BABY,' said Jo-Jo. 'Please be a *très sage* Baby, all the time.'

'Bye-bye, Tullia,' said Ptolemaeos. 'Good-bye, Canteloup.'

Ptolemaeos shook hands with Canteloupe. Jo-Jo tilted her head and put her tongue as far down Baby's throat as it would go.

Jo-Jo and Ptolemaeos were at Heathrow, seeing Baby and Canteloupe off. In the end it had been decided that Baby and Canteloupe should fly to Marseille, hire a car in which to drive to Saint-Gilles, meet Ivan there that evening, spend the following morning making any investigation in the area which Ivan might deem necessary, and then drive north to Dieppe through the afternoon and the night in the hired car, leaving Ivan's Land Rover in Saint-Gilles for later collection. This was very different from the original scheme, whereby Baby, Canteloupe and Ivan were to have rolled north at leisure, examining all important places on Xanthippe's route by the way. Such a dilatory proceeding was no longer possible because of the restorations imminent at Arques and the necessity (as Ptolemaeos insisted) of their being there eight days before these began.

'In which case,' Canteloupe had said, 'there doesn't seem much point in our meeting Barraclough down there. Just send him a wire at the hotel and tell him to meet us in Dieppe.'

'No,' Ptolemaeos had replied. 'In the first place I want to preserve the pretence that Ivan is your valet – and this will be possible only if you arrive in Dieppe with him. Secondly, I want someone on the spot in Saint-Gilles when he gets there to emphasise the new urgency imposed by the restorations. And thirdly, I want you there to signal me in case he doesn't appear at all. He has been . . . diverted. Not radically, I trust, but one can never quite tell in this sort of a circus.'

'And so,' Ptolemaeos was now saying to Canteloupe as he shook hands with him at Heathrow, 'telephone me at once if Ivan is not there by the time you have finished your coffee and cognac this evening.'

'I think I shall have Marc this evening. They do it rather well down there, you know. Roughish, of course, but very euphoria-making.'

'Then have two large glasses of the stuff,' said Ptolemaeos, 'and if he's not there when you get to the bottom of the second, get on to the blower. Ivan is the most punctual man in the world and allows ample margins. If he's not there by the end of dinner, it means he won't come. Which in turn means that he can't.'

'Wow,' said Baby, as Jo-Jo at last withdrew. 'You shouldn't do that to a girl at Heathrow. It makes her go all funny in front of all the people.'

'You're sure you still want to go,' said Jo-Jo, 'after all I told you?'

In accordance with her agreement with Ptolemaeos, Jo-Jo had reported to Baby the entire tale of Xanthippe's death and subsequent disposal, and had thus given her full warning of the kind of thing she really might be in for at Arques, which wasn't just acting as upper-class cover for Ivan Barraclough. But Baby had said that she had always really suspected this and found the prospect quite exciting.

'I only hope poor old Canty doesn't get too bored,' she now said to Jo-Jo as they all moved toward the passport barrier, 'but he can always go to the Casino. . . Oh good: here's that heavenly Len with my novel. I'm glad *he*'s popped up.'

'Me too,' said Jo-Jo breathlessly.

Len gave Baby a paper bag.

'They hadn't got *Middlemarch*,' Len said, 'so I settled for *Deronda*.'

'Blissikins,' said Baby. 'All about a young girl who marries a crinkly. I shall read it aloud to Canty.'

She blew out her cheeks and pointed to one of them. Len kissed it in elegantly caddish style and then shook hands with Canteloupe.

'Ta-ta, you two,' said Len.

'Cheery-bye,' said Jo-Jo, and sniffed loudly.

'Chin-chin,' said Baby, and to Len *sotto voce*, 'You be *molto gentile* with my *dolce* Jo-Jo.'

'*Ciao*,' said Canteloupe amiably.

'Go well,' said Ptolemaeos to Tullia and Canteloupe as they passed through the barrier.

THE FIRST TIME Ivan had used Aristarchos' herb, on the Messenger on the island in the lake at Ioannina, he had been lucky. For in fact the Messenger, as he himself admitted to Ivan, had clandestinely read Hubert of Avallon's Appendix while on a visit to Ptolemaeos. He should therefore have known all about the herb and its powers, in which case he should have been on his guard against them. But evidently his reading of the Appendix had been so hurried and jumpy that he had omitted or failed to retain the passages about Aristarchos. This being so, Ivan argued to himself (as the furry paw of his second gaoler caressed the phylactery), this being so, none other of the conspirators could know anything about the herb or what could be done with it. None of these four men in this low-built house could know that the herb, self-administered, enabled one to command one's soul, and, if deliberately administered by oneself to others, enabled one to command theirs. Thus, they could not know that, if they tasted the herb at his bidding or suggestion, they were his, body and spirit, for at least forty-eight hours.

The furry paw found a little spring. One end of the cylinder flipped open. The frizzy-haired man now took over, shaking out what looked like green cigar leaf into his palm.

'What advice can be here?' he asked.

He called a third man, handed him the tongs, bade him re-heat them.

'What advice?' he repeated.

'To find what you seek,' said Ivan, 'you will need vision.

This will give you that vision. You must surely remember, you have surely been told, that this matter is a mystery which has to do with a Lady who died of a broken heart.'

'So you have been saying since we took you. I tell you, English, all this talk of mysteries is just to confuse and hide. We are men of reason' – he tapped its seat beneath its frizzy hair – 'and we talk of bearings and measurements, of distances along and across and down, not of mysteries.'

'Then you will find nothing.'

'Suppose,' said the second man, 'that we trusted you. How is this advice sought?'

'By chewing the leaf. It conjures vision and from vision comes advice.'

'From the dead Lady?'

'Perhaps.'

'We could reach her from here?'

'Only with difficulty. It is easier if you are closer to her tomb. And in order to address her it is necessary that you should know many things about her. But you can make experiment here. You can chew the leaf and raise the vision. If the Lady does not answer you in the vision, you may still converse with another, alive or dead, whom you know or love.'

You can emancipate a peasant from poverty, ignorance and disease, Ptolemaeos used to say to Ivan during their travels, from gross diet and even from insanitary habit; but from superstition – never. Well . . . one would see.

BABY AND CANTELOUPE drove from Marseille to Saint-Gilles by way of Arles and being in no hurry went to look at the Arena there which now serves as a bull ring.

'Got the guide book?' said Canteloupe.

'You know better than that, Canty. You know very well that one should look at the guide book before and after but never when one's actually there. While you're there you must use your eyes, not glue them to print.'

'Yes. I remember your saying that in Venice. That was when I first began to love you. What a funny little thing you were in your tartan skirt and your kneesocks. Full of guts.'

'Silly Canty. Now just sit quiet on this stone and hold my hand, and I'll tell you a poem. It's about Arles, though not about the bit we're in now.

'"*Dans Arles, où sont les Alyscamps,*"' Baby began, and then continued to the end of the poem, which said that when one is among the tombs or monuments of the dead one is apt to feel very keenly the joy of living, and that then, of all times, one should beware, treading humbly and talking low.

'I DO NOT TRUST IT,' said the man with the frizzy hair.

'So far we have got nowhere,' said the man with the furry hands. 'Why not give this a try? If one of us tries it, whatever happens there are still three of us to take care of him.'

He pointed down at the bound and supine Ivan.

'If you are going to try it,' said Ivan, 'it is better that two of you should. With two of you together the vision will be more powerful. If you first agree whom you wish to summon, and summon him or her together, your call will have the power, not of two, but of four.'

'Could we summon the Lady from her tomb if there were two of us?'

'Perhaps. You would be more likely to succeed if we were in some place in which the Lady had actually lived, like Ilyssos, or which she had passed through on her journey, like Bari or Corfu, because a summons from a place known to her would travel more easily to her. But even from here, if there were two of you –'

'Did the Lady travel to Venice or Trieste?'

'No,' said Ivan, gratefully noting that the question implied proximity to these cities and thus confirmed his hope and supposition that he had been brought north, near to the Italian border. His plan now was simple. If he could persuade two of his interrogators to taste the herb of Aristarchos, he could command them to overpower the other two and bring him swiftly to his trysting place in Saint-Gilles. He was due there that very evening for dinner: punctual he could not be, but since he would need only hours to cross Italy and drive on to Saint-Gilles, he could be there before the night was spent (having telephoned the hotel to put those whom he must meet at ease), yes, he could be there before dawn tomorrow . . . if only he could get away now.

'No,' he repeated. 'The Lady did not travel to Venice or Trieste . . . but she *would* have passed through Venice had her Guardian not been warned that there was plague in the city. So you might say there was an association with Venice. How far are we from it?'

'About fifty miles,' said the blubber lips, grudgingly.

'Not very helpful. Still, if there were two suppliants. . . Anyway, what can you lose? I am powerless, and there would still be two of you to keep me so.'

'Why are you so eager that we should take this herb?'

'Because it may give you information . . . or at least advice . . . which I cannot give, and thus save me from being tortured to no purpose.'

The two faces (ferret snout below frizzy hair, black-speckled chin below labial droop) bent over the green shreds. You can wean a peasant from wife-beating, incest, hoarding grain or clipping coin, Ptolemaeos had said years ago, or even from his atavistic greed for land; but only when fishes lay their eggs in trees will you wean him from superstition.

'Very well,' said the ferret snout, he that was leader of them all: 'very well. We shall try it. You two,' he called to the couple by the fire, 'keep good watch and heat those tongs white-hot. And now,' he said to his lippy companion, 'you taste first.'

'I THINK I'D LIKE to come now,' said Len.

'No, no, no,' said Jo-Jo. 'The whole point is that you *don't* come. You get quite near coming, then you stop and let it all die down, and then you start again and get quite near coming, and then –'

'You go stark raving bonkers.'

'It's all a matter of discipline. It's often better to stick to a kind of skin massage which eases rather than arouses. Then there are all sorts of ways of tickling which are simply delicious but wouldn't make you actually come in a hundred years. So don't keep concentrating on my clitoris the whole time: play with my bottom instead.'

'Lovely little bottom. Strong and tight.'

'That's better. And in the same way I'll leave your foreskin alone – though I love the way it slides up and down – and play with your backbone. There are so many marvellous things to do,' said Jo-Jo, 'things which can go on for hours and hours, that it's quite absurdly wasteful to knock ourselves out with spurts and spasms after only a few minutes – or indeed at all.'

'And this is what that Ptoly's taught you?'

'Yes. This is what that Ptoly's taught me.'

'Well, I don't say but what there might be something in it, though a fellow likes to squirt his nuts off from time to time. Does Ptoly mind . . . our being together like this?'

'No. You heard what he said. He's not a jealous man and he knows that people need a change from time to time. Ooooooh. Do that again – at the bottom of the crack.'

'You know . . . all you need is a prick and you'd be a lovely boy.'

'That's what Baby Canteloupe says.'

'Never mind her. Do that thing with your tongue – between my shoulder blades.'

'WHAT A BLISSFUL DAY it's been,' said Baby as she poured the coffee in the Hotel Cours in Saint-Gilles. 'I know they say the Camargue is dreary, but there's something about those salt-marshes. Childe Roland country.'

'We can see more of them tomorrow,' said Canteloupe. 'The idea is that Ivan Barraclough may want to examine something or other here in Saint-Gilles, or nearby, before we leave. If he doesn't need us, we can go for a drive.'

'We'd better take care not to take the wrong turning,' Baby said.

'What can you mean?'

'If you take the wrong turning in Childe Roland country,' Baby prompted him, 'and if you go so much as five yards down it, you can never get back on to your proper road. It's vanished.' Baby giggled. 'You go back and look for it and it isn't there. All there is is a flat plain of mud, stretching for ever in all directions, oozing fog.'

'I sometimes wonder if we haven't taken that turning already. This whole business: Xanthippe and her soul and her treasure: there's madness here – or worse. Can we ever get out of the fog, one asks oneself, and back on the proper road?'

'We came in with our eyes open,' Baby said.

'And of course Ptolemaeos has been very obliging over the money. But it was really only a small private thing. Our Stately Home Corporation,' said Canteloupe, 'has always been in the best of nick. All I needed was a cure for a small bout of financial hiccups – something to do with a bad year on Lloyd's, a sum low in six figures. Was that worth getting us into this weirdness of Ptolemaeos Tunne's?'

'Anyway, we are in,' Baby said, 'so we'd better make the best of it. And now I'll tell you another thing. That's your second Marc de Provence.'

'You've taken to counting?'

'Just for tonight. Your second Marc, nearly finished, and no sign of Barraclough. You'd better ring up Ptoly.'

'Give him a few minutes more.'

'Certainly. Until that Marc's actually finished. Then you ring. That's what Ptoly said, and that's what we'll do. If you stray down the wrong turning in Childe Roland country,' said Baby, 'then the only hope lies in strict discipline.'

WHEN I WAKE UP, thought Jean-Marie Guiscard, there will be just nine days to go before we start on the Castle. Nine days before I start positively disobeying the voice that begged me to desist. Will the voice speak again? Or will the soul which (according to the eighteenth-century chart) is imprisoned somewhere between the donjon and the tilting yard and 'shapes the air around it by its virtue' – will this soul make some pronouncement, express some sentiment of pain or anger?

If it is confined, thought Jean-Marie, then pronounce is all that it can do. Or is it? If it can 'impose shapes' upon the air in the vicinity, might it not, even although it is immobile, be very active in its own place?

M'sieur Socrates, thought Jean-Marie, as he switched off the lamp in his bachelor bedroom, thinks that there is rich scandal here. For myself, I think that there is great sadness. But what there most certainly must be, sad or scandalous, grim or gay, is a mystery: who lingers in September Castle, and why?

'ANOTHER SNAG,' said the Marquis des Veules-les-Roses to the Princesse d'Héricourt-en-Caux, as he returned to the breakfast table from the telephone room.

'More trouble from the Department of Monuments?'

'No. They are giving neither less trouble nor more. They start their work in nine days' time, and that is that. What is new, Magdalene, is that Ivan Barraclough has failed to arrive at Saint-Gilles. Ptolemaeos has just told me that his friend Canteloupe rang up from there last night, and then again, as instructed, this morning: still neither sight nor sound nor sign of Barraclough. Since this Barraclough is a man of a punctuality positively officious, and since he is well versed in the use of European systems of communication, it is to be assumed that something . . . untoward . . . has occurred.'

'And is that something likely to make itself felt this far north?'

'One cannot be sure. Meanwhile, the operation must continue without Barraclough. To postpone it now would be to abandon it for ever.'

'THE THING IS,' said Ptolemaeos to Len, as they watched the morning fog billow along the lawn, 'that without Barraclough we are also without the herb of Aristarchos. He had been especially charged to collect a new supply as the last lot we had had crumbled to dust.'

'The herb of Aristarchos,' said Len carefully. 'Let's see if I have this right. It was to be used – was it not? – to gain control over recalcitrant elements, and, more particularly, to gain control of the Despoina Xanthippe's soul and then command it to free itself from her body . . . this in despite of her gaoler or guardian, Hero, and her daemon, Masullaoh.'

'Correct . . . always provided of course, that those sort of terms turned out to be relevant. Myself,' said Ptolemaeos, 'I think it most unlikely that they are relevant, most unlikely that the explanation of the whole affair is *of this order*. But it was as well, Ivan and I had agreed, to be prepared, and therefore to cull a fresh supply of Aristarchos' herb.'

'And now,' said Len, 'no herb and no Barraclough.'

'Giving you your big chance,' said Ptolemaeos, 'to prove your assertion that you could be of use to us.'

He paused while this sunk in.

'So far,' said Ptolemaeos, 'your only contribution has been to swear to us, from your specialised knowledge, that the explanation of the burrow which led beneath the donjon could not possibly be rats. Now you will have the opportunity to go and find out for yourself exactly what it is instead.'

'All right,' said Len: 'I'll have to go. Providing Jo-Jo comes too.'

'Tullia Canteloupe was to have helped Ivan.'

'And now it's to be Jo-Jo helping me. Baby too, if she wants, but I will have Jo-Jo.'

'Very well. But we must think how to fit her in. You will be joining the Canteloupes at Marseille this afternoon. Your flight is already booked, and a car to take you to Heathrow will be here in an hour's time.'

'You can fit Jo-Jo in on all that.'

'Oh yes. But remember why you are going all the way down to Marseille. It is so that you can drive up to Dieppe with the Canteloupes overnight, thereby giving substance to the pretence that you are their servant – the camouflage which we had devised for Ivan and which will do as well and even better for you.'

'Go on: rub it in that I'm common.'

'There is nothing common about being valet and courier to a nobleman. These days it is an extremely rare profession. But the question is, as I say, where do we fit in Jo-Jo? Is she to be your fellow-servant – Tullia's maid, perhaps? Or is she to retain upper class status?'

'She'd like looking after that Baby,' said Len reluctantly. 'They'd have a high old time prinking each other up.'

'This is no time for frivolous diversions. I want everyone's attention on the task. Nevertheless, I think Jo-Jo had best be lady's maid to Tullia. If they want physical proximity, there will be no way, however we cast Jo-Jo, of keeping them apart.'

'That's what I'm afraid of,' said Len.

'Stop snivelling like a jealous schoolboy,' said Ptolemaeos, 'and listen to me. In under an hour, you and Jo-Jo will leave here for Heathrow and Marseille. At Marseille the Canteloupes will meet you – in a bigger and faster hired car, which they will have changed for the present one at the airport. *You* will then drive the party through the night to Dieppe, and when you are there, at the Hotel Présidence, you will comport yourself courier-chauffeur-valet, while Jo-Jo will assume the role of lady's maid to the Marchioness. So far, it's all very simple. What is very far from simple is the instruction which I now have to give you about how to proceed in the Castle during the eight days and, more particularly, nights that will precede the start of the restorations. Ivan knew it all by heart. He also had the advantage of years of research into the habits and progress of the Princess – research of which his recent journey was to have been the culmination. Ivan was soaked in the whole bloody business, Len: he ate it, drank it, breathed it, slept it. Your situation is very different, and I must therefore request your closest and most intelligent attention to the schedules and techniques which I shall now propose to you. . .'

'THE KING wanted a harbour down here,' said Baby, 'so that he could assemble a fleet for a Crusade. In those days the sea would have come almost up to these walls, or at any rate there would have been creeks and channels through the marsh deep enough to float the kind of ships which they had then.'

Baby and Canteloupe looked south from the ramparts of Aigues Mortes, over the salt-marshes and towards the distant gleam of the sea.

'Aigues Mortes,' said Canteloupe. 'Dead Waters. Aptly named.'

And indeed nothing stirred in the scrub beneath the walls nor in the reeds beyond. Funny, thought Baby: as everyone knew, the marshes of the Camargue were full of wild life, carefully fostered and guarded; and yet here, between these ramparts and the sea, there was a stillness as of world's end; it was as though God had gathered up all his creatures from this place and carried them hence in his bosom to some new country far away.

'So,' said Canteloupe, wishing to break the forlorn peace, 'a change of plan. Ivan Barraclough will not come. We shall be working with Len instead.'

'When Xanthippe landed at Saintes-Maries-de-la-Mer,' said Baby, 'and travelled across the swamps towards Aigues, these walls were hardly begun. And yet she must have seen them. According to Hubert's Chronicle some guardian angel or spirit kept them safe from the sloughs and quicksands, and brought them past here and on to Saint-Gilles.'

'Ptolemaeos says we must hire a larger car at Marseille,' said Canteloupe, 'as Jo-Jo is coming as well. I think Avis can run to rather a swish BMW, with plenty of room for four bodies and their kit. But they're probably in short supply. Perhaps I should telephone ahead to book one?'

'When they saw these walls,' Baby said, 'or rather what little there then was of them, they should have known that they were over the worst. Even in those days, from here to Saint-Gilles must have been relatively easy going. But did they realise that? Did they say to themselves, from now on there will be well-marked tracks, and ploughed fields, and dykes where the swamps still linger? Or did they regard these walls as just a mark of distance covered, beyond which there would be so many miles more of treacherous quagmire and creeping fever?'

'We must go, darling. Whether or not we ring up the Avis people in Marseille, time's getting short. Len and Jo-Jo should be landing at just after three.'

'Xanthippe is riding with Hubert,' said Baby in a small, precise voice. 'The men at arms in the party are too afraid of the marsh to ride in front, so Xanthippe and Hubert are leading. She, being a Princess of the Mani, must show fear of nothing, and he, being her knight, must ride with her for very shame. But inside her, her heart is full of fear; fear of the Dead Waters and of the spirit that has guarded them thus far.

'Just behind her is Hero, who is cold of heart yet honours

190

Xanthippe as her mistress and pities her for what she is else. With Hero is Lalage, whose heart I cannot read. Behind them are four more hand-maidens, singing a round song.

> In my father's garden
> There is a wood
> Where young men and maidens
> Sport as ne'er they should.
>
> Under the green leaves
> In frolic they moan;
> But when the leaves have fallen
> The maidens cry alone.

'It cannot be a song of their own land, my lord; for in the Mani there is no autumn as we know it. Perhaps Hubert of Avallon has taught it to them or composed it for them. They love Hubert and they are happy to sing his song, trusting him and their Princess to bring to safety.

'I do not feel the presence of the spirit who has guided them, only Xanthippe's fear of him, and also Hero's. In both of them the fear is mixed with longing. I still cannot read the heart of Lalage.

'Whatever their other fears and troubles, Hubert and Xanthippe are glad to have reached this place, because they have been told that from here on the journey will be easier. Already their minds are opening to Saint-Gilles and the many towns and cities beyond, and Xanthippe is questioning Hubert about the country and the Castle for which they are bound . . . and for which we too are now bound, my lord, we too, Xanthippe,' called Baby, waving over the Dead Waters, 'and I shall find you there.'

III

The Agape

'*CARTE POUR LE PREMIER TABLEAU*,' intoned the croupier, '*et carte pour le second. . .*'

But before the cards could be issued the banker must show his hand.

'. . . . *Et neuf en Banque*,' the croupier concluded.

'That's the third natural the Bank's had in the last four hands,' said Canteloupe to Baby, 'and his ninth win running. What's more he's already had a winning run' – Canteloupe consulted his record – 'of seven, during this session, and one of *fifteen* during the previous session. I think he must have a pact with the Devil.'

Canteloupe was having a hairy time opposing the Baccarat Bank in the Casino at Dieppe, while Baby was sitting behind him and making sympathetic noises.

'It does seem rather fierce,' she said now, 'but that banker's such a dear little man that I'm sure he'd never deal with the Devil.'

'How can you know?'

'He isn't – well – Faustian enough to look at.'

'Faust started out as a humble scholar. "What a dear little man," I expect his landlady used to say as she darned his socks. The point about dealing with the Devil is that part of the deal is that you don't look as if you'd dealt with him.'

'Faust did.'

'Only for theatrical purposes. In real life the Devil's creatures do not sprout horns or come sizzling up through the floor-boards. They walk in and out the usual way, looking pretty much like anybody else.'

The door at the far end of the *Sal des Jeux* now opened to admit Len. Dressed in striped trousers, Marlborough jacket and winged collar, he stalked majestically past the roulette tables to the *Table de Banque*, where he came to an almost military halt and made a courtly bow to Baby and Canteloupe.

As the French began to giggle and mutter, variously in amazement, amusement and suppressed admiration, Len articulated:

'My lord marquess, will it please your lordship to instruct me as to your wishes about your evening repast.'

'I shall dine presently in the *Restaurant des Jeux*,' said Canteloupe. 'Please to escort her ladyship back to the hotel, where she will require a light collation in her suite.'

As the French goggled and scowled, Baby rose, Len bowed once more, Baby moved past him, Len resumed the upright and turned to follow her, and both marched in immaculate time and stride towards the doors, Len a yard behind and a yard to the right of Baby. As they passed the Black Jack tables their seigneurial progress was nearly obstructed by a crossly departing loser, whom, however, Len removed from Baby's path by a flick of the fingers.

'I THOUGHT THE IDEA WAS,' said Baby Canteloupe to Len, 'that you should use your position as Canty's valet to camouflage yourself. If you go on like you did in that Casino just now, you'll be the most conspicuous thing in Dieppe.'

'Oh yes. A gentleman's gentleman – not what people expect to find these days. Major-Domo, courier and personal body servant all rolled into one. A figure from an Edwardian romance (*Belchamber*, perhaps), stately suave and loyal, dedicated to the service of the House of Canteloupe yet with a persona and integrity of my own –'

'You're reading too much into the part –'

'And in no case the sort of character you would suspect of sneaking away up to this donjon with his mistress and digging holes by candlelight.'

'Torchlight.'

'Don't be so literal,' said Len. 'We need all the poetry we can get in this dump. How am I getting on?'

Baby played the torch near the bottom of a large bush which

was rooted in the side of a small hollow, and together they surveyed a hole some four feet deep and two in diameter.

'How far down do you suppose . . . it . . . will be,' said Len, 'and precisely what are we expecting when we get there?'

'The remains of a mortal body and a priceless artefact, an indefinite distance down and not far off the shaft of that well.'

Len leaned on his shovel. 'Doesn't it strike you,' he said, 'that there is something anti-climactic, something positively bathetic, about this performance? I mean, all those years of scholarly research, all those agents posting hither and thither all over the Balkans, a huge paraphernalia of manuscripts and monuments and mediaeval chronicles – and at the end of it all just this, you and me like joke grave-diggers in a 'B' Movie, scratching away with a garden spade.'

Baby looked at the rough towering walls on every side. She walked up out of the hollow in which Len was digging and looked at the jagged wall-head, some ten yards away across a patch of wild grass. She looked up at the misty three-quarter moon, and down at Len, and she listened to the remnant of the sea-wind as it gratefully settled and died in the trees on the ridge.

'We're here to start things off,' she said, 'to stir it all up.'

'Stir what up?' said Len, peevishly poking the earth.

'There is a Lady buried here with her treasure. It is said that her soul is somehow confined to her dead body. It is also said that there is a Guardian who will be roused if anyone comes deliberately seeking the treasure.'

'Do we believe any of this?'

'We do and we don't.' A cloud obscured the gibbous moon. Baby came down close to Len and shone the torch on his spade. 'We allow for the possibility of some of it being in some sense true. And then we tell ourselves that if there are (in some sense) souls or Guardians, which may be (in whatever fashion) disturbed or roused, the thing to do is to send some intelligent people – us – to disturb or rouse them and so get the party started.'

'So Ptoly's throwing us in as ground-bait?'

'So I judge from what Jo-Jo told me. That was always the idea, even when Ivan Barraclough was to have done the digging, only of course he knew more about it all than you, and he would have had those herbs to help him.' Baby glanced over her shoulder and lowered her voice. 'The thing is,' she whispered, 'that if once you rouse a Guardian, then (a) you know there's something there to guard, and (b) there's a good chance that the Guardian, without meaning to, may lead you to it.'

'This is our second night here, sweetheart. No sign of Guardians.'

'I'm not so sure. You saw what happened to Jo-Jo last night.'

'Sure. She got a little sick. The curse coming on, she told me later. That's why she's not fit to come up here to-night.'

'Jo-Jo never worried about the curse in her life. Anyway, we're neither of us due for three weeks. She just got bad vibes, Len.'

'You mean . . . that you think . . . that she thinks . . . that you're angry with her for having it away with me?'

'No. I've told her I'm not angry. And I know that you're not really having it away. She's just doing with you what she does with Ptoly: teasing and being teased. I'm the only one with whom she crosses the line, Len. She keeps the real thing for me. So I'm not jealous, and I wish her all the slap and tickle in the world until the time comes for her to be together again with me. And then she'll come to me, Len, as she does to no one else – and all this she knows very well for herself.'

'All right,' said Len crossly. 'Then what did get into her?'

'Whatever it was got into her on the other side – on the outside – of that wall.'

Baby pointed to the north wall of the donjon.'

'When we were leaving,' Baby said, 'she stopped, went stiff . . . and then sort of retched.'

'I thought *you* were meant to be the psychic one.'

'I didn't feel a thing. But evidently Jo-Jo did. I asked her later what it was, but she wouldn't tell me. Nothing, she said. But I know my sweet Jo-Jo, and I know better.'

'I think,' said Len, 'that we'd better take a breather and go and have a look at the place . . . where it happened to Jo-Jo. That might help . . . "get the party started" . . . as you put it.'

'I think our hosts will proceed at their own speed,' Baby said, 'and in a way of their own choosing. It begins to seem that Jo-Jo is what they've chosen. But in any case at all I agree with you: we should go and take a look at the place where it happened.'

They climbed out of the hollow, walked along a path which skirted the wild grass round the well, climbed a low but steep bank and descended on the other side of it, then came to a gap which had once been a gate in the east wall of the keep. The moon reappeared and helped light them on their way to the north-east corner and then along the north wall.

'It happened about twenty yards further on,' said Baby. She shone the torch ahead. 'By that bump in the ground.'

The sea-wind rippled in the trees and was still. A gull who had sailed inland on it trilled in the dark.

'Poor Xanthippe,' said Baby. 'Salt-winds and cliff-birds flew all about her Castle with their messages of the sea that was just beyond the hill; but never a sight for her of a single wave.'

'Beware of pity,' said Len.

'If you do not pity, you cannot love.'

'Then summon her,' said Len: 'if here indeed she be, summon her with your love.'

WHEN THE *TABLE DE BANQUE* was prorogued, Canteloupe changed his mind about dining in the *Restaurant des Jeux* and went to visit Jo-Jo, who had stayed in all day and was looking dreadful, strained, sweaty and pale yellow.

'Come with me to the hotel restaurant,' said Canteloupe, 'and try to eat. Or at least drink some wine.'

'All right. I couldn't feel worse.'

'What's up?'

'That's the trouble. I don't know.'

While Canteloupe whacked into a comprehensive menu,

Jo-Jo picked at a sole, sipped Vichy and occasionally tried some of the Montrachet which Canteloupe was having with his first two courses. Half way through the second of these the manager brought him a card.

'Ask M'sieur to join us,' Canteloupe said.

A few minutes later a dapper, spare and slightly stooping figure appeared by their table.

'Des Veules-les-Roses,' said des Veules-les-Roses. He kissed Jo-Jo's hand, grasped Canteloupe's, bowed gracefully when offered a chair, and (rather creakily) sat.

'I am sorry to disturb you at your dinner,' he began, 'but I have news which you should know. M'sieur Jean-Marie Guiscard of the Department of Monuments is in Dieppe for the night. Normally he drives over from Eu, which is not an hour away, for the inside of the day. It follows that if he is staying the night here he must be planning something novel. A moonlight visit to the Castle, perhaps?'

'Why should he plan that?'

'Because he is in love with the Castle. He is a very good sort of young man, Jean-Marie, if to us an annoyance. He loves the Castle and the Lady and the Ballad; and like all lovers he wishes, I expect, to pay his court by night.'

'Ah,' said Jo-Jo. 'Where is he staying?'

'In a little place by the port, my spies tell me. The *Hostellerie de la Manche*.'

Without saying anything more, Jo-Jo left the two men at table. She ran along the Boulevard Verdun, turned right down to the Ferry Port, enquired frantically, and was directed to the *Hostellerie de la Manche*, where a sour-smelling man behind a zinc bar emitted a globule of something unspeakable and told her the number of the room of M'sieur Guiscard. She climbed three flights of decomposing stairs, knocked at a splintery door labelled 12bis, and was admitted by (she presumed) M'sieur Guiscard, who was getting himself up, in three sweaters and a jerkin, to go somewhere. Jo-Jo very much liked the look of his round farmer's face, his bushy tow hair, and his rather shambly arms and legs, but she was not there, she reminded herself, to enjoy his appearance.

'I had a French nanny,' she said, 'whom I very much loved

and from whom I learned your beautiful language. Hear me, then.'

Jean-Marie bowed to Jo-Jo and indicated his one lop-sided chair. But she chose to stand in the middle of the floor.

'Last night,' she said, 'I went to the Castle at Arques to help despoil it, to help find and steal the Treasure. I would be there again tonight, were it not that something happened to me which warned me to stay away and at the same time compels me to speak to you as I am speaking, although in doing so I must accuse my friends.

'As we were leaving the Castle last night and passing along the wall of the keep, I felt suddenly as though I had stepped into a vacuum. My whole body was jolted and for a moment felt as if it must explode.'

'"The confined spirit which shapes the air by its virtue."'

'What?'

'This happened near the *north* wall?'

'Yes.'

'If I am right,' said Jean-Marie, 'that is where the Lady – you know of whom I speak? – was laid to rest. There is, it appears from a chart in my possession, some old story that her soul, or *a* soul, is imprisoned there and makes influence on the air around.'

'Ah. Then she could have made the vacuum into which I passed. Whether she intended it for me or for one of my friends, I do not know; but in any case they felt nothing. As for myself, after I had been threatened with explosion and then, just as suddenly, released from the threat, I felt . . . I felt sick, all here about my heart.'

'No voices, mademoiselle?'

'No voices. Only sickness and despair. For I now knew that there would be misfortune and misery for all concerned if I and my friends continued as we were. I knew that there was something wrong, not necessarily about what we were doing, but about the manner and the spirit in which we were doing it. I knew it was essential that I should stop my friends, in order that we might stand back for a while and take thought. All day I have been wondering how I might do this, and indeed whether I could do it at all; for the search is dear to the heart of a man whom I greatly love and who will be hurt and angry if I cause delay. But when I heard you were here, I saw how it must be. You love the Castle, and must come with me to save it and all those in it from this clumsy meddling of my friends.'

'God help me, I was going to meddle there myself. In a few days, mademoiselle –'

'What matters is now. You must come with me now, Jean-Marie Guiscard, before the daemons are roused and revenge is sought.'

'What daemons? What revenge? I know there are some sad tales about the Castle, and some very odd ones too, but I have heard nothing of such evil as you suggest.'

So as they went, Jo-Jo told him what Ptolemaeos had told her, compressing it as best she might into the twenty minutes or so which it took to find and activate his rattly car and drive it through the October night to September Castle.

'WHAT SHALL WE DO?' said Canteloupe to des Veules-les-Roses.

'Nothing.'

'But what does she want with Guiscard? Somehow or other she may give the game away. Ptolemaeos will be furious with her. His own niece.'

'Mademoiselle has a face which betokens determination and truth,' said des Veules-les-Roses. 'When confronted by such a combination, one is well advised to sit still and let the thing go on as it may.'

JEAN-MARIE STOPPED HIS CAR with a clank on the patch of rough grass in front of the Castle gate. He then, after considerable trouble, managed to light a storm-lantern, with the aid of which Jo-Jo and he padded through the barbican arch.

They made towards the central archway. Through it they saw a torch flash, far off by the tilting yard. A little later they heard a light high keening, which grew in strength and pitch as they passed under the archway and began to cross the court of honour.

Then the three-quarter moon, which had been doused by mist since their arrival, suddenly re-kindled, and what they saw and heard was this:

Baby Canteloupe, chanting over and over again, to the tune of the famous spiral passage in Fauré's Requiem, the words 'Come, Xanthippe, come Xanthippe, come Xanthippe, come', was dancing such a dance (thought Jo-Jo) as Nausicaa and her maidens must have danced on the beach of the magic island of the Phaeacians, swaying and fluttering and gently twirling, in the area immediately below the wall of the donjon and at the bottom of a slope. Standing nearby, in the posture of an umpire, was Len: standing behind Len, on a little bump in the ground which stuck out like a peninsula from the slope, was a tall lady all in white.

Jo-Jo shuddered and grasped Jean-Marie's hand. Jean-Marie crossed himself with his free one. Baby twirled again, saw the lady all in white, abruptly checked her chant and ran towards the lady, holding out her arms and smiling with great tenderness and joy.

'Welcome, oh welcome,' Baby called.

As she came close to the lady and made to embrace her, their shapes seemed to merge, and Baby dropped to the earth.

203

ON THE FIRST DAY OF FULL TERM, the assembled Council of Lancaster College, Cambridge, voted that the Provost, Lord Constable of Reculver Castle, being about to reach the age of retirement, should cede his Lodging, his authority and his title as Provost on the following Founder's Day (December the sixth) in favour of some person to be elected by the Council during the intervening eight weeks.

When Lord Constable rose to address the Council there was a murmur of affection and sympathy from most of the elder men present, notably from Tom Llewyllyn the historian, Ivor Winstanley the Ciceronian, and Balbo Blakeney the Custos Conviviarum (i.e. Steward in charge of College Feasts and Celebrations), while many of the younger men, by contrast, exchanged looks of spiteful jubilation. Lord Constable began by thanking his Fellows for their loyalty and support during the period of his incumbency, which had lasted for close on twenty years. He went on to say that he had given much thought to the question of a suitable successor, whether they should select him from among their own ranks or from the world outside, and whether –

At this point a pimply face on a stove-pipe neck popped up to remark that the election of Provost Constable's successor was a matter for the individual consciences of the members of the Council, who had no need of Provost Constable's dissertation in the matter.

Since this interruption appeared to the majority of those present, even the most disaffected, to be unnecessarily discourteous and dismissive, Provost Constable was invited to resume. What harm, after all, could he do them now, the radicals were thinking: he was going, he was making no trouble about going, and it might not be unamusing (for he had been a doughty and subtle Councillor in his time) to hear what he had to say about the succession.

Provost Constable thanked his Fellows for their kind permission to continue. He was glad the word 'conscience' had been aired: he had recently had pressing cause to investigate his own. His problem had been whether or not to exercise his Special Prerogative.

There was a puzzled silence while the phrase hung in the air above them.

His Special Prerogative, Lord Constable now repeated: his Special and unquestionable Prerogative, virtually unknown but absolutely conferred by a royal statute of 1782, never repealed if never applied. The reason why it had never been applied was very simple: there were narrow and exigent conditions as to its application.

The Royal Statute of 1782, *In Patriae Salutis Causam* (in the interest of national security), laid down that when a provost of the college was also a peer of the realm (a case which, in the event, had not arisen until now), such a provost, being a Lord in Parliament and Privy to the Councils of his Sovereign, and having therefore an especial obligation in duty and in honour to ensure the loyal service and lawful demeanour of the College which he ruled – that such a Provost, be it hereby decreed, was fully empowered and absolutely commanded to advise the Sovereign of the day if, in his expert and conscientious opinion, there was risk that an election of his successor might install *hominem quemlibet vilem, hostem et Legis et Monarchi* (some low fellow hostile to Constitution and Monarch) who might seek to subvert the Crown and frustrate its servants. In such case election should be barred and the succeeding Provost should be appointed by the Sovereign, in close consultation with the decedent. He, Provost Constable, now begged to produce the Statute before the Council.

A scroll was now placed in the centre of the great table by the Senior Fellow. From the bottom end arose a peevish and incredulous mutter, such as one may hear from the lower class of spectator on a race course when the popular favourite has just been beaten by a short head by an outsider at 66 to 1.

'Which things being so,' the Provost pursued, 'after a long inquisition of my conscience and experience, I at last decided to seek audience of Our Sovereign Lady the Queen, and to advise Her that the Council of Lancaster College, as at present constituted, is only too liable to elect a new Provost who would indeed seek to subvert the Crown and insult its dignity. In subsequent consultation with Her Majesty I have most earnestly put forward for the Provostship, and Her Majesty has most graciously accepted, the name of Thomas Ethelrydd Llewyllyn, Companion of the Order of the British Empire, *Doctor Litterarum* and *Litterarum Doctor*, better known to all of you round this table as plain Tom Llewyllyn.'

IT WAS BAD LUCK, Ivan Barraclough reflected, that the first chappy to chew Aristarchos' leaf (blubber–lips) had proved allergic to it, or so he must suppose; for instead of becoming Ivan's immediate slave of mind and muscle, he had gone straight into a rabid and maniacal fury in which he started to claw the skin from his flesh and then the flesh from his bone. As a result the leader, who was about to take the herb himself, had very sensibly changed his mind, called up his two other colleagues to secure the first, and then destroyed the remains of the leaf in Ivan's phylactery. There had been no further possibility of escape; and by now Canteloupe and his wife must long since have given him up and left Saint-Gilles, presumably for Dieppe. What would happen to them there without him, Ivan wondered.

And come to that, what was going to happen to himself? It was now seven days since the violent miscarriage of the Aristarchos scheme, seven days during all of which he had been closely confined to the low-built house. Although his bonds were sometimes taken off or loosened to allow him to stretch a little, they were always replaced within the hour. The unfortunate fellow who had chewed the herb and gone dervish had been removed and had not reappeared; the rest ignored Ivan totally, save when his bonds must be loosened or replaced, or when it was his (once daily) feeding time, or when he asked to be led to the bucket which served as a jakes. He had the impression that the leader with the frizzy hair had sent away for instructions and would do nothing until he received them. Why they had suspended their intention to torture him, he did not know. Possibly the hideous effect of the herb on blubber-lips had caused them to suspect him of having further and similar resources which he might apply if too far provoked.

This reminded him of Ptolemaeos' uncharitable remarks about peasants' incapacity to shed superstition; and he was just considering the possibility of renewing his attempts to exploit this ancient debility, when the leader, who had been out for nearly four hours, strode into the room, smacked him three times over the chops (the second blow being a backhander) and then began to untie his ropes. When this was done, he helped Ivan to his feet, led him to the door, blinked rapidly, shook his head and pushed Ivan out into the night.

'Go,' said the leader: 'it is finished.'

From somewhere below came a light splash of water; all about him was a rustle of pine.

'Where am I?'

'What does it matter? In the morning you will see, and then you will use your money. Nothing can matter much to a man as long as he has sight and money. That is why we needed you – to tell us where the treasure was so that we might take it and have money. But now all that is over, at least for us.'

'What happened?'

'I do not exactly know. But for us it is over.'

'Why have you not taken my money? It would have been some sort of consolation.'

'When a man has been close to a mine of gold, English, he is not happy with pilfering small copper. Later, no doubt, we shall change our minds, and think how foolish, since the treasure is denied us, not to take what he had from the English. But as it is we have not the heart to trouble, so go now while you still may.'

207

'CONGRATULATIONS,' said Ivor Winstanley to Tom Llewyllyn as they left the Council Chamber. 'If only the Angry Brigade in there doesn't assassinate you.'

'They haven't the guts. But they may make themselves very unpleasant, Ivor, so I'm slipping off for a day or two. My daughter Tullia hasn't been at all well – some sort of brain fever, I gather – but now she's out of danger and recuperating at Ptolemaeos Tunne's place near Ely. I'll go there for a while and see her. I hear Ptolemaeos has got some intriguing guests as well as Tullia, including our old chum, Len. . .'

'ALL WAYS ROUND, a fascinating experiment,' Ptolemaeos said.

For now the fight had been fought and already the wounds were healing; now half way between golden Michaelmas and grey Hallows, the season when campaigns cease and men sit over the grateful wine, it was time to debate the matter of September Castle. The usual rectangular table in Ptolemaeos' dining room had been replaced by a far larger one, round. In honour of the occasion Jo-Jo had prepared blinis with red caviar and sour cream, a soufflé of tench with a sauce of *écrevisses*, sorbets of Calvados (to refresh the palate), partridges stuffed with chestnuts, pancakes *framboise*. Since there were many people present, and since Jo-Jo must take a prominent part in the debate which would accompany the meal, the dishes were being served (very efficiently) by octogenarian twin sisters from a nearby village. (If one lived to be sixty in the Fenland, Ptolemaeos used to say, one was thereafter indestructible.)

Present at this collation were Ptolemaeos Tunne; the Marchioness Canteloupe (on his right); Jean-Marie Guiscard (on her right); Madame la Princesse d'Héricourt-en-Caux; Tom Llewyllyn (Provost Select of Lancaster College in the University of Cambridge); his newly appointed *Custos Arcanorum* (confidential secretary and hatchet man) in the person of Len; Monsieur le Marquis des Veules-les-Roses; Madame Jean-Marie Guiscard (née Jo-Jo Pelham); Ivan Barraclough (rather battered after a difficult journey); and Captain the Most Honourable Marquess Canteloupe of the Aestuary of the Severn, to give him, just for once, his full and proper title.

Ptolemaeos had ordained that after the sorbets of Calvados there should be an interval, before the partridges, of forty-five minutes, during which he would open the debate and conduct the earlier stages. It was not only a debate but also an enquiry. 'What,' Ptolemaeos was saying now, 'has really been at the bottom of it all? It was to find out this that I first went into the thing.' Yet always contiguous with this enquiry must be the debate, he continued, because his guests would find, as one after another of them made his or her deposition, that there were (if one allowed for minor variations) two possible explanations of the whole affair, the first entirely logical, mundane and rational, the second very much the reverse. It would be for those gathered at the round table to debate and to decide which must prevail.

'Perhaps as good a starting point as any,' said Ptolemaeos, 'will be a review of the events which took place on the second evening of the dig in the donjon of the Castle. Len . . . if you please.'

Len now told the company how Baby and he had discussed the evident absurdity of what they were doing ('Joke grave-diggers in a "B" Movie') and had reached the conclusion that they were there as ground-bait just to get the local queer fish biting. And now they came to think of it, there had been a bite already: on the previous night, when they left the donjon, Jo-Jo had suddenly gone very peculiar, had had a kind of fit, as they passed a certain spot (a slight bump in the ground attached to a more prominent slope) near the north wall of the donjon.

They had therefore decided to take another look at the ground in that area. As they approached it, Baby had been much moved by the rustle of the spent wind from the sea and the cries of sea-birds, and had given voice to her pity for the poor little Greek Princess who had been tortured by these tokens of the element which she yearned for but was no longer allowed to look upon. Hearing the true love in Baby's tone, Len had told her to use that love to summon the Lady's soul.

'We had been told that her soul was in some fashion imprisoned in what was left of her body,' Len said. 'It seemed to me that the way Baby Canteloupe felt she might be able to set the Lady's soul free – if there was any truth in the tale. "Summon her," I said. "Summon her with your love." So Baby started. She found a suitable and simple phrase and a tune to go with it, and she chanted away under the moon and then began to dance.

'Soon after she began to dance the moon went in. But we had a torch and I could see her pretty well, and it seemed to me that whenever she danced actually on the little bump in the ground she became more excited, more kind of vibrant, as if she were feeling a response. A little later she danced some paces away from the bump and I turned to watch her. Just then the moon came out again, and when this happened Baby suddenly seemed to see something behind me, on the bump perhaps; she rushed towards it and passed me with her arms outstretched, calling out cries of welcome – then dropped flat and didn't stir. It was just about then that Jean-Marie and Jo-Jo showed up –'

'Cut right there,' called Ptolemaeos. 'We'll continue with the further events of that evening in a little while. But first I want you all to hear Jo-Jo's account, and Jean-Marie's, of what *they* saw when they arrived up there near the donjon.'

Jo-Jo now reported that she had arrived with Jean-Marie during the concluding stages of Baby's dance, just as the moon came out. The scene had been very much as described by Len, she said, except that she suddenly became aware that behind Len was standing a tall Lady in white. It was in order to welcome and embrace this figure that Baby had rushed past Len. It seemed to Jo-Jo that Baby had, as it were, stepped inside the Lady in white, so that for a split second a white margin had flickered round Baby's whole body . . . after which the two forms merged into one – Baby's – and that form fell to the ground.

Jean-Marie supported Jo-Jo's account in every particular.

'Well now,' said Ptolemaeos, 'before we pass on to the later developments of that evening, I have just one question for my niece. Jo-Jo, darling Jo-Jo, heart of my heart of my heart, *why* did you go running to Jean-Marie and blow our whole box of tricks wide open? You are the most loyal and loving girl a man could know . . . and yet you split on your Uncle and your friends like a rotten banana.'

Jean-Marie made jerky manual gestures towards Ptolemaeos, as if to say, 'Don't you dare bully my wife', but Jo-Jo soothed him down with her little-boy smile across the table, and then answered Ptolemaeos:

'It's exactly as I told Jean-Marie, Ptolykins. As I walked along the donjon wall, just by that bump which Len talks of, I felt a terrible jolt, almost as if I was being blown apart, and after that I absolutely knew that nothing but wretchedness could ensue if we went on digging in the manner and the spirit in which we had started. I knew that it was imperative that I should make everyone at least pause and think what he was doing. I thought how upset you'd be, my sweetheart, and I agonised all day, but when M'sieur des Veules-les-Roses told me that a man from the French Department of Monuments was in Dieppe, I knew that this must be my cue.

'So I tracked Jean-Marie Guiscard down in his hotel, and he came with me to the Castle, and later on he was so kind and trusting and loyal and understanding that . . . that . . . that. . .' Then Jo-Jo ceased to falter and said in a low clear voice:

The die is cast, and thus the matter is:
My true love has my heart, and I have his.

There was a murmur of pleasure round the table, after which Ptolemaeos smiled at Jo-Jo, blew his nose rather loudly, and then:

'So there we are,' he said. 'Baby flat out in the moonlight, Jo-Jo and Jean-Marie advancing over the old tilting meadow, and Len already bending over Baby. Had *you* seen a Lady in white, Len?'

'No. Strictly no Lady in white from where I stood.'

'And yet you had turned as Baby ran back past you, so if the Lady had been there you must have seen her?'

'You'd certainly think so. But as far as I was concerned Baby was just embracing the air.'

'I see. Jo-Jo and Jean-Marie, could you have been deceived by some trick of the light? After all, the moon had only just come out again and there was mist about. Perhaps you saw a refraction of moonbeams?'

'Perhaps,' said Jo-Jo, 'and perhaps. But if so it was a powerful enough illusion to make me shiver like a fen-willow and to set Jean-Marie crossing himself like the Baptist. You should also remember that Baby obviously saw someone there behind Len . . . as Len himself will allow.'

'*Certes*,' said Len.

'What do you say, Tullia?' Ptolemaeos asked Baby.

'I'm afraid I don't remember,' Baby whispered wanly.

'I'm not surprised. It was only a split second before you passed clean out. But in any case,' said Ptolemaeos, turning to Jo-Jo, 'you agree that any sign of this Lady had vanished by the time Baby fell to the ground and Len started to bend over her.'

Jo-Jo, Jean-Marie and Len all nodded.

'Very well,' said Ptolemaeos: 'Jo-Jo, you take it from there.'

'Baby was right out for the count,' Jo-Jo said, 'and nothing made any difference. She was breathing heavily and regularly, as though she were merely asleep, but nothing could wake her. Len had some Cognac, and he got the flask into her mouth and poured some down, but she slept as deep as ever. I tried tickling her' – Jo-Jo flushed slightly – 'where I know she's sensitive, and Jean-Marie blew in her ear –'

'I wish,' said Baby perking up, 'that I'd known about all this at the time –'

'– But simply nothing happened. Eventually we all agreed that she must be allowed to sleep it out and should not be moved. Jean-Marie put his jerkin under her . . . and then we all – well – huddled together for company, to keep the cold away. I shared Jean-Marie's jerkin with Baby, and the other two put their arms round us. They must have had a horrid time on the damp grass – but it didn't last long, because Baby started talking. When this happened she knelt at first and then stood, so of course we all stood up too.'

Jo-Jo paused and frowned, weighing some nicety.

'It was Baby's voice,' she said at last, 'but it wasn't Baby. This inclined me to think that . . . whatever it was . . . could not be bad. If something bad talks through the mouth of a person, then it talks in its own voice. Since we were hearing Baby's voice, I was reassured. In any case it was soon clear that the speaker had good intentions. She said . . . she said that she was called Hero, once upon a time the chief lady-in-waiting to the Despoina Xanthippe of Ilyssos. She said that Xanthippe had devoured her – or rather, that the daemon Masullaoh had devoured her, using the body and organs of Xanthippe, and that her immortal spirit had been appointed by Masullaoh to keep company with that of Xanthippe after Xanthippe's death. She wasn't actually gaoler to Xanthippe's spirit because Masullaoh had imprisoned it in Xanthippe's corpse with so powerful a spell that it could never in any case escape. The point seemed to be that Masullaoh, though angry with Xanthippe for wishing to break away from him and though determined to punish her most horribly, nevertheless loved her as he always had and wished in some way to mitigate her sentence. So he gave her Hero's soul for company, and also let her keep a miraculous image of a water-creature which he had brought to her in a dream.'

'I see,' said Ptolemaeos. 'With very slight differences Hero was taking the same line as Hubert's Appendix.'

'Yes. Masullaoh had been coming to Xanthippe ever since she was thirteen; he had presented her with the jewelled horn to intensify her orgasms (which were also, in a sense, his own, because he entered her as they took place); his visits were sudden and could be embarrassing; he demanded meat, which he consumed through the mouth and entrails of Xanthippe; he brought intelligence both of Heaven and Hell – and so on and so forth. Pretty much Hubert's line, as you say.'

'Not rationalizing? Not suggesting any commonsense explanation? Paradoxical as it sounds, you know, ghosts sometimes do.'

'Not this one. She told us – Hero did – that she had certain powers and privileges. Unlike Xanthippe, she was not tied to one place. She could move, at any rate to the ground above what had once been Xanthippe's shrine. She could make her wishes felt over quite a distance – if given someone sensitive with whom to communicate.'

Jean-Marie nodded. 'That morning under the ramparts,' he muttered.

'She could also sense any threat to her mistress's remains of dishonour or interference. Over the centuries she had been, in effect, the Guardian of Xanthippe's resting place and whatever was inside it –'

'The miraculous water-creature? The *Écrevisse*?'

'At first, yes. Thus she had been responsible for the death of the soldiers who tried to loot the shrine shortly after Xanthippe was confined to it. She had so possessed them that they savaged each other's throats with their nails and teeth. Then again, when she felt the more massive threat posed by Lord Phaedron and his men –'

'She never suggested that the *Écrevisse* might have belonged to Phaedron?'

'Certainly not. In Hero's version Lord Phaedron had heard rumours about what was in his daughter's tomb and was coming to grab it. But it wasn't his. It had been part of no dowry. It had come out of another world as Masullaoh's gift, and it was Hero's duty, with such assistance as Masullaoh might offer, to defend it. But this time the opposition was very formidable, and on Masullaoh's advice Hero decided that she and Xanthippe and the *Écrevisse* had better take refuge deeper in the earth. So Xanthippe, who was still in one piece and animated by the soul which could not leave her corpse, scrabbled and clawed a kind of tunnel down through the soil and under the donjon wall. Down this tunnel she escaped with the *Écrevisse* (only just in time, Hero said, just like it happened in Henri Martel's saga) to a lair near the well shaft, where her remains and her *Écrevisse*, with the soul of Hero, would pass the coming eternity.'

'But were very nearly found, even there.'

'It seems Masullaoh told them not to worry. The searchers would never reach them where they now were, he said. And of course we know from Henri's poem that he was right. But there was now another threat looming. Masullaoh had been disgraced. He had abused his privileges as an emissary who could move between God and Satan: he had tried to violate an Angel in Heaven, and had been sentenced, by God and Satan in concert (for they were strict respecters of each other's ordinances) to be confined for a millenium of millenia to the Nethermost Pit.

'He paid them a last visit, Hero said, on parole, so to speak, before his final committal. Hero and Xanthippe begged him to release Xanthippe's soul from her poor mouldering corpse, before he was put away, and to release Hero from her distressful charge, but he refused. If he must suffer confinement for the next million years, he said, so could they. What was more, he would need distraction: Xanthippe and Hero had each other; he would have nobody – so he would now take back the *Écrevisse* into the realms from which he had first brought it, in the hope that its brilliant presence and its haunting song of forbidden pleasure would lighten the weary centuries before him.

'How weary these would be,' Jo-Jo continued, 'Hero now understood well enough. For she and Xanthippe had passed only seven centuries together in the earth, a tiny fraction of what Masullaoh must endure, and both of them had long since desired to be utterly extinguished. For Hero it was a little better: she could at least rise to the surface, to the old entrance of the shrine of which she was Guardian, and there she could feel through the pores of her spirit (her expression) the passing of the seasons and the advent of the spent winds from the sea. But for Xanthippe . . . she was chained to her skeleton in the lair near the well shaft. The days had long since passed when her soul could bring her corpse into effective movement, for whatever her will might be the crumbling limbs were no longer capable of response. From time to time Hero tried to accost those who passed near the little bump (the sole relic of the shrine) where she was permitted to station herself, in order to rouse their pity or ask their help. But all she succeeded in doing was annoying or bewildering them: none knew the full tale, few knew any of it, and those that did thought it was the spirit of Xanthippe that was trying to speak with them, the sad ghost of the girl who had died for want of the sea; and so such men would shed a tear for her and pass on their way swiftly, having sorrows enough of their own.

'But then at last Hero the Guardian received warning that for the first time in many centuries men were coming to seek the *Écrevisse*. That it had long since gone, taken by Masullaoh, made no matter: the soul of Hero had been endowed with an instinct that told her when there was threat to the *Écrevisse* or to her mistress, and such a threat, in intent, now approached. But she also realised something else through her instinct: that these seekers, unlike those who passed over the shrine from time to time and could not understand what she would tell them – that *these* seekers all knew the full history of her mistress, and there was one among them who might, at last, be able to bring help.'

Jo-Jo paused and looked at Baby, who seemed pre-occupied.

'Did you know you were saying all this?' Jo-Jo asked.

'I knew it was being said to *me*,' Baby replied. 'Or rather, it wasn't actually said, but somehow the sense of it all was communicated.'

'So you acted as interpreter,' said Tom Llewyllyn, 'and passed it on to the rest of them?'

'I suppose I must have done, since they all heard it.'

'Can you remember,' said Jo-Jo, 'what was communicated to you next?'

Baby nodded, wary and somewhat embarrassed.

'Hero had sensed,' said Baby, 'that I had a special love for Xanthippe . . . which Hero thought might save Xanthippe, might indeed save both of them; for if Xanthippe could be released from her prison, then Hero would be released from her duty as Guardian and companion. And so Hero asked if I would come with her to meet Xanthippe; and when I told her that I could not physically accompany her into the earth, she began to plead.'

'You heard this, Len?' said Ptolemaeos.

'Sure I heard it,' said Len. 'It was heartrending. Hero was saying that here at last was someone who might be their saviour, someone whose love might break the bonds of Masullaoh's forging – and now this person refused to come to Xanthippe. You see, Hero seemed to think that Baby could just scrabble through the earth like the corpse of Xanthippe had done, when seeking a deeper lair. Hero had been so long dead that she had forgotten the limitations placed on the human body. So here she was, pleading and howling at Baby – and this was the more horrible, because Baby was still inter- preting and was therefore pleading and howling at herself, if you get me.'

'Yes,' said Ptolemaeos: 'I get you. What happened then?'

'What happened,' said Jo-Jo, eyes shining, 'was Jean-Marie. He doesn't speak much English yet, but I was keeping him *au fait*, and when he realised what Hero wanted and why Baby had to refuse, he said to me: "You are close to this lady, I think, this little Canteloupe. Can you make yourself heard by her . . . while she is in this state?" And I said I thought I just might, although I had failed before, when the trance first came on her. "Then tell her," said Jean-Marie, "that if she is willing, I can bring here tomorrow men who will make a path to this . . . this place where dwells Xanthippe; and then she can meet with her. For I too love Xanthippe," said Jean-Marie, "and now that it is at last clear to me how things are with her, I would well wish her to be freed."

'So,' said Jo-Jo, 'I came and stood very close to Baby, who was still pleading and whimpering to herself on behalf of Hero, and I did something to her which she really goes for – not just the half-hearted kind of goosing which I'd tried before – and I did it with all my knowledge and my love of her. She stopped quarrelling, went limp, said my name. Then she went horribly taut, as though something inside her was insisting on her attention. So before things could get any worse, I spoke Jean-Marie's message into her ear, hoping that she would hear it and translate it to Hero, or that Hero would contrive to pick it up, that *somehow* it would get through. And so it did, thank Heaven. Baby was still again. I knew everything was all right because she kissed me, kissed me like the first time we were ever together, such a kiss as there are not many in a girl's life . . . and just as well, perhaps.'

And then Baby had drawn Jo-Jo to her once more, as the two men left them. For a long time neither spoke, until at last Baby said:

'Hero is content. She says that Xanthippe and she will wait patiently, now that they know I am coming. Oh hold me, darling Jo-Jo, for I am so afraid.'

SINCE THE AGREED FORTY-FIVE MINUTES after the sorbets had now passed, the partridges were served.

'Well,' said the Princesse d'Héricourt-en-Caux to Provost Llewyllyn, 'what shall we think of all this?'

'I think,' said Tom, 'that they are telling the truth . . . what they believe to be the truth.'

'But as that M'sieur Ptolemaeos, he says, there will be another way of explanation.'

'No doubt, Madam. My worry at the moment is that my daughter may be worn out if we continue to pursue this one. She has been quite ill with it all, you know.'

The Princesse peered left, past Jean-Marie, at Baby, who was eating steadily but keeping an uncharacteristic silence. Then Mme d'Héricourt spoke crisply to Jean-Marie, received a careful and even earnest reply, and turned back to Tom.

'That young Guiscard, he says the little Canteloupe will be all right. He was worried, he says, that she might be jealous and unhappy when he took her Jo-Jo. But that is all *en règle*.

The little Canteloupe wants her friend to have a husband, that she may stand as godmother to the first-born infant. As for their loving together, it has come to a splendid and wonderful ending, and now they can be friends of the heart, one with the other, and never so much as hold hands.'

'I see,' Tom conceded. 'But how and when did this . . . wonderful ending . . . come about? That night near the donjon? After which Jean-Marie perhaps insisted that they should cease to be . . . what they were to each other?'

The Princesse gave Jean-Marie a patrician tap on the shoulder, took aim, and let him have it right between the eyes. Jean-Marie look rather hurt but answered civilly enough. Mme la Princesse turned once more to Tom.

'Jean-Marie, he says that he insist on nothing. It is not his way, to insist. Things happened as they happened, as you shall hear after these so delectable *Perdreaux*.'

THIRTY MINUTES were to be allowed between the partridges and the crêpes for the continuation of the debate. As the two octogenarians carried the last cleanly-picked carcass from the dining room, Ptolemaeos invited Jean-Marie to describe how the emergency team which he had assembled probed the ground for Xanthippe's lair.

'The problem was,' Jo-Jo translated, 'whether to follow the route supposedly taken by Xanthippe herself, from the crypt of the shrine, under the donjon wall, and then towards the well; or whether to adopt the method which Len had been told to adopt and dig straight down inside the donjon.'

'Easier, surely,' Len interposed.

'Yes . . . *if* they could get the mechanical excavator into the donjon, through the gap and over the ditch, and arrange it in the correct position. In the end it was decided that it would be preferable to tunnel under the donjon wall. For technical reasons there was less chance of damage being done to – er – to what they were looking for, if they came in on the flank. On the other hand the exact question of the depth at which their quarry lay was a difficult one. They did not want to tunnel over, or under, Xanthippe and straight on into the well.'

'Should have gone down like me,' Len said.

'Unlike you,' said Jo-Jo, 'they got on with their work, and when they had cleared the foundations of the donjon, Baby heard Hero again. She was calling this time from a distance and could only make herself fully understood, she said, if Baby came to the bump in the ground, the old entrance of the shrine, where she had seen and heard Hero last night. So thither Baby went, and from there relayed through me to Jean-Marie quite helpful instructions from Hero as to how to approach . . . *chez Xanthippe.*'

And so the day had gone on in a pretty humdrum way. Baby called out directions, for all the world as if she were an overseer instead of the medium for a long dead girl from the Mani, whose remains had lain in the Castle moat for over seven hundred years. Baby called out the directions, and the manipulators of the mechanical shovel responded, and the spademen sifted the earth carefully at the shovel's side and in its wake, and as the afternoon drew on they came to what they sought.

'A skull, separated from the backbone,' said Jo-Jo prosaically; 'a pelvis, still attached to the backbone, but separated from the thigh bones, which were in turn separated from the shins and feet. Two arms, still attached to the collar-bone; two little star-fish claws for hands, detached at the wrists. The Despoina Xanthippe of Ilyssos, Princess of the Mani.'

'Who spoke to me,' Baby said, 'much as Hero had spoken. But with Xanthippe I had . . . I had to touch her, touch the skeleton so that the soul imprisoned there could flow into me and tell me her message.'

For a long while she was silent. Tom sat strained and white; Canteloupe sat with two huge tears poised on his lower eyelids. Minute succeeded minute.

'And the message, Tullia?' Ptolemaeos very gently said.

'Already I had asked Jean-Marie to go away and take the workmen. Then I asked Len to go. Then Xanthippe told me I must ask Jo-Jo to go too, and I said no, Jo-Jo must stay, I wasn't quite sure why, but she must stay, at least for the present, until I had learned more of what Xanthippe would tell me.

'After this she seemed happy about Jo-Jo's staying, and then she began. Once or twice Hero tried to correct or interrupt her, but when that happened Xanthippe always put her down, not nastily, but reminding her, as she must have done when they were alive, that she should not interrupt her mistress, however concerned she might be for her, however good her intentions. I thought this was a bit hard after all that time Hero had stayed there for Xanthippe's sake, but Hero herself took it as a matter of course, and after all it wasn't as if Hero had stayed voluntarily . . . though I suppose she might have, if the question had arisen. For she was all loyalty; loyalty but not, I think, love; loyalty to the House of Ilyssos, not to Xanthippe alone . . . more to her father Phaedron, I think . . . and there seemed to be some other, a son of Phaedron's, perhaps.'

Baby looked distressed.

'I could not make that out,' she said.

'Tell us,' said Ptolemaeos, 'what was it the Lady Xanthippe wished to say to you?'

'Ah. She seemed to think that I could plead with God on her behalf. Masullaoh had been a neutral spirit; he had offended God but was currently imprisoned in the realm of Satan. Either God or Satan could undo what Masullaoh had done, but surely God was the more concerned with mercy. She had prayed to God through the centuries and he had not answered; but then why should he, for after all she had been a poor thing when alive, a poor thing who had been enticed by a jewelled trinket, an enamelled image of a water-creature, instead of looking to her soul when it was in danger; so perhaps Masullaoh's sentence had had the approval of God. She had rebelled against Masullaoh, or tried to, because neutral or no he had too much of the Devil in his conversation and activities: but he had coaxed her back to him with a dream and the gift of this golden and ruby and sweet-voiced creature of the waters, which came, she knew, from the realm of Satan. So she had been untrue to both – to Masullaoh and to God, and perhaps God

221

had approved the sentence passed upon her by Massulaoh. At any rate God had not answered her prayer, had not perhaps even heard it. Perhaps he would hear and answer mine – the prayer of someone that loved Xanthippe and was pleading for her; for surely God prized such love as this.'

Baby drank off a glass of deep red wine, then looked very thoughtfully at her father, Tom, and after him at her husband, Canteloupe.

'When I was still very young,' Baby said, 'my mother used to tell me what it would have been like for me if I'd been born a little boy. I should have had this interesting thing which went stiff, she said . . . and so on and so forth. Later on, when I first knew Canteloupe, he sometimes used to talk of the Greek word "α'ναγκη", which meant "necessity", or the "necessary structure" of a situation, what is *given* as they used to say in the geometry books, either because it is there in a particular case or is axiomatic in the general condition. Thus my mother's hypothesis, "if you had been born a boy", was irrelevant, worse than irrelevant: it was a denial of order, even a blasphemy, because it ignored reality, it ignored what had been *given* by God. On the other hand, it had a powerful magic as a source of erotic musing and constituted an ingenious effort to establish, if only in the imagination, an alternative and private world – a rival to God's.

'Now, with some shift of emphasis,' Baby went on, 'there was a hint here as to what might be done about Xanthippe. It was clear to me that God had forgotten her, or simply did not care about her: for that an innocent girl (*in herself* she must have been innocent) should have been condemned to such a hideous fate and then left unheard and unheeded for so long was quite unthinkable – unless one assumed either that God no longer knew of her predicament or that for some reason of his own (very difficult to fathom) he had deliberately put her out of his mind. But surely God was omniscient, could never forget anything: therefore his heedlessness must have been purposeful. Perhaps her innocence really had not been enough to recommend her to his mercy: perhaps he felt that she should indeed have struggled harder against Masullaoh: perhaps he thought that since Masullaoh had found her attractive and had come to her in the first place, she was somehow tainted from the beginning (if by no fault of her own) and must be excluded from his charity, thrust out from his kingdom lest she contaminated it. In which case it was clear that no amount of *pleading* on my part was going to move God; He would have to be *shamed* into saving Xanthippe.

'In order to shame him, I thought, one must show him what human love could do. One must deliberately do what my mother had done (though with a different emphasis and from a very different motive) – one must create a rival world, a private one, which defied necessity, went beyond the bounds which God had ordained, and so protested against his law and its vile application to Xanthippe. If we, out of love for Xanthippe, can do this thing (we should be telling God), braving all your most terrible sanctions in order to bring Xanthippe to your attention again, surely you, in your charity, can at last relent and release her. So the central element in our protest or blasphemy (there are times when the two words mean much the same thing), the central feature of our whole endeavour, must be a specific denial of Necessity, an assumption, so whole-heartedly acted upon that it would amount to an assertion, that something, which was not and never could be the case, nevertheless *was* the case.'

'You say "our",' said des Veules-les-Roses; 'you say "we". You were not to do this by yourself then?'

'I might have done, but I had not the strength or the courage.' Baby rose and walked round the table to Jo-Jo, on whose shoulders she lightly rested both hands. 'It needed a stouter heart than mine. I had love; I needed will. Tell them, my darling,' Baby said to Jo-Jo, 'how you gave me that will.'

Punctual to the second, the crêpes were served.

'TELL ME,' said Len to des Veules-les-Roses, 'how much do you know about the other side of all this?'

'The other side?'

'The other, the rational, explanation.'

'A very great deal, as it happens. But we must not antici-pate.'

'Dear me, no,' said Len. 'It's just that I'm bothered about one little thing. When I first got into this, we were discussing who made that burrow under Xanthippe's shrine . . . the one through which she and the *Écrevisse* supposedly made their way to a lair near the well. Now, on Baby's showing so far, Xanthippe dug it – while she was still sound enough to activate her limbs by the power of her soul. But in a rational and realistic approach something else will have to be proposed. The strong suggestion here the other evening, when I was first allowed to join the party, was – rats.'

Des Veules-les-Roses nodded.

'Someone was bound to mention them at some stage,' he said.

'Oh yes. But you see, although I don't want to boast, I have to tell you that I have a kind of empathy thing with rats★ – or did once – and I just know, as I had to tell Jo-Jo several times (she was so insistent), that this *could not* have been their work. They'd never heave a heavy metal object about, for one thing. A body, yes, in certain circumstances, but not this *Écrevisse* that's talked of. So . . . strictly no rats here.'

Des Veules-les-Roses nodded again.

'Why are *you* being so insistent?' he said.

'Because although I'm happy to wait long and patiently for the other explanation, I don't want any time-wasting when once we get to it. So please assure me, since you know a thing or two about what's coming, please assure me if you can that when we arrive at a second and "natural" explanation of that burrow, no one is going to spout bloody balls about rats.'

'"Bloody balls"?' M. le Marquis said.

'*Merde.*'

'I can absolutely assure you,' said des Veules-les-Roses, 'that nobody is going to spout *merde* about rats.'

★See *The Roses of Picardie*

224

THE PORT was put on immediately after the crêpes in order that a health might be drunk to Our Lady the Queen and those present might now be free to smoke if they wished. The next stage of the debate was to take place while the decanter circulated for thirty minutes, after which there would be a service of coffee, Cognac, Armagnac, Calvados, the Marcs of Burgundy, Champagne, Provence and the Loire, Vieille Prune, Poire William and Framboise. Rightly or wrongly, Ptolemaeos opined that the later and more rational depositions that were to be made, being of their nature comparatively sober, could only be improved by strong drink.

But meanwhile, after the royal health had been drunk ('God bless Her Majesty,' called Captain the Marquess Canteloupe, with the privilege of an officer of Horse), Jo-Jo resumed the story as Baby had asked.

'By now the afternoon was well on,' Jo-Jo said. 'Jean-Marie had seen the workmen off, and had returned to keep "Cave" with Len. There were quite a few people around in the warm autumn evening, and they were made curious by the tunnel which led under the foundations of the donjon. But Len and Jean-Marie, who had a very fierce official card with him, let none of them beyond the tilting yard, and inside the four walls of the donjon Baby and I were left in peace.

'The assumption, the assertion, that had to be made was that if Xanthippe's soul was still attached to her body then she was still alive. What Baby and I were going to say to God was this: human love requires us to treat her as a living human being, and if you don't like it you have only yourself to blame, because it is all the result of your cruelty. So now take heed: repent and let her go. This was the way in which we were going to shame God into freeing her.'

And so as the shadows gathered in the donjon Baby and Jo-Jo made love to each other and to the poor broken bones of

Xanthippe, talking to her the while, clasping her head and caressing her arms and thighs, taking care she had close part in all their pleasure, plighting their love for her by making her privy to their love for one another. As they came towards their goal (which men call the little death), Xanthippe's voice was joined with theirs in celebration, until she cried out that she must leave them, and her presence ceased.

★ ★ ★

'Time to toast Xanthippe,' said Ivan Barraclough, 'and wish her a good deliverance.'

The decanter went round in silence. When they had all filled, Potolemaeos said:

'I think we should know one thing more before we drink. What, meanwhile, was happening to Hero?'

'She thanked me for what had been done,' said Baby, 'and told me that although she was now free of her charge, for the time being at least she could follow her mistress.'

'Where to?' Ivan asked.

'Hero said that first of all Xanthippe would do what many souls of the Maniots did: she would visit the places where she had lived, in order to see with the eye of her soul what her soul could not see while in the living body, since then it had been dead. "And then?" I said. "When she has been back to Greece and to Ilyssos, will she journey across the Wilderness and approach the Throne?"'

Baby paused and giggled.

'"I do not know," Hero said, "for myself or for Xanthippe. You see, gratitude requires that if we do indeed voyage over the Wilderness, if we do indeed enter the Courts and approach the Throne, then it must be the Throne of that Being who has heard your cries of love and been moved to pity and release us – the Throne of Satan."'

INVITED TO COMMENT on Baby's and Jo-Jo's depositions, which were corroborated, in most matters of circumstance, topography and appearance, by Jean-Marie and Len,
the auditors gave various opinions. Ivan Barraclough remarked that everything Baby and Jo-Jo had vouched for was
entirely consistent with the Appendix to Hubert's Chronicle,
with Henri Martel's eye-witness if rather frenzied account of
the opening of the shrine by Phaedron, and with such pieces of
inscription, sculpture and monumental masonry as he himself
had often inspected in Greece and beyond, and had indeed
been inspecting once more when interrupted in his recent
journey.

Ptolemaeos countered this by saying that if anything the
girls' account was *too* consistent with the sources cited. Two
impressionable and romantic young ladies, excitably in love
with each other, one of them about to fall in love with
Jean-Marie as well, both of them no doubt sexually disturbed
by the Mephistophelean attractions of Len – two such young
ladies, being emotionally stirred by the tragic tale and hideous
situation of (so to speak) a spiritual contemporary, might well
begin to hear voices, see figures and feel presences and com-
munications of just this kind – which were all, in fact, derived
from the basic matter of Hubert and Henri. This had been
deeply absorbed by the two girls, had been processed by their
subconscious minds to include their *egos* and fit in with their
fantasies, and had only too obviously been delivered back
again in their recent imaginative and indeed hysterical projec-
tion.

When Baby and Jo-Jo looked sad at this, Ptolemaeos tem-
pered his judgment by saying that theirs was a poetic and
intuitive version, containing an important message about the
human heart, but not constituting the literal truth . . . if only

because it was demonstrably and damnably inaccurate in one very important instance.

'Before the coffee,' said Ptolemaeos, 'we have a dish not mentioned in the menu.'

He made a sign, whereupon one of the twins brought in a nobly canopied silver dish. It was set before Ptolemaeos, who grasped a handle in the shape of a salamander and slowly lifted the canopy . . . to reveal a giant *Écrevisse* of gold, ruby, diamond, emerald and finely-worked enamel.

'So you see,' Ptolemaeos said, 'whoever removed it from its hiding place in the Castle, it cannot have been the daemon Masullaoh, nor was it taken to the Nethermost Pit . . . unless, that is, I have procured it thence on loan, which I assure you is not the case.'

THE RE WAS NOW A SERVICE OF COFFEE and digestifs. Nobody said anything after the production of the *Écrevisse*, until Len at last enquired:

'Can it still move about and play its music?'

'No. The mechanism was a kind of clockwork made of relatively perishable materials. Gold and precious stones can survive almost anything, and enamel can survive a good deal so long as it is not deliberately battered. But the metal used in a piece of clockwork – no. The little bells survive on which the tune was played; but not the clappers which played it nor the cogs which moved them.'

'Just as well, perhaps,' said Ivan Barraclough. 'To judge from Hubert's description, that tune would not have improved the moral flavour of the occasion.'

'I don't know,' said Ptolemaeos looking slily round the room. 'I should have thought it might have been rather appropriate.'

'The object is . . . genuine?' enquired Canteloupe diffidently.

'Undoubtedly. It corresponds exactly with the description in the Byzantine Catalogue of the Artefact made for the eighth-century Sebastocrator Demosthenes Commenos, from whom it was subsequently looted at sea by a piratical ancestor of the Lord Phaedron of Ilyssos. The metals and the stones have been checked by experts whom I had down from London yesterday, while the insurance premiums, so long as it remains in this house and not in a bank, are positively cosmic. Its identity and its value – now perhaps as high as ten million sterling – are beyond any possible dispute.'

'So,' said Len, 'now you've got the bugger, what are you going to do with it?'

'A very nice question,' Ptolemaeos said. 'In any case whatever, I am first going to tell you how it comes to be here, and in the course of the story to propound a theory about the mystery of the Despoina Xanthippe altogether different from the one which we have just heard. As I say, I think it possible that Tullia and Jo-Jo may have divined an important truth about the human heart and the human soul (if any); but they, so to speak, have proposed and elaborated a metaphor, while I am about to construct a scientific explanation.'

Ptolemaeos poured himself about a decilitre of Vieille Prune, then selected, listened to and lit a cigar. He began:

'M'sieur le Marquis des Veules-les-Roses; Madame la Princesse; Mister Provost; my lord, ladies and gentlemen: my dear friends:

'As Ivan Barraclough has observed, the story told by Tullia Canteloupe and my niece Jo-Jo is entirely consistent with his own researches and with the Appendix to the Chronicle of Hubert of Avallon; and it is of course this Appendix on which this whole endeavour has been largely based. But the question we must ask ourselves is whether it is to be interpreted literally, whether we are to take at face value the visits from Masullaoh, and the imprisonment of Xanthippe's soul in her own rotting corpse, and so on and so forth; and the answer must almost certainly be "no". Discussing this matter with Jo-Jo the other day, I proffered the following theory. First of all, I said, Hubert dictated the Chronicle of Avallon, a work quite well known ever since, the official handout about the

Lady Xanthippe, more or less in line with Henri Martel's equally well-known Ballad on the subject, but containing just a hint or two, for the sake of verisimilitude, that all was not entirely well with the Despoina, that she was not at any rate perfect.

'Next, I conjectured, he was attacked by his conscience, which told him he must tell the whole truth; and the whole truth was that the Lady suffered from a species of epileptic mania which caused her to masturbate in frenzy (and often in public) and then to devour raw meat like a beast of the jungle. The disease also had such ancillary symptoms as feverish dreams, when the fit was over, and an obsessive urge to steal and sequester glittering or colourful objects, a grave embarrassment when she was visiting the houses or castles of others. All this was closely controlled or concealed by Hero, called her chief maiden-in-waiting but in truth her nurse, who could usually recognise the signs of an approaching seizure and get Xanthippe out of the way before its onset, who helped her to masturbate as fiercely as she was impelled to but without harming herself, provided her with raw meat, heard her and soothed her after her dreams, and gave her pretty things to play with (often from her dowry chest) in order to keep her from expropriating those of her hosts. These were the facts, as I conjectured to Jo-Jo, which Hubert felt should go on record in order that history and truth might not be mocked; they need not be made public, these facts, but they must be recorded.

'The trouble was that Hubert could not bear to record them. He tried; he started; but when it came to the point he could not dictate, to the learned monk who was writing down his story, such squalid and degrading things of the young Princess whom he had guarded and loved. And so, I speculated, he transformed the Despoina's pitiful and horrible illness into something dark and mysterious and grand and powerful. Instead of masturbating she now offered her body that a daemon might enter it; she did not gobble raw flesh, she devoured whole sheep or oxen to refresh her daemon lover within her; when she dreamt, she was transported to Heaven or Hell; she no longer craved or pilfered pretty trinkets, she was handed strange and magnificent gifts while lingering in her dreams by Styx or Phlegethon and allowed by special favour to carry them back with her into this world.

'In this way, I surmised, Hubert salved his conscience by describing something like her actual behaviour but at the same time saved her face and served his love by transposing it into something magical, something unearthly, something almost numinous. Served by spirits and privileged to converse with angels, Xanthippe was not just a wretched little epileptic frothing at the mouth: she was Medaea, she was Hecate of the Three Ways, she was the Witch of Endor; and to top it all, she met an end far more haunting and appalling than that of Faust himself. This was the illusion which Hubert wished to promote; but all the time, of course, she was in reality the squalid and violent victim of the falling sickness which he wished to conceal. She was ill – no more and no less. Surely such a conclusion,' said Ptolemaeos turning to Barraclough, 'would be consistent with *your* researches.'

'Broadly, yes,' conceded Barraclough. 'Obviously the depictions and records of Xanthippe's progress through the Peloponnese and elsewhere were based on her *observed behaviour*. As far as this went, although the impression she gave was not entirely wholesome, and although superstitious idioms or images were occasionally used in describing her (e.g. the imp who is stimulating her genitals at Karyteina), it is nevertheless clear that she is regarded as being abnormal or pitiable *on a human scale* rather than as the grand supernatural phenomenon of Hubert's Legend.'

'So you have no complaint about my interpretation of the Appendix? That it was, to sum up, a hyperbolical and metaphorical device to conceal a pitiful illness?'

'You have yet to prove this interpretation,' said Ivan Barraclough, 'and in this connection there is one surviving monument which must be carefully considered. The Chapel of Our Lady of the Sea-Marshes, near Dubrovnik. There is an effigy of one of her ancestors, resting on its own tomb, which she naturally visited while in Dubrovnik with Hubert. The effigy would appear to have been so shocked, so horrified by whatever was . . . informing or attending her, surely in this instance something more sinister than mere illness . . . that its shape and facial expression were fundamentally altered. I have examined them several times myself, and I can only describe them as tormented.'

'Time, weather, salt and damp,' said Ptolemaeos. 'There is also, I think, some question of an earthquake – almost certainly, at that latitude, of many earthquakes.'

'I think the burden of proof, of your interpretation of the Appendix, still lies heavily on you.'

'Granted,' said Ptolemaeos. 'And I can't possibly prove the version I've just given because it simply isn't true. I gave it only as an *example* of how the allegories of the Appendix (for allegories of some kind they must surely be) *might* be translated back into natural, worldly terms. Let us start again – when we have recharged our glasses. This time I shall be aiming to kill.'

'SO WHAT DO YOU THINK NOW?' said the Princess of Héricourt-en-Caux to Provost Llewyllyn, as the chariot of digestifs clanked round the table.

'I have always pinned my faith in rational deduction from proven evidence,' said Tom, pouring himself a royal measure of Marc de Champagne, 'and I do not expect to be disappointed tonight.'

'And yet,' said the Princess, 'you would not, you could not, repudiate the suggestion that chance, the most fiendish and improbable chance, may have been at work even within a logical and rational context.'

'I should expect any rational solution, even of a baroque affair like this one, to be, *at bottom*, pretty commonplace and prosaic.'

'But surely,' said the Princess, 'you are famous for your books on the *Random Nature* of things. Of power, for example. You believe, you do not, in strong elements of the unexpected.'

'Only because there are so many factors which we must try

to anticipate that we cannot compute all of them. Inevitably there are omissions, even gross omissions, and the factors omitted are in that sense unexpected and are therefore seen as random. In reality they have merely been overlooked, and are as commonplace and prosaic as any other.'

'Perhaps they deliberately camouflaged themselves,' teased the Princess.

'Not a rational conception,' said Tom.

'No? Well then, perhaps God deliberately camouflaged them?'

The Provost Select smiled in polite scepticism.

'You wait and see, my learned friend,' Madame la Princesse said.

'WE HAVE JUST EXAMINED,' said Ptolemaeos, 'the possibility of Hubert's having deliberately dictated a text which was false as to fact but significant as metaphor or allegory. We have also examined one set of possible motives for so doing. But although I think I was right about Hubert's technique of falsification, I have already admitted that I was wrong in my interpretation of his saga and I now further and freely admit that I was wrong in the motives which I imputed to him. In order to understand the full truth which lay behind his lucubrations, we must now take an entirely new point of departure. Aristarchos of Thessaly,' Ptolemaeos said: 'the Mage Aristarchos.

'This gentleman encountered Xanthippe on Corfu, saw that all was not well with her, and offered her a supply of a herb which he had gathered on the island in the Lake of Ioannina – in exchange for her own confidential account of her clinical symptoms. In none of this need we doubt the word of Hubert.

'But his account of the properties of Aristarchos's herb must make us blink a little. Apparently it enables a man to exercise total control over his own soul, and through the soul of his

233

body, if he administers it to himself, and total control of the soul and body of another if he himself administer it to that other. Rather a long order, one tells oneself. Why should a herb which grows in the fabric of a little chapel on an island in a lake possess these powers? Well, I reply, and why not? I have friends nearby who own a meadow in which grows a certain type of mushroom: eat it raw, and you will be entertained, for some hours, to the most brilliant hallucinations. So why not a herb that possesses the soul instead of deluding it? In any case, Aristarchos' herb has been tested. Some time ago now Ivan sent me a sample which I submitted to a discreet aquaintance in the laboratories in Cambridge. The scientific truth about it is very simple: it heightens the *ego*, it enormously strengthens the *ego*'s command of mental will and bodily effort – but it also transfers control of that *ego* to the person who has the power to apportion and administer the herb. If I administer the herb to myself, I retain control of my own *ego*, which enormously gains in power. If I give it to another his *ego* falls under my control, because he has accepted the herb from my hands, and he will obey my most trivial or most abominable command.'

'As I have seen for myself,' Ivan Barraclough said, remembering the fat Greek with the winkle-pickers on the island in the lake.

'Why this transferred control of the *ego*, you may well ask? The crude answer,' Potolemaeos pursued, 'is that Aristarchos' herb operates, in some respects, rather like certain truth drugs: just as these latter induce psychic subjection to the interrogator in the person who is being interrogated, so this herb persuades him who tastes it to subordinate himself, his *ego*, his soul, to the donor. Or again, the working of the herb may be compared with an Amazonian drug, sometimes used as an anaesthetic, which paralyses the body and renders it immune from pain but otherwise allows it to retain full consciousness and powers of perception.

'Such, then, were the powers inherent in the herb with which Aristarchos furnished Xanthippe in exchange for her description of her illness, which was, we postulate, an intense form of epilepsy that had troubled her from her early pubescence. The herb might help her, Aristarchos said: it would enable her to govern her soul. Let her chew the leaf when she felt herself about to succumb to one of her fits, let her command her soul, and through her soul her body, to be still, and she would find peace. And with that, exit Aristarchos. Xanthippe now wonders what, if anything, to do with the herb and consults Hero. Clearly, Hero says, no herb can give Xanthippe or anyone else power over a soul which they know, from their religious teaching, is dead in the tomb of the body and will not be awakened or released until the physical death of that body. But might the herb not work on the living spirit which controls the body, Xanthippe now suggests: for they know that there is a kind of substitute soul, the "*thymos*", which operates the brain and the nervous system in the absence of the soul itself; might not the herb give her powers over this "*thymos*", and thus enable her to check the horrible fits?

'At this stage, we may imagine, Hero becomes the heavy nanny, and treats Xanthippe as if she'd been accepting sweeties from a strange gentleman. Who is this Aristarchos, Hero would like to know, and just what is he up to, we don't know anything about him or his herb, God knows what will happen to Xanthippe if she starts eating that sort of rubbish. There are worse things than fits, when all is said, and they've learnt to deal with them quite tidily, thank you, and if my Lady knows what's good for her, she'll throw those nasty little leaves away and forget them.'

'Hero was quite right, in a way,' Ivan Barraclough put in. 'She instinctively felt what I myself discovered by accident only the other day. That herb can raise sheer disaster if given to someone who is allergic to it. If Xanthippe had taken it and turned out to be allergic to it, she would indeed have learned that there are worse things than epileptic fits. The chap I gave it to nearly tore his own eyes out.'

'In fact,' said Ptolemaeos, 'and as you will learn later, Xanthippe was not allergic to the herb: it worked on her as it was meant to work, as Aristarchos said it would work. But for the time being, Hero's natural caution prevailed; and although Xanthippe did not throw the leaves away, she put them up in an onyx box and for a long while she thought no more of them.

'But none of this had gone unremarked by Lalage, the second lady-in-waiting, or by Hubert. And it was at this stage that Lalage began to work on Hubert (who was, let us remember, in overall charge of the party) and to propose a scheme inspired both by vindictiveness and greed.

'You see, Lalage hated her mistress. Why should she serve anyone so disgusting simply because of an accident which made her inferior in birth and rank? And again Lalage, who came of a relatively poor family, needed a dowry: why not possess herself of part at least of Xanthippe's? And yet again, Lalage knew that Hubert was in trouble. His business on his estates in Avallon, the ostensible reason for his voyage, was trifling – not the kind of thing to bring a man all the way from Achaea to Burgundy: what was really in train (so Lalage had heard from one of Hubert's pages in exchange for a round of hot cockles) was an ecclesiastical suit which was being secretly threatened by the Bishop of Sens. Unless Hubert provided a very substantial sum of ready money as a "gift" to one of my lord Bishop's "Charities", the Bishop was going to charge Hubert with having married within the prohibited degrees of consanguinity, a conviction on which ground would make a bastard of his young son and heir and would in any case lead to the immediate forfeiture of all the lands and honours which this son stood to inherit. So Hubert was going home to bribe his way out of this fix, and Lalage reckoned that he would be only too happy, in all the circumstances, to grab the opportunity she was about to offer him.'

'Now just stop there,' said Ivan Barraclough. 'All this is the purest speculation, based on nothing whatever.'

'It is indeed somewhat conjectural,' replied Ptolemaeos, 'but it is a plausible introduction to what is coming next, and *that* I can prove absolutely.'

'Then kindly do so,' said Ivan. 'I don't think you are entitled to go a step further with this rigmarole without offering concrete evidence.'

'Very well,' said Ptolemaeos. 'Madame la Princesse d'Héricourt, we hang upon your lips, Madame.'

'A mile or two from the little town of Cany-Barville in Normandy,' the Princess said, 'stands the house in which I live with *M'sieur mon frère*. Five minutes' walk from that house, over a meadow and at the junction of two little rivers, stands our Chapel, which is generally known as the Église of Barville. Just opposite the south door of this chapel is a small house, in which lives our – er – dependant, who is called Claudine de la Cochonerie. She is cleaner and caretaker of the chapel, and is charged to ensure that the wrong sort of person does not get inside it.'

'The wrong sort of person?' queried Tom Llewyllyn, the residual socialist.

'People who would not appreciate it, M'sieur.'

'And how does Claudine tell?'

'She has developed a nose over the years, as sutlers develop a nose for corked wine. There are, you see, certain curiosities about this chapel which we would not wish to be tampered with. It is now mainly of the fifteenth century, though the chancel is much earlier (of brick, which is rare for the region) and goes back to the thirteenth. In the chancel there is a set of fourteenth-century misericords under some of the seats in the choir stalls. The most famous is that of a lady, who is flagrantly amusing herself on the rampart of a Castle. It is popularly supposed, though the misericord was carved over a century after the death of the Lady Xanthippe, that the sculptor had the Lady in mind, for there was considerable local lore about her.

'Now the other day, despite the vigilance of Claudine, this misericord was damaged by two of the wrong sort of person, and we had to call in Jean-Marie Guiscard to treat it. *N'est-ce pas, Jean-Marie?*'

'*Mais oui, Madame.*'

'While he was there, he also gave treatment to the other misericords, which for sixty years have been obscure to look upon and the more obscure as the chancel of our chapel has one great peculiarity – there is no east window.★ Now, however,

★As he who goes to Barville may see for himself, if he approach the Chapel from the road to the east of it. He is unlikely, however, to be able to verify the interior features described by the Princess, as the Chapel is nowadays kept locked and Claudine has been instructed to open it to nobody – for reasons which will become abundantly plain before this narrative concludes.

S.R.

in honour of this good young man's clever work, lanterns and torches were brought to the chancel, and the misericords, which we had all but forgotten, my brother and I, were all looked upon with great interest and esteem. Next to Xanthippe, and east of her, was one of a sea-monster ridden by two mermaids; then one of a man and a woman, who are attending a dead or sleeping body; another one of the sea-monster, who is this time devouring the mermaids head first; and one of three small crowns, which exactly resemble the three crowns carven on the stone shield in the exterior wall just above the south door.* Another matter of interest was that the mermaids with the monster were executed in very much the same style as two mermaids that are carved on another stone over the south door,** flanking a Baron's helm beneath which appears the motto of the Martels of Longueil and (later) of Les Veules-les-Roses, *Mihi Placet* (I Decree). The chief point of resemblance between the mermaids carved in wood and those carved in stone lay in the tails, which were crustacean rather than piscine, the inference being (as from the resemblance between the two sets of crowns) that the same man who had carved the misericords also carved the exterior tablets.

'None of which you may consider much to our present purpose, or indeed to any purpose. But the matter fascinated Claudine, who is of surly and obstinate temperament, very persistent when her concern or curiosity is aroused. Who were these mermaids, she wanted to know, and what were the crowns? The answers which we proposed to keep her happy were that the mermaids were there for the fun of the thing, a sport of the mason who had carved them, and that the three crowns were those of the Three Kings who came to adore our Infant Saviour on the Twelfth Night – for so my brother and I had always been told as children, and had continued to believe (as one does, if firmly instructed in the tender years) for all our lives thereafter. By why, she urged, were the mermaids in control of the monster on one misericord but being eaten by it on a later one? Because, we said (as our nursemaid had

*Still prominent.
**Still prominent.

instructed us) they had gone too far: not content with riding on the monster's back, they had made injurious remarks about its personal appearance.

'Claudine accepted these answers *pro tempore* and went away to mull them over. Four days later she appeared with a very peculiar look on her face, compounded of insolence, apprehension, self-applause and something like awe, and invited us to the chapel to be given a true interpretation of the carvings. Tomorrow, we said; but she was exigent: a duty was owed, she told us, that could not wait. When we still demurred, she became very insulting' – the Princess exchanged a wry look with her brother – 'as only she knows how to be, and when this threatened to become intolerable, we put on our walking clothes and went with her to the chapel.

'First she halted us by the south door. Three crowns, she said: the sign of the Three Kings, as if to say that there is something within which is worthy of adoration or amazement.

'Mermaids, associated with the baronial helm of the early Martels, she said, must mean creatures of an extraordinary kind somehow connected with the fortunes of the house, probably creatures who had come from afar by sea.

'Then she led us inside, and took us through the misericords from west to east.

'First, the rude picture of the Lady from Greece, she said: we all know *that* story. The two mermaids riding the sea-monster: this must betoken some monstrously evil action on the part of the two creatures who had come from afar and were somehow connected with the fortunes of the Martel family. Claudine did not pretend to know who they were or what, precisely, they did, only that the misericord proclaimed evil intention. Next, a man and a woman standing over a body. The man and the woman were probably the evil creatures symbolised by the mermaids, and here they were, either having killed or being about to kill a fellow human being. Next: the two creatures being devoured by the sea-monster – clearly, announced Claudine, their evil actions are now destroying them. They have come – how you say? – unstuck. And finally, the three crowns again. These must indicate the proximity of whatever

239

there was to adore or wonder at, a prior advertisement for which had already appeared over the south door. Well, we said, what was there to adore or wonder at?'

'A saint, she said: she had found a saint.'

And then Claudine had led the Princess and the Marquis to the blank, the windowless east wall, only a few feet from the easternmost choir stall, the one which housed the misericord of the crowns. She flashed her torch on the wall just behind and above the altar; a very faint mural depiction of three crowns appeared. Claudine moved between altar and wall, put her hand out to the three crowns, which were about chin height, and removed a block of bricks.

'*Mama, Papa, regardez*,' she had said in a spiteful triumph (though the Princess, in telling the tale to Ptolemaeos and his guests, emended the mode of address).

'And now,' said Ptolemaeos, 'after a further service of coffee and the rest, we shall be further enlightened by M'sieur le Marquis.'

'I DO HOPE,' said Canteloupe to Jo-Jo while the ancient twins brought fresh cups and coffee, 'that you're not going to throw Baby over altogether.'

'Of course not,' said Jo-Jo. 'It's just that I don't need her *like that* any more.'

'She might need you.'

'No. Not after what happened in the donjon. It had to end there.'

'But what's Baby going to do?' said Canteloupe miserably.

'Len,' said Jo-Jo. 'He's great fun, is Len. I had a nice try-out with him, so I know. I've already given both of them the tip.'

'Thank you,' Canteloupe said.

'The trouble is, Len says, that Tom won't like it. Tom's very keen on Len, he's made him his Private Advisor and all that in Lancaster, but if Len should so much as touch Baby

Tom will tear him to pieces. You see, the one thing which Tom can't stand is that Baby, his daughter, should have it away with any man except her husband. He doesn't mind me because girls don't count. Remember that business of Diana and her band of maidens? Though they fingered each other until they turned somersaults, they were still considered chaste. That's pretty much how Tom sees it: anything goes, so long as there's not a prick on the scene – unless of course it's yours, and I think he's a bit tetchy even about that.'

'What does Baby say about all this?'

'Baby says it's absolutely splendid. In order not to hurt her Daddy's feelings she and Len will have to go right away from Tom whenever they want to do it. Since Len is Tom's Private Advisor and whatnot, that will be quite difficult to arrange, so they'll only be able to do it very occasionally, which means, on Ptolemaeos' theory, that love will last much longer and lust, when it happens, will be fifty times as much fun.'

'A very sensible solution of the whole matter,' said Canteloupe. 'As I have always said, there is nothing like being together to drive two lovers apart.'

'A SKELETON IN NUN'S HABIT,' said M. le Marquis des Veules-les-Roses, 'walled up. Wrapped in the folds of the habit, that object.' He pointed to the *Écrevisse* which flashed and shimmered in the candlelight that had replaced the electric after the second service of coffee. '"A Saint," said Claudine; and then, when she saw the *Écrevisse* "What a pretty reliquary. Can I have it?" "No," I said; "it is too holy; I shall have to take it to the Pharaoh." "The Pharaoh?" "I mean, of course, the Pope. Meanwhile. Claudine, you must swear to keep all this a secret." "If I swear, can I keep the beautiful reliquary in my house, until you take it to the Pope?" "Yes," I said. After all, I thought, who would look for such a thing in Claudine's home?

'So Claudine bore away the *Écrevisse* while my sister and I got down to work. First we dismantled the rest of the wall behind which the nun had been immured. Then we examined the little chamber in which she had died. Clearly it had once been an alcove with canopied sedilia of Caen stone. The nun was sitting at one end of the sedilia; all over the rest of it (seat, front and sides) were crudely scratched letters, possibly done with the jewelled claws or antennae of the *Écrevisse*, in any case quite indecipherable – until we realised that they were Greek.

ΕΓΩ ΛΑΛΑΓΗ ΤΟΥ ΙΛΥΣΣΟΥ
ΓΠΑΦΩ ΤΕΙΧΟΣ ΠΟΙΟΥΣΙΝ

I LALAGE FROM ILYSSOS WRITE THEY BUILD
THE WALL I SHALL HAVE ONLY CANDLES SHE
HAD GODS SUN ALSO BUT SHE HAD NOT
SINNED TO HUBERT I SAID WITH THE LEAF THE
FISH-TOY CAN BE OURS

'That was the starting point,' said des Veules-les-Roses. 'Lalage's original idea had been that somehow they could co-operate to exploit Aristarchos' leaf in order to possess themselves of the "Fish-Toy", the *Écrevisse*, which was hidden away in Xanthippe's dowry chest. The early stages should not be difficult, once they had dealt with Hero. The difficulty would be to silence the rest of the hand-maidens and such other servants as might know what was doing, and subsequently to dispose of or disperse the ingredient materials with the maximum profit and without incurring suspicion. It was Lalage, of course, who knew of the *Écrevisse*. Hubert, though he knew of the dowry chest, had no idea that anything of such immense value was inside it, and was not properly convinced of it until Lalage, having briefly purloined the inventory from Hero, showed him the entry on the list. At first Hubert was reluctant to join forces with Lalage (for quite apart from anything else he had been very fond of Xanthippe); but eventually he was won over by the thought of the sum of ready money he was going to need to bribe the Bishop of Sens –'

'Who, let us remember, is sheer conjecture,' said Ivan.

'– Who represents, for the sake of argument, Hubert's unknown motive. *Some such case* there must have been, to make Hubert act as he did. Lalage is not precise – she had neither the time nor the space, only a surface of Caen stone and a few candles. So she simply records that Hubert was badly in need of ready money and at last consented to assist her in this theft. Piecing together Lalage's crude and scattered phrases – higgledy-piggledy, all over the sedilia and some of the canopy – the subsequent series of events would seem to have been in this wise:

'Lalage, knowing that Xanthippe kept the herb in her little onyx box, purloined some of it. She then administered it to Xanthippe, in her food and drink, and instructed her to believe that her epileptic fits were in fact visitations from a daemon named Masullaoh. Long before they even reached Rouen, Lalage had contrived to establish, in Xanthippe's mind, a whole paraphernalia of spirits and supernatural emissaries and celestial fields and satanic coasts. Hero, worried by this sinister and (to her) inexplicable turn in events, kept getting more and more valuable and decorative objects out of the chest to keep the fractious Xanthippe happy, but would not play when asked by Xanthippe (on Lalage's instructions) to release the *Écrevisse*. Meanwhile Xanthippe herself now became intermittently miserable about the manner in which her whole being was dominated (so she thought under the influence of the herb) by Masullaoh and his associates; and in desperation she decided to take some of the herb on her own account (not knowing that she was being fed it already) and to try to stir up her soul, dead as it might be on the Ilyssan theory, in order to resist Masullaoh. This plan suited nobody. It outraged Hero, who disapproved of the herb and thought it was blasphemous to attempt to rouse the soul prematurely; and it disarranged Lalage and Hubert, because the good God alone knew what would happen if Xanthippe voluntarily took a dose of the herb in addition to what had already been put, so to speak, in her soup. As fortune would have it, however, a fit was now imminent and Lalage and Hubert decided to take their chance. This time they instructed Xanthippe to kill Hero (by tearing out her throat) while the fit was on her. They took the keys to the chest off the dead Hero, removed the *Écrevisse*, and placed it by the comatose Xanthippe, for her to find when she awoke; and then they began to consider the last and far the most embarrasing problem, which was how to get the *Écrevisse* into their own keeping (for subsequent disposal) without being denounced by Lalage's four remaining colleagues or any such senior servants as might also have cause for disquiet.

'At this stage Xanthippe awoke and was *boulversée* by what she had done. She had assassinated her old friend and attendant (whose body was later consigned to the moat) and she had had (influenced by Lalage again) the most unsettling dream, wherein she had beheld the aboriginal Devil. She was also (at first) horrified by the *Écrevisse* and its *petit chanson*, although she had craved for it earlier, because she now believed that it was a dream-gift from the Realms of Lucifer. She was now determined, she said, to sample Aristarchos' herb and to command her soul (dead or not) to resist and reject Masullaoh. But *hélas*, the onyx box has disappeared, apparently appropriated by Masullaoh . . . who is displeased, she hears, by Xanthippe's rebellious attitude. Xanthippe is commanded to yield to Masullaoh's will and to reconcile herself to adoration of the *Écrevisse*. So Xanthippe is put down and becomes docile once more; all is for the moment quiet . . . when Hubert conceives a really hellish notion which, he tells Lalage, will solve the knotty problem of finally securing the scaly treasure.

'Let them injure Xanthippe, using the claws of the *Écrevisse*, in her sleep; and then, when she awakes, let them persuade her (having administered a very powerful dose of the herb) that she is in fact dead, killed by the *Écrevisse* as agent of Masullaoh, and that her soul, having duly awoken at the death of her body, nevertheless continues to be imprisoned in that body – this on the orders of Masullaoh who has been most mightily offended by Xanthippe's thoughts of rebellion. In his wisdom and his anger (let her be told) Masullaoh has appointed the soul of Hero to be gaoler to Xanthippe's, which is now condemned to remain for eternity confined to her cadaver. If they once establish this strongly enough in Xanthippe's drugged and helpless mind, Xanthippe will make her situation known, out of sheer despair, to all those around her; and then they, Hubert her Guardian and Lalage her chief maiden, will have an absolute excuse for putting her away, *in special circumstances*, and also, at her piteous request, for putting the *Écrevisse* (the murderous but beloved gift and token of Masulloah) safely away with her. Had she merely died, this would not have been possible without arousing suspicion. But as it is to be, no hand-maiden or servant will question the procedure. Their mistress, they will realise, must be disposed of before her flesh begins to decay, but since she is still in a sense alive she must have something to comfort her – if any comfort be possible in her hideous predicament. What is more, Hubert tells Lalage, all concerned can be bound on oath to secrecy, lest the House of Ilyssos be shamed by such a tale of one of its daughters; and then the *Écrevisse* can be sealed away beyond the world's knowledge or anybody's reach (except that of the conspirators) for an indefinite period – for as long as suits their convenience.'

'What got into that nice Hubert?' said Jo-Jo.

'Fear and desperation,' said M. le Marquis. 'Also, the more doped and feeble, the more wan and whining, the little Xanthippe became, the more she would have aroused his irritation and disgust, until finally he would have become indifferent to her claims as a fellow being and thought of her merely as a pile of rubbish to be removed as soon as possible.'

'Well yes . . . I can understand that Hubert wasn't quite himself by now, what with the Bishop or whatever breathing brimstone down his neck. But to condemn a girl he had once loved to die inch by painful inch, lonely and immured . . . thinking herself to be a rotting corpse from which she could never escape for all eternity. . . It takes a lot of fear and desperation on Hubert's part to excuse that,' said Baby Canteloupe.

'Excusable or not,' said des Veules-les-Roses, 'it is nevertheless the case – unless Lalage was scratching lies on the Caen stone sedilia, which is very unlikely, as she was there causing herself to be bricked up alive as a penitence for her part in the affair. But this is to anticipate. . .

'What followed on Hubert's horrible resolve? And how did

he persuade Lalage to assist him? This latter we shall never know, but persuade her he did, for she herself relates the ghastly events which ensued: Xanthippe's revelation to those about her, that she was now of the living dead; the obscene vigil while the shrine was prepared; the farewell Xanthippe spoke through lips which she said were already poisoned by the worm. About all this Lalage, if we make allowance for her hasty short-hand, gives very much the same impression as we get from Hubert's narrative of the same happenings.'

'*Except*,' said Ptolemaeos, 'that Hubert owns to no guilt. In Hubert's version, Massulaoh exists, he is not an illusion conjured by Lalage, Hubert and the herb. In Hubert's version Xanthippe's soul is really and truly confined to her corpse – not tricked into believing this by her own hand-maid and her own guardian. And here, of course, we have the explanation of Hubert's technique. His motive was *not*, as I once hazarded, to make a more mysterious and awful figure of Xanthippe (though he in fact does this), but to explain everything that occurred, if ever he should be called upon to do so, in terms of factors and forces which are beyond his control or understanding. Thus Hubert hoped to stand exculpated from the whole filthy business – and indeed did so stand until the unfortunate Lalage, with her *ad hoc* exegesis, turned up again in your chapel' (he bowed to des Veules-les-Roses) 'so pray resume your story.'

'As we know,' said des Veules-les-Roses, 'the Lady was taken to her precinct or shrine by her weeping companions, who left her there with that jewelled creature which is before us. A great interdict is put on the shrine. Henri Martel turns up again, is not told the truth or any part of it, and writes his sad little Ballad. The days pass. And now, Lalage and Hubert tell each other, Xanthippe will be dead indeed. They go to the Castellan, of whose services they have need now and will have need in the years to come. They tell him what is in the shrine. "A third of all this may be yours," they say, "if you will help us." The Castellan is an honest old soldier and like all honest old soldiers has his price, which is not a high one as the world wags, though it may be by the standard of the *poilu*. So the Castellan will help them. He picks a small party of diggers.

They go to the shrine. They dig down deep, and they take from the crypt of the shrine the dead (yes, now really dead) Xanthippe together with her brilliant toy, and they stow them right away down by the well shaft (though not *too near*, the Castellan will see to that). Lalage then uses the last of Aristarchos' herb on the diggers and commands them to tear each other to pieces. Thus their knowledge of the affair dies with them, and they also make a colourful warning to the curious not to trespass on Xanthippe's precinct.

'The shrine is re-sealed. Hubert and Lalage and the handmaidens and the baggage train depart with Henri. All are scattered. Hubert goes to Avallon where he satisfies "the Bishop of the Sens" for the time being by giving him some stones which he has taken (with the consent of Lalage, who has done likewise) from under the tail of the *Écrevisse*.'

Des Veules-les-Roses leaned across the table, gently tilted the beast by its tail, and showed eight empty housings.

'More than these they dare not trade as yet. They have taken only minor stones: the greater might be recognised. But the honest Castellan will guard them in Xanthippe's tomb till the time is ripe.

'Lalage, with Henri, goes on to Greece. They have congress together and are married. The Lord Phaedron inspects his dead daughter's dowry, finds that it is *en règle* except for the *Écrevisse*, hopes in vain that her spirit will come to him with news of it, decides to go to Arques to investigate, and takes Henri as a companion. Henri as yet knows nothing of the *Écrevisse*. Lalage, of course, says nothing, trusting in the honest Castellan.

'Many weeks later Lord Phaedron's party arrives at Arques, Henri Martel by this time knowing pretty well what Phaedron is after. The Castellan, after a show of reluctance, allows them to open the shrine –'

'AND WHAT HAPPENS?' cried Jo-Jo triumphantly. 'According to Henri's poem, he, Phaedron and the priest all *saw* the *Écrevisse* under the altar – before it was removed or scuttled off. Either way, your version must be wrong, because according to you the *Écrevisse* had already been hidden away under the donjon with the remains of poor Xanthippe.'

'Oh dear,' said Ptolemaeos, 'the dismal state of female education. The priest,' he said kindly to Jo-Jo, 'didn't really know what he saw. Phaedron, and Henri too, by now, were both expecting to see the *Écrevisse somewhere* around. So what more natural than they should have thought they saw it, when in truth they saw the brilliant spectrum of the sun's rays, which were striking through the thick plain glass of the shrine's east window from the direction of south–south–east and an elevation of seventy-five degrees?'

'How can you know all that?' said Baby.

'I don't. Not exactly. But I do know that the appearance of a spectrum at the foot of the altar is at least scientifically possible, whereas any idea that the *Écrevisse* had come out of the earth to station itself in that place, and had then, in whatever manner, vanished from it, must be sheer lunacy. On my explanation the sudden disappearance of the vision is easily explained by a cloud over the sun.'

'I'm afraid I must agree, my ladies,' said des Veules-les-Roses courteously. 'The glass of the window must have acted as a prism and splashed a rainbow at the foot of the altar. Lord Phaedron, nevertheless, thinks that he has seen the *Écrevisse*, and the hunt is on. The honest Castellan allows it to continue until it is approaching its quarry, when he very correctly forbids further excavation lest the donjon's water supplies be endangered. Phaedron has poor Henri killed in a fit of pique, and then skulks off back to the Mani, where Henri's widow, Lalage, is waiting with a fine baby son. Although she gets up a bit of a fuss about "What happened to my darling Henri?", and although she learns that Henri wrote some poems which annoyed Phaedron and so might explain his demise, she is far more interested in the Prince of the Morea's plans for recognising and providing for his infant kinsman and the infant's mother. Before long she is despatched to Henri's manor at Longueil, where she will live and hold the lands in trust for her son until he comes of age, carefully supervised in this and all other matters by a warden or "Vidame" appointed by the Villehardouins.

'Carefully supervised in all matters except one: her great secret. After a discreet interval she summons the Castellan from Arques, under the pretext of wishing to greet an old companion. "*Alors, mon vieux,*" she says, as soon as they are alone in the rose garden, "and is that *joli Écrevisse* still where he should be?"

'"*Mais oui, Madame.* After Lord Phaedron came and went, we dispersed the materials of the shrine, as this had been totally dismantled. You would not now know, except for a small bump in the grass, that there had ever been a monument to the Lady Xanthippe . . . who sleeps tight under the donjon with the creature she loved."

'"Very soon, honest Castellan, it must be taken from her. Can you extract it without making works in the Castle that will be heard of over half the dukedom?"

'"Very easily, Madame. I can announce that I propose to strengthen or repair the shaft of the well in the donjon. I can then descend, by myself, as though to investigate. It should not be difficult to burrow from the shaft to where the Lady Xanthippe is resting with her toy and to extract the latter, which I can hide in my tool box when I ascend."

'"Bravo, honest Castellan. Now, if you are wise you will leave the disposal of the jewels to me. It will be a difficult business, because some of them are famous from ancient records, while in those places where they are not famous there will be only poor, dirty, ignorant people (like the Scots or the Irish) who have no money to purchase them. Nevertheless, if I sell them one by one on certain markets I know of, we should both be very rich – in time."

'"I have little time left, my lady. And incidentally, where is Messer Hubert of Avallon?"

'"Messer Hubert took to bad courses. He is dead in Argos . . . of the Crusaders' Malady. They say that a bad conscience drove him to debauchery."

'"A bad conscience?"

'"He had married a close cousin, in defiance of the commands of Holy Church."

'"It is certainly imprudent to disregard them. . . And so, my lady, only you and I are left?"

'"Evidently, Sir Castellan."

'"And yet I am old and tired and need but little. I shall claim but one jewel, Madame, which I shall ask of you when I have taken the creature from the earth and brought it here to you. This will be in one month's time."

'"That is good. Go well, honest Castellan."

'"Stay well, noble lady."

'And now,' continued des Veules-les-Roses, 'we come to something of the bizarre. The Castellan duly went back to Arques, unearthed the *Écrevisse*, brought it to the Lady Lalage at Longueil, and claimed the jewel he wanted, which was, as you will have guessed, the pearl between her thighs. Old soldiers are often oddly innocent in their corruption. The Castellan seems to have had little idea of the immense value of the prize which he had guarded so faithfully, and he also appears not to have realised that he could have had the randy widow at any time, just for the asking, without surrendering his share of the treasure. But this is by the way. He came, he asked, his suit was granted. After he had made love to her with the precision and gusto of a drill serjeant, and just as they were warming up for another bout, Lalage noticed two small, raw, pussy patches on the insides of his hands, and asked what they were. Whereupon he told her, in his naive old soldier's way, that in the course of extracting the *Écrevisse* he had disturbed the corpse of the Lady Xanthippe, since when he had had a slight itch in the palms which would doubtless go away before long. And now, if the lady would care to lift her robe once more. . .

'Lalage did not in the least care to do any such thing. One did not have to be a doctor of medicine to know the probable state of poor Xanthippe's flesh after the period she had been inter-red. Realising, with a combination of superstitious horror and forensic divination, that she too might have been infected, she sent the Castellan packing, applied every unguent in sight to herself, spent the night in prayer, and found in the morning that she already had patches of decay on her breasts, arms and thighs, patches which seemed to grow in size and purulence even as she looked at them. She then bethought herself of making penitence before it should be too late: she draped herself in a religious habit and wrapped the sharp-scaled *Écrevisse*, as cause of her crime and burden of her guilt, within

250

the folds next to her bosom. She then had herself scourged along the high road from Longueil to Barville (twenty-five kilometres; poor, plump Lalage) where was a chapel in a demesne which subsequently came to our branch of the family but was then owned by a cousin of Henri. She beseeched the cousin to give permission that she should be mewed up in the chancel of his chapel, for only so, she said, could she atone for the vileness of her life. And so, like Xanthippe, she passed her last hours, walled up and slowly weakening, comforted, perhaps, by her candles, as they shone on the beautiful and pernicious work of art for which she had destroyed her life, but in all things, so far as she could, condemning herself to the same agonies as those to which she and Hubert had consigned Xanthippe. True, she was not under the same unspeakable illusion as Xanthippe, that her soul must stay among putrescence for ever: but then she, Lalage, must *watch* the decay of her contaminated flesh, as it spread and devoured her, whereas the body of the entombed Xanthippe must have remained fresh until it died and she with it.

AFTER SOME MINUTES' SILENCE, during which Ptolemaeos' guests digested these remarks, Madame la Princesse said:

'The immediate problem was how to get our find out of France. If once that article was known about, the Government, in the person of the Minister of Monuments and Antiquities, would have seized it the next minute. Now, we made the discovery the morning after Madame Canteloupe and Mademoiselle Jo-Jo (as she still was then) had their vision together in the Castle. My brother spent the rest of the morning deciphering the characters on and round the sedilia, while I considered the question of the *Écrevisse* and its security.

'Since no one else except Claudine, who would be silent if so commanded, knew the thing had been found, it should not be difficult, I thought, to smuggle it out of France. The Fat Pharaoh – M'sieur Tunne – surely deserved a sight of it, after all his effort and expense of many years, and also a share of it too.'

'You needn't worry about that,' said Ptolemaeos. 'Although I pretended to be in the hunt for the money, *pour encourager les autres* who hoped for some, I always knew that an object like this could never be sold . . . or not without breaking it up, which would be a crime of the first magnitude. I was in the chase for the fun of it and out of pure curiosity about the fate of that poor little girl from the Mani.'

'Darling Ptoly,' Jo-Jo said.

'So in deciding to bring it to you, I was right,' said Madame la Princesse. 'After all that you have done, and after such a speech as you have just said, you deserve the privilege of sitting in judgment. Come then: let us all debate further, and then let the Pharaoh, Ptolemaeos the Judge, pronounce: to whom does this creature rightfully belong? and who shall have it at the last?'

★   ★   ★

'It belongs to France,' said Jean-Marie Guiscard. 'Had I known that it was travelling over in the same ferry as myself and my bride, I should have warned my Department before we left.'

'That would have been very tiresome of you, darling heart,' said Jo-Jo. 'You know that it would simply have been used by that horrible Directeur, or whatever you call him, to get himself promotion.'

'Even so, it would have been where it belongs – in France,' said Jean-Marie stoutly; 'and I am minded to alert the French Government by cable to set about retrieving it this very minute – were it not,' he said, bowing from the shoulders to Ptolemaeos, 'that this would be to breach M'sieur Tunne's so elegant and generous hospitality.'

'Your courtesy does you only less honour than your patriotism,' said Ptolemaeos. 'I am glad my niece has chosen so decent and thoroughly amiable a man as her husband – although I shall greatly miss her cooking. But see here, Jean-Marie, if so I may call you: if we all debate this matter, and then I, as Madame la Princesse suggests, shall judge it, will you accept my judgment?' After all, as the Princess has remarked, I have spent much money and labour in the search – even thought it was not, in the end, my agents that found the prize.'

Jean-Marie looked round at the faces of those who would argue the matter and then at the face of the Pharaoh who would finally give verdict. He thought of M. Socrates, his Director, not an unsympathetic man but somebody to whom the Lady Xanthippe had simply been a possible factor in his career as a scholar and a public servant; he thought of his colleagues in the Department, conceited, quarrelsome, envious clock-watchers, who boasted about their weekends in Trouville with their silly, brittle wives; he thought of his landlady in Eu, and of her sour complaints about the electricity he used in late reading; he thought of Sunday luncheon with his mother and father in the suburbs of Clermont-Ferrand.

Having thought of all this, he looked once more at those assembled. He looked at Jo-Jo, whom he had begun to love, overwhelmingly, for her gallant service to Xanthippe. He looked at her friend, the little Canteloupe, who out of a loving heart had conceived this service, though it needed the courage of Jo-Jo to bring her to it; at the little Canteloupe's father, the scholar who held that history depended on the factors which men, by chance, forgot; at the old man who was the little Canteloupe's husband and wanted only her happiness without regard to his own *amour propre*; and at the young man, Len, who might now become the little Canteloupe's lover, a common man, as they called such men in this country, but far from commonplace. He looked at Madame la Princesse and M. le Marquis, whose ancestor had ordered herself to be buried alive as the only fitting penance for her worse than murderous cruelty and greed; at Barraclough the Voyager, who had come from the land of Agamemnon and Odysseus; and finally he looked once more at the sweating, fleshy face of Ptolemaeos, 'the Fat Pharaoh', who had sat in these Fens for so long, teasing out the mystery of the little Despoina of Ilyssos.

'Yes,' said Jean-Marie to Ptolemaeos, 'I shall hear their

argument and accept your judgment. But you will permit me to enter my own for France.'

Ptolemaeos nodded.

'Naturally,' he said. 'But let us now ask ourselves, not where, but *to whom* this work of art belongs? Apart from eight minor jewels purloined from beneath its tail, and apart from a clockwork engine now destroyed by rust, it is just as it left the hands of its anonymous artificer in Constantinople. *He* had constructed it of materials which had been looted from Trebizond by his employer or patron, a Sebastocrator in the strategic service of the Emperor. In so far as looting is – or was – a legitimate part of warfare, the materials and therefore the work itself rightfully belonged to the Sebastocrator as the spoils of battle. Did he have heirs? If so, where are they now?'

'The last male in his line deceased in 945,' said Ivan Barraclough, 'leaving issue one daughter who was married to Nicophoros Philotimos, Count of the Thracian March. Since she proved sterile, he put her away.'

'Away?'

'In a cemetery. There are therefore no heirs either through the spear line or the distaff line to the Sebastocrator Demosthenes Commenos.'

'And so,' said Canteloupe, 'since privateering is time-honoured as a profession, this creature became the property, *de facto* if not *de jure*, of the Lord of Ilyssos who first won it at sea, and of his successors. The Lord Phaedron was the last of these actually to possess it, but it still rightfully belongs to his heirs, if any.'

'The Lord Phaedron had a son,' said Ivan Barraclough, 'the man who gave Henri Martel's poems to the monks. This man in turn had two sons, both of whom, like their Aunt Xanthippe before them, suffered from epilepsy. The blood of the line was running sour, you see. The father of these two degenerate boys put them away –'

'In a cemetery? –'

'– In a monastery in Armenia, much the same thing, where they could not embarrass him. Not that they would have done so for long, as they both died under sixteen years of age. Their father had no further issue. The Lordship of Ilyssos devolved on a distant cousin, whose entire family was wiped out, as quislings, by the first Greek Emperor who finally dispersed the Franks of the Morea. Lord Phaedron, then, has no heirs to inherit the treasure.'

'But one could make a case, I suppose, for giving it to the people of the Mani, of the Peloponnese, or of Greece as a whole,' said Baby, 'since that's where it came from.'

'No,' said Ptolemaeos. 'It was among my Greek agents that dissidence and disloyalty started. They gave me a lot of trouble – in return for liberal dealing.'

'They were hardly representative, Ptoly, of the Greek nation.'

'Anyhow,' said Ptolemaeos, 'the *Écrevisse* came originally from Constantinople, which is now in Turkey. No one, I take it, would entrust such a marvel to the Turks?'

'It seems to me,' said Jo-Jo, 'that on the form the Marquis des Veules-les-Roses has as good a claim as anybody. He is the descendant of the Lady Lalage, who has nursed it for all these centuries.'

'Having originally stolen it,' said Canteloupe.

'And having paid an appalling penalty for so doing.'

'To say nothing,' said Jean-Marie, 'of successfully concealing it from Phaedron – but with the assistance of two Frenchmen, the Castellan and Hubert of Avallon. In all the circumstances, one might say that the Lady Lalage has been holding the *Écrevisse* in trust – for France.'

'Why not give it to your old College?' said Tom Llewyllyn to Ptolemaeos. 'After all, you've borne the brunt of all this, so the *Écrevisse* should go somewhere that is acceptable to you. Now, if you give it to us in Lancaster, we shall place it on loan in the FitzWilliam, which will in turn lend it all round the globe. This way there will be a social benefit – the thing will be seen and enjoyed by millions – and also two personal benefits.'

'And what might those be?' enquired Ptolemaeos.

'One to me. Amusement at the annoyance which this magnificent benefaction will cause among my left-wing Fellows, who will want to sell it to build hostels for sub-cretinous students and crêches for unmarried student mothers –'

'And give the rest away to terrorists –'

255

'– But will be prevented,' said Tom, 'by the terms legiti-
mately stipulated by the benefactor . . . to whom will come
the second personal benefit to which I refer, in the form of an
Honorary Fellowship awarded *propter gratiam donorum*.'

'I don't think your left-wing Fellows would stand for *that*,'
said Ptolemaeos equably.

'With Tom as Provost Select,' said Len, 'and with Constable
and me advising him, there's bound to be a way of fixing it. I
defy any shower of Grots and Trots to get the better of us.
Just look at the way Constable wished Tom on to them, for a
start.'

'And once appointed,' said Tom to Ptolemaeos, 'you could
leave this unwholesome Fen of yours and come and live in
College.'

'Which sounds even less wholesome. Anyway, I love my
Fen. I thrive on it.'

'It will be lonely now Jo-Jo's going.'

'It was lonely before she came. I thrive on my own company
– much as I've loved hers.'

'*We* would appreciate your company, Ptolemaeos,' said
Tom. 'There's not so many of us left, you know. The old
gang's dying, my friend. As Provost from next Founder's
Day, I shall need your help.'

'Hear bloody hear,' said Len.

'The sea,' said Baby Canteloupe; 'I hear the sea.'

So did they all, as it pounded against the shore below
Ilyssos. The *Écrevisse* shifted across the table and began its tune
of lust . . . lust that knows no limit, no frustration, no
prohibition and no death.

'Her soul went to Ilyssos,' Baby said, 'as Hero told me it
would. She is crying out from Ilyssos for the companion that
was taken from her grave.'

The waves crashed and the gulls cried. The *Écrevisse* moved
towards Baby; its tune spiralled and rippled, conjuring the
delight of the unspeakable.

'Whatever may have been proved among you,' Baby said,
'however and by whomsoever that magic thing was taken
from the earth, Xanthippe claims it for her own: it must be
carried to Ilyssos.'

The waves and the sea-birds and the music ceased.

'Very well,' said Ptolemaeos. 'Though some Greeks in my employ did me an ill turn, they were not, as I am reminded, representative of their nation. From Ilyssos this creature came to France and England: to Ilyssos let it now return.'

Then there was silence, the silence of assent.

'JUST A LITTLE LOWER DOWN, sweetheart,' said Ptolemaeos to Jo-Jo: 'that's it – just under the sack.'

Jo-Jo and Ptolemaeos were having one last little time together, by special permission of Jean-Marie, who much admired Lord Canteloupe's unselfish attitudes in these matters (as reported to him by Jo-Jo) and thought that this was a very stylish and aristocratic way to go on.

'And anyway, darling,' Jo-Jo had said, 'it simply doesn't count with Ptoly because neither of us ever comes – nor ever has.' Even so, Jean-Marie privately thought he was being pretty daring and emancipated. Whatever would his parents in Clermont-Ferrand, or his landlady in Eu, or even the sophisticated M. Socrates have thought? O brave new world that had such people in it!

'We reached a good decision tonight,' said Ptolemaeos, paddling his fingers in Jo-Jo's modestly ripening breasts.

'I thought you were against giving it back to the Greeks.'

'I said I was at first in order to make it appear that I was open to other views. But in fact Greece was what I wanted. And of course that performance of Baby's was a help. All those suggestive noises.'

'What was behind all that, do you suppose?'

'Collective sensibility,' said Ptolemaeos glibly.

'Or could it be,' said Jo-Jo, 'that those two old women were up to their tricks? It wouldn't be the first time they've entertained your parties – by special prior arrangement. Anyway, why are you so pleased that thing is going back to Ilyssos? No one there will have any use for it these days. They won't even have a proper place to put it.'

'Precisely, my little juice-pot. (Just round the corner – that's my girl.) So some bossing official, some odious and conceited Greek version of that Director of Jean-Marie's, will come nosing round and take it off to Athens.'

'And what's so splendid about that? Jesus Christ, Ptoly Tunne, no one can tickle a girl there like you can. Just what's so kosher about that *Écrevisse* going to Athens? After all your trouble.'

'I once made a vow to Athene, my own heart's darling Jo-Jo. In return to her gifts to me and to all men, in return for her lessons of tolerance and sweet reason and moderation – the lessons that save those that hear them from utter destruction of mind and spirit, and have certainly saved me despite an arrogant disposition and enormous wealth – in return for these her gifts, I say, I vowed to Athene that I would give to her the most beautiful thing that came into my possession before the end of my thirty-fifth year, which has now come and will very soon be gone. For a long time I thought I should have to give her you; but now I have decided that she – or at least her city – shall have the *Écrevisse*. It is a gift worthy for a goddess.'

'I wonder whether I should have been. How would you have gone about . . . making me over?'

'I should have had to sacrifice you, I suppose.'

'I'm quite glad you didn't. I've got a lot to live for just now.'

'You know,' said Ptolemaeos, 'since this is the last time we shall ever be together, I'm absolutely going to break my rule: I'm going to come.'

'Not just yet, I hope.'

'No. Very slowly and with great relish.'

'Then so shall I. Very slowly and with great relish. There . . . *there* will be best for me, my darling, and I think that . . . there . . . will be best for you. Oh Ptoly, Ptoly, my own angel of evil and of love. But one thing you must promise me, before I begin to lose myself: never tell my beautiful Jean-Marie: I will not have him hurt.'

' A PITY THAT PTOLEMAEOS wouldn't take up my offer of an Honorary Fellowship,' wrote Tom Llewyllyn in his journal the last thing before he went to bed; 'but at least I've made an excellent recruit in Ivan Barraclough. I'm sure that Constable and Len and I between us can get him on the books by the New Year . . . which will give him plenty of time to clear up his household and other affairs in the Peloponnese (which include a boy, I gather, but a purely domestic one). Not only is Ivan a distinguished scholar of Maniot folklore and religion, but he has the manners and address of a gentleman. Dear God, how one does long for these nowadays in Lancaster.'

'DARLING CANTY,' said Baby, 'I do like stroking your hair.'

'What's left of it. Will you mind stroking a pate?'

'I shall always adore stroking anything of yours. You are my first love and my last.'

'I'm glad you manage to fit a few others in between . . . though now I come to think of it a bit more, I'm not all *that* keen on Len. A bit – well – creepy?'

'Very fetching. Oh yes. There's something compulsive about Len. But perhaps he isn't altogether suitable . . . to father a future Marquess.'

'My darling girl?'

'My lord must have a son,' said Baby. 'You shall choose the father: I shall love the child as yours for your sake, and you shall love it as yours for mine.'

259

'Well, well. Tricky problem. Choosing the sire, I mean.'

'Don't let's leave it long, Canty. I'm sick of voices and visions.'

'What have they got to do with it?'

'Auntie Isobel – she gets them too, you know –'

'I well remember –'

'– Auntie Isobel says they stop when you're made preggers. What a relief that will be.'

'You really drummed up something this evening. *Aida* wasn't in it.'

'It was all faked,' said Baby. 'The only true sounds were those I heard inside me, which started just before the rest of it. That was the work of those two old women. They've got a local reputation as witches, Jo-Jo once told me, but really they're just natural conjurers, and they're very clever at operating all Ptoly's electronic equipment. I expect they thought that my starting up was as good a cue as any . . . though quite what it was all in aid of is hard to say. Some plot of Ptoly's, I suppose.'

'Anyway, one result is that the *Écrevisse* is going back to Ilyssos. You must be glad of that.'

'Yes. . . I was with her, Canty, looking down from the hills to the sea. She told me that now she had come back to Ilyssos she was going to stay there. She was not going to attempt the Wilderness, because for one thing there would be no sea. Then she said that she knew, she sensed, that the *Écrevisse*, her beloved friend and toy, had been released from whatever place it had been taken to from Arques. She yearned for it in Ilysssos, as Hero had now left her to seek One or Other Throne (she was not quite sure which) on the far side of the Wilderness, and she was lonely without her. The sea was a great comfort and happiness, but she missed her Creature, her gift from the Rivers of Death. I'm telling you the truth, Canty. But all of them tonight, they have found – and can prove – another truth. Do you think I'm potty?'

'I think . . . that there are many truths, and that in places some of them overlap. They have found signs; they have read inscriptions, made logical inferences, infused some plausible conjectures, and in the end they have arrived at an explanation which is probably fairly close to the physical and historical facts. They, in short, have deduced the plain man's truth. But you . . . you have *perceived* your own truth in all this, just as Henri Martel, the sweet singer, once perceived his.'

'Thank you, dear Canty. I still think I shall be better off when preggers and off the air. There may be some distressful messages coming up later, which I should really prefer to miss. I mean . . . when that Creature reaches Ilyssos, which hardly *exists* any longer, so Ivan Barraclough says, some busybody is going to grab it for the swish museum in Athens. Now, if they are right, if their literal and scientific terms are the true ones, this won't matter much to anyone. But if *I* am right, it will matter a lot to Xanthippe . Oh, poor Xanthippe.'

'Not so poor,' said Canteloupe, 'thanks to you and brave Jo-Jo, who gave her back her sea.'

April, 1981, to May, 1982
Dieppe, Deal, Hove, Corfu,
Cortona, Dieppe.